Mikhail Kononov was born in 1948 in Leningrad. He studied Russian literature, then enrolled in the army and was exposed to missile radiation which has severely affected his health. He is a teacher, editor, artist, garden designer, and English translator. A member of the Russian Writers' Union, Mikhail Kononov is the author of numerous short stories and essays. *The Naked Pioneer Girl* is his first novel. He now lives in Germany.

THE NAKED PIONEER GIRL

Mikhail Kononov

Translated by
Andrew Bromfield

Library of Congress Catalog Card Number: 2003111414

A complete catalogue record for this book can be obtained
from the British Library on request

The right of Mikhail Kononov to be identified as the author of
this work has been asserted by him in accordance with the
Copyright, Designs and Patents Act 1988

Copyright © 2001 by Limbus Press
English translation © 2004 Andrew Bromfield

First published as *Golaya Pionerka* by Limbus Press, St Petersburg

First published in English in 2004 by Serpent's Tail,
4 Blackstock Mews, London N4 2BT
website: *www.serpentstail.com*

Typeset at Neuadd Bwll, Llanwrtyd Wells

Printed by Mackays of Chatham, plc
10   9   8   7   6   5   4   3   2   1

Translation funded by the Arts Council of England

With whom shall one talk of olden times,
if the peach and the plum do not speak?
(Kenko-Hosi, 'Tsurediuregusa',
14th century)

THE NAKED PIONEER GIRL

OR

GENERAL ZUKOV'S
SECRET ORDER

A breathtaking battle piece and erotic extravaganza
in eight positively vulcanic-vulvaic chapters
with a cheery war and a proud blockade,
pure love and dirty sex,
and thunderous psychopropedeutic salvoes
discharged point-blank from the hip by General Zukov
and, in addition, a documented appearance
of the Most Holy Mother of God
and the strategic night flights of
AN ABSOLUTELY NAKED PIONEER GIRL!

Chapter 1

In which General Zukov himself, the sweet darling,
proposes a *living* Midge for a *posthumous*
Order of Hero of the Soviet Union.

Brightly whistling the catchy tune of 'Rio-Rita', without bothering to wipe away her sticky tears, Midge trudged along to her execution down the familiar German rammed-earth road to the village of Shisyaevo, where Smersh-with-the-Portrait was waiting for her.*

Couldn't tempt any of that lot down to the front even with a tasty loaf, the egotists, every one of them playing the big von-baron, literally. Setting up their own selfish interests against the collective, worse than any peasant farmer. And all because of his high and mighty lordship devoted trench-soldiers had to waste their time wandering distances like this on fool's errands. Not even the chance of a dance would have got her plodding this far, let alone some rotten old shooting. And it still wasn't guaranteed for certain to start with. He only needed to get some piss-stupid idea into his head – which was more than likely with his lot – and he'd decide not to waste a slug on a miserable beggar like Midge, just give her a good tongue-lashing and send her off with a knee up the backside. That'd be a turn-up, eh? Might as well string herself up on the first stick of wood after that. Then all the excitement would just have been a rotten waste of time. It wasn't likely, mind you. But you could never tell what side the freak had got out of bed on. If it was the left, he'd chew you out for a couple of hours, then give you a clip round the back of the head – and *auf Wiedersehen*. And how could you look your regimental mates in the eye after that?

---

* SMERSH, an acronym from the Russian words 'smert' shpionam', meaning 'death to spies', was the name of a department of the Soviet intelligence service during the Second World War.

They'd given her a send-off for a genuine, honest-to-goodness execution, the whole company had pulled together for Midge, done it right, filled her pockets up to the top with sunflower seeds, and stuffed them with sugar lumps, and someone had stuck some captured biscuits and spare knickers down the front of her jacket just in case, and then, oopsa-daisy, Midge goes and turns up without so much as a scratch on her — take me back, lads, just like the old times. Never once in a whole two years had she demonstrated that kind of lack of political awareness, never once put the collective on the spot like that. There she was day after day trying to keep everything squeaky clean, always trying to justify their trust, because everyone knew what a bad effect undesirable cock-ups had, even though she might not really be to blame for anything at all. And from that point of view you never knew which way to spread the straw for these rear-line rats, they were always trying to trip the class-conscious soldiers up, every step they took. And what's more, there was no comeback against any comrade who cut loose, especially in front-line zone conditions. Out here Smersh was tsar and god, top of the heap. And they weren't ashamed to make the most of it, driving folks this way and that, anything to avoid getting up off their own déclassé backsides and facing the bullets. What was General Zukov thinking about at all? If he got in touch at night, she had to brief him, so he could analyse the question concerned properly. And here she was soaked through from all this pointless walking of theirs, hell's bloody bells, she was so angry she could burst!

But then, that still wasn't the thing she was most afraid of — getting executed or even having to stand through some deadly boring tongue-lashing, she could put up with that all right. But if Smersh-with-the-Portrait decided to check out her papers, everything was shot to hell. He'd spot a fake straight away. And then, of course, he'd tie her in knots and start picking her to pieces, set her head spinning so fast, before she knew what was happening she'd get cold feet and break, like some rotten squealer. He'd wheedle it out of her that she was still just a kid, only fifteen, and then she'd be for the high jump, for certain. No discussions, they'd just pack her off back to the rear in the first truck going that way, like some greenhorn school-kid – it was terrible to think of it, she'd never outlive the disgrace of that, and then there was the moral trauma. This was her second year living at the front line, after all, and she'd only just started feeling like a real human being, a member of the collective. She'd got used to people, and they were getting to be nice to her too, they believed she wouldn't let them down, that she'd provide all the support she could if an officer needed warmth and female affection. And what's more, they were doing their best to show her some consideration as well – they were world-class lads, a really choice bunch. So choice that sometimes she could have up to two dozen spare pairs of knickers stashed away in her kit bag. It sometimes made her think that even after the victory she'd never wear them all out. Although from a practical point of view, of course, it was naïve to think like that. Sometimes during redeployment, when the ranks were swelled by reinforcements, she could change up to three pairs a week. But then the only reason for that was the elastic. That was the whole problem: industry was producing elastic that wasn't strong enough – our side and the Germans, we both had the same problem. Somehow they just couldn't get to grips with the question and sort it out. It obviously hadn't been properly planned for front-line conditions yet, they hadn't really geared that area up for war. Someone ought to drop a hint to Stalin about it, or at least to Hitler. All those marshals probably never thought about anything but cannons and planes, but if you happened to be a girl you had to juggle the whole lot of them the best way you could, grip the broken ends in your teeth if you liked, and go wandering around like some crazy-woman with shell-shock, pioneer's honour!

On the other hand, it was better to fight without any knickers at all – begging your pardon – for a hundred years than spend the whole war living it up in the rear, like some high-class deserter, hiding behind her granny's skirts. 'Ma-sha, oh Masha! Quick, drink this nice warm milk with the skin on it!

Drop that yoke, I'll fetch the water myself, you've got weak lungs, if you're not careful your 'berculosis will come back...' She'd be damned if she was going to go choking on boiled milk and guzzling fish oil – better to be shot every day of the week! Only bags, of course, on one condition. Not out in the sticks somewhere, to give the rear-line rats a good laugh, but right here where the action was, in the glorious machine-gun company, in the bosom of her own beloved, close-knit collective. When she started thinking how they'd all feel for her, the entire company to a man and every soldier individually – of course they would, after all, they all knew she was innocent, they hadn't even found any body, or any evidence against Midgy, so they'd all listen to the sentence with their heads hanging, and Midge would be standing out alone in front of the company, where everyone could see her, like an Honoured Actress up on the stage. And everyone would try to look into her eyes and give her a wink – to keep up their comrade-in-battle's spirits at the crucial moment. When she started thinking about that, even now it brought tears to her eyes. Although the question of the execution still hadn't been decided yet. But for happiness like that – to merge in one mighty surge of feeling with the entire red-banner collective, take your nine grams of lead right there in front of your tried and trusted friends and die with honour – for that you'd gladly give up your whole life, never mind your bloody knicker elastic!

Everything she dreamed about had come true! Midge's luck had held good every time, literally! Something terrible it was, if you really thought about it: what had she done to deserve such happiness? Before the war, to be honest, she'd thought her life was a waste of time. After all, she hadn't served with Budyonny in the First Cavalry Army or gone to the North Pole with Papanin's team – nothing but vulgar bourgeois idle time-wasting, in fact. And now here she was blazing away with a 'Maxim': Anka the machine-gunner in person, and what's more even Osip Lukich's moustache was exactly like Chapaev's, only, of course, it was grey. She'd been longing to go to the front to avenge Alyoshka and then – the gates had opened! She'd dreamed of becoming a genuine soldier and setting an example for all the new recruits – and it had all come true down to the last detail. In the last few months the company commander, and the political deputy commander and the Komsomol organiser who was dead now, had all repeated with a single voice at every meeting: 'Mukhina can be trusted with any assignment, day or night, if only you were all so dependable!' If only Walter Ivanovich could have heard that, how happy it would have made him! But in the beginning she'd worried herself sick, like some crazy-woman, not knowing how to prove that a girl-soldier was no worse than a man, that she could be trusted with a gun and eat gruel from the same mess-tin as the others and she could down a hundred grams without even batting an eyelid – but everything had gone as smooth as bloody grease, hadn't it! And then when fate had brought her and Lukich together, she'd learned to reel the spiel as good as any hood, when before that she couldn't say a single word simple and straightforward, like a normal human being. One thing, though, they hadn't managed, the parasites, and they never would either – to get her to curse and swear like some lousy deserter in solitary. What damn point is there, dear comrades, in defiling your own tongue? Oh no, *merci beaucoup* with tassels and knobs on! And anyway, in the first place, it was disgusting. If you're already used to it, by all means, *bitte-dritte*, curse and swear yourself blue in the face, but don't you go besmirching a young girl's reputation – that's not right. And, in the second place, where did you ever see a well brought-up, conscientious Soviet Young Pioneer girl, even if she hadn't managed to join the Komsomol yet – but that was due to circumstances beyond her control – suddenly out of the blue start going around blinding and swearing left and right? It was just plain bloody absurd! There you are, for instance, sitting in the cinema, enjoying *Volga-Volga* in a fine cultured manner – and suddenly up there in front of everyone blonde, slim Lyubov Orlova starts bawling out her beloved Leonid Utyosov in filthy language, just like our own lovely medical assistant Svetka. You'd be the first to take offence, no two ways about it! And what's the point of whistling your time away here and tramping around wearing your boots out, if you can't take a single step without swearing? Take it and stuff yourselves with it, if you've got no manners. But you'll waste your bloody time trying to get Midge to show her ignorance like some foul-mouthed tub of lard. The number of rows I had with the lot of you before you accepted me as one of your own and began to really respect me. And not for using foul language, that's the point that needs stressing, but for my genuine Leningrad education and culture, which is something Svetka, the slut, never had and never will, with a fanny — begging your pardon — like she has. Just you ask anyone about Midge, the whole regiment knows the score: when you write a letter to the girl you love, you need to do a special rush job on it, but so it still turns out literate and cultured, proper like. Midge will always dictate it for you and check all the mistakes. She has to give the rank-and-file some kind of moral support as well, doesn't she? The officers will take from Midge what their rank entitles them to from a girl. But she's no stranger to the common soldiers either, thank God, there's enough of her to go around, she even surprises herself. Lukich was dead right that time when he said about Midge: 'She's carried a heart of pure gold in her breast ever since she was a child!' And as for that, there wasn't a single man who called her by her surname, as though they'd all just forgotten it, but the entire regiment knew Midge and respected her. And if anyone from the new recruits took it into his head to call her 'Moll' like some bandit and sing some hooligan song, the regulars would soon set that wise guy right and tell him to keep his hands off! And as it happened, her authority ran beyond the bounds of the regiment. Anyone in the division would confirm that Midge was a world-class girl, one of our own through and through, not like Svetka the medical assistant. She'd hang herself for an extra pair of stockings, that battleaxe, she'd already been hauled over the coals more than once at the Komsomol bureau for noxious conceit, but that was water off a duck's back to her! And wasn't it typical, by the way, that it wasn't Svetka the divisional commander sent his personal MK automobile for on his bath day, on Sundays, but Midge. And why, what special reason was there for it? Svetka had an entire dairy tucked away inside the front of her jacket, her medals lay there flat like they were on a table, literally, and she had a backside like a self-propelled gun – so how come a little squirt like Midge had got hold of him? Because in the first place, you shouldn't go round making yourself out to be all frothy and fancy, being picky and choosy, that was the first thing. And at the same time you shouldn't go skulking in corners and cut yourself off from the collective. And in the second place, of course, you shouldn't always be wagging your tail in front of the bosses, tip-toeing around, arse-licking and kow-towing all the time. You had to be closer to the masses! After all, what is it the Party teaches us future Komsomol members? Just the opposite, you have to merge with the collective, make every nerve in your body part of it. Be honest with every one of its members, be as open as if he was your own brother, or even closer. And then, perhaps, they'll say it about you too: one of our own through and through, bloody well right! Well, and for those words, of course, any normal Soviet person wouldn't just be glad to die – they'd happily burn to ashes on a campfire twenty times over, and not think twice about it!

The stupid freaks, thinking they could frighten her with an execution. Like the old saying – frightening a dame with a big, fat prick! What is there to this execution business anyway, comrades, if you figure it out calmly? A puff of smoke – and you're gone. Nothing to it really, no real hassle, pioneer's honour! When they shoot you, you've no time to feel pain or cry out – she'd watched it often enough. Provided, of course, they shoot straight, so all the bullets hit the target, in a tight bunch. And as for that, they ought to appoint Sanka Goryaev and Selivanov and Frolov to carry out the sentence. And Kostiu Zhokhov, of course. He's a top-class Siberian, a man of the taiga and one of Voroshilov's riflemen too, he can hit a squirrel in the eye at three kilometres, he let that slip one day when he had a bit too much to drink. But will Smersh ever really listen to the opinion of the men in the ranks, will it ever really bloody consult with them properly?

And then anyway, if you looked at things straight on, generally speaking wasn't there a whiff of egotism about all this – going to get herself shot voluntarily when tomorrow or the next day wasn't she supposed to carry out a strategic operation, complete her secret mission? And there was no one else who could get the job done, only Midge herself in person, maybe she was the only one in the whole Red Army who could pull off such a feat of heroism. Eliminating the chief German Fascist Dragon – that was a lot bigger trick, comrades, than pulling the legs off a bloody crayfish! In fact with that to be done it was downright shameful to be thinking about going and getting herself executed when the mission still hadn't been carried out. If General Zukov himself hadn't placed his hopes in Midge, hadn't put his secret trust in her, then she wouldn't feel responsible to him like this, and to the whole country, if she was really honest about it. Well anyway, she wasn't any empty-headed schoolgirl, she'd caught on ages ago: up at front HQ and back in the Kremlin itself they were already in the know about Mukhina's mission and they backed the activities of the invisible flying agent code-named 'Seagull' absolutely one hundred percent. But the order still hadn't been carried out yet. A tip-top secret order it was too, and mind you, that was only typical. How could there be any blasted talk of execution, when the girl had to fly a secret raid almost every free night? And, what's more, without any aeroplane at all and practically completely unarmed. And they hadn't sent her to study on any kind of courses, she hadn't even read any instructions on the tactics of this kind of work, or on strategy, or on the *matériel* required. If anything went wrong up there in the sky, there was nothing for her to grab hold of, something terrible that would be. None of your motors or wings like normal fliers had, no trusty 'Walther' pistol in her back pocket, not even – begging your pardon – any pants, like some kind of crazy-woman. And no link with the ground except for General Zukov's voice: 'Forward, Seagull! For Stalin! The

Motherland hears you – the Motherland knows!' It was a sacred duty. The meaning of her entire life. The justification for everything – for the forged documents, and for being so short, and most important of all, for the fact that you could never, no matter how bloody hard you tried, never ever be a man. So there couldn't be any more talk of executions for the time being, she'd have to wriggle out of the whole thing as best she could. This was for real, not a dream, General Zukov couldn't give her instructions, he couldn't help her out. Walter Ivanovich would have been glad to help, but where could she find him now?

Then again, no matter which way you twisted it, it was the same thing all over again as Pavka Korchagin went through: of course, dying was far easier and much nicer, but you try holding out and winning – even when you're weeping tears of blood. What is it Pavka teaches us? 'Know how to live even when life becomes unbearable.' But excuse me, comrades, hang on a moment! Just what do you see that's so unbearable for Midge right now? She's got clothes and shoes, for a start. Right? And chow as well, almost every day, top quality, stuff your belly till it bursts. And second, she's surrounded by people who are pure gold, real lively lads, as the people call them. So that's two, right? And she's got a mission. A special one! Secret too, the kind lots of folks dream about. That makes three, right? No, that's not three – it's a hundred and three! It's thirty-three million! Just get on with your life, you parasite, and be glad. And get those treacherous dreams of execution out of your head, you egotistical imbecile! Did you know her knicker elastic breaks! Why don't you stop being such a dozy sloven and get your knickers down in time before it can break. You know what a nervous state they're all in, vulnerable, it's about bloody time you got used to it!

But you know what was really annoying? Like a fool she went down to the river specially and gave her neck a thorough scrubbing, did it right. Only without any soap, of course. The last little slip of the grey stuff, transparent it was, leapt out of her hands like a frog and went floating off downstream.

Couldn't go back to the dug-out for a piece of trophy soap now, could she? Especially with it having that pretty coloured picture on the wrapper, it was a shame to tear it open: that petite blonde sitting by a river on a shiny German rock, the whore, with those shapely legs pulled up under her, seductive like – really classy! And, by the way, the name was thought up by Heine himself, Hans's own biggest classic, back in school Walter Ivanovich had made them learn that gibberish off by heart – *Ich weis nicht was sol es bedeuten* – God rest his soul – 'Lorelei' it was. Midge's hair was blondish too, but always with some odd touch of colour about it: either the ends went yellow like old straw or next time you looked it was all green, like mermaid's hair, literally. But the German Lorelei girl's hair was smooth and soft and bluish in the moonlight – you couldn't take your eyes off it! She washed it with that soap, make no two ways about it!

Anyway, she'd had a wash. And put on fresh white trophy knickers – just to be on the safe side. Firm elastic, not stretched yet, pleats in the silk like it was starched, real stylish – *immer-aligant*! Lieutenant Volodya had presented her with three pairs that had never been worn just last Thursday after the battle – a world-class lad, modest and reliable, the real thing. Because that was the tradition in the company: once you'd got well in with Midge, then please, dear bosom buddy, be so kind as to deal with the trophy underwear problem – she wasn't taken on to tie knots in her elastic every morning thanks to your loutish lack of manners and the officers always being so impatient. Thank God they'd finally managed to grasp the basics at least. What an effort she had to make with them, drained her almost dry, they did, before she could teach them to behave themselves properly – if only when it came to supplying knickers – something terrible, it was! They were living at the bloody front line, after all. Not to mention bras, couldn't find them for love nor money at the front, especially size two, the most popular. She couldn't remember when they'd finally ripped her last one to pieces. Her nipples itched all day from one night to the next, and her tits were all black and blue with nothing to keep those suckers off them. Some of the comrades would go without bread for a chance to suck on a breast – and it was a long time since they were babes in arms, they were fully certified dads now, liked to tell her about their kids in between times, show her their snaps – real freaks they were, honest!

But not any longer, comrades, it's all over! Smersh-with-the-Portrait's going to shoot your Midge – then you'll have no one to show your snapshots to. So you can stick your teeth back on the shelf, you smelly old goats, and forget all about young girls' titties. You won't even have an itsy-bitsy little piece left for a souvenir. Then it'll hit you time and time again how you didn't know what you'd got till it was gone.

Oh, how tired I am of the lot of you, really and truly! It's awful! Sometimes some rough rider or other, some fat hog or billy-goat, shakes me about, sucks me to death and squeezes me black and blue so I can't even lift up my head in the morning. Then Lukich doses his half-dead Midge with strong tea with vodka. Holds her head up like she was some sickly five-year-old. And he has tears running down his moustache. I should be feeding him from a spoon, the doddery old granddad, but where would I get the strength? I'm all squeezed to death, crushed and shattered. One of those mornings I'll get the mean idea into my head that life in the next world has got to be better than this. Especially if you've been honest with people in this world, tried not to get detached from the collective. It's like they say, everything's for the best whatever happens, including shooting in some particular cases. Some nights, especially after a battle, certain comrades have no conscience at all, the next in line's already waiting at the door, playing pocket billiards to pass the time, while the first one's almost ripping off your elastic with his teeth, like death itself is right there on his heels, but if he can just stick his johnny into you in time he'll be saved. You can feel all of him there inside you, with his boots still on, groaning and squealing like some sulky little kid, and he gasps out: take pity, save me, you're my only hope. And outside the tarpaulin you can hear the third one's rolled up for his midnight vigil, and the fourth: 'Who's last in line for Midge, comrades? I'm after you, then, Lieutenant! Hey, mate, let me finish your fag!' — 'Where d'you think you're going? Can't you see there's a queue here?' — 'Ah, but I can jump the queue, I've got connections!' — and they laugh, the great studs. Like some kind of massed offensive it is, literally! They should give it a try themselves — no breaks for a smoke for a start, and always on the go all the time like a blue-arsed fly. By the time it gets near morning you don't know what the hell's going on, can't remember anything, can't feel anything — you're stiff as a board all over, hard as a drainpipe, and it just goes on pouring through you, pouring and pouring …

But then of course, all that's just weakness and nothing more. If you get right down to it, do a bit of real soul-searching, you can see it right away: one — it's moral degeneration; two — it's alarmism; three — it's betrayal of the common interests of the collective. The kind of attitudes that have to be swept clean out of the ranks, the way you were always the first to demand. And anyway it's not really hard to nip your own weakness in the bud. You only have to remember that during your night flight you'll hear General Zukov's painfully familiar voice again: 'Forward, Seagull! You're our only hope!' — and straight off you'll get this warm feeling deep inside, there'll even be tears in your eyes, literally. After all, it's them you're fighting for, these idiots, these rotten goats, so what's the point in taking offence, when you're surrounded by such world-class lads? Take a look inside yourself first, root out those failings, you can start making demands on others when you're already perfect. That's what Stalin wrote, isn't it?

Anyway, she had a quick wash, army-style, got changed, ate a solid breakfast just to be on the safe side and she was sitting there quiet-like on the tree stump by the dug-out, winding up the phonograph. Hoping like some top-class crazy-woman Smersh-with-the-Portrait would turn up right there at our position, settle the business there and then like a man, with no messing about and dispatch her to the next world straight off, no complications. Then Lukich appears out of nowhere like a crazy jack-in-a-box: 'Let's say goodbye then, girl! You've got to tramp all the way to Shisyaevo, so wrap your feet up properly. Yashchenko the signalman came round: Smersh wants to see you, he's going to decide the matter on the spot. Chin up, you'll come back safe and sound. God'll watch over you and keep you from harm.' First she thought he was having me on like he always did, the old dog, spinning a line. He was always prattling on, a real top-class trickster. But he took off his cap and came to hug her with his face all twisted out of shape like he was at her funeral, just about to burst into tears. What a freak, pioneer's honour! He even made the sign of the cross over her three times seeing her off. He had tears glittering on his moustache – all those shell-shock victims have boggy eyes just waiting to overflow.

She wound up the old phonograph for herself one last time before she left, as tight as it would go, the whole way. And to keep her spirits up she put on that cheerful 'Rio-Rita' – the one that she danced to with Alyoshka in the village club. She kissed Lukich on his nose, as cold as a dog's. Of course, she could have said to hell with it and stayed home in the company – if only as a matter of principle! After all, she didn't do anything wrong, anyone could tell them that, the whole company was in the know. And Smersh too, he might be as ideologically principled as they come, but in the first place he was an officer too. He was used to having everything served up to him on a plate – just hand it straight over!

She shuffled her feet along the smart, straight German road through the young birch forest. The Hanses had put their hearts into building the road: they'd been counting on staying here for ever. And now when they'd finally been driven out, and Midge had done her bit too, how stupid it was, comrades, to just go and die for no reason at all! Tears, cold and sticky, crept into her nostrils. The brazen May sun baked the back of her head: it was high noon.

But that 'Rio-Rita' tune was really catchy – something terrible it was! You just kept on and on whistling it and you couldn't stop. On and on and on. Never mind though, it made things a bit more cheerful …

But rumbling and creaking ever more menacingly in the girl's chest, cutting across the persistent rhythm of 'Rio-Rita', was a lurching, leaden-footed funeral march. With a vague, greedy feeling of joy Midge saw herself in a red general's coffin. A petite little coffin, just the right size for Midge. Comfy, with cheerful lace frills, suspended on gold chains from crystal columns. The columns were faceted, like the stems of the pre-revolutionary goblets her granny used to have in her sideboard. Solemnly, in time to the swooning rhythm of the march, the sleeping Queen Midge is carried along by quiet Sanka Goryaev, himself as long and thin as the crystal shaft in his hands, and his dead brother Sevka, who was shot right through on the volleyball pitch in forty-one, and the sobbing commander of the machine-gun detachment, Osip Lukich Plotnikov. The fourth column with a chain squeaking in its hook-eye had been entrusted to – Oh, my goodness! – could it really be General Zukov himself? Never in her wildest dreams could she have imagined such a final honour for herself!

And look at the poor general, just like that other time, working that soft-pink, triangular, clean-shaven jaw of his round in figures of eight – he's in pain, the brave warrior! With his mouth twisted out of shape like before, the way Midge remembered him in forty-one. Once again the poor martyr can't escape his suffering for the senseless losses in our ranks of steel …

And what a wave of tenderness, of sudden pity, for him, swept over Midge! She could have sat up right there in the coffin and shouted right in their faces: 'What do you know? Which of you has ever suffered for his dear Motherland the way he has? Showing no pity to yourself or anyone else – literally! Aha, not got the guts for it? That's right! The only thing you're good for is to slander the hero, you lousy lot!' Straight up, that's the way she'd fling it straight in their rotten, lousy faces. If it wasn't for the flowers. Who wouldn't feel sorry to throw them off? Heavy pink roses on Masha Mukhina's chest, pierced through by Smersh's bullets, and on her belly. And roses covering Masha Mukhina's legs in the new officer's boots. A dead girl covered with bouquets of flowers, like a fancy New Year cake from the 'Nord' shop – it made you feel afraid to touch.

And Zukov, the sweet darling, had flown in specially, by emergency flight, to honour Midge in person for her top-secret night flights after all, better late than never. But the divisional commander had come through too, the fat hog remembered the way Midge had scrubbed his back last Sunday and given him a damn good steaming – and so he goes straight up to the general to report. 'This and that, Comrade Commander in Chief,' he says, 'permission to present my report! Permission to recommend machine-gun company Private Soldier Maria Mukhina, for implacable valour shown in combat with the invading parasites and also for her top-class individual heroism in carrying out her special command mission exactly two nights ago, right here and now, without proper investigation, for the award of the title of Hero of the Soviet Union – posthumously, all right and proper!' And then there'd be nothing left for General Zukov to do but salute smartly, take out his revolver and join in the immediate general salute in Midge's honour and modestly take his turn just like everyone else in the guard of honour round the petite little red coffin.

'Rio-Rita' clacked her castanets, trying to liven up the dreary funeral march. And the spring forest was flooded with sunshine, every black twig gleaming as if it had been varnished, the blue-tits were chirruping away fit to burst, and the little yellowish leaves were literally unfolding as she watched. Now the whole world, right down to the last blue-tit, knew what a devoted comrade her regimental brothers had lost in Midge. But so far, apart from General Zukov, of course, Lukich was the only one who'd understood everything ages ago – what a world-class girl Midge really was – that was why he was crying openly like that without feeling embarrassed in front of the officers and shaking the tears off his grey moustache. He was old already, forty-two, he'd be the first one Midge would forgive.

Or maybe she shouldn't forgive him just yet? If only out of educational considerations! There was the rotten old blockhead bawling away as if it wasn't him who'd fetched her such a belt yesterday at lunch – something terrible it was! His vodka ration had come spurting straight back out through Midge's nostrils. She didn't have enough time to down his hundred grams of commissar's special while he was bending over and fumbling in the top of his boot for his fork. And all those times he'd poured Midge's rightful ration into his own mug, bold as brass, right there in front of everyone: young pioneers aren't allowed, he said – and that's that! You swore a solemn oath, he said, always to be prepared, so hand over that vodka and don't break your word. Children aren't bloody well allowed, he said!

Chapter 2

*In which Midge is astounded by Soviet officers'
childish habit of toying with a woman's breasts,
and also by their treacherous attempts
to kiss a girl directly on the lips.*

...Ah, not allowed, isn't she?

And worming your way into sleeping pioneers' knickers in the middle of the night – you reckon that's allowed, do you? Which internal services regulation is that in then?

The number of times she'd brought the matter up: why's it such a problem to wake a person up in time, comrades? What do all these top-flight egotists think they're up to, rushing straight in without so much as a simple hello or by-your-leave, worse than some rotten white guardsman with his dander up, pioneer's honour! But they know, don't they, no two ways about it, the entire regiment knows – Midge sleeps like a log, and when she's out she's out. In the beginning soft-hearted Lukich used to raise the alarm every night, the freak. Came dashing across, pulling and tugging at her, yelling in her ear: 'What's wrong, haven't gone and kicked it, have you, little Midgy, Mashenka?' He used to pester her in the mornings, why, he says, don't you breathe when you're asleep, you've got no pulse and you're all cold and green like a corpse – what kind of ghoul have I got myself lumbered with now? Of course, things aren't so great for him either. Reinstated in the Party when he's only just recovered from shell-shock and the company commander threatens to throw him out again almost every day: 'You watch it, if that Midge of yours runs off or goes and hangs herself I'll have your Party card on my desk quicker than you can blink!' Keeps on telling him and poor old Lukich stammers and his eyebrows jump up and down and his eyes dart all over the place and he's shaking all over like he's going to fall to pieces any moment. The poor sod crosses himself and gives Midge another look like he's thinking of bumping her off only he hasn't quite made his mind up yet exactly what for. But then Midge doesn't exactly feel great about it all either. Looked at one way, it seems like everything's in good shape: the order's clear, and you go flying off on your mission, just like you should. So how come when you leave your body unplugged like that while you're away, it acts like it's not even human? What has she done wrong? She does what the top command ordered, and the general couldn't make a mistake, he'd be the first to put her right if she was doing something wrong, wouldn't he? So all her doubts are pointless. He'd said it, once and for all: the Motherland hears, the Motherland knows, and that was that, no ifs and buts about it! But from a different angle she could understand Lukich too: he wasn't in the know. Anyway, in the end she had to let the soft old fart in on it, and clarify the situation for him – about how these strategic dreams of hers had started in forty-one under the sympathetic personal direction of the legendary commander General Zukov. Lukich had sworn to God to keep quiet about Midge's special mission till the day he died, sworn on his Party card and given his word as a communist of twenty years' standing, except for those eight years he'd sweated out on a bunk in a camp. And he'd started giving Midge his sugar lumps at breakfast, regularly, without needing any reminders. He even stopped blinding and swearing when she was around and started fencing off his bunk with a tarpaulin at night. He'd never been afraid of Midge's visitors, but her dreams terrified him: that's what a concussed noggin does for you! Never mind, anyway. When it comes down to it, what he does isn't important, but our mission, in the first place, is of strategic importance and in the second place it would be good if she could catch up on her sleep at the same time, which is what normal class-conscious soldiers are supposed to use the night for anyway. We're not suffering from insomnia yet and, by the way, it's not my business to keep watch all night like I'm lying in wait to ambush the next billy-goat who comes trotting in. I never made a date with any of them, God forbid, the suckers, and they'll never get me to either. I'm not concussed yet either, thank God, I don't go around like Svetka the medical assistant, inviting guests round to visit her for a screw, making eyes at every little lieutenant, just begging for their Gestapo-style tortures – *merci beaucoup* with knobs on! It's only for their sake you put up with it all, the parasites, children they are, literally, even if they are officers in their souls. So just what's so difficult about giving a girl a belt across the shoulder or a tug on one leg or the other before you get started? Do you think it's nice, comrades, being woken up by your crude tickling? Try looking at it from a practical point of view! Have you ever, even once, had some strange man start fumbling and raking around with his hands in your knickers without the slightest warning and make a grab at your hairy fanny? Well? I can imagine the kind of scandal you'd kick up, you great warrior, you'd have the entire division up on armed alert you would! You're all so smart at saying what's allowed and not allowed, all got so used to spouting your top-class demagoguery. And in the very same combat conditions Private Soldier Maria Mukhina carries out her duty modestly, without making a song and dance about it. Ever heard of that old phrase – 'duty first'? But even at the front there are some folks who just look after number one, never put themselves in anybody else's place. Only as it happens, by the way, facts are the most stubborn things in the world, Comrade Stalin himself has pointed that out more than once. And in that connection the company activists, the healthy core of the personnel, and every single private soldier among them, is always ready and willing to give his very last drop of blood at the very first order, without retreating a single step, literally. And by the way, at the level of social responsibility, it's nine months without a break now Midge has been one of the editors of the company battle sheet: drawing Hitler with a red Army bayonet stuck through him, or Stalin with his moustache – easy as pulling a leg off a crayfish, three seconds flat. And Thursday before last at the activist cell meeting she was even elected agitator – unanimously! Just try finding the time to do all that lot, running around – begging your pardon — like a blue-arsed bloody fly. That's why the command are always satisfied with Midge, always holding her up as an example to all the politically ignorant men and national minority members — the ones who are all used to pretending 'me you not understand'. Although of course, not every last one of the minority men is a weirdo. For instance the company Komsomol organiser Lieutenant Svinadze, he's dead now, said it at the last meeting, literally: 'The command knows: Mukhina is dependable, she's easy to work with, you can count on her.' He was an interesting sort of brown-haired man. Big, white teeth, a black, miniaturish sort of moustache, the night before he died he recommended Midge for the Komsomol and next morning a stray bullet cut him down, rest his soul. And the way he danced the *lezginka* whenever he got a letter from home — Assa! Assa! Fill the glasses! Made you feel faint all over: Stalin's double he was, a perfect copy, something terrible it was! Although of course it isn't right to go comparing anyone with him, especially a simple Georgian, after all maybe Stalin came down from the mountains too, but by nationality he was definitely absolutely Soviet, despite his accent.

And in general, in principle the national question makes no odds anyway. As it happened Walter Ivanovich was a German, but he was a Soviet teacher, though he taught German, not drawing or any stuff like that. Maybe it doesn't make any difference now for teachers either. But if it didn't, then he'd still be alive, wouldn't have got arrested the stupid way he did, like a German. The fact of the matter is that every Svinadze needs a girl's tender, loving friendship at least once a week, on the same terms as everyone else, in his rightful place in the organised queue. All of them are the same, even the Tartars, not to mention the Armenians. That Captain Sedlian got blown up by a mine not long since, a quartermaster he was, got torn to pieces. And he was such an interesting man, rest his soul! The first time with him she almost choked herself laughing, literally, got the hiccups. Midge had hardly pulled off her tunic and laid down when he blew out the lamp — and suddenly something wet and cold flopped slap on to Midge's breast! A frog! Oh, hell's bloody bells! And it lay there without budging, the little horror, just lying low and huddling down. Oh no, it must be dead! Or maybe it's not a frog? He's a quartermaster after all, he must know what he's doing! And then he roars in the darkness and throws himself on her! Starts gnawing on the frog, literally, with his teeth! Right there on Midge's chest, just under her throat. Sinks his teeth into it, growling and gurgling in his throat like some kind of janissary from the zoo. And he hasn't forgotten to put his tool in either, he remembers what he came for, so he can't be completely crazy. How was she supposed to understand a phenomenon like that? It was afterwards that Midge split her sides laughing, of course, but at first it all seemed sort of weird: what was the frog doing there, dear comrades, have you got any grasp at all of the situation? A quartermaster especially shouldn't really be all that hungry, should he? He confessed afterwards, even apologised, the freak — it was a habit he'd had since he was a child, it was the only way he could get laid, it was no good unless he screwed the girl and chewed raw meat at the same time. Seemed meat was the only thing that set his tool up right, meat and blood. So every time he brought a lump of beef in his officer's map case — as an appetiser. She got used to it, of course. But even so, sometimes she'd laugh fit to burst, just couldn't stop, literally, it was almost frightening: what if you ended up like that for the rest of your life, with your gob stuck wide open! It was sticky, in the first place, and it tickled, the blood ran down her neck and under her arms, and he just carried on toying with it, growling and chomping away until he'd poured out all his ferocity. She felt sorry for him, like he was sick. It wasn't his fault, the freak, if he had a special character like that, was it? The others were worse, they could bite her breasts or her neck or her shoulder so hard that they bled. But why did this one deserve the mine? For half a kilo of beef? He only ate it so he could get the job done, not because he was a glutton and he enjoyed it. Rest his soul …

So nationality is strictly secondary. The main thing is for an officer not to have a character that's too hot-headed. For him not to go grabbing for his holster at the slightest thing, not to threaten you with court martial if you won't let him in the back way or you don't want to toot on his flute: you ought to be ashamed, comrades, even if it is dark, we have to keep up some kind of standards. But you'll always forgive him for his nationality. Just look at the number of nationalities we've produced in this country – something terrible it is! A real live Yakut even turned up once. At first she thought he was Chinese. He spoke the same way, like he was sucking on every letter: 'Meetch, Meetch, jussa secon, jussa secon …' And he was short too – they say that's typical of them – just about up to Midge's armpit. He got himself settled in somehow with a bit of a struggle, slumped on to her, stuck his johnny in, jerked it backwards and forwards a couple of times, squealed like a shot hare, then flopped over and started snoring like a real rough rider. And Midge was glad: it was all so quick and easy with him, not even enough time for her to wriggle around a bit. The little darling stuck his nose in Midge's belly-button and went out like a light. Only his heels were sticking out from under the padded blanket – little miniature heels. And yellow too, like mandarins, with the light from the oil-lamp shining on them. Mukha felt happy: she'd made friends with a real live Chinaman! From an oppressed country. Back there they exploited him any way they fancied, treated him like he wasn't even human, and now we've even given him epaulettes and we treat him like an equal, like he's a real man. And he is a real man, not some kind of wind-up doll, is he? Almost like a genuine officer, his noggin's in the right place, his eyes just haven't come out properly. And his heels aren't standard issue either. Like they've been pickled. Ah, you little love! She took hold of his ear, pulled him out of her belly-button, tugged him up a bit higher, woke him up politely and considerately, and of course she asked him how they said, for instance, 'long live friendship of the peoples' in their language, in Chinese. But the stupid freak took offence! Would you believe it? 'You nashty wady!' he yells. 'You bad whou!' Real nasty, eh? You can't treat them nice, everybody knows that – the Yakut in them surfaces straight away. How is she supposed to know in advance if you're some shell-shocked Yakut or maybe some Japanese they didn't finish off on Halhin-Gol lake? When she lays out her money-box for you, and doesn't even have enough time for a couple of words of conversation and it's not written on your forehead what nationality you are, maybe you're all Eskimoes or Karakalpaks or something, Lord only knows. And anyway, so what? Nationality isn't catching, they proved that ages ago. We haven't all turned slanty-eyed yet from being around you, and we won't turn slanty in the future either, and our Soviet heels won't turn yellow from being near your pickled mandarins. And the Yakut with the high cheekbones pulled on his little boy's boots and cleared off to his little Chinese dugout. It was next morning that Lukich put Midge in the picture about the Yakuts: two of them had arrived in the fourth company with the reinforcements last week. And he told her about the free life the Yakuts lived up beyond the Polar Circle. And the things their slanty-eyed pride drove them to: eating reindeers raw right there in the middle of the tundra, in the middle of the snow, they even used to give Lukich raw deer meat and blood, still warm, that was why he was still alive, he said, everyone was starving to death in the camps: but as yet Soviet power couldn't do anything with that kind of savageness, it just shrugged its shoulders and gave those lucky Yakuts real reading and writing, we even shared our own Russian letters with them, because after all they are a peaceful people, harmless, only the freaks drink neat alcohol all the time and die of tuberculosis. So what's the national question got to do with anything, that's the question. Seems it turns out that in the north and in the south the male sex simply can't live without raw meat, although most of them try to hide it of course, they're ashamed of their ill-bred manners. But you can try as hard as you like, you can't keep something like that secret. When he slips it in and shags you gently for a few minutes and then suddenly goes wild and comes at you hammer and tongs, howling and growling and grinding his teeth like he's having a fit — even if he's a plain ordinary

Ukrainian or Belorussian or a native Muscovite — anyway, comrades, from the outside the whole thing's obvious straight away, the way you'd all gnaw on a girl's flesh and sink your fangs into it, something terrible, if you were only given a chance. That's the nature of your male race — predators. Even if to look at you seem like perfectly tame domestic animals: one behaves himself a bit like a fine young stallion, but the slightest thing and he's rearing up at you; one's a real top-class ram — it makes no difference, you can try all night and still not get him to admit Comrade Leshchenko sings sweeter than Vertinsky, more soulfully. And one's an absolute billy-goat: no doubt he'd be proud as a peacock if he had any stars on his shoulder-straps, pile them on. Or take meek and mild Lukich now — he's a grey gelding, of course. Broken to the bridle, won't lash out, pulls his load along slow and steady, and the yoke won't chafe his withers, his skin doesn't feel it, it's tough as oak. That's how he got his rich experience of life, of course. As smart as a yid, got an entire Palace of Soviets on his shoulders, not a head. He'll always explain the situation to you and help you choose the right tactics, no two ways about it.

'You've got to understand the most important thing, you crazy-woman,' Lukich says. 'So far there's really only two nations on our Planet Earth: men and women. Women run away like they're supposed to, with their skirts held up, of course, and men go after them. But not at a gallop. Always at a canter, every time: if I don't catch her, at least I'll warm myself up a bit, like. That's the circle this life of ours has been running round in since the dawn of time, like a squirrel in a wheel. The scientific word for it is progress. That's why any old officer comes creeping in to see you with his big fat prick — that's your female lot, the way things have been since the world was created. When you reach a mature woman's age, then you'll be reconciled with God's providence, but in the meantime you have to be patient. There's nothing the two of us can do about it anyway. They'll carry on pestering you the way they always have, that's a fact.'

Lukich himself has never pestered her, thank god, she

doesn't mean him in this case. Lukich doesn't need it. He's a saint, everybody says so. Because of his concussion. But anyway sergeants aren't supposed to screw the officers' girl, the number of times he's said it himself: 'What the priest can do, the deacon can't!' And once, talking about the officers, he said: 'Their lordships are all anointed with the same oil. They scratch each other's backs all right, everyone knows a raven doesn't peck out another raven's eye. But who gains from the whole business? You're the only one who gains from it, Midge. After the war most of them will have nothing to be proud of. The entire officer corps has been serviced by just two skirts, yours and Svetka the medical assistant's, that two-legged stud-mare, that double-barrelled trollop. But now you're a rich woman for the rest of your life: you've had a whole harem of boyfriends, like the Shah of Persia. And you've got the experience to handle anything life brings, and all the advantages. When you get old you can always remember how the majors and lieutenant-colonels ran after you in herds, not to mention the green lieutenants. And your granddaughter will envy you, and maybe your great-granddaughter too, you bloody well mark my words!'

But after all it was a matter of principle: was it allowed or not? In the first place she was under age. But in the second place it was a long time now since she'd been a greenhorn in the army, she wasn't some kind of novice or skivvy. It said it in black and white in her soldier's identity papers: number two in the machine-gun detachment. And there was nowhere it said specially that female personnel weren't to be given their hundred grams, it was the legitimate daily norm for every individual in the field – this was war after all. Not allowed! And swapping chocolate for the non-drinkers' vodka and pouring it into a trophy flask with a swastika, like Saint Lukich did, and then every Saturday night getting tight as a newt on the quiet up on his bunk behind the tarpaulin – was that allowed? What if they went into battle during the night? Those reptiles don't follow any rules, but if you're not in the Komsomol yet, then anyone can order you around any time of the day or night — right? If it hadn't been for Commissar Chaban, in forty-one I'd have taken my female revenge on all you horny goats for the rest of my life. There's my pistol, always with me, tucked away in my back pocket, warming my backside even at night, until some heroic soldier pulls the pants off me. Stick the barrel in my mouth — instead of your bitter cream wafer! Take a good last bite with my teeth so they'll remember me all their lives and — bang-bang! Let the court figure out afterwards which of you is first to have his prick ripped off for a young girl dying so unforgettably — you've all shown lack of discipline, the whole bunch of you, every one of you deserves it! But there has to be someone who feels some kind of class-consciousness, doesn't there? Especially if you're dreaming of joining the Komsomol, the way you should. The Komsomol organiser himself has already signed the recommendation, did it just before he died, rest his soul, a real world-class lad. His signature will never wear off: he dashed it off in indelible pencil! She licked the stick for the weirdo herself, while he was smoking, after his fifth time round, wasn't it? He'd already played frogs with Midge, and pendulum, and bent her legs up and given her a taste of his cream wafer — she put up with all of it without a single squeak, and he stuck his corn-cob in everywhere he could, playing his games. Morally, of course, it's very hard. If, that is, you don't know what you're fighting for and can't see the grand goal ahead clearly and don't have the true Komsomol flame burning in your heart. But when the goal is clear, when your comrades trust you, when the top brass is pleased with you, anybody's life immediately acquires deep meaning, that's clear enough even to a Yakut. And if it's not clear to you, we'll teach you. We'll make you understand! The whole collective together, the whole bloody country! You've got to grasp the main thing: the whole meaning is in the struggle, in the front ranks, alongside Pavka Korchagin! I can't, you say! You've got to get past 'I can't'! That's what the Party teaches us, and our beloved Komsomol too. You've got to realise it for yourself: your biggest enemy is your own weakness, your flabbiness, your lack of discipline, your political immaturity and petty-bourgeois opportunism. Basically, you are your own biggest enemy – day and night, round the clock. So you've got to struggle against yourself in the first place, you crazy freak! Until you nip all your philistine prejudices in the bud: about being under-age, and about your belly aching and all that stuff. Oh, they're so nasty to her, the giddy flirt – what a poor little girl! You think Korchagin had it any easier? A hundred times worse, a thousand times, make no mistake about it. Just try it, compare who he is and who you are. And for all his worldwide eternal fame he was so modest there are just no words for it. He never forgot for a moment that the phrase 'duty first' exists in the world. That's how the individualistic egotists take advantage, of course. They know that for you the collective always comes first. So of course they try it on. You wake up and grab hold of your knickers – hang on, I'll get them down myself, I'm not going anywhere, if it's your turn now, whatever your name is, Kolka, Sashka, don't tug them, hang on a moment, let me just give my eyes a rub! But it's done already, the elastic's broken again, and the end's disappeared into the hole, it'll take a safety pin now to get it back out …

And just what is it they're all looking for under the knickers that's so marvellous and wonderful? Of course, in any house in Leningrad all the normal boys play hospital in the yard – giving injections in bare bums – but they're just little children, right? The kids are just curious about the way people are made, they're being inquisitive, the way a class-conscious future pioneer and Komsomol member ought to be. What kind of nuts and bolts and tubes is he actually made of – our Soviet man? After all, he's a machine as well, isn't he? And a top-class mechanism too: he moves around in the first place, and he can talk like a radio, in different voices, and he can work as well as any old lathe, especially if he's been given the honorary title of shock-worker. On the other hand, take a doll, for instance. Even if you stick a pin in it or twist its head off, it won't say a single word. But do that to a man and for some reason he's bound to start yelling like a stuck pig, you only have to jab him a bit stronger with the pin if the cheat's jumped the queue for his injection. But just how much he can stand, unfortunately that's something science still hasn't established yet. That's why every future soldier has to develop a real soldier's endurance from childhood. Even though our tanks are fast, like it says in the song, just to be on the safe side anyway. You could end up getting caught like Kibalchish by some samurais or other and they'll start pestering you with those stupid hara-kiris of theirs: betray your comrades, you pioneer swine, or it'll be worse for you! After all, nobody knows who you might have to fight tomorrow: the whole world's ready to gang up against the land of the Soviets, it's a bone stuck in everybody's throat, every bourgeois does nothing but dream of attacking us, and in the most treacherous way possible, something terrible it is! And that's why it's so necessary to train yourself all the time, so that no torture means a thing to you, so that Stalin can always rely on you when he thinks up a new military secret, the most invincible of all, to frighten his enemies with. That's why Timur's gang chose Midge as chief surgeon: for purposes of education in steadfastness and heroic courage she always had a safety pin in her knickers, specially blunted a bit on the asphalt so as not to draw blood when it pricked you in case anyone still happened to be afraid on account of being too young and still hadn't developed their willpower to maximum strength. Even the big louts, six or seven years old, tried to force their way past the queue to see her, started fights, literally, they could fight half the day over who Midge was going to give an injection to next, and they always insisted on having it without anaesthetic. And of course you did your best to meet that kind of class-conscious fool halfway, because you could see the man had a goal. After all, endurance doesn't just depend on willpower, a man has to have a goal in his head – to become the man with the most endurance in the world, a genuine Bolshevik, made of flint and steel, or at least of wood for a start. And they pricked Midge herself last of all, each of them three times. But she only allowed that as an incentive for the ones who stood it themselves and didn't start blubbing. She never squealed even once – it didn't hurt the slightest bit, just imagine! She was chief surgeon until they accepted her into the Young Pioneers. And then for a whole year the little kids trailed around after her: hey, Aunty Masha, let's give you an injection, hey, just once! The little shit-faces were used to the idea of Aunty Masha being more fearless and better at bearing pain than anyone else. And that was why her senior comrades put their trust in her and gave her a red tie to wear as a model activist. Now she had to teach every little boy and girl in the yard what was what one by one: you have to understand at last that young pioneers aren't interested in children's games, they have their own laws of collectivism and genuine grown-up principles, friendship's all very well, but it's for kids.

But at the front she realised straight away that grown-ups were even worse than little boys. Something terrible it was! Worst of all, most of the officers had done anatomy at school, but they all imagined they could unearth some miracle down there – under a normal, ordinary person's knickers. Like some kind of crazy idiots, so sad it was enough to make you laugh, pioneer's honour! Even worse than children – a hundred times! Any normal Soviet Timur, even if he was a top-class snitch, say, and a desperate liar, a whinger and little mummy's boy, even a traitor like that would still never think of sinking that low – breaking the elastic in your knickers or sinking his teeth into your bare breast. Because he'd collect a smart smack round the ear that very second. And he knew that perfectly well and he wasn't going to set his milk teeth to work, not even if they were itching for it, especially when they were just about to fall out. It's not allowed and that's that. He's not a little sucker any more, not a baby. Hospitals or mothers and daughters, it's all the same – you don't go making up your own special rules, nobody gave you any right. The rules in any game are the same for everyone: if you want to get an injection – join the queue the same as everyone else. If you don't know how, we'll teach you, if you don't want to – we'll make you, all nice and quiet, like. But if, my fine friend, you go trying to pinch people with a clothes-peg or torture kittens or blow up a toad through a straw, or if our common rules don't suit you – then sorry, out you go, citizen, you've got the wrong address, as they say, find yourself different company to keep. Where they'll let you bite people and break elastic – only just next door in house number fifteen, they're all like that – déclassé and disenfranchised, every one: some have dads who are known enemies of the people, some have uncles who are kulaks and some have been excluded from the pioneers – like the whole gang of them was put together specially, something really terrible it is! But in our house there isn't a single alien element left on all five floors, they've been exterminated as a class. And if someone from our yard behaved like that just once, the entire collective would react instantly. World-class our lads are, they'd give the crazy freak a good kicking all right, and then Aunty Masha would never give him another injection, even the simplest, in his bum or his belly, let alone let him see her titties – she wouldn't even let him into her sight. Because he's a genuine crazy freak. No class-conscious Soviet kid would go sucking on your nipples – think about it for yourselves, dear comrades! It's impossible to imagine it, a nightmare it is! Never mind an experienced young pioneer – in our yard any snot-nosed little twerp is always able to figure things out, size up the situation and get a proper grip on himself, even though he's still only knee-high to a grasshopper.

But these freaks, they're running wild, out of control, pioneer's honour! Worst of all, it's not just the green lieutenants either, they really are still wet behind the ears, they still haven't forgotten their mother's breast yet – it's the senior command personnel, that's what's so amazing! And the middle level's even worse. To look at, someone like Major Khriukin is a regular officer, decorated too, with white teeth, large ones, still an interesting old man at forty. But in fact it turns out he only has one thing on his mind all day long from morning till night. Before you even get undressed he snatches so it takes your breath away! As though his hands were just itching to grab hold of them! And then of course he'll start pushing and pulling you about, squeezing and stretching – kneading you like dough until your tits are swollen all over. And then suddenly he'll pounce and start sucking on you like a crazy man – something terrible it is! I've tried explaining to them like normal people: I haven't got any milk in there, don't try to squeeze any out, you won't get a drop, I've checked it plenty of times. Khriukin just growls like a hungry little animal and starts in with his teeth. Chewing and biting and sucking and licking like you're an ice cream or a crème brulée – sucks you in like a dummy, till you feel like you're inside his mouth, all of you sucked inside, boots and all – that's enough of that, Comrade Major, it's a waste of time; if you'd like some condensed milk I've got an open tin under the trestle bed, I'm fond of it too, just reach down and feel around a bit – but he doesn't hear. He slurps and snuffles and whines – just like a little kitten or a blind puppy sucking on his mother. And the worst thing is, those painful groans of his make it sound like the freak's actually sucking something out on the sly – couldn't be my blood, could it, bloody hell? The number of times I've checked afterwards. No blood, not a single drop. Just red bruises – from all that greedy grasping and sucking of theirs – it's been like that for more than a year now. And my nipples are stretched, like a suckling bitch or a nanny goat – sticking out like they're pointing and telling you to get lost, Comrade Major, no sweet milk for you – go suck on a dummy!

I'm used to it – in principle. Only it itches all the time and in the morning I feel thirsty, something terrible, like I've got a hangover. Lukich laughs, the parasite: 'What is it, Midge, guts on fire because you drank too much? How many times do I have to tell you: drinking with the officers is just a waste of booze.' He laughs and rubs his concussion tears into the corner of his eye with a finger. Of course, he feels sorry for Midge. At night behind his tarpaulin he hears everything, but he can't help, his hands are tied by the regulations. But as soon as an admirer gets off her trestle bed and gets dressed and clears off back home and Midge finally gets to close her eyes – Lukich hops straight up off his bunk. He comes over and straightens Midge's padded blanket, tucks it in at the sides, strokes her hair gently, makes the sign of the cross over her and crosses himself too, the fool: 'Our Father, Who art ... Mother of God, rejoice!' He may be concussed, but he's a good man, he tries to understand her. So why at such a good moment does she suddenly feel like cursing and swearing at him? But at the same time Midge realises that if she had the strength, if Major Khriukin hadn't spent half the night drinking blood from her breasts again, then she'd immediately feel ashamed of her unforgivable desire to swear at the kind old man who isn't to blame for anything, of the incomprehensible spite she feels for saintly Lukich, make no mistake about it, she'd blush and ask him to forgive her. She would – if only ... If only, if only – but she hasn't even got enough strength to move her leg or cover up her bare breasts. There's no point in being shy of Lukich, and her nipples seem to itch less in the air than under the blanket, they're swollen that badly. Although you couldn't say that Major Khriukin is such a wild and greedy sucker as Lieutenant-Colonel Bykovsky, for instance, who always tries to stuff both her nipples in his mouth at once and gets very angry when he can't manage it. And he accuses Midge of losing weight, although never once has he brought the girl any chocolate, not even a tin of condensed milk. How can you build up your body for all of them, if you have no supplementary rations, with such responsible duties? Who's worked out how much you lose just by sweating? But you've got to give everybody a nice, soft, well-fed, strong body so it feels good to grab hold of your boobs and any other part of your young girl's anatomy. So why not bring some chocolate regularly, what's the problem? No, they'll eat the chocolate themselves and then blame you because they can't stretch your second tit into their jaws at the same time – you've got so thin. Making themselves out to be big von-barons, every one of them! And if Khriukin did bring any chocolate once, he'd remind her for a whole year afterwards: lie the way you did when I brought you the chocolate. As if now Midge had to keep spreading her legs for the rest of her life just for that chocolate – what a miserable cheapskate, eh?

In general you can almost always tell from his habits – from the way he presses on you, the way he puts it in and gets hot and excited and finally shrinks away to nothing – you can always make a good guess from those data at what kind of officer he really is – a greedy egotistical individualist or maybe not a total von-baron after all, but a comrade with at least a little bit of class-consciousness. But then, to tell the truth, with most of the officers, you couldn't really tell: he might seem to be paying attention to a girl and he'll talk to you like a comrade, without any hurry, so sometimes you even think: at least here's one of them who doesn't need that childish nonsense, a real adult, a serious man, so you can even just lie there beside him and talk with him like a brother, or at least a cousin – what a pleasure – and your elastic won't get snapped either – wonderful! Then he'll suddenly leap on you like a Cossack leaping into the saddle and setting off at a gallop. It's like he's been changed into someone else, a pure stud – at least thank god they haven't shoed his feet or he'd trample you to death. And then, when it's all over, he seems like a human being again and you don't bear him any grudge or feel angry with him for being such a coarse lout and egotistic old goat. It's easy, when you know what's most important of all: and for you that's service, work, your duty to the Motherland and your beloved Party, but for him, the freak, it's either a chronic disease, or maybe a fit, and what demands can you make on a sick man? Especially since he's practically a child, how can you take it seriously?

Senior Lieutenant Sbruev, for instance – he's a real world-class lad now, isn't he? Young, but already respectable and dignified. And there's really nothing at all surprising about that, because he's a Siberian, came here from close to Krasnoyarsk itself, they say they're all the same there. It doesn't do to fuss and fidget in Siberia: the taiga is the law and the bear is the landlord. Sbruev served his national service before the war and then spent two years swinging a hammer in a collective farm forge. He's got shoulders as broad as that and he walks like the bear that he once went for with a forked pole, one against one. But when he starts settling himself down on a girl's trestle bed, if you were asleep you wouldn't even feel it, he's that gentle! And he'll never ever try to get into your knickers – begging your pardon – while you're still asleep. He'll act disciplined and sit there beside you smoking his 'Little Star' cigarette, quiet as a mouse, waiting for you to wake up on your own. And without making a single sound either. Only occasionally he might scratch his hairy chest with a sigh like a creaking or chirping sound – open those shaggy blacksmith's bellows of his like an accordion so that a hot wave of air wafts Midge away and pins her up against the wall by accident – what a freak, eh?

'Sbruev, is that you?'

'Yes, Midge, who else? Sporting greetings!'

'Hi! Back again quick as a flash.'

And she'll give a quiet, hoarse laugh, immediately feeling her body, deadened by her strategic dream, beginning to thaw and recover in his expansive warmth, the body that was no use to anybody just a minute ago, while she was flying on the course set by General Zukov's voice – then suddenly it was like she hit an air pocket or something. Instantly she started dropping towards mother earth, tumbling over and over on her way down, but as it happened she fell with terrible precision straight into herself, Midge, pinned against the wall by Sbruev with the full force of his breath. Midge warms up, hurrying to get her fill of the warming comfort of his chest, before the moment of inevitable torment arrives, stretching as she gets used to her body again and settling into it as comfortably as she can, she curves herself out like a cat then curls up tight again, tickling the massive bull with her claws and at the same time pressing her sniffling little girl's nose, cold from sleep, up against him and wiping her innocent little snots on his red-hot shoulder, as big and round as a volleyball, with the pure smell of sporting strength and strong 'Chipre' male eau-de-cologne. She'll toss about, the little baby, spinning from one side to the other like a top in the generous peace of his deep, subconscious heat – and warm her thighs against hot stone-hard hips and trustingly stick her buttocks, like cold hard beans, into his belly, with the back of her head resting on his chest, in that undergrowth as thick as grass – so delighted she doesn't know what to do with herself. Just as if mummy had taken little Masha into her bed on her day off work and she could bask in the lovely warmth for half an hour. Midge knows she'll never be allowed such happiness with anyone except Sbruev and she nestles against him, and suddenly presses her cheek against him, even strokes him in a childish fashion, like a pet dog or perhaps even like her daddy when he used to bend down to his little girl and ask: 'Come on then, Midge, show me how you love your dad, will you?' – and she didn't want to kiss him, no matter how much her mother tried to persuade her, she would just stroke his cheek and run away. And the young pioneer, chilled through from her dreams of flying, goes on drawing life from Sbruev's firm hips and now she shakes and wiggles the icy cold cheeks of her little bum – all the time stroking her friend, lying there as still as a house, and tickling him a little bit, distracting her future tormenter with conversation – any other man wouldn't put up with her empty chatter and midgy droning even for a minute – rattling on and on to put him off starting for as long as possible. Sbruev's virtually the only one out of all of the men she's got used to sharing her hard trestle bed, her brief sleep and the eternally cold dwelling of her soaring spirit with, who listens to Midge's childlike chatter and spellbinding babble without irritation. And it keeps on and on, pouring out of her rounded little mouth, that rambling stream of names, coquettishly extended vowels and pathetic exclamations with a genuine tear in her icy eyes. In the rounds of her hasty speech the names of human bodies and inanimate objects are all no more and no less important for her during these brief minutes of daughterly joy than the trills, modulations and flourishes of some simple happy little robin's song repeated down the centuries in the July noon. The melodic Morse code of a languishing Nature that seems not yet to have acquired a sufficiently accommodating receptacle for all the ciphers and codes of the all-wise Logos, not to have set human vocal cords up according to His blueprints and not to have poured into our skull of clay a sufficient measure of that still liquid brain, but still scattered the hardening convolutions thickly, as though with stars, with the self-love of the All-Powerful that nags us ceaselessly and masks man's fear in the face of his own insignificance. And the complaints about the elastic that has been snapped again are drawn like a red thread through the tumultuous, greedy, cowardly and proud, vague and monotonous monologue, interrupted by squeals of outrage, snorts of laughter with a hand held over her lips and mischievous slaps against the smooth skin of the patiently sighing Sbruev. Intoxicated already by her corporeal satiety, the little chit talks about the regimental news – the icicles are no longer visible in her eyes, only the pupils are left, sucking the living warmth directed towards her into a black void. She talks on and on and on – choking, spraying cold drops of spit, swallowing words, losing track of a thought that perhaps never even existed. She talks about herself – what she ate today, and who tried to court her – that is, put his hand over her mouth and dragged her into the bushes, after ambushing her behind the little hillock where she usually goes to pee – but she'd sent the cheeky swine packing pretty smartly, because privates are still nobody and nothing, but they still want the same as everyone else! She talks about her Lukich, the wise fool, about his drunken fancies and his drunken, glorious, holy-seer pronouncements – for Midge is the only one in the entire regiment who doesn't dismiss his boring sermons out of hand. And the girl will talk about Hitler too. And about the company commander, who has radiculitis at present – to Midge's delight, it's more than a week now since he's been able to pester her, the old goat, but before he used to send for her to see him after lunch almost every day – afterwards she had to rest up until the evening, her belly went hard as a brick with the pain, literally; the commander might not have turned out too tall, but like they say all the growth had gone into the branch – she wished that branch could be torn off him, cut away by a piece of shrapnel, sawn off – begging your pardon – by a burst of machine-gun fire.

And Midge also talked about how incredibly happy she was to be living and fighting side by side, shoulder to shoulder with people worth their weight in gold, like the company commander – he might be an old goat, but of course he was a world-class commander – bold, decisive, independent, never paid any heed to the number of casualties, for him an order was something sacred, something terrible that was! And what about Regimental Deputy Commander for Political Affairs Inokhodtsev? In one and a half years not once had he ever let her leave his office in the staff hut without two pairs of Lisle thread stockings and a few bars of chocolate into the bargain, even though he didn't keep her for more than fifteen minutes, she didn't even have to get undressed with him, just stroke him, waggle him about a bit and lick him a couple of times – he said that was the Muslims' custom, the way required by the Shariah law. A real freak, eh? Or maybe he was lying when he said it was their custom and he was simply old and lazy already. After all, Senior Lieutenant Svinadze came from a national minority too, almost a Muslim he was, with those tidy little miniature moustaches, but if he dropped into your dug-out in the night, once his piglet got stuck into the cabbage he'd keep shagging away all night until the dawn, until the cold just before morning set Lukich tossing and turning on his bunk.

Sbruev sighs silently and shivers a little, and Midge won't notice the way his powerful breath suddenly falters for a moment – he'll finish off his cigarette in two long drags and light up a new one straight away from the butt. And the monologue creeps stealthily on, stretching out and flowing avidly towards the eternal ground of female self-delusion – towards that radiant high point where the girl herself will suddenly realise clearly what a petite, delicate little blonde she really is, and in the future she could be a film actress but for the time being she's just a well-tested comrade, modest and reliable, in the first place, and in the second place the most beautiful girl, of course, in the entire division, and maybe in the entire Red Army – wasn't that the reason why General Zukov had chosen her, of course – begging your pardon – he was in love with her too, head over heels, no two ways about it, but as yet there was no way he could strike up a proper friendship with Midge, all that was available to the general was a secret service operation with the girl he loved, a shared feat of geographical heroism for the salvation of our own dear Motherland.

Her incoherent speech flows and streams on. As though the half-starved family favourite, a pretty tortoiseshell cat, grown skinny during the week she's been away wandering God knows where – she got lost, she's a house cat after all, not like the wild street cats who couldn't give a damn about anything – is back home lapping up her milk again, see how the poor thing has stuck her nose into the milk saucer, pressing her torn little ears back guiltily, the way she has directed all her seething, cold, feline tenderness to herself – her kind mistress will take her low growling for affection, for gratitude, for love.

Sbruev will finish smoking with a sigh that is almost a sob, spit neatly on the butt, toss it under the trestle bed into a tin can that Lukich will shake out into the stove in the morning – and then sweep Midge up in one arm with a sigh – a light one this time – and sit her astride his body. The way when he was in a good Sunday mood her daddy used to dandle her on his knee. Sbruev will sigh easily and tell her: 'I'm knackered today, Midge. I was taking the company political classes – instead of that captain of yours. I'm dog-tired. Jump up and down, play around a bit. I know you like that …'

That first time, six months ago, when Sbruev appeared in the regiment, how Midge had fluttered and trembled when she woke up in his arms! She froze and withdrew deep inside herself when those immense, hot palms lifted her up as though on a plate and set her down, daddy's little daughter once again, to ride her dashing mount, and the fire-steed Chestnut-Grey had gone charging off at a gallop. Sbruev's tall hips begin curving up and down in a wave and there's nowhere Midge can go, mounted firmly for safety, she just grabs hold of the wool on his chest and makes sure the wind doesn't blow her off on the corners. Sbruev just slightly tenses his back, his buttocks and his hips, and Midge – on daddy's knee – soars up to the ceiling with her eyes half closed and falls back again, into the broad, comfortable saddle – and then the leap and the flight through the air come over and over again. Now it's as though the little girl with flushed cheeks is soaring upwards and plunging back down on a swing and Sbruev is not playing like a comrade any more, tricking her by curving up sharply out of rhythm, or shifting to one side so that Midge almost falls off him, her heart plunging down into her heels – and she feels so happy playing the game: the lithe little tomboy, the little live wire, shrieks, gasps and curses – she forgets all about the war, and her never-ending tiredness. The little girl is in a desperate hurry to get her fill of playing the game, to stock up her lungs with a store of childish joy for the future, this is something that only happens to her with this freak Sbruev – quick, quick, she has to gratify her frisky impish body with the childish effort of the game. More fright! More fun! Hup! Hup! Hey. Hey-hey-hey! Get on, Chestnut-Grey, you handsome sorrel steed, dash on at a trot, rush on at a gallop. Hey-hey-hey!

If only that idiotic blunt bayonet didn't prevent her from soaring even higher – it's like you're sitting there screwed on to it, it's a real pain. But Sbruev seems to prize it just as much and think it's just as important as all the other officers do. In fact it's the real reason why all this jumping and jerking about is going on in the first place. And if you were born a girl you had to spin round on it all the time, following its blunt-headed will, like a butterfly pinned up in a herbarium, literally. And an officer doesn't even know himself what else she can do to please him, how else she can help him with something apparently so important that a man is incapable of even thinking about anything else until this most important thing is over and done with. After all, at first it seems just as simple as taking a pee. But that's not the way things are at all! A man can't deal with it on his own, he has to be helped out by some girl he knows if his wife isn't around, and not just with words, with action. You can't fob him off now with jokes or conversation, you have to roll up your sleeves and finish the job according to the letter of the rules. And then you'll do anything for the good cause, bending this way and that way, twisting like a snake, literally, sometimes even hopping like a frog. There are plenty of ways you can deal with him, your body will tell you how, just don't be too lazy in twisting and turning and especially remember: until the job's done there'll be no peace for you or your comrade in battle who has turned to you like a sister for help with this, who trusts you and is sure you won't let him down. And when you make an honest effort and the freak doesn't understand that you're trying to do the best you can for him, often you feel like laughing at him and the insult brings tears to your eyes because he's still not satisfied, you can tell straight away. He swears and starts pinching you and hurrying you on – he can't wait, you see, just can't wait until his pump works automatically the way it's supposed to. No, he wants it faster and faster, emergency speed! Then of course he'll grab your backside with his huge great hands and start pushing you up and down, up and down on his pole – something terrible it is! And he'll keep trying to slap you down tighter on to himself: Slap! Bang! Plonk! – a blacksmith from hell, trying to turn you into his bloody anvil! And what sturdy stuff an officer's made of! A three-edged bayonet would probably have snapped by now, but it's like this thing has a spring inside it, the way it rings! Your buttocks will start to ache, you'll get cramps in your thigh, but he keeps on flapping your numb backside up and down and hammering in his hellish pile, the freak – you can't tell any more if he's sticking it into you or himself, your head's turned to cast-iron ages ago, it's a copper boiler chiming like a bell and making your young girl's body tremble all over: boom! bang! boom!

But all this is only just the beginning, you can put up with this easily enough, the worst is still to come. Actually it's world-class that the chiming in your head makes you a bit crazy and you even start thinking that now you can go on swaying to and fro in the saddle for an hour, or two, or all night long, without thinking about anything – and letting your empty, chiming bell-head joggle feebly to and fro without a single thought in it, letting the incandescent piston that has almost chiselled right through your empty body carry on sliding backwards and forwards as long as it wants – your body doesn't feel any pain or heat inside. And now the sick feeling's gone away and after that you'll suddenly get your second wind, like a good runner, and then suddenly it's fun again, like being on a swing – as though you wake up all over again – and you get new strength from somewhere, you're weightless, empty, happy – just like a balloon on the First of May! – and you go flying on and on: 'Long live the workers' holiday! Proletarians of the world, unite!' You don't notice the time any more or the jolting and itching inside, you don't feel your numb knees or your breasts turned to wood, squeezed tight like sponges in the blacksmith's massive palms. You go on bounding and swaying, bounding and swaying.

But it's like that freak there inside was just waiting for you to get carried away and let your guard down, close your eyes and start feeling good, as if daddy was still alive and you never left Leningrad and you're flying round and round on the carousel and afterwards daddy's going to take you to ride a pony, and then on the carousel again if you want – why not, twenty times if you like, only the endless steep curve takes your breath away and makes your head spin – you keep leaning over sideways and clinging on, squeezing your knees against the sides of faithful Chestnut-Grey. But suddenly he'll rear up as though he's frightened, suddenly start swelling up and getting all stubborn and rise up like a monument – the von-baron blockhead – who wants the great mushroom for a rouble – for twenty bloody roubles! And then he'll get all haughty and start pushing harder, like he's really got right up on tip-toe – what an arrogant sod, a real individualist! You can feel all his spite and fury – absolutely raging he is, ready to tear anyone who comes within reach to pieces. And of course his owner will start grinding his teeth and tossing his head about – all that bestial ferocity is transmitted to him – and Sbruev's face will start to look as though he's just about to die, his last hour has come, any moment the man will start twitching and shuddering and that will be the end.

Well, you started the job, so now hold on. Like they say, if you're a mushroom, then get in the basket. But it's the other way round, he's the one who's the mushroom, sticking up like that! Even in these final, most labour-intensive, like they say, minutes you still can't get swinging and bouncing properly, he has to get in deeper, where it hurts more, as though his only genuine joy is buried there inside where your pain is. But he'll soon pretend to be gentle again, the traitor, the moment you show some soldier's savvy and seize the right moment just when it seems that if his mushroom giant grows even a little bit more it will rip you open at the seams, stab through right up to your throat and hit the ceiling and then probably break through the wooden beams above your head, force its way through the false ceiling and the earth mound outside and carry on growing out as far as the Great Bear itself, swelling right across the universe until the terrible moment when it spouts a jet of new stars up into the night sky like the sparkling 'Samson' fountain at Peterhof – blue ones and milky-white ones and pink ones like blood mixed with milk – but I don't think so, hang on, Brer Rabbit, no hurry now, when you're all cocked to fire – suddenly when you're not expecting it your skilful, faithful comrade in battle Maria Mukhina will pull off a little trick for you, just like that! – and squeeze everything inside tight like in a fist. Then you'll scream, Sbruev, you'll bellow and start shaking your head about and biting your lip until it bleeds and a mysterious, righteous force will arch you into a bow, lift you up in a bridge on the back of your head and your toes, tossing Midge up to the ceiling for the last time. You'll scream out loud when that invisible bullet hits your belly, and in a long, lingering spasm your pump action flame-thrower will start firing blast after blast in a stuttering stream of flame, releasing all the heat and fear accumulated under the faithless sun of war by your Siberian body fed on bear meat, and letting it out in the death roar of bull laid out for slaughter that Midge catches in her childish palms as she stops your mouth: she wouldn't want her game of carousel with Sbruev to disturb Lukich, or her game of swings at the Sunday zoo, where the well-fed pre-war animals haven't remembered yet how the terror of hungry oblivion used to roar inside them when they were free...

Like a dead man, scarcely breathing, the great Sbruev lies there in front of Midge, now cheerful at last – Sbruev the freak, who only a minute ago was ready to scatter flocks of new-born constellations across the sky in a single salvo – he lies there with his eyes closed and his arms crossed on his chest, a dead man, literally. He says nothing. And you can't hear him breathing. And the fury of his pacified flesh slowly settles and is absorbed back inwards. Midge is still sitting astride him, observing curiously with her own body how ticklishly Sbruev's strength carries on subsiding and slipping away and disappearing. She feels sad and disappointed because the game of carousel didn't last very long. And she runs her finger across the giant's skinny belly, taking offence, only not at him, she can't tell at who or what.

'Midge!' Sbruev calls quietly, barely parting his lips. 'Midge! Did you – was today the same?'

'What? Today? Aha, are you still going on about that?'

Midge stretches, yawns and lifts her right leg over his convex chest like it's a hummock on the ground, then settles herself beside him. 'Just drop it, will you, Comrade Senior Lieutenant! Why do you want to keep rooting around and getting all worked up? I'm not doing anything wrong, am I? If I am, then tell me, order me, hell's bloody bells!'

'You do everything right, my darling, my only love!' he sighs noisily, like a bull. Nuzzles into her armpit and sighs again.

'That's good then! Isn't it?' She yawns again, with a groan and a quiet, good-natured oath.

'But didn't you feel anything today either, Midge? I tried so hard!'

'I enjoyed it, Comrade Senior Lieutenant, it was great fun! Pioneer's honour!'

'Maybe I'm too rough, Midge?' he puts his hand on her breast.

'You're a freak, honest you are! You're my most world-class, most cultured boyfriend, my most reliable comrade!' Midge reassures Sbruev with a yawn. 'Only I'm tired. Let's sleep, ah?'

'All right. I'll just kiss you a little bit more ...'

And then it starts. She could rip his balls off for that!

Gently, indecisively, guiltily he will touch Midge's breasts with the plump lips of a kind man. And her guts will knot themselves together in her belly and her stomach will leap up into her throat like she's being tortured on the rack. What else is it he wants? What is she supposed to feel so that he won't torment her afterwards and tickle her till she feels sick? What has she done wrong? Or is he just sick like the others? O God, what has she done to deserve this?

Wet and hot, passionate and weak, spiteful and tender. Making Midge feel hot and cold, drenching her from the inside with a dark shower of contemptuous repulsion as he warms the girl's skin with his breathing. Squeezing until she has to bite her lips and releasing into the open all her hate for the greedy male tenderness that never reduces a man to a child, but only lays bare his weakness, the concealed cowardice of a petty, insignificant being. All he's capable of is taking, taking, taking – and his hot and bitter juices are no use to a girl's body – you can pour a bucketful into a hoop without filling it up, an entire railway tanker full if you like, you horny goat! It's a miracle they haven't ripped the girl's purse in half yet, impossible to understand, that is! Almost every night – grabbing, tearing, nearly pulling her to pieces with their hands, lips, fingers and the leaden weight of them, if they were like Sbruev, sucking you in and gnawing you, breathing you in with their nostrils and their eyes that flash in the dark like a March tom-cat's.

And just what else am I supposed to feel with all of you, hey god, you sod? What else do you want? You're a man too aren't you, why don't you tell me? Nothing to say? Well sod you then. Why did you make me a woman, a girl? Why didn't you hang a big heavy prick between my legs like every normal man has? You've probably got millions of them. Why did you give me a slit of a cunt and leave the gates to the bottomless money-box wide open for the rest of my life – a ferret could climb into the burrow, or a piglet – you didn't put a lock on it, you forgot. I hope the night will be over soon, and my whole life too! Help me, you bastard! Although I don't believe in you even a little bit, and I never will believe, I'd like to spit on you, with your little lead soldiers! And now he's trying to kiss me on the lips too – yuck, bloody yuck!

But honestly, the only thing they can say is 'give'! And you will, of course, in the end, you'll break down, you feel ashamed to play the miser. But afterwards almost every time you get a nasty aftertaste, that's typical: no, at least once you should have taken a principled stand! Especially when he tries to kiss you on the lips too – that's disgusting! When you get right down to it, dear comrades, it's just not on! Why should anyone have to put up with you and your slobbery lips as well? You're convinced she has to go and kiss everyone at the first glance, emergency speed, just like some slut. You treat him like a human being, that's all, and straight away he gets a big swollen head: she's fallen head over heels, the daft thing, she's his little pussy cat. You keep your mouth covered with your hand all the time. What else can you do? You can't start teaching every one of them how children really get born. If Walter Ivanovich hadn't explained in good time, she probably still wouldn't have guessed for herself. And all these freaks, every one of them, are convinced that a kiss there has nothing to do with it. It isn't explained properly in any of the anatomy text books either, there are drawings of tadpoles everywhere to distract your attention, and an egg, like a chicken's, as though Midge isn't built any more cleverly than some village farmyard bird.

But essentially that's the way it ought to be, so that every woman can only find out from her own experience and it's a secret for men. Nature has fixed things specially so that they don't have everything their way after all, and in the end it depends on you first of all whether there'll be a child or there won't. She ought to have guessed it sooner! When Walter Ivanovich gave her a friendly warning she didn't understand, the fool. It was only after the business with Rostislav, rest his soul, the headless martyr, that she learned a bit of sense. Now, of course, you're worried every time, you beg this shock-worker to put those massive lips of his somewhere else. He takes offence, the freak, and swears and tries to bite so it hurts. The main thing is, how does he see it? If you're an officer, you can do anything you like! So he launches straight into full frontal attack. You're lucky if he's a serious comrade and doesn't like to draw things out for too long and once he's got his officer's job over with quickly – he's off. Goodbye, darling, we part like ships at sea! So there won't be any problems for him or for the girl. But that's only when he's already a regular combat officer, a top-class front-line soldier with serious experience – he understands the way things are at the front, he knows there can be all sorts of undesirable complications, up to and including a strict reprimand from the Party, and for her in her own combat collective as well. Especially since the divisional commander's personal gratitude to Midge was announced on the First of May, written in the certificate it was: '... for exemplary fulfilment of a soldier's duty and valour shown in action'. So the top brass seemed pleased with her all right so far, touch wood, Midge was in their good books, her authority among the men in the unit was deservedly high, she had to take good care of her reputation. Stalin was right when he said: take care of a dress from when it's new, and your honour from when you're young, bloody well right!

But unfortunately not everyone here knows how to demonstrate their class-consciousness yet, especially if they personally don't need it. For instance, when a kid's still only a lieutenant, no one and nothing really, first in line for the ranks of the dead and, God forbid, arrived straight from college with the reinforcements, then you'll have no end of trouble with an inexperienced little chick like that, no two ways about it. They're the ones this is really all about: what's allowed and what's not. They're the ones who cause all the confusion and unnecessary casualties at the front, the manky beasts.

He'll turn up, our Ilya Muromets from the well-fed rear-line, strawberries and cream, like he was only born yesterday –

please take good care of him for us! Not a blind bull's notion about tactics or strategy! No good for anything but saluting and signing death notices, and subtle as a flat iron in his approach to the personnel, especially the women — something terrible it is! Why can't he turn up like a respectable seasoned officer in the evening after dinner and take you gently by the hand: this and that, comrade soldier, a sensible proposal has been advanced to go for a stroll to the nearby wood, behind the small hill, territorially speaking only a stone's throw away, you know all about it, of course. There's some bully beef by the way, and salami sausage — we'll look for blueberries, polish off a bottle of red in the fresh air — 'Abrau-Dursot', an extremely subtle bouquet! And you won't want to, but you'll smile at him in reply — he has such a lovely smile, gleaming teeth, broad and even like they were specially picked for the set, and that narrow little moustache, like a thread … His name was Seryozha, wasn't it? Or Vitya? Anyway, in this case it makes no odds. So what's the point? When they invite you politely, proper-like, you feel like being nice to them yourself, even if you maybe didn't get enough sleep last night because of some lemon-coloured Yakut and you're not in the mood. What is it Stalin teaches us? Even if you die for it, lend your comrade a hand. But a cultured admirer, by the way, will be the first to show some attention: are you feeling well, and how are things going? His considerate words just make you melt and then it's typical that everything turns out very easy with him, and it almost doesn't hurt at all. Not like with those young ones — that's the only reason they turn up, just to put everyone's nerves on edge before the first battle and catch themselves a bullet once and for all. Stalin was right when he wrote about them: if you've no brains you can't buy them at the chemist's. Straight out of the blue, without any agreement in advance — bloody hell, what does he know about 'Abrau-Dursot' and its bouquet — he comes barging into the dug-out in the middle of the night, the freak, with his helmet still on and his machine gun in his hand. At least he's not in a tank! And every time he's bound to stumble over the garbage pail at the door and startle

Lukich, of course. But Lukich, to be honest, will only half wake up and cuss a bit and carry on snoring in the same direction. He's got used to it, he's given up on the lot of them. On the other hand, you can understand him too: how long can he spend sitting in the guardhouse because of these Don Juans? There's no end to them, literally! No matter where the company might be stationed, even out on the far wing of a division stretched right along the front – the very first day they'll penetrate Midge's cover – they have their own reconnaissance and communications, the parasites. At first Lukich used to throw himself at them like a dog, he laid one senior lieutenant out with the butt of his rifle one night last summer. Now all he'll do is cuss out each one of the louts as he arrives and pull his great-coat up over his head: I'm not really here and it's not my dug-out anyway. Or does he deliberately put the bucket on the step for them? Say a single word to an officer and you'll end up in the guardhouse the same day, or even, if you're unlucky, in a penal battalion. But this way, in the darkness, you can cuss the commanding officer out of it world-class and you can't be charged. And it's one more reason for taunting Midge: 'You've started wandering around in the night again, daughter, like a lunatic. You kicked the bucket over, stopped an old man getting his sleep. I'm going to leave you and move to Sanka Goryaev's place! Their top bunk's been empty for two weeks now since Seryoga Vysev ...' – he's lying, the old prattler, he won't go anywhere. But of course Midge is overwhelmed by shame for her deadly dream anyway, for showing such coarse lack of concern for an old man and commander in the same person. After all, he's been like a mother and father to her for more than a year now, every since he picked Midge up on the volleyball court that time she survived by a miracle.

One Saturday night when he was drunk, Lukich read her an entire lecture, all about Midge's special talent for sleeping soundly and how it ought to be understood in the broadest historical context: 'The machine-gunner's sound sleep is our surest guarantee of rapid and total victory! So you take your sleep in good cheer, daughter, in unshakeable faith. When you're sleeping your childish body is still growing and developing, it couldn't give a damn about the war. You're not even fifteen yet! And there you are off flying almost every night, you told me so yourself. And that's the surest sign of all that you've still got to keep on growing and growing, nature will have its way, you can't outwit it. And secondly, remember, if someone sleeps soundly, it means his conscience is absolutely clear. And you thank God that so far he allows you to sleep like a log after all the torments you're forced to go through, and forget yourself completely, at least in sleep. Because if you're not suffering from insomnia, it means there's no wrongdoing put down to your name, no sins, you're pure. Only don't be proud, don't you go pointing your little snub nose up at the sky. A clear conscience isn't your own doing, it's a gift from God. You've not really got anything to do with it, it's all just God's providence working itself out, we're all his servants. If God tells you to, you'll steal and kill and betray your own father. But if you're not commanded to take any sin on your soul yet – rejoice in your heart and thank the Creator unceasingly. But don't go thinking you're the only one like that in the world. Everywhere life has taken me I've met plenty of these pure-hearted sleepers. Even in the far North. And in the transit prison, in a common cell for sixty souls. One cropped convict beside me tosses and turns from side to side on his bunk all night long, counting fleas, his conscience won't let him be. But there's another one who looks like a real hard case, a thief and swindler who could be doing time for some bloody murder – and he sleeps like a little child, just beaming with holiness. It's so obvious a blind man could see it: in the eyes of the Almighty this comrade isn't guilty of anything. And the life ahead of him is probably bright and easy, even if he's stuck in jail for the rest of his days he'll get himself set up as a trusty medical orderly or a bookkeeper or a clerk – who knows where the Lord can find a place to shelter a man of God in his bosom? – and the Creator himself will choose a kind death for him too. Either he'll take him while he's sleeping – simply drink up his breath and take the pure soul to himself. Or if it's at the front, our Saviour will send a stray bullet at a quiet moment after a heavy battle straight into his heart so he won't even have time to sigh or cry out. So you sleep as much as you like, and don't have any doubts. It'll be time for you to grow up soon. Develop your body and be a mother. When we smash the Germans we'll get you married. To a general with stripes on his trousers. And you won't have a worry in the world, guzzling anchovies and having red-haired sons to delight all of us, your eternal regimental comrades. So when the next war comes, the Third World War, God grant, and even in the Fifth, there'll be someone to stand up for Russia – may the Blessed Virgin protect her, our holy whore. So get your head down and catch up on the sleep you need, daughter – for the glory of the Motherland and a rapid victory!'

But Midge doesn't need any persuading.

Chapter 3

In which Midge is now Seagull,
flying without any wings or propeller,
under the personal command of General Zukov.

She only has to lay her wild little head on the hard duffel-bag, curl up in a tight ball under the padded blanket and pull her pointed little knees up to her belly, and her ice-blue eyes instantly roll into oblivion. And almost immediately the glorious warrior Maria Mukhina, the faithful little wife of the regiment, radiant bride of her own death, sets off, flying out on a night raid along the route laid down by General Zukov and approved, naturally, in the headquarters of the Supreme Commander in Chief, in the Kremlin. It is even just possible that He Himself signed it after perusing the plan of the secret operation 'The End of the Dragon'. What if he even developed the plan? Oh, better not think about that!

It started happening to her at midnight in August the year before last, after Midge burst into laughter when she saw the bullet holes in Sevka Goryaev's back by the light of the headlamps of the general's MK. She could still remember it: she didn't laugh that time because she was stupid, it was out of absolutely genuine human happiness — a deep personal happiness, at that — at suddenly meeting the glance of the great man and instantly realising that in another second, death would fuse her own soldier's soul with his, which was practically another soldier's soul, even if it was a general's. After all, if even he had tears in his eyes now, then he would never forget the sight of Sevka's blood gleaming orange-gold on the ground in the light of the headlamps — a little pool that lay there without soaking away, as though it was calling on them to spill the enemy's blood on the trampled earth of the volleyball court. Only that would dim and extinguish the yellow highlights on the little crimson lake, and the crimson

[51]

sparks of the tears in the general's eyes that were blue like Midge's. She laughed, fell down and died. And when she came round a day later, burst into tears and fell asleep, as though everything was calm and peaceful now, in Lukich's dug-out — because he had picked her up — she still didn't suspect that from that moment on her dreams were no longer just dreams but also part of her duties, an even more important and honourable part than when she was awake.

And for more than a year now, almost every night, every time like the one before, like the first time, with amazement and a brief terror, the weightless and incorporeal girl called Seagull has risen up, absolutely naked but almost invisible even to herself, and for other people even more so — as insubstantial as her own breathing in the night. With no sound or effort she floats up above the heavy slumbering flesh of her poor sister Midge. With transparent fingers Seagull gratefully touches the short, singed eyelashes of her snoring guard, the blessed Lukich, with her bluish little palm she strokes the soft transparent glow surrounding his wise old bald patch like a head on an icon, so bright on the nights of her flights that she can see every knot in the planking wall at the head of the holy man's bed. Sometimes, when he is very drunk, Seagull is afraid his head and its good thoughts might burn up in the fire of his holiness: the flame above the bald patch flares up in purple patches, black arrows with coiling crimson tails come flying out of the bald dome and bore straight through the wall. The light and airy Seagull pities him and then, drawn on by the Supreme Will, slips quietly past the door curtained off with a waterproof cape, which for some reason is forbidden to her on her night flights, and follows the stream of air through the little hole in the iron door and into the heat of the small stove stoked up by Lukich, without any fear of the fire that she can't feel or any concern about her mysterious route. If her way lies through the stove, so be it, the command knows best, of course, who has to keep what secrets and leave without being noticed when they go out on a secret raid.

The semi-darkness under the soot-blackened vaults of the

stove is full of mystery. Like in the famous Sablin caves where she went on a hike with their pioneer troop leader Volodya on the first day of the summer holidays in nineteen forty. With a single candle for the entire group, deliberately with only one, to make it more dangerous. And when they went in under the vaults, by the way, a bat immediately grabbed hold of Midge's hair. Everyone was envious of her, literally! And they took turns trying to feed the tiny little fidgety dragon saveloy sausage and sunflower seeds and black sticky grains of repulsive pressed caviar: the grown-ups adored it, and maybe it was grown-up too? And Senka Egorov even tried to get it to drink cream soda from a teaspoon. The little mousekin choked and snorted, twisting its head with the big ears, squeaking and wriggling, wrinkled all over like a little old man. In the little flyer's huge, round, bulging eyes, as wet as black ice, Midge could see her own tiny face lit up by the candle – white hair and a red tie. And Volodya explained that bats are immediately blinded by the light, science had proved that, and so they ought to let it go. 'Let it go, let it go!' Lipuchkina started shouting. 'It's probably got children!' Volodya took the blinded flying creature and carried it into the depths of the cave. Of course the whole troop moved in after him. And then those mice with wings came raining down on the pioneers! Like hail, literally. The little grey bundles came hurtling out of the darkness, making the damp air tremble in front of Midge's half-blinded eyes and tickle her ears and neck. Huge shadows leapt across the walls. Someone dropped a knapsack with a mug that clattered against a rock and Svetka Lipuchkina squatted down and put her arms round Midge's knees. Then, speaking loudly so as not to feel afraid in the cave, Midge said: 'It turns out bats have collectivism too – isn't that great! And they maintain the honour of their troop too – right?' – 'Oh, that's my girl, Mukhina!' said Volodya, and he gave her a firm, friendly hug round the shoulders, and stroked her bare cheek too. 'You look at things from a class position! Demonstrate a mature attitude! But perhaps some of you others are afraid, eh? Own up, comrades! I won't expel anyone from the group for that – if you own up honestly, of course …' Midge stopped breathing. And down below Lipuchkina stuck her nails into Midge's leg and bit her knee. Then with a sudden *huff*! – Volodya blew out the candle! In the darkness Midge imagined that now all the bats in the cave would immediately throw themselves on her from all sides and start snatching at her hair and her ears, and grabbing her nostrils with the little prehensile hooks on their wings, with their little fingers and claws and sharp, brazen little teeth, and start clambering and scratching and gnawing and squeaking and they'd get into her ears, complete with their prickly, webbed dragon's wings – the same way she'd barged in uninvited into their dismal cave with her red drum over her shoulder. Senka Egorov dropped a bottle of cream soda and of course it smashed against a rock. It splashed on to Midge's bare legs and tickled and she shuddered all over. And somehow her throat suddenly began singing as loudly as it could: 'Flutter your glowing camp fires, blue summer nights!' And of course everyone immediately joined in. Although not quite immediately: 'The pioneer's word is always be prepared!' They stood there in the dark and sang. When they came out of the cave into the light, Volodya took Midge by the shoulder and said: 'You'll be chairman of the troop! I think the comrades will support your nomination. I've had my eye on you for a long time, Midge.' And he straightened the tie on her chest. Smoothed down the ends carefully, like with an iron. She felt all ticklish inside with joy, or maybe with fear again. Or maybe with shame. Midge was the first in her class to start wearing a bra and she was very shy about her newly protruding breasts: in the first place, they were completely useless, they got in the way, and in the second place she felt ashamed in front of the boys, like she'd changed somehow, and you can't go around all the time letting everyone know you're still the same as before, you have nothing to do with these stupid bumps and don't intend to have anything to do with them – *merci beaucoup* with tassels on for the lovely present!

And now in the small stove, as Seagull, shrunk by a mysterious power on the orders of General Zukov for the sake of secrecy, drifted above the suddenly massive charred timbers of ordinary logs, above the spots and patches of fading heat, Midge remembered her pride and her shame and the frightened little mousekin with the beautiful-fairytale, evil-dragon webbed wings and the darkness of the tall cave where she sang in order to stop herself blubbing, and she remembered the campfires of those pioneer nights, the flame of the candle stump, the shadows on the walls. Now she would probably think the dragon's cave was small and not frightening at all. But here in the stove it was so spacious and so comfortable that the thought suddenly occurred to her: wouldn't it be nice to live here for a while and take a rest? Read a book – Jack London or Jules Verne. There'd be more than enough light from the embers and no bombing would mean a thing here in this little iron shelter. But the mission comes first, ahead of everything else. Ever heard of the phrase 'duty first?' Or have you forgotten it, Mukhina? Come on, stop playing the fool, you crazy-woman, you'll have time to rest when you report to General Zukov in due form: 'Your orders have been carried out! The Red Army is victorious!'

But meanwhile, streaming and coiling over the bluish embers with the last thin wisp of choking smoke, she moves directly to the hole in the vault. And slipping like a grass snake through the long, jointed, sooty pipe – as though she is finally wriggling out of her last material mantle, her enchanted frog's skin – Seagull bursts out into naked open space stretching out to the horizon all around. The sparsely scattered early stars gaze at Midge ecstatically, like kittens. Now there is no more to her than a breath in with no breath out. And there is no need for her forgiven heart to shudder and shrink, giving painful, hapless life to her soldier's body – she has no heart. If only it was like that when she's awake, eh?

Low, low at first, just above the grass. Drawing in the satisfying scent of the mature inflorescences of St John's Wort, without breathing, with nothing but trust, drawing in the scent of mint and meadowsweet and celandines – every flower turns its little corolla with its little glow of rainbow aroma towards the flying girl, hurrying to share its secret power, like some crazy freak, for the good of the common cause. The long little azure cloud floats and streams and drifts above the grass and herbs – across the little gully before the firing line, where the final scented warmth of the day just past still hangs in the windless air. Feeling no warmth without any body or skin, in her enchanted dream the cloud-girl sees ever more clearly the flowing patches and the waves expanding in rings and the subtle coiling filaments of scents. The tansy sparkles on the hummocks – a scattering of polished copper buttons, broadcasting rapid green needles in every direction. A silvery cloud glows above a clump of cool, dewy michaelmas daisies. A bank of thick blue flame rises straight up above a little meadow with tall pink fountains of willow herb. A subtle green rainbow hovers above a white umbrella of goutweed. A thick, sleepy, milky haze swirls above the reeds of a shallow little swamp. And every splash of soft, untroubled, peaceful light, every weak, fleeting spark of a little rainbow above the flowers and plants gives up a portion of its strength to the girl flying past, equipping her for battle.

When she feels the currents of deep waters drawing her down to the earth itself, through the clay and stones, in the depths the girl can make out a colourless, sluggish underground stream – she can clearly hear its cool bluish ringing. Bearing their silver gleam between the subterranean boulders and blue blocks of clay, the serpentine branches of the torrent rise to the surface in springs, feeding the bog and the stream that curves round the regiment's front on the left flank. And deeper still, the heat of the earth's inner depths bursts through a stony layer of compacted clay in barely perceptible sparks. As though below the very deepest depths, in some giant witch's stove gigantic logs are radiating crimson and purple, burning on throughout the ages without being consumed. Or maybe it's Satan himself fanning the flames beneath the cauldrons in the caverns of hell – something terrible that would be! No, best not to glance that far. Of course, there is no devil either, if god doesn't exist, but anyway, all the same, just to be on the safe side ...

As Seagull flies she can see the breathing of every iris in the bog, every silvery little bell with precisely scalloped edges, hanging on its slim twisting stem as thin as a thread. She can see and hear the ringing and rustling of the underground waters and the sighs of the blue-tits sleeping in the bushes and the disgruntled snorting of a mole – there's a real world-class miner for you, eh? – a Stakhanovite, on the night shift he digs himself a new passage from his burrow to the surface, where the little wild strawberries are lying like the scattered sparks from an extinguished cigarette – in the daytime Midge wouldn't have seen them in the thick grass, she'd never have found them. Only when you fly at night can you see how bright everything on earth really is, how it gleams from the inside – except for the stones and the ground itself, they're dull and dark, blind and silent. If only she could stay for ever in this transparent world, among the translucent rainbows, the gentle glimmerings, the sparkling patches of light – but these are things you can only see and feel in a dream, not in the daytime, when you're awake, it's not allowed. And you can't bring anything back with you from a dream, she'd realised that when she was still a child. So all day long you keep looking at the sun and trying to hurry it on to sunset so that the genuine, normal life can start as soon as possible, the life when every flower's glad to see you and you have honourable secret duties …

A crimson sky in the west. Orange clouds like garlands of New Year mandarin peels. And inside her, it's starting to seethe, like the bubbles in fizzy water, about to burst out any moment – the delight of limitless height. But somehow all the same every time without fail she wants to fly somewhere else before crossing the firing line – either to say goodbye to her friends, just in case something happens, or to convince herself once again that Seagull is invisible, that the dream will not deceive her this time either, that it will carry her, lead her to where she needs to go – her direct course to combat. And in her low-level flight, as they call it, Seagull will glide on, very nearly tipping the crumbly parapet of the freshly dug trench with the machine-gun nests on its flanks, where Sanka Goryaev and Fyodor Shumsky are on guard, chilled through from the night dew, and red-haired Olezhka and Stepan Fomich Muziukin, and Kolyvanov and Starostin, the inseparable pair. Smoking up their sleeves, glugging down the drink in the flasks they had stowed away. Starostin's a well-known coward, the light above the top of his head's already so thin, so dim and smoky you can barely even make it out. But even that's something to be thankful for, at least he's half-alive, even if he is afraid – thanks entirely to a swig from his flask. He screws the cork in, and the pale luminescence above his forage cap starts to shrink and darken, on the point of dying completely. Starostin obviously hasn't got long left to walk the earth, she's seen plenty of these dim-glowing men, ours and the Germans', all of them the same – doomed. Just look how the writhing black arrows come swarming out of nowhere to the weak, pitiful light of his flesh – they stab the poor man in the head, and he doesn't feel it – right in the very top, pointing out the target to death. Obviously there are limits measured out and procedures defined for death too – if he took each and every one by turn then what kind of war would that be? Starostin's been pining away for more than a week already, she noticed, look at him pressing up against Kolyvanov, and earlier he used to run after Seryoga Rysev like he was tied to him, and he managed to do it, the parasite, guided his own death to take his friend. Surely he won't manage to hand over Kolyvanov too? He keeps trying to lean against his broad back or embrace him as though he's joking. Kolyvanov, thank God, has almost got his own individual sun rising above his head, and his entire powerful body radiates crimson heat – it would probably be enough to warm the entire company, and not just Kolyvanov, in the face of inevitable death. That's probably the way Walter Ivanovich would shine, if only he was alive. And of course, he would have been like Kolyvanov, a knight of the order of the Red Banner, or maybe even a Hero ...

And flying over Kolyvanov's head, Seagull is unable to resist. As though by accident, as though she doesn't really notice it, with just the very tip of her invisible little finger she touches the springy crimson wave round Kolyvanov's shoulder. A light, momentary burn tosses Seagull upwards like a trampoline. Thanks, Vasya! Sorry I didn't ask first, of course. If you were an officer, I'd know how to pay back the debt to your generous body ...

And there's Sanka Goryaev, a green glow-worm counting the first stars with his head thrown back. His eyes don't see the heavenly, transparent Seagull and as she lingers above him she makes no attempt to check her inaudible laughter – Sanka's familiar face seems terribly stupid to her, the freak can't even spot her at the distance of a bayonet thrust. Pressing her cheek against his and then recoiling, Seagull flicks him on the nose and snorts in his face to make sure that Sanka is deaf and insensible to her affectionate mischief. She tugs on his arm as well, blows in his ear, turns a somersault in the air above him and Olezhka, leaving a train of dissolving azure sparks that they can't see and then, feeling frisky now, she flies straight through their bellies and through the tall parapet of the trench – whirling like a top, already faint from bliss, literally. She's free! Completely, finally free! Now you can all go jump in a lake!

Seagull knows that General Zukov can't see her undisciplined jokes, she's not in his field of view yet – and he can't hear her soundless laughter or her swearing or her secret thoughts. But soon, just as soon as that steely voice of his gets a fix on her line of flight, she'll shudder all over at the command 'attention!', feeling annoyed that she can't click her heels because she hasn't got any. And just what kind of walkie-talkie is it that he has anyway, hell's bloody bells? She can hear every order even without an aerial. And how does Seagull herself receive his voice while she's in flight, anyway? With her ears? But she doesn't have even one ear, comrades!

Meanwhile, without feeling any shame or disappointment, she'll fly on, not yet subordinate to anyone's authority, over the ravine and over the river and over the thin birch forest where she went the day before yesterday, wasn't it, 'gathering blueberries' with some lanky man, as stiff and skinny as an anti-aircraft gun – it was as though it wasn't her remembering the way the buckle of his new belt that was still stiff pressed against her bare belly. No it wasn't her it happened to, it was that other one, that Midge sleeping like death in the dug-out — sleeping with a bloodless white face and a body sweaty with the cold dampness of the earth, gritting her teeth, and painfully grinding through the customary dark confusion of her heavy friendship duties.

Higher, higher! General Zukov has probably tuned in his apparatus already! Quickly, further and higher — to the west! There are the clouds, orange with shaggy lilac wool on their bellies. Motionless, like barrage balloons. The sunset, gently pink, with a faint green sheen on top, can neither burn them up nor tear its way through them. It suffocates under them and goes out, inundated from above by the lilac cold of the August night. But Seagull senses exultantly that her flight is becoming smooth and irresistible. If only she didn't have to fly like this alone, if only she could fly with Walter Ivanovich for her partner, eh? Hell's bloody bells!

Above the village of Shisyaevo, occupied by the Germans — there's no Smersh waiting for Midge down there yet, and the surviving window panes in the huts glitter in gay flashes of gold, reflecting the red-banner sunset. And it's hard to imagine that down there in the class-conscious Soviet log huts roofed with dried-out, peaceable shingles, the lanky, white-haired Hanses are sleeping all mixed up together with the occupied collective farm workers, and every one of them in white woman's knickers — what a top-class chuckle! Just think what a final stage of human degradation that brainless Hitler has reduced his healthy nucleus of the German working proletariat to — the people have had even their very simplest class instincts taken away from them. Literally! Snoring away like that, the shameless freaks — only two paces away from the living builders of advanced socialism. See that old man and his wife keeping warm on the stove, and those others on the bunks and on the floor — Seagull can see through the roof as easily as she can through the earth. And isn't it just typical that somehow not one white-headed turkey cock is woken by a normal sense of oppressed solidarity with the advanced and almost completely literate Soviet rural population. Not one of them, literally, will leap up and go dashing off to fraternize with his Russian brothers from the poorest peasantry, getting a move on, before it's too late – not one, it's hard even to believe things could have gone this far! Hell's bloody bells, in your fascist place I'd have pulled off my knickers ages ago – what a white flag they'd make! – and I'd have surrendered my stupid machine guns to the granny and granddad. Who's stopping you, dear comrades? Who's preventing you from showing rational initiative? Right here in the hut, without even lighting the kerosene lamp so as to keep things secret you could call an improvised meeting of a united Soviet-Fascist Party cell, chaired, for instance, by that old granny – after all, you're all communists in your hearts, every last one, it's Hitler who's duped you by force and driven you to the front, we know all about you, don't you worry. And you could vote unanimously: all of our officers who are especially stubborn and will vote against, up against the wall; the collective can take responsibility for the further re-education in the spirit of loyalty of the ones who abstain. But that's a strictly individual matter, of course, exclusively according to the wishes of the masses, if there aren't enough cartridges or perhaps a comrade was particularly class-conscious and tried to show his best side from the very beginning of the war, agitated against Hitler like he ought to and bided his time, sabotaging his own side the best he could: derailed all sorts of military trains as often as possible, blew up store depots, threw dead cats into the Germans' wells and so on – after all, there are a lot of class-conscious communists in the German army, and the heart of every one of them longs for some real work to do. We've spared the lives of some of them ourselves – the specially active ones. Yes, don't keep putting it off, the old granddad could soon have everyone lined up in a column two wide, in pairs, German with Russian, the way they always put a boy with a girl in kindergarten, because the swines can't be trusted and you have to keep the reptile in your sights all the time, just in case, it was no accident when Stalin said: 'Trust them – but check them!' And then a forced march straight through the allotments, across the ford of the river, not forgetting to carry granddad and his granny across piggyback, so the prehistoric old shit won't accidentally go drifting off downstream – and then territorially speaking it's only a stone's throw to the forest, and of course in the forest there are partisans sitting around under every bush, in bad need of reinforcements. Just send five agitators to the villages round about – to accelerate the growth of class-consciousness and further mobilisation into our ranks of steel. Or maybe it's best not to waste time dashing around the forest for six months until you stumble across a partisan camp. What good is a German for a partisan? Hans loves order and conveniences, he won't last long on starvation rations with practically nothing to do almost all the time in the partisans: he'll want ammunition, then he'll want bully beef. They don't know how to fight like normal people – modestly. Oh no, you give your Hans world-scale war straight away, as an absolute minimum. Well if that's the way they feel, take them and stick them all in the first unit of the Red Army you can find and the whole lot of them can join the ranks, even in our machine-gun company if you like – big ships are for big voyages, like Stalin wrote. We'd accept them like our own, no two ways about it! The granddad would be put forward for a medal straight away and granny would get a cow, of course, or a hog. So what's the problem? Comrades German workers, I think you're being addressed! They're asleep. Come on, wake up, my darlings! Take a look around, hell's bloody bells! Do you really not want to live a comfortable and prosperous life, like our collective farmers? Soviet power's given the peasant everything, everything, literally! There's a calf in practically every hut – there it is, munching the straw under the bunk, it's stuck its horns out – Seagull can see everything through the roof, especially since the roof's like a sieve. And there's a chicken for you as well – it'll lay you an egg straight into the palm of your hand if you're not too idle just to reach out. And there's a tub full of kvass by the door, even though there's not enough bread in the villages nowadays – drink it when you've got a hangover, take a bath in it if you like and blow bubbles – if only I could dunk your face in that tub, you sleepy-head, to sober you up once and for all, you rotten dragon spawn! Those German turkeys are snoring away even louder than granny and granddad – so what can you do about it? If only she could dive down on those sleepy-heads and put the village in proper order at last! Even without her favourite Walther, even without fists she could easily cope alone with a whole platoon of Hanses, no two ways about that! What would you like to bet?

The important thing is to get inside him, the Hans – into his throat or his belly, or into his head through his ear – it doesn't matter where! She flew through the stove didn't she? She did! The hole in the door was no wider, was it? You have to get yourself into his most ticklish place and then act according to the situation, and it's in the bag, he's out like a light, as they say. Us Seagulls are no fools, our battle-readiness is well tested. She tried out the method once – when she was in a good mood. Some drunken little major or captain settled in slyly beside her one night and started snoring away – but she didn't hear him turn up. She was sleeping away peacefully and carrying out a strategic raid at the same time – and he disrupted the operation right at the very beginning, the traitor! And worst of all, he flung his arms and legs right across the trestle bed, the egotist, she couldn't budge him, something terrible it was! Every time they do nothing but show off their lack of culture, the amount of trouble she's had with them – she can't even put it in words! And with this one as well. She kicked and kicked him with her boot until finally she got tired and dozed off, really annoyed. And when she took flight again in her dream and felt she was free, the first thing she did was flit into that major's shaggy, hairy nostril. She went in as far as she could over the broken terrain, chose a securely protected position – practically a ready-made little trench – and just simply sat there. Modestly and perfectly politely. Under a bush, like a rabbit. Now let's just have a look see how he'll react, the great billy-goat. The great von-baron sprawling there, taking up the entire trestle bed. OK then, our little goat, jump a bit! She straightened up there in the darkness. Huddled down and straightened up again. And she waved her hands around this way and that, the way she used to on athletics parade, oh hell's bloody bells!

And then it started!

Effectively, if you thought about it, it was just like a perfect developing attack – according to what it says in all the rules and the instructions. On our side the absolute minimal force is brought into play, no more than a single soldier, in fact. But in response the enemy suddenly exposes his full fire power, the full complement of his garrison and also the fact that he has ammunition, if you do the job right. That was what happened! As soon as Midge finished doing her exercises in the nostril, things started rumbling and crashing and that major's damp-old-mother-earth started trembling under Midge and then the blast wave broke loose – centuries-old oaks would have been bent to the ground, never mind the grassy little hairs on the steep slopes of the nostril. The freak started sneezing so hard the entire dug-out shook, literally, sand trickled down from the ceiling. Crash! Bang! Ba-boom! Midge herself is fond of a good sneeze, if truth be told, but she can't manage an a-choo that powerful yet. Lukich leaps up, gets tangled in his tarpaulin and grabs his machine gun – thinks they're being bombed or shelled. Assesses the situation, spits, lies down and carries on snoring. But the major, he carries on blasting away with his large-calibre shells and demolition bombs – like an earthquake, literally. It's amazing she didn't go flying out of his smooth-bore nostril like a shell. But she held out and carried her developing attack through to total victory: the sleepy-head woke up.

What lesson must we draw from this particular combat episode? A strategic one! She didn't make any practical effort, she simply sat in the nostril and did the opposite, she had a rest, a good one too, and the results are plain to see, right? Another five minutes and she'd have made the man bloody well sneeze himself to death, something terrible, eh! And moreover in this particular exceptional case there was quite clearly a very warm, entirely comradely attitude to the invader, it was all simply for a joke and for education with a pedagogical purpose, so he wouldn't go wandering around other people's trestle beds when he was drunk and occupying their territory, and so he'd turn up to see a girl according to the organised queue that Lukich had written down on a piece of paper, like everyone else, and what's more in smart, neat officer-like condition, the way an attentive boyfriend and Red Army battle commander ought to – hello and welcome, hell's bloody bells! And it was typical that even with such comradely relations a billy-goat like that barely survived, that should be emphasized too. But as for the Hanses, the genuine die-hard invaders who were snoring away in the huts in Shisyaevo, no two ways about it, Midge would do things very differently with them, for sure.

But anyway the main thing's quite clear enough: even if she only used the one tried and tested manoeuvre she used on the major, except at full power, of course – how many Hanses could she make sneeze themselves to death in one night like that? You count it up for yourselves, dear comrades, and the world-class figure will set you laughing worse than any tickling, literally. If you take half an hour per head as usual. Eh? Seven hours of fascist sleep and we write off fourteen Hanses, as a minimum. Territorially speaking, from one nostril to another is only a stone's throw, there's no point in adding in any time for flights. Fourteen altogether, eh? What kind of Fedosii Smolyachkov will lay out half a platoon for you in one night? And here you are fighting without a rifle, so there's a saving on ammunition as well, and just at the moment, by the way, that's the most important task for all of us, socialist competition has just been declared in that area and our entire personnel is making a great effort, because the question of cartridges is still at the stage of being solved, which is why hitches are not infrequent. And it doesn't bother anyone if you have to make bullets out of shit when a German's closing in on you – more like some cheap private shop than a real army, pioneer's honour! And so, of course, you're ready to try everything, you rack your brains day and night trying to learn somehow to shoot without any cartridges or shells. And in this connection, of course, it would be good to disseminate the experience of the night flights, so that Seagull wasn't the only one to have the additional opportunity of exterminating the enemy's manpower with her bare hands, and even without any hands at all (invalids with no arms would be able to do it as well) – with just their class-consciousness, the way it really ought to be. They could fly out at night on raids on the enemy rear lines, at least a platoon of sleeping soldiers from each company – so who wasn't allowing it? After just one week, literally, the entire cocky 'Centre' army group won't exist any longer, because it will be eliminated as a class. And after two weeks at those work-rates we'll reach Berlin already, and together we'll tickle Hitler himself all the way to hell in every single hole he has in him – he won't even have time to sneeze, if we set about it with proper organisation, on a count of 'three'.

At present – and let's look the truth squarely in the eye, so far no one is listening – there is no other chance of a rapid victory, considering the shortage of ammunition and also the lack of sound elastic for knickers, which has already been emphasized. So what's the snag then? Can it really be that difficult for General Zukov to give the order? They ought to organise short courses for the emergency training of correspondence students, Seagull could be the instructor. How many volunteers would be gathered in a week? If we multiply fourteen nostrils by thirty trainees, we get more than four hundred heroic young nostril-raiders for every platoon. An entire German regiment wiped out! And without anyone even losing any sleep. Firstly a saving in ammunition and secondly a simultaneous improvement in battle-readiness by means of profoundly refreshing rest: that certainly couldn't do any harm. But if just one platoon or so of our invisible airborne heroes can do away with an entire regiment of Germans that easily, that means a company can do away with a division, right? And a regiment of sleepers trained by Seagull could annihilate something like Guderian's tank army in just a couple of ticks – quietly, modestly and economically. But in the Kremlin the marshals are probably racking their brains, wondering where to get more cartridges from. Well, comrades Red commanders, here are your cartridges, open your eyes and look! Every soldier is as good as a cartridge, if you think about it properly. And not just a single cartridge, an entire clipful! He can take out seven a night, just give him the nod to fly. In your place I'd have gone round to General Zukov ages ago and begged him on my bended knees before it's too late: save our Motherland for us, our brave falcon! It should be dead easy for you, hell's bloody bells! But some chance they'll go begging to him! They're probably still writing anonymous reports about him, the freaks, whispering behind his back: we still don't know how this risky project of his with this little schoolgirl might end, we just hope it doesn't turn out badly, they just might demote us or put us in jail, like before the war when they put all the generals and marshals away. You cowards! You don't have an ounce of faith in the soldier – that's why we're retreating! Only General Zukov knows how to really believe. He proved that in forty-one, on the volleyball court. You should have seen his saintly eyes then, his tears! But what's the point of explaining things to you, you're all officers, not people! Only the private soldier can really assess, understand and justify.

And in that connection, in accordance with the priority of the basic order, of course, you might wonder a hundred times over whether you ought to continue your flight on the course set or dive down for a minute after all to liberate at least one village as an example – then General Zukov would mark a tick in his commander's notebook and he could report to Stalin: one-nil, Comrade Stalin! And then the collective would change its attitude towards him all right, even the cook would happily tip an extra ladle of wheat porridge into his mess tin, so maybe she should take a chance and make a stop at Shisyaevo?

Oh no, dear comrades, that's not the way we'll get the job done! Onwards! Onwards and upwards! Always remember the most important thing: we are born to make a fairy-tale reality! Those words of Comrade Stalin must become the motto of every soldier and general – every single one without exception! So dedication first, and iron discipline second.

Otherwise tomorrow or the next day Stalin will run out of patience because you still can't carry out your piffling little mission after more than a year – and then you'll find yourself under court-martial, my little darling, with your beloved general there at your side, hell's bloody bells! So onwards, Seagull, onwards!

Over the long, wide, deadly bog, white in the moonlight, with round black 'windows' and old flooded log paths, where the bodies of stuck one-and-half-tonne trucks are rotting and the short barrels of forty-five millimetre cannon stick up, abandoned by units breaking out of encirclement back in forty-one – if only the surrounded soldiers had known then the justice that was waiting for them on the volleyball court! And, by the way, Midge ought to have been lying in a bog like this one now near the river Mga – with her little, pale, surprised face, well preserved in the peat. If it wasn't for Sevka Goryaev, who came back for her: the girl had fallen behind the division to do a number two and stepped off the rotten log path into a 'window'. She'd struggled until she had no more strength left, choked on water until she couldn't shout, only cough, with the peaty sludge seething in her throat as the bubbles of swamp gas burst, so how had he heard her? She was floundering, tearing the floating moss with her feeble fingers, hobbled tightly by her lowered breeches – the Walther in the back pocket was pulling her down as well, apart from the ooze sucking her down into the depths, something terrible it was! Sevka had almost pulled her out when she remembered about her pants! – her entire backside was naked! And of course she pushed him away again: she wanted to adjust her equipment properly under water. She was young and bashful then – something terrible! But he didn't let her drown, he grabbed hold of her hair, the freak, she thought he was going to pull her head off, he made such a world-class tractor! And he did turn away when she was pulling up her pants – some individual soldiers do have a conscience after all, not like the officers. She thought then that Sevka was bound to die soon, they always kill the good ones first – the way it had to be, they're in the front ranks, they don't spare themselves. And she was spot on: exactly three days later Sevka was killed on the volleyball court and Midge was suddenly transformed into Seagull. Straight from being a frog in a bog, hell's bloody bells! So that was what fate spared you for, for a feat of heroism, so you just fly where you're ordered, you toad, without any cheeky talking back, and don't go hanging around over every village and every bog for half an hour. That's not what Sevka gave his young life for, so you could catch crows up in the sky and get lost in your dreams while you're on a mission. Onwards, for Sevka Goryaev!

Onwards above the distant pine wood and spruce forest, already indistinguishable in the gathering dark below. As though in pursuit of Seagull, the moon slips across Khistyai lake like a light boat and the glass-panes of aeroplane cabins glitter on the western bank, where the Hanses have an aerodrome. Never mind, just wait, you webbed bats, and we'll deal with you too, I'm sorry, madam, but we don't have time just now. Every minute is precious! Quick, faster, absolute maximum speed! You know, everything depends on a single second! Oh no, comrades, no more of that disgraceful behaviour, really! The operation was broken off last night and the night before that, and a week ago, and a month ago – every time since the night flights began, but today it's bloody curtains for the enemy hydra! The important thing is to understand what the snag is here, not to let yourself get duped again. Change tactics in time and the success of the operation is guaranteed. Hitler kaput.

Or maybe that was how the general planned it? For Seagull not to take on the black dragon in combat straight away, for her to acquire adequate experience of night flights first? What did the fliers call it – putting in the hours. But just how many of these useless hours of yours can she put in, dear comrades? The amount of fuel you'd use up alone! And while she's hanging around here pointlessly with you, like a turd joggling in an ice-hole, he's doing his black business, no two ways about it, he's not called a dragon for nothing, is he, hell's bloody bells? And by the way, Leningrad's been blockaded for more than a year now, and the only one who can sort out this whole disgraceful situation once and for all, and set everything back right side up, is Midge, that is, Seagull of course, begging your pardon. So how long can you carry on putting a girl off, why such lack of trust? I'd like to toss the mother-truth of it right in your face, don't take offence, Comrade General – you haven't thought through this particular little question, your intelligence is obviously not on the ball. Otherwise they'd have reported personally to you how many acrobatic manoeuvres Seagull has mastered and perfected in just the last month. Anything to fill in the time, as they say.

And Seagull calmly directs the azure cloud of her impatient loyalty upwards, moving swiftly over and down and looping the loop, trying in the process not to lose sight of the only reliable reference point – the fiery strip of sunset dividing the sky from the land. A loop backwards, another loop, and another, every time seeing either her own trail sparkling in the air or a sort of train, looking very like the long, long legs of the actress Orlova, the kind she always dreamed of having, only in this particular case they're a transparent blue. They shimmer and quiver in the air like a gauzy, weightless scarf. Now if she could fly in at Walter Ivanovich's little window at night with legs like that!

If only she knew where that barred little window was, in which jail. If he's still alive, of course, the crazy freak. And if not then she could always turn up to visit the dead man underground, she stopped being afraid of corpses ages ago, and she'd confirmed her own penetrating capabilities plenty of times, flying straight through hillocks and little hills in her sleep, and even the stone walls of buildings in Leningrad. So locating him in his grave would be as easy for Seagull as pulling a leg off a crayfish, in her dream she was omnipresent and armour-piercing. She'd knock on his coffin politely, like knocking on the classroom door. Excuse me, Walter Ivanovich, *bitte-dritte*, I'm late for class as usual. There's something I wanted to tell you, well for instance: *Ich weis nicht was sol es bedeuten* ... But why are you so pale, by the way? You look really terrible – literally! Exactly like the genuine classic when he's composing one of his 'Loreleis' about love, the freak. Yes, you don't look too good at all, I must say. And there are little worms crawling around in your eye sockets instead of those dreamy clear-blue eyes of yours I used to adore. And you're grinning for some reason. Showing off those regular, wide teeth, all the same – you were an interesting man all right, no doubt about it. Only what on earth possessed you suddenly out of the blue to call a simple Soviet schoolgirl a 'Valkyrie'. No, I'm not offended, I got used to it, I even like it. So thank you very much, *bitte-dritte*. Well all-righty, I'm sorry but I've got to fly: military duties. I'm on a secret mission, and you're a German, that's why you're suffering down here in proud solitude, so I can't let you know too much, it might be bad for your health. *Auf Weidersehen, meine liebe Knabe*, my beloved boy. I'll just give you one kiss in farewell, I'm not afraid now. It's very handy the way your lips have already rotted away completely or else who knows, hell's bells, I might have had a mole or a worm from your underground kiss, like some crazy freak! We ought to have kissed earlier, much earlier, my one and only Walter Ivanovich – only don't tell Alyoshka, if you happen to meet him anywhere over there ...

But unfortunately, it's all just an empty childish dream, and where, territorially speaking, she should look for his grave, which could very easily already exist, obviously no one could tell, and that was right: an enemy of the people is an enemy of the people, a dog's death for a dog. Although personally Midge had been certain they would let Walter Ivanovich go the next day. They'd figure out that his German language was for teaching, not for spying, and let him go straight away. She'd only been convinced he actually was an enemy of the people when the chairman of the collective farm told everyone so at a special meeting, with the man from state security sitting there, although he was in civvies, and afterwards when he interrogated Midge, and she was the only one of all the kids that he praised, for not trying to hide how under the influence of her teacher she'd listened to symphonic records of the main fascist composer Wagner, and so she'd been a great help to the investigation and made things easier for him too. After all, hadn't he confused everyone, duped them and seduced them with those big dreamy eyes of his? If she met his executed soul in the sky now, she'd throw the truth back in his face all right: say what you like, as a teacher you ought to know, but I believe in principle that's not the way to behave yourself with girls! If you have a spying mission, then go ahead, who's stopping you, but then why go looking like that with those eyes? Thanks to you even now I still feel like I'm drilled right through by those eyes of yours, even in my dreams, while I'm on duty!

She flies on almost at the same level as the loose, woolly clouds, feeling with her incorporeal body the prickly December smell of unfallen rain. From up here she can't distinguish any trees or human habitations, and she wonders what height it is – a kilometre, two? The flaming border ahead of her traces out the wavy edge of an immense grey-blue plate, and the seemingly motionless Seagull glides above it, alone in all the heavens. Exactly like a circus girl dangling on a cable up under the big top. And by the way, for some reason the horizon doesn't get any nearer, not even a metre. Down below it's absolutely dark, and she can't feel any headwind: hell's bloody bells, she's got nothing to feel it with! If only there was some little reference point. In General Zukov's place she'd have set signalmen with pocket torches all along the route – to make absolutely sure. Fliers probably have everything they need: they're in reliable radio contact and their map-cases are stuffed so full of maps they're bursting at the seams! And here she is without any wings or any motor, and they've got her roaming blindly around the sky like some disorganised crow. They appointed her Seagull, so it's up to them to do things right with supplies and such. That's always the way on our side: there are some who are used to getting everything just handed to them, and the majority has to suffer because of those individualists – with just one rifle between three even now, the same as in forty-one. There was no order then and there still isn't, anyone will tell you. Ah, look, at last there are some lights on the horizon.

The night battle zone moves close instantaneously, in a just a few seconds, and she realises with pride that she's covering the kilometres like a shell from a long-range cannon. Hurtling over the line of fire, Seagull has time to notice that the explosions come bursting out from under the earth in clumps of lilac-white, crimson and orange roses. Rotten roses. Either frost-withered or gnawed away by black cobwebs. Suddenly it seems like the entire earth is sick with a great, deep, secret conflagration, and if it bursts out all at once, the planet will blaze up from horizon to horizon in a flash.

She passed something that looked like a wide body of water – for a moment the scent of the water, as dense as laundry bluing, washed away her unease. Maybe it was Lake Ladoga, Seagull didn't know. It could even be the Baltic Sea and she could be flying straight towards Königsberg or even Berlin itself – the way she'd already been carried off once in stormy weather – how could you tell? Her only hope was that General Zukov would speak up and give her orders in time, the way he always did. Provided, of course, she hadn't already been wafted into Germany or America, or into the tundra to the Yakuts with their frost-bitten heels ...

But then over on the edge of the world, just to the west of the sunset that has crept to the north and been almost completely curtained off by dark clouds, a milky-coloured, living haze emerges. On the edge of the sky there is a weak hint of dull mother-of-pearl. As though beyond the horizon, or maybe under the ground, an immense silver flower is blossoming – any second now it will open its bud and grow up to the sky, lighting up the whole earth with a gentle glow that the darkness can't dim.

How many times when she was little she'd seen a dome of light over the black ravine on her way back home from Grandma Alexandra's on the night train from the Valdai Hills – exactly the same glow, only much brighter. Sometimes it was like the top of a huge balloon, or the peak of a snowy hill, or a white ship with wide sails.

Bluish, gently tinged with mother-of-pearl, the dome of light rises and expands. The light above the city flares up in crimson patches and dies away again. It seems to flutter and tear in the gusts of a tremendous, ragged night wind. A heavy, coal-black wind, sweeping in from the depths of the sky, where the stars are already enthroned and the emancipated moon glares into Seagull's eyes like a searchlight, but there is too much swampy, empty space. It trickles down thickly on to the earth, heaps up on top of the dome of light and presses down on it, any moment now it will crush it. It's as if the black wind could extinguish all the lights on earth and carry away its light completely. It could blow the earth itself away, tear the globe off its axis and set it rolling like a ball through the deadly bog of the boundless night to the childish laughter of the stars and the murderous hooligan whistle of the one-eyed, drunken moon.

Seagull is prepared to wear herself to a frazzle to prevent such a terrible disgrace. And we'll manage it all right, don't you worry about that, we'll manage it on our own, even if no one else helps. Over that way she can already make out the air defence barrage balloons and luminous milky-white columns. Searchlights. Right now, dragon-features, watch out! As Stalin wrote, have you prayed for the night, Deadly Moaner!!!

Only first, of course, she'll go home, to Suvorov Prospect, to Lusya, just for a moment, literally …

'Seagull, Seagull, do you hear me, come in!'

She stumbles in the empty sky and comes stiffly to attention.

If Seagull had a heart, then at this moment it would have simply burst from happiness, like a hand-grenade. And from that point of view, of course, it was a very good thing she didn't have a heart and it had been left behind in sleeping Midge's chest.

An orange flash of triumphant loyalty erupts within her, lighting up the sky far away, like the golden summons of the pioneer bugle. The bright rays of her future glory enfold Seagull, frozen in flight, like the detonation of an anti-aircraft shell. And instantly all the light and the non-burning heat of the transparent fire condense inside her into a cast metal shot of new strength, linked by the thread of a high, confident voice to the will of her commander and god.

'Seagull, Seagull, this is Number One! This is Number One, come in, Seagull!'

His voice runs right through her. As though the commander's sharpened bayonet can enter her backbone without any pain, in fact it's a pleasant feeling – a long-awaited, dependable reinforcing rod for her selfless devotion and courage. Recovering her wits, she is already continuing her flight, gradually gathering speed again. And Seagull's voice rings as it reports in, answering her controller. It comes bursting out of the very centre of the metal shot that takes the place of her heart, of all her desires and her reason: 'This is Seagull! This is Seagull! Number One, Number One, this is Seagull! Always prepared!'

'Seagull, here are your orders! Commence operation 'Black Dragon'!'

The commander is calm. His voice rumbles smoothly, secretly, sternly. General Zukov is pleased, the signalmen have done a world-class job, the connection is clear. He's perfectly calm, absolutely, it's frightening. As though it's not Seagull who has to carry out the mission, with her clumsiness maybe risking her own life, so precious at this moment to the Motherland, but him, Zukov, so failure's quite impossible.

'Seagull, Seagull! Set your course by the Pole Star! Take it steady, little daughter! Ready! On your marks! Get set! Ma-arch!'

Compressed by speed, space comes at her whistling and howling. The pillars of light over Leningrad rise up higher than the Great Bear, higher than the Pole Star. And through the whistle of speed she can hear the dull groan of old torment and tribulation – the voice of the besieged city. Seagull is approaching her goal.

The black height draws her in and the light is left below. The waves of darkness spin her round and toss her up, as if she's bumping over potholes in the back of a truck. She sees the earth above her head or behind her. Then once again the whole of Leningrad goes zooming downwards and the columns of the searchlights turn into thick, blurred, electric-yellow spots. From here she can see that the city is covered with a transparent dome of interlocked rainbows. As if two immense palms have embraced Leningrad and come together above it, sheltering it like a weak candle-flame against the wind. It must be some new secret defence. Invisible from a distance, the armour protects the city like a helmet.

Seagull flies in circles round the tall rainbow dome of this strange temple that has suddenly sprung up over Leningrad, tens of kilometres high and as round as the head of St Isaac's Cathedral. Blinded by the sharp flashes, sparks and arrows of light, she finally soars up above the very peak of the cathedral and falls like a stone towards the glowing spire – as though the same force that drew her out of her body for the night flight is casting her down to certain death. But His voice is with her again: 'Seagull! Seagull! We're approaching our goal! For the Motherland, for Stalin! Full speed ahead, hell's bloody bells!'

Hell's bloody bells! How does he know her favourite expression? See, miracles do happen, comrades!

'Yes sir, hell's bloody bells!' Seagull responds, and she hears his affectionate fatherly laughter – the general is wagging a finger at her, shaking his head: we know all about you, little midget Midge, our people in Smersh are invaluable!

She's known for a long time that in the centre of the rainbow dome, in the middle of the tall golden spire, there's a narrow secret aperture – a way through. About three millimetres wide. She has to slip in through that. The number of times in the beginning she went skidding off full tilt across the dome, slithering down on her belly like she was on a toboggan slope – until she learned to plunge straight in at the first go, like a cleaning rod into a machine-gun barrel.

Right, Comrade General, you're my only hope, don't let me down, correct the trajectory a bit on entry. Here it comes now … Oi, oi-oi, hell's bloody bells! Now where have I got to? Oh, not again! No don't, Comrade General! I won't do it again, pioneer's honour! Don't, I'm afraid! Do-o-o-n't …

Chapter 4

In which Midge is appointed acting Holy Virgin,
and as a result she is fortunately obliged
to offer heartfelt thanks to an old oak divan.

As though she is suddenly pulled up short by an acrobat's cable attached to an invisible belt, her flight halts just two metres above the spire. A crude, insistent force draws her back. Seized treacherously round the middle from behind so that her body is almost snapped in half, Seagull flaps her invisible, powerless little arms like wings, struggling towards the glowing pipe. This has happened several times before in her dream, and she knows she hasn't really been lassoed from above, but from the ground, from that lousy damp trestle bed in the damp dug-out, where poor trapped Midge is already groaning before she wakes up. The expanse of the heavens instantly contracts and coils tight around her body, her head begins to spin and she falls down like a stone into the depths of a dark well-shaft, slipping through the narrow pipe, drawn by the noose that has cut off her breathing and her will, rapidly and terrifyingly taking on her full human weight. The pipe turns through a sharp bend, and then another – and before she even has time to recognise and remember the familiar stove-cavern with its dying embers and bats lurking in the corners, Midge finds herself back on the hard boards, not breathing, with her heart tight and pounding. Something heavy slumps over and presses down on her and, still unable to believe that she has failed to reach her objective again, she opens her eyes and sees the timber ceiling of the dug-out.

Surely not that again? Oh yes, and he's all set to go, back in there again, hell's bloody bells!

Heavy as hell, and worst of all, like some wounded corpse. From the voice it sounds like she's seen him before somewhere. But maybe it's some brave warrior she doesn't know at all who's collapsed across her, snorting away, and is working his way under the elastic that's already been knotted together in two places: 'Midge, my beautiful little love, I love you so very much, you know, from the very first glance, I'll be careful, the lads told me you're kind, you help everyone out, give me just a little bit too ... I'm not like the others, I really do love you, I'll just sip a tiny little drop off the top, OK? Hey, Midgy, don't sleep! Oh, how good you smell, my only love, my first, oh, I've broken your elastic, I'm sorry, forgive me, I'll bring you another piece, I'll give you mine from my underpants, I'll put it in myself, I'm sorry, I won't do it again, let me try ...'

Oh yuck, what a half-baked twerp! And what a dream he interrupted! There, have it! There, take it, just stop whining! Go on, go on, go on ... Hey, but don't go sticking your fingers where they don't belong, they still don't know what they're doing, but he's straight in there like the rest, the little brat! How'd he like to be jerked around by his prick in the middle of the night to make it grow a bit longer, and he's sticking his hand well in there like a grown-up officer. Maybe I should offer you my backside too? You're not a man, you're a ponce, a fat-arsed little goat, you ought to be studying the regulations, not groping my cunt, you beginner! Reckon you've found yourself a cheap whore — as if I'm going to teach every little kid, every desperate wanker and tosser, how to get his end in and how to screw — try the infirmary, Svetka the slut'll teach you all about everything down there, she's the one with the slit that's always itchy, not me ... What are you doing groping at the gates again? Hands out of the short and curlies, you scum! Don't fiddle with the strings if you can't play the guitar! The jockeys have already chafed my minge raw, undermined all the foundations ... Take your rotten stump out, I told you. What a little scamp, did you ever see the like? Young, but so advanced for his age! Just feel the way his balls have swollen up, he's a lively one all right. Well all right then, let's see you go to it if you can ... Hey, what are you rooting around for now, miner-boy? Not with your hands! Stick it in quick! All right? Take your grabbers away! That's ticklish for a girl, how many times do I have to tell you freaks? What's this strange habit all you new recruits have? All picked up the stupid fashion, every one of you! At least turn your face away, you rotten lousy gent, don't breath down a girl's nose! 'Oh, how I love you, Midgy, I really love you, honest and true!'

Not a chance in hell he'll listen to you! He's off and running, no controlling him now. Right, settled in now, have you, rammed home your cartridge? What are you doing still groping around in there, you crazy freak? Get a move on, I've still got to catch up on my sleep after you, I'm not made of triple-core cable, you know! Quickly now, my sweet little lieutenant, I'm asking you as a comrade, it's disgusting, can't you understand ... Oh, sure, he'll understand, only don't hold your breath! Or does he really not know how to do it after all? Is he afraid? Couldn't be, could he? No, he's just some kind of sadist, pioneer's honour, worse than any fascist! Why the hell is he starting all that childish hugging and squeezing, now he wants to kiss me — vodka, onion, beef: 'I'll marry you, I love you, believe me! You've not got the clap, have you?' — 'No, I haven't, ask anybody you like, your clap can't get a hold on me, the entire division's amazed. Get on with it quick, military style, stop holding back! And stop tormenting me with that drivel, act like a man ...'

You bite your lips until they bleed, literally, and the leech tries to suck them, slobbers wet kisses all over your cheeks, puffing and panting, something terrible it is! You're my very first, he says, Komsomol honour, I'll submit an application to the colonel tomorrow, and we'll sign the register, like normal people. Midgy, Midgeling, little Midgelet, you and me, we'll never die, we won't even get wounded, no bullet or bayonet will ever get us, you'll see, because it's love, and after the victory I'll take you home with me to Kondopoga. My mum'll like you, she's blind, she can see through anybody from a mile away, you can't fool her, she'll know straight away you're not just some girl or other, I know ...'

What a bloodsucker, eh? Try to treat him like a human being and it's like he doesn't even hear you! Oh, why don't you just shove off back to your bloody blind, deaf, Finnish Kondopoga, I wish I'd never laid eyes on you, you slimy little wimp ...

Last summer Midge was tormented for almost a month by a little lieutenant like that, Rostislav. When he turned up the first time, he spent almost half the night stroking her cunt and droning away. She listened to his endless stream of psychopathic drivel, cursing and swearing and praying under her breath to any god or devil who would finally clamp his chattering jaws shut and take him away home – she couldn't say it out loud, after all he was an officer, even if he did only leave college yesterday – and the torment was too much for her to bear, she fell asleep. When she woke up in the morning, her knickers had been pulled back up into place, and the elastic had even been knotted together with a childish double knot, and her breeches had been put on too. And, by the way, the swine had pulled her belt so tight she couldn't even get her breath! And it was tied in a knot too. A spot of sealing wax and Midge could have been a top secret package.

Of course, she immediately boasted about the mad freak to Lukich, how he'd offered to marry her at first glance and how he'd trussed her up when he left – she almost shit her pants in the morning before she could get untied, bent over double and tugging the knot open with her teeth, but the cunning Yid scratched his head and came straight out with it: 'Right then, so his lordship's a dog in a manger: if I can't eat, nobody else is going to either. You get shut of him right away, my girl, and forget all about him. So there'll be no tears shed afterwards, God forbid. Hopeless cunt-struck idiots like that catch a bullet in their very first battle – that's a scientific law of nature. You'll remember what I told you, you'll see, this fiancé of yours won't keep his head for long.'

And he was spot on! In fact the holy scoundrel was so right it was funny.

Every evening, literally, when he escorted her under armed guard to the woods, Lieutenant Rostislav started up his hurdy-gurdy again: 'Only, Midgy, don't you go doing anything with anybody else, you watch out now!' And the halfwit slapped his gun-holster. 'You understand me, eh? Do you promise, my darling?' And he's already unfastening his holster. 'I promise, I promise, leave me alone,' says Midge, yawning. 'You can stand me up against a fir-tree right now, if you like, so as not to waste any time. I'd only thank you for it. I'm absolutely sick and tired of the lot of you. Why are you holding a knife to my throat?' – 'No, you swear!' And he grabs her elbow, hard. 'All right, I swear, bloody hell! Happy now?' And Midge tries to turn away. Rostislav won't let her. Fingers like a vice, a real spider! Used to play in the volleyball team for that Kondopoga of his, the egotistical individualist. 'No Masha, not like that. You give me your Komsomol word of honour!' And he goes red all over and clutches at the pocket where his Komsomol card lies next to his heart the way it's supposed to. Midge catches her breath too, her voice starts to tremble: 'I'm not in the Komsomol yet. I didn't get a chance to join, you remember, I told you about it. Do you want my pioneer's word of honour instead? I'll give you that. I'll even salute at the same time!' There were cold shivers running up and down her spine. 'All right, go on then. Like they say, when there's no headed paper, use the plain. Well?' – 'I've given you my word.' – 'Don't try to cheat! Give me your word like you promised – out loud, with a salute!' And he reaches for his holster again. 'Pioneer's word of honour! Always prepared!' Midge salutes, lifting her five dirty digits with the nails bitten down to the roots so they look purple in the evening damp up above the star on her forage cap. And Rostislav is absolutely beside himself with delight: 'How I do love you, my little Midgy, who'd believe it!' and he starts trying to kiss her again, starting his soppy calf-love nonsense. If just once he'd think about whether it was easy for a girl to go against the collective because of his personal egotistical demands. In effect he's encouraging her to break with the masses! It's a good thing that Colonel Konogon died the death of the brave only the other week: a stray shell hit the headquarters hut during the night – the whole HQ staff had just been drinking to his latest decoration – and Major

Poprugin was killed too, and Adjutant Serenka Sedelnikov, he had those dainty little moustaches, and such a lovely smile ... Rest his soul, he was a fine jockey. Yes, if they'd all heard Midge now, swearing to be true to no one but Rostislav, they wouldn't have let the matter rest, oh no. And what can she say to Khriukin? How can she look Captain Gartsevalo from the reserve regiment in the eye? And Quartermaster Khvostenko? And Junior Lieutenant Udilian? Especially since he has a big family, six boys at home in Tashkent, and his older children are dying to get to the front, the man never has a moment's peace, he showed her a photo, the whole family round the table, with a dainty little melon in front of every one of them – he even cried, great huge tears he wept, and Midge wiped his nose with her own handkerchief, she could hardly help crying herself, the world-class way he sang those Tashkent songs in some strange language or other, and kissed all her fingers one after another – the thumb, the forefinger, the middle finger and the little finger, three times in a row. Only he missed out the third finger. 'Here you wear ring, when you grew,' he said. That was what he said – 'grew'. The national minority men are all especially kind somehow, she feels particularly sorry for them. She felt sorry for Udilian. Even though she'd blacked out underneath him three times when he started shafting her rear: his piglet is too fat altogether, it rips you open, and you start bursting at all the seams. He even apologised for it afterwards, when he woke up. Of course, you always forgive considerate officers like that, if they're not jumped-up Yakuts or something of the sort, altogether too big for their boots. And it was just typical too, that not Khvostenko, or Colonel Konogon himself – a really impressive officer even if he was a bit bald – and least of all Udilian – not one of them ever, even once, so much as mentioned all these idiotic oaths and promises. After all, all of them remembered how Pavel Korchagin's beloved Rita answered him when he got it into his head to start insisting on a wedding at the very height of the world revolution: calm down, Pavlunya, she said, now's not the time. And right now's a revolution too, isn't it? The world-wide conflagration has practically only just begun burning up the whole world. They all understand that and they try to put themselves in her place, demonstrate their class-consciousness. They don't bother her too often. And afterwards Lukich guzzles so much chocolate he gets diarrhoea for three days on the trot if the regimental command's been to visit Midge, or even for a whole week, if it's a division-level visit. And what's the point anyway with this poor peasant Rostislav? All he ever does is scowl at everyone sullenly and follow Midge around all day to make sure she doesn't happen to smile at any of his army mates – he'd like to have every one of them packed off to the penal battalion, the rotten freak! It's odd the way a man can ever let himself go to that extent, shows his lack of culture, his plain ignorance – after all, we're in the collective all the time, day and night. And by the way, what does the pioneer salute mean? The five fingers clenched above your head, they're the collective, the views and the needs of the collective, which are much higher than all our individualistic caprices. But this turkey cock? Making himself out to be some old-regime type von-baron – he ought to find himself some fancy tart in Lisle thread stockings, she'd swear to him all right, oh sure she would, he'd be sharing the whore with every truck driver in the place and he wouldn't even dare squeak about it.

But then, you know what's the most annoying thing? On the second night she already explained to the thick-lipped little ram that kissing on the lips and all those code words of his like 'I love', 'darling dearest', 'kondopoga', 'mum' and the rest – they're only for the couple of days just before the genuine Soviet registry office and the official marriage registration, everything right and proper – there has to be a white veil and 'brut' champagne, to show them all, hell's bloody bells! Everything else – by all means, as much as you like, three times a night if you want, she'd teach him herself, the little sucker – guzzle it down with a spoon, like they say, that's not what makes you put on weight. But not the other way round! Because kissing on the lips as good as means having children, and a future Komsomol member's only supposed to do that with her one and only legitimate husband – those are the directions Stalin gives us: when the job's been done, then have your fun! Of course, in a case of extreme emergency you can do it with your one hundred per cent engaged fiancé, but then everything has to be agreed in advance with the parents, rest their souls, and the rings have to be bought already. Naturally, the rings are purely according to the wishes of the respected parents, because after all that's a bourgeois prejudice, alien to members of the Komsomol. But if you let everyone kiss you on the lips before, then that's unhygienic, in the first place, for the oral cavity. And anyway, as far as kissing was concerned, Walter Ivanovich opened Midge's eyes to that phenomenon a long time ago, and she'd never forget his most important lesson as long as she lived. And then try to figure out whose child it was you had, you great sloppy sloven! And in general, it's not allowed, full stop. What actors get up to in some of their pictures, that's one of their special privileges. Especially if you take into account that, in the first place, you can't have children from that kind of artificial cinema kiss, otherwise Liubov Orlova and all the other beautiful film artistes wouldn't be able to give birth fast enough, literally, and Leonid Utyosov could never earn enough to pay all his alimony. So let's not go confusing ourselves with film actors: they can do it, but not us, begging your pretty pardon, dear Comrade Lieutenant Rostislav Ovietsky! Even your name's like it's got something missing, got no head to it somehow. If only you were, say, Sovietsky, all present and correct – you wouldn't suddenly get carried away like that: I'll marry you, and take you to Kondopoga, up north to the Yakuts. Just take a look at yourself. Some Utyosov you are! He probably kisses a hundred actresses at every rehearsal just for practise, before the bosses let him loose on Lyubov Orlova. And what's he let loose for? Just to give her one single little kiss, and not even for himself, but for the viewers, that's what's typical about the whole thing. That's the whole catch, that's the sign that divides people into good and bad – look to see who a person's making an effort for: for the viewers, that is for the collective, like the actor Utyosov, for instance, or like Maria Mukhina all her life – or for their own individualistic satisfaction, like Lieutenant Ovietsky in this particular instance. And please don't go confusing these two completely separate differences, because in actual fact it's not really a personal matter, it's a question of politics, of principle. Of course, in real life Utyosov is probably a tall, interesting kind of man, with nice broad, even teeth, and even Midge would kiss him a thousand times, especially in an urgent emergency for the pictures, for millions of viewers. That's art, but this is life, and especially as there's a war on let's try to keep them separate somehow at least. And in the second place, please don't go confusing a genuine family wedding with simple comradely front-line friendship, when a girl understands out of a feeling of duty and personal responsibility that if they aren't getting it the officers go crazy and that reduces their level of battle-readiness – there's no denying that. Of course, only when you're in the mood and it's not raining, so as not to lie on the damp ground and get your back and your backside all wet – then try drying your clothes out on your own body for two days, till you give yourself a dose of pneumonia – terrible! I've tried that already, more than once – *merci beaucoup* with tassels on for the wonderful attention you pay to a girl, no matter what the weather's like, you rotten goats!

And all the time, despite his meek-sounding name, this Ovietsky keeps taking offence and trying to educate Midge – a real cranky freak! 'I'm looking after you specially,' he says, 'so there were won't be any complications, to avoid having any abortions, and you don't appreciate it. What kind of wife are you going to make in the future?' When he wears her out completely, Midge unbuttons her collar and lets him kiss her on the neck. But only just once and no love bites allowed. But Rostislav Ovietsky simply goes crazy. Almost rips open her tunic – tries to twist at least one of Midge's breasts out from behind the cloth, like a goat – take it out and give it to him just like that! Just keeps showing off his own plain ignorance all the time of course, the same as any loutish officer. And again she has to beat it into his head, patiently and simply, like a political instruction class for retarded half-wits in kindergarten, hammer into his retarded male brains the things that couldn't be any easier to understand: a woman's breasts, naked, both left and right, it makes no difference, both of them, according to the laws of nature are only intended for a little baby and no one else, for a future son or daughter, and perhaps even for twins who Midge would have from some legitimate husband later, after the wedding. Because after all, two breasts had been provided, not one, and not six either, like record-breaking sows had – you couldn't feed six kids at once even in peace time (and when did we ever have that, the people have already forgotten what it is, what with all these officers' wars of yours, Civil and Spanish, and we had to push the Finns back from our borders too, and at the same time liberate our brother Slavs and our dear Baltic friends from oppression – the amount of effort we made for them, it's incredible!). And by the way, if a Finnish mine, say, or a Bessarabian one, tears off one of the breasts – then there's the second one, even bigger and stronger than the other one on the right. Get it? So they'll both be well fed and healthy, the twins, because nature's provided for everybody in advance for everything life can throw up. And she's also provided for you as a man to receive something from a woman, so there's no point disenfranchising yourself, hell's bloody bells, pull yourself together, and show you're a genuine world-class lad!

No sooner has Midge calmed down her little lamb Ovietsky, sat the freak down under a pine tree and wiped the sweat from his burning forehead with her clean handkerchief than he starts up again with his questions. 'But who did you love before me, Midgy?' – 'I've never loved anybody at all! It's too early for me yet, understand? I'm under age. What kind of crazy freak are you!' – 'Well then … How can I say it? Right! Who've you done it with before me?' – 'Who with? Who with? Nobody, that's who with! Satisfied?' – 'But how d'you mean, nobody? You know what the entire division's saying?' – 'That's right, believe all the rubbish they talk. I told you – nobody, and that means nobody! I was sick! Sick for almost a month and a half.' – 'With the clap?' Ovietsky turns as white as a sheet of paper. 'You've got the clap, I knew it!' And he clutched his head in his hands. 'You idiot. You're the one with clap. Ordinary bloody pneumonia, the injections almost killed me. And it's so boring in that infirmary – something terrible! In your own close-knit collective, of course, it's a different matter altogether!' – 'Hang on, hang on, Midgy!' Lieutenant Ovietsky wipes his stupid ram's forehead. 'So that means it's two months now you've been a virgin again … Oh, how I love you, my own little Midgelet!' – and then he has to have her neck again, opens Midge's button himself without even asking – what a nerve, eh? 'I'll take care of you right up until victory day, you just believe me …'

He took care of her all right. Thanks a bunch! She wished she'd never laid eyes on him.

But didn't Walter Ivanovich warn you, you stupid fool! Might as well talk to the wall, literally, you're as stubborn as a mule.

That evening as usual they walked to the wood, picked out a dry spot under the thick trunk of a pine-tree and sat down. Then Rostislav suddenly launched into reciting this poem to Midge off by heart, putting a bit of real feeling into it too. And it wasn't any of that banned vulgar bourgeois tripe, either, not that Esenin with his filthy drinking-house talk, not that Severyanin with his chrysanthemum, that was the whole thing about it. It wasn't anything like that, it was a politically literate and correct poem, with proper patriotic content, real odd it was to hear it. He'd read it in a newspaper ages ago, he admitted that much later. What was really good was it was written so it was easy to understand, the feeling was so strong, there's no way to describe how strong, something terrible it was. Wait for me, it said, and I'll come back. Only wait with all your heart, not just playing at it, like. Wait, it said, even when the yellow rain – odd, that was what the poet had, yellow, she spotted that straight off, maybe it was some kind of chemicals, but then every other way it was just plain ordinary rain – makes you feel tired and miserable, and wouldn't it, lashing down day after day like that, just lashing down, enough to depress anyone, that! He had snow swirling around in the poem too, then a bit later the weather suddenly changes to the exact opposite and it's hot and close, so you can't draw breath, exactly like Tashkent really is. And the main point, the thing Rostislav stressed with his voice and that soulful look, was it said to wait for me even when everybody else has given up waiting for anyone ages ago. What an egotist, eh? Pity she couldn't remember the name, which poet it was Stalin had told to write all that. Or else she would definitely have sent the curly-headed writer greetings from the front. She'd have written it just like Stalin teaches us: love the book, the source of knowledge! And they'd have struck up a real lively exchange of letters straight off. After all, a rear-lines rat of a poet would feel flattered to have a pretty light-haired girl writing him letters from the very front line by the light of her smoky oil-lamp, and all the lads in the company would laugh at his daft love-sick scribble, every letter a hundred pages long and, of course, every word of it in poetry. And of course the entire company would write back to him with poems the like of which he could never have dreamed up in a lifetime: take your girl to see your mum, to Kondopoga at a run ... But just at the very moment when Lieutenant Rostislav was reciting the most jealous line of the lot, even if nobody's waiting for anyone else, it said, you keep on looking out for me anyway, you bitch, she suddenly saw he was going be killed soon and almost burst into tears. At first when it happened, she thought it was just her being stupid, or else it was the poem, the sudden upsurge of powerful feeling. What happened was that Rostislav's head just went bobbing up into the air. His real, actual head, literally.

Midge cleared her throat quietly into her fist so as not to upset him or put him off or spoil his passion and delight. But that empty head of his, once it had risen up into the air, just carried on hanging there, hanging there and repeating: wait for me, wait for me, wait for me — something terrible it was! About ten centimetres up above his shoulders. Or maybe eight. Room enough to get your hand through, anyway. And to spare. A moth actually flew through the gap, a grey one, right through between his shoulders and his neck. Midge put her hand over her mouth to stop herself shrieking out loud. A live moth! One of those fat-bellied slow ones, those stupid one-day wonders that loved to fly full-tilt at Lenin's light-bulbs during the summer, even killed themselves in the process. What's more, it was guaranteed for sure she wasn't asleep right now, Rostislav would confirm that, if only he could keep hold of his head after all these goings-on. What reason could there be for such a vision happening? It must be nature starting to play some kind of unscientific tricks on people, but anyway apart from that it was just plain frightening to think about it afterwards, a living head ripped off and hovering over the shoulders of its rightful owner, repeating to itself over and over again: wait for me, wait for me... Why, hell's bloody bells!

And the freak just kept on and on spewing it out like he had it written down, looking up at the sky and the stars – it was a fine evening at first, bad luck, not a cloud in the sky. Even if my son and my mother start believing I'm dead, even, it went on, if my friends get drunk at my wake like they're supposed to, don't you go drinking, you keep yourself in hand so I won't have wasted my time over here spilling my blood by the sackful – still harping away at his same old tune. And then Rostislav's head set itself back down on Rostislav's shoulders where it belonged. And it grew back without any scar, would you believe it? She checked it for herself later with her fingers and she took a really close look the next time he stretched his neck out in those high-flown unnatural feelings of his. He really was worried about Midge though, afraid she wouldn't be able to withstand the pressure of the masses, or she might let some major with a big holster have it. But still he wasn't actually paying any attention to his little darling-Midgeling with her belt pulled in tight, none at all, as though he wasn't actually addressing the poem to her personally. That was really annoying. Anyway, from that minute on Midge could always see that torn-off head in front of her eyes. She guessed what it meant straight off: Rostislav didn't have much more time left for messing around with the girls, seeing as she'd had a vision like that his days were already numbered. It wasn't the first time she'd had that kind of premonition of trouble ahead. And if that was the way it was, it only meant there was all the more reason. If the man had only a few days left on earth, he could at least pay a bit more attention to his lady-friend!

Then suddenly he, Rostislav that is, said to her: 'As if that poem was written specially about you and me, eh?' 'How's that?' she said, thinking Ovietsky must be pulling her leg. But no, he was serious. 'The waiting, I mean! Meaning we should wait for each other right to the end, and then we won't get killed. It's about you and me, don't you see? Don't you feel it, Maria?' 'I think you're wrong,' Midge objected sharply. 'In the poem their story's quite different. He's supposed to be out at the front, but she's sitting in the rear somewhere in Tashkent, stuffing herself with melons for want of anything better to do. And there are all these officers, rear-line rats with dainty little moustaches, the whole garrison's from Tashkent down to the last man, because they're the most extreme national minority of the lot. Interesting men they are too, regular soldiers, and their teeth are all white from those melons, so perfectly regular you'd give them everything just for a smile, literally. And of course the entire pack of them is after her, naturally enough; a pretty young blonde and a slim little thing with it, a bit like Lyubov Orlova, especially if you dress her up in a Civil War padded jacket. So he's suffering a bit, it's only natural, and he wants to warn her off, nicely like, even though he's no more than a young lieutenant who can't even grow a moustache yet. Nobody and nothing as a matter of fact, and not even from Tashkent, but from somewhere up in the north. But all the same he's no fool and he knows his chances are about as good as a snowball in hell, if that. So it's weakness makes him threaten the girl he loves: if you get mixed up with any of them, you rotten whore, he says, when I come back from the war a cripple, even if I've got no arms or legs, all the same I'll never let up on you, there'll be no mercy, and don't you forget it, you slippery slut! But when you get right down to it, she couldn't give a damn, territorially speaking she's a thousand miles away from him, maybe not even in Tashkent, but in old Ashkhabad itself, that's where all the bigwigs are after all, all the big classics are taking it easy out there in the evacuation, and all the actors and all sorts of scientists in pince-nez, guzzling down their special rations without even choking on them while I'm stuck out here feeding the lice for them with my virginal white body. And the poets' wives are the worst of all over there in Ashkhabad. That's what's they're appointed for anyway, to be top-quality muses. The dust never gets a chance to settle, the kind of tunes they dance to over there nowadays! That's why their husbands write them letters from the front saying wait, wait, wait ... But what's that got to do with you and me, Ovietsky, my bosom buddy? Open your eyes! We're still here, aren't we, side by side?' 'Side by side,' he said, 'and a thousand miles apart! Even worse! You've got moustaches on the brain you have, Midge. Dainty little ones! Pah... I might as well reach for the moon as you, Midgy, you're that far away!'

He stretched his arm up towards the sky and clutched at the empty air, as though he wanted to grab hold of the moon, the freak. He laughed a sour, bitter, twisted laugh.

Midge was so insulted her belly leapt up into her throat, literally, so she choked and couldn't get a word out. How do you like that! The bloodsucking reptile! He's taunting her, the little cry-baby, the soft kid, the little mother's boy fresh from music school! Every day he accuses a girl of being unfaithful, although no one else knows anything about it, although the bloodsucker's been told that she's never loved anyone in her life and never intended to love anyone either – what else is it they want, these studs? Today's not so bad, but yesterday he was at her throat with his knife again: confess that you didn't want to do it with them, that they forced you, they took advantage of your situation and made you do it. I spent two years studying in the law department, I know all the laws, and I'll find a way to make them pay! What a provocateur, eh? Only interested in one thing, just like a saboteur. The only thing he wants is for Midge to break down and betray her army mates, slander them blind and get all those world-class officers court-martialled for rape and disgraced for the rest of their lives – no one would believe it! Rostislav's jealousy's turned him into an idiot, he'd happily betray the Motherland. Stalin was right when he emphasised the point: a gossip is a real godsend for the enemy! And not only does this one talk through his hat, he's always blubbing and sobbing and won't look you in the eye, and just keeps on saying it over and over again, the thick-headed billy-goat: 'You're not going to be crucified under them any more, I won't allow it, I won't let you, you're the purest, you're my only love, you're the very best, I can't allow just anyone to treat you like a cheap whore, I'll drag you out of this filth and take you away, we'll transfer to another unit, I'll make you pregnant and they'll demobilise you, because you're breaking my heart, I can't bear to see you humiliated like this ...' And then Midge slapped his face, the way you're supposed to when people swear like that. And she didn't just give him a simple little slap, she enjoyed it, took pleasure in it. She swung at him real hard – and she laughed. Because, of course, she immediately remembered Walter Ivanovich – and instantly her heart was washed clean of all the filth of his foul, treacherous words that defamed the entire Red Army all at once, every single soldier. But a lambkin is still a lambkin, and even hitting him is almost pointless, the beating doesn't really get you anywhere. He didn't say a word, just took hold of Midge's hand, still wet from the tears on his own cheek after the slap, and kissed it. In gratitude, was it? Then what for? Or was he simply asking her forgiveness for his stupid, malicious words, after all he'd made Midge feel really bad, because to be quite honest she'd really belted him hard in the kisser. After all, you can put up with anything as long as you know you're in the right, but being to blame for anything – *merci beaucoup* to you with tassels on for that kind of disgrace. How do you carry on living if you really are to blame? Anyone can laugh at you, if you're to blame, can't they? At such a petite, pretty blonde? You must be crazy, citizens! Anything at all, but not that! And so she belted him, of course. And next thing she felt his warm lips on her cold palm — a kiss. A stupid, sheepish kiss. Rostislav didn't say anything, he only smiled. That meant he recognised the error of his ways and his short-sighted political immaturity, the weakness of his initial positions. That meant the man's character wasn't entirely rotten, there was hope he could be reformed — that was what Midge thought yesterday. That was when he said quietly: 'I'm sorry' — and kissed her hand again. The same hand, the wet one. And he went away.

But then today he started in singing the same old song. Maybe he really was a saboteur? There'd been any number of cases! The warning signals came in almost every day, hell's bloody bells! No two ways about it, Stalin had really thought it through when he wrote his remarkable words, that was why they'd become everyone's motto: the enemy never sleeps! And if Rostislav didn't actually usually go to sleep when the night was almost over, for about an hour and a half, then she'd have decided straight off that he'd been sent on a special mission — to undermine battle-readiness from within by underhand means. But when he was dozing on Midge's breast, the girl couldn't take her eyes off the handsome young man: a tall, interesting officer, and with white, even teeth — he looked Russian, not like a Hans. And his name was almost Sovietsky. No, that would be the absolute final degree of human degradation, to go sliding shamelessly down that slippery slope. To have the nerve to work for the enemy openly and select the most vulnerable spot in our ranks of steel for the successful execution of your sabotage — our knicker elastic! It's clear straight off that for the black heart of a man like that nothing at all is sacred apart from his hostile spite and his disgusting mission to give girls as many kisses on the lips as possible. And so she'd have to go to the people in Smersh and report in due order: this and that and a disguised enemy has penetrated our ranks with boundless cunning. When she wrote her report on Captain Baranchikov the year before in connection with his similar unacceptable remarks about the officers (odd they were too: you poor wretch, he said, the commanders have turned you into their own plaything, a miserable trollop, don't even pay you for it) no one bothered checking up on his details, all Smersh needs to catch on is a hint. They came for him the same night. Broke into the dug-out clandestinely, without knocking, Lukich didn't even wake up and they lifted that freak Baranchikov straight off Midge. Carted him away in nothing but his drawers. The poor old man never took his drawers off, the sweet darling had to watch out for his radiculitis from the trenches, always afraid of getting a chill, he was, the egotist, that was why Midge always felt sorry for him, always sighed and gasped. He groaned real bad every time his whole body, rheumaticky waist and all, started twitching when he came, and often afterwards she gave the nice man's entire left buttock a full frontal massage, he taught her how himself, following his own former wife's recipe, she was killed by a bomb in the Leningrad blockade with the children. So now who was going to be giving the sick man his tender loving massage? But that was the way life worked out sometimes, and all just because of some stupid thing you said, that was the point that had to be stressed. He was wearing those drawers of his in a punishment battalion somewhere now. Or maybe he'd already been cured of his radiculitis for ever by a bullet, one of the Germans' or one of ours, it made no difference which. The best thing, though, was they took him at the beginning of the night, so Midge had managed to catch up on her sleep as well, done two good deeds at once, killed two birds with one stone. All fair and square and above board. What was it Stalin had said once and for all? Said it specially for those rotten whinging traitors who were still wasting their time trying to undermine our principles and our front-line friendship cemented in blood? He'd told them all straight: 'Don't eat cat at Christmas, don't defile the festival!' The people had even taken it up as a folk saying because it was such a catchy phrase, a real bull's eye!

And so Midge tried to figure out how that Rostislav would look with his wet cheeks, when two hefty Smersh men suddenly appeared from behind that thick spreading fir tree over there and twisted his arms behind his back — that wouldn't be like sitting in Kondopoga with mummy scoffing soused cloudberries with blind undercooked and burnt-black pancakes, would it now? And, like they say, Midge would sprinkle pepper on his tail too: 'Don't eat cat at Christmas!' It was just a pity that this time the ram wasn't in his underpants, but dressed in full uniform, shoulder straps and all, like a genuine officer. She wished she'd never laid eyes on him, the jealous Othello! Look how tight he'd got her by the throat, wanted to take her freedom away altogether and take her for his own individualistic use, turn an activist into his own individual lambing ewe, hell's bloody bells!

Midge suddenly put her arms round his head, which thank God was still firmly screwed on to his shoulders, and kissed the treacherous fool right on the lips. And she bit him as well – just to teach him!

Of course, she leapt back straight away. She felt ashamed – something terrible it was! After all, it was the first time in her life! She could have died! And worst of all, it happened without any warning, as if she didn't do it herself but somebody else had nudged her from inside – played a cunning trick on her. Now she'd ruined everything all because of a silly Tashkent poem from a scrap of newspaper good for nothing but wiping your backside. Oh, hell's bloody bells!

But what was amazing was Rostislav didn't even seem to have noticed the kiss. When Midge leapt away from him and hid behind a pine tree – just keeping one eye on Ovietsky – all he did was shake that head of his that was hanging by a thread, literally, as though he was feeling sleepy, and go on spouting poetry out loud. And the magpie repeated the same thing over and over, on and on, on and on: wait, wait, wait … And what's more he wasn't looking at Midge, but at the moon. The sky-gazing astronomer! Midge snorted, and of course she started staring at the moon too.

And just at that precise moment in time the moon peeped out from behind its idiotic black clouds – as white as a target in a shooting-range. Like seeing the way out shining from deep inside a black cave. There you've been plodding on and on through the labyrinth with a little stub of a candle, stumbling over stones and dodging the bats like a crazy-woman, bumping into sharp corners, and then suddenly there's the way out, it was close by all the time, you were looking for it round the wrong bend. So run to it then. Fly! You know how, after all, it's no problem for you, just close your eyes and you're there, free, where the bright-white day is shining for you, and the pure snow and the clear winter sunshine – and all around everything's as white as white, a bright holiday light. New Year, probably, mandarins on the tree, and mum's there with you, and dad too, and Lusya, of course, in her corner, gazing happily at a plump little mandarin – fly, Midge, after all you're not only Seagull when you're asleep, are you? Why can't you hear the order? Give me the OK, Comrade General! Where are you out there? After all, it must be possible to fly a little bit for the sake of ordinary human life as well, especially if it does no harm to official duties, or any damage to military secrets, surely?

Silence.

The bright light of the moon hurts her eyes with its loud ringing. And the dark clouds are already drifting over its white edge, covering it, blocking off the narrow way out. Well? Well then? We can even squeeze through a crack, if only we're not too late. We won't be gone long. Just three little minutes, literally. Only out there and then straight back again. After all tomorrow or the next day Rostislav will be on his way to heaven and he won't be coming back. If only she could have pleasant memories of him – a peaceful flight together, three minutes without any war, without slobbery lips, without all the cowardly quivering and the pedantic poetry – just break free, the two of them, and for once breathe their fill of that pure light, both of them breathing it in a single breath – after that they could face up to the bullets, or a bomb – one for both of them. After all, what was there that was any good, here on this side? How could you really love anyone here – at war, in an endless lie, where not one single person believes in any other and they're used to it, they don't know any other life ...

No, all the good things were over on the other side, that's where they were all gathered, in the dream, where the flowers sing ... Well? Are you too mean then, Comrade General? Eh?

The clouds covered the moon, crushed it and buried it under great slabs of dung. The light fell silent.

And Midge felt so hurt, even more hurt now, that Rostislav wasn't paying any attention to her. That during his last few days he looked past her and didn't even notice her kiss, after he'd been begging and pleading for it for so many days.

And she kissed him again, the freak, on the lips. And she felt her heart skip a beat and tremble as it hung on its very last thread. And again the moon blinded her and brought tears to her eyes – Rostislav threw her on her back – and the light went into her and pierced her through and struck a bell inside her – like a shot from an artillery gun. She couldn't move a muscle. His lips drank in the booming of her secret bell – blow after blow – and the pulsing of two lives mingled in her breast, and now the moon turned warm, like fresh milk in a glass. Midge heard someone inside say: 'That's it then, hell's bloody bells!'

'And you were afraid,' said Rostislav, helping her up from the ground. 'I told you, I can always control myself. So now we've kissed each other, see! And now you're my fiancée – the moon's a witness ...'

So he never unfastened her belt that evening. But he could have done! She'd have stripped off herself, if he'd given her a sign. But he didn't, the stubborn ram!

It was more than a week now since that first night with him when Midge had made a man of young Rostislav and then woken up with a pre-revolutionary-style waistline pulled in furiously tight by the righteous hand of her protector, and for him that canvas trouser belt had remained sacred and inviolable. Lieutenant not-Sovietsky avoided visiting Midge in her dug-out as a matter of principle. He decorously invited his beloved to go for a walk to the wood, as a rule after supper, and beneath the shelter of the trees, taking her delicately by the arm; with forceful ardour he sketched out for his bride-to-be his strategically sound plans for their tranquil and fruitful married life in a cosy log house on the outskirts of Kondopoga, which abounds in mushrooms, cloudberries, cranberries, fur-bearing animals and red-fleshed fish. Windows overlooking Lake Onega! With a geranium on the window sill and five feather pillows fluffed up blindly by his mum at the head of the bed with a special little carved bench with steps for the young wife to clamber unimpeded on to the bottomless feather mattress of the very lightest swan's down – instead of a hard trestle bed. At first Midge hemmed and hawed. Then she started getting bored. But then she got used to it, started to enjoy it, and with an ardour borrowed from this raving ram of a man who lived in voluntary monkhood, she began answering him back in their discussions of the artistic details of the lacy design on their future napkins, towels and sheets, as well as the imminent and inevitable little bonnets of the two rosy-cheeked twins as neat and robust as firm little mushrooms, and famous for their excellent appetite. Rostislav absolutely refused to settle for a single heir, evidently inspired by Midge herself and a fanciful vision of his own full double-breasted Madonna with himself imagined as both little suckers at once.

Something absolutely incomprehensible began happening to Midge. One day before she went to sleep she suddenly barred the entrance into the dug-out by nailing two crossed planks over it. That very night, having flown off with unprecedented speed, Midge immediately spotted below her an unfamiliar little town on the shore of an immense lake – Lake Ladoga, it had to be. Plank-walled, two-storeyed barracks-like buildings, tall log-built houses, pitiful sawn-off little huts from the destitute times of the old regime. Here and there on the streets and by the station dim street lamps were glowing and she made out low, stocky dray horses harnessed into green vans with the inscription 'Bread', in which they were ferrying the wounded from the railway station to the hospital. But she decided that somehow or other she must have been transported to one of Leningrad's Lake Ladoga suburbs because General Zukov hadn't managed to tune in his apparatus in time: there hadn't been a single command yet, although he usually greeted

Seagull with his cheerful, kind voice when she was still making her approach to the city, fifty or sixty kilometres away.

And then she started to sing, chanting to the entire vault of heaven in her deep general's voice husky from a cold – Midge's future Onega mother-in-law, Domna Dormidontovna Ovietskaya in person, the entire massive Kondopoga presence of her, no doubt luxuriating on soft feather mattresses at that precise moment.

'Oh, I didn't dare hope I'd ever be honoured to admire your lovely face, my sweet darling girl! Why, you tender little white-sea salmon, you white seagull, fleet and subtle of wing, our sweet little bride, our little flying whore, bugger it, *striecher-miecher*! Don't be offended with your old mother for her way of talking, my little white swan! We'll give you a lovely wreath of flowers and a fine feast to celebrate the wedding! Oh yes ...'

'Seagull, this is Seagull!' the invisible girl interrupted the suddenly hoarse General Zukov, overjoyed and reassured at finally hearing the general's voice and his commanding tone, despite his unexpected jokes. 'Comrade Number One! Where am I? Give me a reference point!'

'I will that. I'll give you a deference point, my little child!' the general groaned again, rumbling out his unprecedented folksy lamentations in peals of thunder that split the sky. 'Hurry, come quick, my girlie! Fly to your new loving mother, my little orphan, my under-age darling! Good luck to you in retiring from your soldiering duties, you're our little midge-fly now, our own little whore-fish! No more sweating and toiling for you, our loose little darling. Let that Svetka bitch service them all on her own, it's no problem for her, the whore-madam, the great slut-slit, a pro with an arse like that won't keel over and die, the old hussy's fond of her prick, she won't get tired of showing them her backside, the whore, the man-eater, the shameless deceiver – my foolish little Rostislav would really have been in trouble if Svetka had shown up instead of you! You're my own little whore and plague-spot, forget all about that bloodthirsty general. He's forgotten it now, that woman, that vicious slut, that snake, that lousy informer, the way everyone screwed his arse in our criminal colony. And the rotten jerk didn't even serve half his time, he turned informer, lived in the separate trusties' room behind the barracks. He was a ponce, a mare, a daisy, just you wait, we'll put a scare into him all right! You fly to mama, my sweet seagull-girl, my little daughter, rest on my soft down mattress, lay down your silly little head, my soft little puppy-dog! I'll chop birch logs for firewood! I'll heat up the bathhouse! And I'll choose the twiggiest besom! I'll give the little bride a good lashing and feed her crazy vodka for her hangover, sluice you down a bit out of a little wooden tub – the sinful body with the sinless soul – I'll wrap you in linen sheets! I'll feed your white body with strong-flavoured honey, steam the shame and the filth out of my own darling girl! Whores make the most faithful wives. His bride will be a delight to my son's eyes – whiter than a fancy little loaf of fine bread. Fly, come fly to me, my little swanling, to your mother-in-law in your own true home!'

'Acknowledged – to my own true home!' Seagull responded with a shrug of her invisible shoulders. She had already taken a bearing on the stormy, rumbling waves of the general's bass, disguised for some reason as the soloist in the amateur choir of the Kondopoga House of Culture, Domna Dormidontovna, whose rare artistic mastery of folk keening and songs of lamentation was known to Midge from Rostislav's stories about her – Seagull instantly realised that the stream of slander against the general and glorification of her own sinful self flooding across the sky was being poured out, as if from the mouth of a volcano, from the chimney of a tall, neat wooden house at the end of a wide street on the very edge of the lake. Everything the way Rostislav described it: planking pavements and a vast puddle in the middle of the street. And of course, a geranium on the window sill. But what did General Zukov want with all these weird goings-on – transferring his control-point to Kondopoga? And why would he insult himself? And from Kondopoga of all places? Or was there some code concealed in all this? And perhaps he had guided her flights from here before too, but today he'd decided to call her directly to him? What had she done wrong? Or perhaps it was because of Rostislav? Everything seemed to be OK, there was nothing really wrong... Or maybe it was just the opposite and he wanted to give her an award. Yes, it was an award, it was obvious! All those nights she'd spent on duty – almost without a single deviation from her course, and this was the first time she'd been carried away, so to speak, northwards, but when you figured it out it was him who'd summoned her anyway ...

'Seagull, Seagull, this is Number One!' she suddenly heard his peerless voice, as though from far away. 'Careful, Seagull! The enemy is planning some kind of diversion. Be on the alert!'

She stumbled in the sky and stopped dead. What's going on here, comrades? Oh, but could she really have lost her way?

'Attention, Seagull! There may be an attempt at diversion by the enemy!' she heard again.

'I'll give you a perversion, you bastard,' came the belched reply. 'You rotten prick, you snitch, come to rat on people again! You think the girl will be frightened? Liar, the girl will manage just fine!'

Flooding the sky with a turbid wave of threats and scalding the confused Seagull with a hot blast of shame, what must after all be her mother-in-law's bass voice came bubbling like lava out of the brick chimney stack of the log-walled house with geraniums in the windows:

'I'll teach you to mess about with my girl's head like that! Think you're so smart, you devil! Give me a bit of your brains here to wipe my boot on! And those huge hands of his – just take a look, women – up to the elbows in Russian blood! How many of our fine boys have you got killed, you bloodsucking insect, for your medals, for your jangling metal gongs? How many Christian souls have you defiled? Even in hell you'll never be forgiven, you're an enemy of the people, you shameless bitch! And you, my girl, don't listen to him, the swindler, he wears his prick round his waist like a belt. You come on diving down here under my nice warm wing. And we'll show him up for what he is, just you wait. Ooh, all the shameless tricks you've played, all the sweet people's blood you've sucked – I may be blind, but I can see. I know all about your heroic deeds, I know, remember the volleyball court, you butcher, well then! You can never be trusted or forgiven.'

'Rescind that order!' General Zukov's voice screeched like a nail on glass. 'Seagull, obey my command!'

Seagull couldn't understand any more who she was hearing and who she ought to obey in this situation.

'Drop the whole business, forget about that dragon, my girl,' the mighty mother-in-law's command drowned out the distant general and swept him away. 'The Kondopoga convicts know your general inside out. He did time in our sixth corrective colony for embezzlement, this idle parasite of yours. He was the thieves' pansy, a shameless trusty, lost his fine fat arse gambling with the thieves – so now he's running wild, now he's celebrating his revenge on all the people, the heartless beast! Don't listen to that bad man, little daughter! And you're not his seagull any more, just a little Kondopoga girl, our sweet little berry, come to mama, come on!'

'Seagull! Seagull!' The general's strained voice came from far off, as if the wind was carrying it away.

'I won't give you your seagull back! And she's never going to listen to your vile words again … So there! Haven't you ever seen a Kondopoga woman before? Take a good look, and kiss my slit!'

'Seagull! This is Number One!'

'He's Number One – are you joking? He's nothing but an errand-boy! Here, take that, you!'

The feisty Kondopoga mother-in-law shook the sky with a high explosive detonation.

'Seagull!' the call came almost too faint to hear, as if from out of a collapsed dug-out.

She felt that in one more moment the two feuding wills crossed in the night sky, both furious, and possibly equal in power, would tear in half the little empty cloud known from the south as Seagull and from the north as sweet Kondopoga berry. She hung right above the hut where simple human happiness awaited her, pitiless, prepared to tear off her wings, blindly domineering, greedily anticipating her unquestioning soldierly subordination to its own laws. For who else would satisfy, who else would soothe the massive mother-in-law's sense of injury, alone in her huge empty house, if not an affectionate and submissive little daughter-in-law? Citizeness Ovietskaya's husband, a merchant's son and White Guard in the Civil War and father of the timid Rostislav, who had entrusted the secret of his family line only to Seagull, had disappeared in thirty-eight, denounced by Domna Dormidontovna's jealous unmarried brother, a secret collaborator, and she had been blinded by her tears, but he had been exposed by the security forces only six months later as a Japanese spy.

But Seagull was held back from behind on the slim, taut steel leash-like cable of the heavenly freedom of secret strategic flights – after all it was Midge they'd chosen and named Seagull, and she was the one they'd honoured by granting her the right to seek out and destroy the black enemy dragon with her sincere, wide-open glance – and after all, he might turn out to be all the insatiable malice and death in the entire world. So who should she listen to, which way should she move? In her torment, all she wanted was for one of the two voices to take the upper hand – in the sky and inside her own being at the same time. 'Seagull!' – or was she imagining it? Crrrash! Boom-ba-bang! Sob, glug, splash – then once again the landslide rumbling of her mother-in-law's living howitzer – like a crate full of rifles crashing down off a two-wheeled cart and a simultaneous shrapnel burst in the air. And Seagull finally realised what weapon the long-range Domna Dormidontovna was using for her blind bombardment; according to Rostislav's reminiscences, she was very fond of spending her free time sitting in the private meditation room – the massive mother-in-law suffered from constipation, and something really terrible it was too.

Another explosion! And thunder in the sky again. And again, and again ...

Suddenly Seagull, stretched as if between two rubber bands, gasped with all of her little sigh of a body and went hurtling towards the ground faster than a bullet, because the pull from the invisible General Zukov had broken off with a twang. Flying up to meet her came the planking roof of the wooden house that was now already home. Seagull squeezed her eyes shut when she saw the ten-ton Domna Dormidontovna on her feather bed through the boards and the ceiling. Her mother-in-law was snoring and whistling with her face buried deep in five pillows, and her buttocks rose up under the eiderdown like the two halves of the globe, sundered by the efforts of her husband and brother and still wailing and muttering in offence at each other, and trembling so powerfully after the invisible duel that they set the indestructible merchant's house creaking and swaying.

Horrified, Seagull woke up, as always, as Midge.

The trestle bed was still quivering and squeaking under her. And Midge was perched right on the very edge, only hanging on by a miracle. But beside her lay Rostislav, thrashing about without waking in the nightmarish visions of his already half-insane, monkish soul. She laughed, unfastened his belt and to make his stupid life easier to bear she did for him what the fat lieutenant-colonels demanded from her, blushing red and threatening her with court-martial, for the sake of which other excessively worldly-wise lieutenants kissed the thin, unwashed little toes on her pale, tired feet, at the same time promising the indifferent Midge a wedding ring and a flat in the centre of Moscow, Tbilisi or Stalinabad, sometimes with a father-in-law who was a people's commissar of food supplies thrown in. Rostislav, the crazy freak, only twitched, smacked his thick sheep's lips and continued with his innocent dream without even waking up, but now without moving, with a drunken, relaxed smile. Midge, for some reason proud of being with a man for the first time, adjusted his uniform herself, but afterwards she never told Rostislav that that night she had practically been his wife, attentive and unsqueamish, the way it's supposed to be – why go wounding a man if he has principles?

In the mornings now Midge woke the cursing Lukich with a jolly shock-brigade song: 'Stalin paints old Kremlin's walls with gentle light!' A timid, weak, but entirely sincere virginal flush had appeared on her face. She was always tidying up the dug-out on her own, without any urging from her bewildered eunuch, who was left with nothing to do in those days, and all day long she flitted about like a butterfly, irritating even the very calmest of the soldiers with her happy appearance. And in the evenings, before her date with Rostislav, from the bottom end of the trestle bed, stuffed full of unused knickers, Midge took out her captured 'Rosenblum' perfume – Lukich had given it to her last year, and it had just been lying there because it wasn't really needed – and reverentially unscrewed the pink plastic top. She thought it would have lost its fragrance already, but the reek from it was so strong the company commander was forced to call Midge in and he yelled at her for a long time about stinking up the company's entire position like a whorehouse, and how it was unmasking the unit and soon the Hanses would open fire, aiming at that disgusting smell. Midge looked at his trousers below the waist and objected calmly and reasonably: the scent was captured, world-class, the smell was German, and the Hanses didn't waste shells on their own, they were economical, not like our lousy gunners, everyone knew what freaks they were …

Three times now Lieutenant Ovietsky had come to his date with her with a black eye. Midge kissed it better. Rostislav spouted his Kondopologa eiderdown ravings, but he never opened Midge's chastity belt. He left staggering, pressing his hands to his voluntary headache and other suffering parts of his body.

The night after that moonlit evening when Rostislav read her the poem about Tashkent, Midge didn't go flying again, but she had an individual dream all of her own, and it was entirely apolitical too. So short on ideology, in fact, that she'd have been ashamed even to tell Walter Ivanovich about it, hell's bloody bells!

What Midge dreamed about was a bizarre little man on a red motorcycle with an empty side-car. His face seemed to look a bit like Lukich's. Only for some reason he had a beard down to his belly-button – seemed he didn't want to shave it – and a fresh white undershirt instead of a tunic, like Saint Nicholas in the icon. But in general, of course, Lukich wasn't really Lukich at all, in fact he was almost Comrade Karl – begging your pardon – Marx, with that huge impressive beard – whether you want to or not, he said, come on, get on with it and unite with all the other countries, like you're supposed to, if you're such an almighty class-conscious proletarian, make all of us sinners happy, or else you'd better watch it, I'll fetch you such a belt with my beard ... But behind the intransigent founding father's back there were genuine glittery-silver aeroplane wings – with red stars! And Midge, instantly aware of herself as Seagull, began to feel an entirely justified kindred trust in the man with the beard and wings. But the things he said plunged the maiden into a state of embarrassment and fear.

'Gather up your bits and pieces, daughter!' declared Marx-Lukich, knitting his brows severely. 'They're evacuating you back home, girl. An urgent emergency order's come for you from dear Comrade Stalin – absolute top speed: you'll give birth to a Redeemer for all of us in nine months, like it's supposed to be, just in time for the May holidays. And a terrible Redeemer too! Invincible! Implacable! You kissed your little lamb of God, didn't you? Offered up your unsullied lips, you little fool? Now for your sin you'll carry a burden effectively in due accordance with the full severity of all the provisions of the regulations and instructions. For it has been said time and time again: your son of man shall be sent to establish a just order throughout all the earth. Through him shall our holy proletarian spirit descend unto suffering mankind – through the final, ultimate and total world-wide war, named after the unforgettable, red-bannered through-and-through, hero-general Comrade Zukov. For Comrade Stalin's world-wide heart craves to accept into itself the vain, irrational affliction of all the peoples – and swallow it up – for the good and the enlightenment of those lost sheep. And since that's going to be the name of the game, as they say, there's no way to manage it without war, think it out for yourself. That's what it'll be called – The World-Class War. Because it shall be given to the world for the total pacification of all the peoples vegetating in obscurity under our hand. Just as soon as we winkle out Hitler, then we'll set off riding round the world on those same old trusty gun-carriages – to bring consolation to all the pure, class-conscious, selfless, humble souls. But we'll talk about the rest of them some other place, now's not the time for that. Remember that, daughter: not the sword, but peace! The first one they sent was that Jesus Christ of yours, with the sword – it didn't work out, he couldn't pull it off. That's why he had no luck, going around the place frightening people left and right: "Not peace, he says, do I bring you, but the sword!" But people are timid folk, petty, people want peace – so now we're going to give them all peace – there, take it and enjoy it! And if there's only a tenth of all the personnel of the whole of freeloading mankind left in that peace – sorry about that, as they say, you got what you were fighting for, you were the ones that asked for peace, you shorn sheep – now go and graze in freedom, heh-heh. From word to deed: not the sword, but peace! Looking at it from the outside there's not that much of a difference, but you can feel it all right from the inside, and don't try arguing, girl, that this is all way over your head. Although you're right about one thing, whichever way you turn there's not much more than a four-letter word to the whole business, so surely we can manage it? There's a phrase – "duty first"! And just in case anything happens, you bear in mind that Stalin invented that phrase himself, before him we didn't know how to explain everything going on around us. But now things are just fine – there's nothing left to explain. So duty first: you shall carry the peace of the world within you! Peace – and our world-wide single truth from the beloved Stalin. And you shall bear it to birth. And you shall feed the sharp-toothed infant truth. And give it to the people. And be not afraid, this time they won't stretch him out and crucify him like a frog. If anything happens, he'll crucify whoever deserves it – he's been granted great power ...'

'I'm not Mary!' the girl tells him. 'Just Midge, and that's all. You're getting something confused, Lukich! Giving birth to gods is an alien class activity for pioneer girls!' – 'But then I'm not altogether Lukich!' says the little man, stroking his fine beard. 'When you wake up you'll understand. All secrets shall be opened to you, all seals shall fall away. If you wake up, of course. But look out, or God forbid you'll sleep through the second coming of our Lord, the final universal resurrection. So keep your vigilance high, hell's bloody bells, and don't destroy us all by sleeping through it, you increate virgin slut.'

Marx-Lukich jerked his polished boot and started up his red motorcycle on half-throttle. He flapped his aeroplane wings, the crazy freak, crowed like a cock just like Field-marshal Suvorov in the film of the same name when he was crossing the Alps, sliding down from the top without any sledges, inspiring his forces with the example of his own fearless backside – and came hurtling straight at Midge, phutt-phutting his motor and farting army peas – the old dunderhead. She had no time to jump out of the way, but the motorbike reared up like Chestnut-Grey, gave a deep bass neigh and roared up into the sky – something terrible it was! As though there was an invisible wall between Comrade Marx and Midge and he'd ridden up it back to his heaven on high. Round, solid, broad little wings, just like a Hawk pursuit plane in the Leningrad sky. It was the roar of the motorcycle – the rumble of an aeroplane – that woke her up.

She came to, and the German spy plane that had flown over the dug-out in the night could hardly be heard, far away in the rear already. But Lukich was there on his knees in front of Midge's trestle bed. Looking at her with tear-filled eyes, crossing himself and whispering: 'Blessed art Thou among women and blessed is Thy Son, Jesus …'

'What's up?' Midge asked him, frightened. 'Have you gone totally crazy?'

'I'm praying. What's that to you?' Lukich waved his hand in annoyance. 'You just carry on sleeping. Well?' He shifted the weight on his knees, grunting and frowning.

'What are you doing, praying to me, then? What have I got to do with your gods? You're out of your mind, hell's bloody bells.'

'None of your blasphemy!' Lukich shouted at her. 'I haven't got an icon, and like they say, in the absence of headed paper … And what makes you any worse than an icon if it comes to that? Paint in a wreath round that empty head of yours, stick a baby on your tit – and you're a perfect Virgin Mary. Relieve my sorrows – just like it says in all the regulations – the same black shadows under your eyes, and as skinny as if you haven't been fed for three years.'

'I'm no Mary, I'm just Midge,' the girl muttered, and at the word 'Mary' she recalled all of her amazing dream at once and felt frightened at her own words coming to her in a dream and speaking themselves out loud – that meant she'd lost her way again, confused Lukich's dreams with her own – maybe that was because she'd nailed up the entrance to the dug-out?

Anyway, while Rostislav was alive, Midge never gave the old man on the little motorcycle another thought. Every evening she went to the woods, as if she was going off on work detail. She came back after midnight, exhausted by her fiancé's caresses, with a heavy weight in her belly, but with her belt still not unfastened. And more than once she kissed Rostislav on the lips. Somehow she wanted to. So that was the way nature had arranged things – it was like science fiction!

But after exactly two short weeks her brave young darling came flying in to see Midge in her machine-gun nest, and kissed her loudly on the cheek. 'I'll be fighting for you, my dearest,' he cried with a sob. Pale as chalk he was – something terrible! Osip Lukich turned away and spat. He only said one word: 'Slop!'

After the battle, which was only arranged on the insistence of the new divisional command in order to check battle-readiness in the flanks, the medical orderlies brought the defender of his homeland Rostislav back on a waterproof cape. And his head separately – in a bast sack. The rule was to bury bodies with their heads, that's what the sacks were issued for. Lukich took the watch off Rostislav's wrist – a dainty little one that glinted bright and pretty in the sunshine.

'Hey look, his ticker's red,' said Lukich with a shake of his head.

'Why red?' Midge was offended. She kissed Rostislav's dead lips and stroked his light-brown hair while no one was looking: turned the head this way and that way, the little fool, but she still couldn't get her fill of kissing it, it was funny, she should have done it before – that's what she kept repeating to herself – you should have done it earlier, hell's bloody bells! And even deeper inside her she realised that if she could somehow take this head she loved away with her and carry it everywhere during the war and kiss it sometimes at night – then she wouldn't need practically anything else, no two ways about it. And so she took offence at Lukich: 'Who's red? We're not red at all, we're genuine brown! Aren't we, Rostik? Tell the man: I'm brown-haired. All right? I'm brown-haired! Say it!'

'Enough tormenting yourself with that nonsense!' Lukich interrupted her. He took the lieutenant's head and put it away in the sack. 'I tell you, his ticker's red. That means gold. His watch. Get it, daughter? I mean his watch.'

Midge nodded her head happily, trying to show Lukich that not only did she understand his words perfectly well, but she'd already realised how stupid and childish her behaviour with Rostislav's head had been. Like some kind of crazy-woman, word of honour!

'You're lucky, daughter!' said Lukich, lighting up. 'At least one man has personally and quite deliberately given his life for you. You'll never get that in peace time, not even if you're the world's biggest man-teasing pain in the neck …'

And later Midge gave the watch to a captain. He was young, but already completely grey. Jolly he was, kept threatening her: I'm going to adopt you! That was a great laugh! The captain kept cracking jokes. Between the jokes and the funny stories Midge had an easy time with him, and everything happened quickly, she didn't have time to get tired and irritable. Quite the opposite, she laughed at the end, when he announced: 'All clear, no mines!' That was why she gave him the watch, because he didn't torment her. All the same, she wondered what he was called. All the good men were either called Kolya or Sasha, she'd noticed that ages ago, Sasha, probably. But no, he was Kolya after all! Nikolai Sergeievich was his name. Oh yes, it was Nikolai Alexandrovich ... Or was he really Kolya? Alexander ... No, he couldn't have been Alexander after all ... But anyway – Kolya or Sasha – he was a world-class lad, that's all, jolly. He must have been killed. He was a sapper, came to clear mines, he was commandeered, only stayed on for three days because of Midge. He was definitely killed. Everyone knew all sappers went the same way. The most terrible way to go ...

No, of course Midge didn't go to her little ram's funeral – *merci beaucoup* with fancy tassels on! She wanted to, to be honest, but Lukich advised her not to, and thanks for that. But in the night she suddenly burst out blubbing like a little girl – it made her ashamed to remember it. Any man who got friendly with her even just once was bound to get killed. Midge had noticed that ages ago. She'd been surprised, of course, at first, but then she got used to it. Lukich, by the way, actually explained the reason for this strange state of affairs. He even started talking to Midge about it himself. Which one of the regiment's officers had caught a stray bullet that day she couldn't remember. It might have been some junior lieutenant, or maybe a senior one. Brown-haired, wasn't he? Yes, curly headed, and with black eyebrows. No, the curly-headed one was blown up on a mine earlier. Anyway, one day after supper Lukich asked: 'Tell me, daughter, do you notice or don't you how fond death is of your boyfriends? Don't you notice that? Seems like he hasn't missed one since I've been serving as your eunuch. Eh?'

'It's the war!' Midge shrugged her shoulders. 'What does the war care? It couldn't give a damn if a man's wearing stripes or shoulder straps with stars. What can I do about it?' she asked sorrowfully.

'That's not what I mean,' croaked Lukich. 'How can I explain? For a long time now I've seen it as a special sign. I even pointed it out to Sanka Goryaev. The moment a man gets in with our Midge, it means we'll be burying him tomorrow or the next day. If he's not killed in action, then a spy plane will strafe him from the air. If it's not a plane, then a mine will finish him off. One time I even started keeping count. But I soon got scared and dropped it. There's a spell on the girl, I thought, best leave that to God in heaven. But it's a great thing that the men receive some comfort before the end. If things were done right, you ought to get a special medal for that and a comradely front-line word of thanks.'

Midge put on a serious expression.

Lukich breathed out heavily and poured out the special reserve from his flask in equal portions for Midge and himself.

'Let's drink to their memory, daughter! All of them together. Rest their souls!'

They drank without clinking glasses. Lukich drained his glass, Midge took a sip.

'Who's put a spell on me then?' she asked, wiping the alcohol off her lips with the sleeve of her tunic.

'That's the whole point: no one! It's much simpler and far worse than that!' Lukich scratched the back of his head and bit into an onion. 'You've got a flaw in you, daughter. A major flaw. You don't get angry about this rotten lousy life of ours.'

'What's that?' Midge yawned.

'Like I said, confess, now: do you ever get angry with them, the officers? Do you ever take even that much offence?' He showed her the tip of his little finger.

'What for, Lukich?' Midge asked, frightened. 'My God, what for? This is war, hell's bloody bells! You think I don't understand that? I understand everything, of course … Maybe I used to get angry before, I don't remember. But now – it's like I don't feel it somehow – I can't work it out myself. How can you make sense of it all? And how can I get angry with the little fool, when compared to me he's nothing but a child, or even worse, a babe in arms! Some of them even take all their clothes off, like when you go to see the doctor. When you look at his shoulders with the knobbly bones, you feel sorry for every part of him! Every day near enough there are bullets flying, shrapnel, bombs, mines, and he's really completely naked, not a single part of him made of metal or even aluminium – right? Nothing but a tunic to cover him – and how much protection is that? It seems stupid, I just can't understand it. They say that earlier people used to fight wars in suits of armour, in chain-mail shirts, with a cooking pot on their heads a hundred times better than a helmet, safer – although there weren't any rocket launchers then, or even proper big guns, nothing but swords and sabres. And now they've thought up all sorts of dynamite, but they've left the man naked – the crazy freaks! That's how I see them all – naked under their clothes. Sometimes it even makes me shudder when I look at some of them – they're so naked underneath. And when I feel too cold looking at one, I know he's going to die soon too, very soon. Why's that, Lukich? And you're not any kind of eunuch, don't give me that. You know how much I value you and respect you as a senior comrade and boss. And in general. Why do you say that? A eunuch's what Khan Girei used to have, I saw him in a ballet, he was horrible, in a massive great turban and he had a flunkey's job: keeping an eye on someone else's wives to make sure they didn't get up to anything. You don't watch what I get up to, do you? The number of times I've got washed in front of you, no bother. God knows anyway, you're like my own father!'

Already drunk, Midge reached across the crate with the oil lamp on it and kissed Lukich on the cheek. She always got drunk straight away from spirits, couldn't get used to it somehow.

'But that's the whole catch: you're affectionate.' Lukich snorted, disgruntled. 'And what's more, you haven't got an ounce of malice in you. If only you'd get just a little bit more angry: you're still living on earth, after all, not up in heaven. Then maybe they wouldn't get hit so hard – not so badly and not so often. After all, it's not all the same to him – I mean God – who a man offends. It's one thing to give that shameless hussy Svetka the medical assistant piss to drink instead of brandy for a laugh when you're drunk – but you're a little pioneer girl only knee-high to a grasshopper. God's no slouch, he sees everything, he takes offence for you, you little ...'

'But who's done me wrong?' Midge smashed her fist down on to the crate, the flask fell over on its side and the vodka spilled out. 'Have I ever complained to you, you snitch? I've never told tales in all my life! D'you think I've got no class-consciousness or what? You know all right: for me the collective is everything! Who have I ever let down?'

'From way up there our Lord couldn't give a damn for your collective.' Lukich spat on the floor. 'But his heart aches for you. He's the one who marks them – to make every one of them a target. And he does right.'

'You're jealous of them, you big boss!' Midge said with a sad smile. 'But god doesn't exist. If god existed, there wouldn't be any war. How do you like that!'

'Well, well,' croaked Lukich. 'You don't know him very well, daughter ...'

The night after the battle when the handsome lieutenant's head was torn off, it wasn't grief for her pale-faced little ram with the big blue eyes that made Midge cry, or resentment against some god or other. She cried out of fear and shame. Because the only person who could help in her situation was the medical assistant Svetka. And of course, Svetka would spread the dirt round the whole division: she didn't like Midge. And Walter Ivanovich had warned her, he'd foreseen the whole thing and tried his best to protect her, fool that she was – she'd completely forgotten all about it with her headless Rostislav. And Midge fell asleep still crying.

But in the morning the order came from headquarters: redeployment.

Chaos, confusion, swearing. Idiotic orders from lieutenants, croaking from Lukich hit by an untimely attack of radiculitis, the destruction of their comfortable little nesting. Annoyance, fear, tiredness, boredom. A long, bumpy journey in the back of a captured truck over rough tracks pitted by shells and cut right across by temporary trenches. Nights spent under the open sky by blown-up bridges. The first early morning chill of frost, hoarfrost on the grass and the flap of your greatcoat. At the new place – digging ditches, shelters and trenches. Cold lunches and hot nights of futile exchanges of fire from the ill-equipped, disorganised firing line. The smell of blood in the frosty air. A yellow birch leaf on the chest of the dead Captain Eremin: but that was absolutely nothing to do with Midge, she hadn't let another man near her since handsome Rostislav's death – and for some reason they didn't pester her. Autumn descended in a sudden cold spell with snow. But in mid-September a calm, azure Indian summer emerged from behind the sheer wall of cold days and hung a sticky little cobweb on the sight of her 'Maxim' machine gun, although only two days had gone by without any firing. Sunshine; yellow woods behind the trench; clean, scattered clouds. Midge felt lousy every half hour now, overcome by the nausea. The poor girl's heart raced.

'Why don't you go and see Svetka at the infirmary, daughter?' Lukich growled when he carried out Midge's bucket in the morning. 'What are you waiting for, hell's bloody bells?'

So Midge dragged herself there.

'Come hopping in have you, froggy?' Svetka stuck her hands against her sides. 'Brought some spawn along, have you? Want to get rid of it? You're round as a melon – anyone can see your belly from a mile away! Which little lieutenant was it put his charge in your chamber? Your face is all puffy and green – toxicosis. Well, where's he got to? They're all great hands at knocking the girls up, but when it comes to getting the papers stamped at the registry office – you can't even drag the billy-goat back by the tail. Of course he'll choose the worst possible moment to disappear – just as soon as you're up the spout. While he's still winding you up, oh no, he doesn't want anything from you – what do you mean? Likes self-service, doesn't he, real clever with his hands he is, but he'll never manage to screw you right – just grab hold of your slit …'

'Couldn't you just give me some medicine, Svetlana Erofeevna!' Midge took off her cap and wiped her feet at the door for the fourth time.

'You'll go under the knife!' Svetka condemned her. 'The way I have all my life. It's time for you to get used to it.

Medicine, hah! Listen to her! There's no such medicine on earth – Comrade Stalin hasn't invented it yet! Give you medicine and you young things'll lure away all my studs! When you're stretched out on the frame and turned inside out, then you'll learn how to love the Motherland ...'

The liquid porridge locked in Midge's throat broke through into her mouth. She held her hands up like a ladle to stop it falling on Svetka's nice clean floor. But of course it still poured through.

'I beg your pardon, Svetlana Erofeevna,' Midge croaked without breathing. 'Give me a rag, I'll wipe it up.'

Midge was reeling. Svetka wiped her face clean. She wiped the floor. Without looking at her she barked.

'Come for the abortion tomorrow. I've got Colonel Orlovets today.'

Midge thanked her and darted out through the door.

'Hey there, come back!' the medical assistant ordered her. 'Give me a hand, here, little girlfriend. I want to move the divan. You take hold of that side ...'

The divan in Svetka's hut was an old one, covered in leather, well known to the whole division. Svetka had dragged it round with her right through the war, and the soldiers were tired of cursing the oak catafalque's unliftable weight. But every time they were redeployed the command was careful to send a truck and five soldier boys to transfer the infirmary. Apart from the divan and two boxes of medicines, the infirmary consisted of three metal-bound trunks containing Svetka's dowry. The medical assistant was heavier than all her trunks, with a squint in both eyes.

'Don't pull it your way, you clumsy sloven!' Svetka commanded, thrusting her hands against her sides. 'Oh no, little girlfriend, we won't get it done that way! We have to lift it first. Lift it from the bottom. Bend down, bend down, what are you afraid of, you fine lady! The number of times I've lifted it myself, and I'm still alive, as you can see ... Ah, you've got no strength at all – I don't know what the billy-goats see in dead carrion like you ...'

Midge was angry. She heaved the divan towards herself and started slowly straightening up, hoisting the massive bulk off the recently painted floor. The blood rushed to her head and swelled her throat tight.

'Hang on there, piss-bladder, I want to give you a hand …'

And Svetka plonked herself down right in the middle of the squeaking divan. Midge held up the huge thing for about five seconds. She was used to people relying on her and to not letting them down. Something jerked and quivered in her belly and her knees buckled from the piercing pain. She fell with her face on the padded arm of the divan, dropping the divan, with Svetka rolling about on it and laughing, on to the empty toe of her spacious boot.

Svetka gave Midge sal volatile to sniff. She led her into a little room with a narrow little window. She undressed her and laid her carefully on a bed with two pillows.

'It's simpler our way, like that, without the knife,' she chirped in a cosy, satisfied kind of voice. 'Now you'll empty yourself all at once, my little under-age double-barrel shot-gun. You're lucky your belly's still weak, like a child's. You probably couldn't beat one out of me with a stick, but somehow I've not had any luck for over a year now. I could have been back home in Tver ages ago … But why didn't you take advantage of your condition? You're not fed up yet of doing battle for the Motherland every night then? Well, that's your business. Was he at least handsome? Did he promise to marry you?'

Midge nodded and burst into tears.

'Here, take a sip of spirit.' Svetka held up a beaker for Midge and supported her head. 'Listen carefully. Now you'll feel like you're dying for a while. You'll have a miscarriage – all right and proper. You can thank the divan for that, go down on your knees to it. God willing, there'll be no need to take you to hospital' – she spat over her left shoulder – 'you'll empty yourself out clean. There's a pot under the bed. But don't put up with too much pain, call me straight away if there's anything wrong. Although there shouldn't be anything wrong, you're not very far gone. Do your nipples get wet, is the milk flowing?'

'Yes,' sobbed Midge. 'It's sweet ...'

'Well, aren't you in a fine mess, you fool! OK, I'll bring you another basin ...'

Midge closed her eyes. She imagined the little child in her belly clutching with its hands but unable to keep itself in there. The dream about Marx-Lukich surfaced from her memory, but then instantly tipped over the edge of oblivion and left only one word ringing round her head, emptied by fear: REDEEMER − RELIEVER − BELIEVER − DECEIVER ... And then silence ...

The medical assistant only woke her the following morning when she began rattling and clanking the empty pots under the bed.

'Where's the miscarriage?' she shouted in a terrible voice.

Midge checked and began laughing. It was just like the time that came round every month − a little drop of crimson, that was all − nothing else. A pleasant warmth flooded her belly, her body felt light, rested, well.

'Are you mocking me, bitch?' Svetka stuck her hands into her sides. 'You malingerer! You wanted to desert − but you're as empty as a flaming drum!'

'What have I got to do with it?' Midge shrugged, fell back on to her pillow and sighed in relief.

'But you were pregnant! I saw it myself: you were all green and nauseous, and the milk ...'

'I was,' said Midge with a guilty smile. 'The whole company knew it. The whole regiment, even. They wouldn't come within a mile of me, as if I had the plague.'

'Then where's it got to? I'm asking you!'

'Maybe it was never there?'

And Midge burst into song: 'Sleep not, arise, my curly-head! The workshops are ringing ...'

'But it was there! It was!' Svetka sat down on the edge of the bed. She thought. 'Hang on, little girlfriend. Maybe it was a phantom pregnancy. It happens sometimes, I read about it in a book. They call it the Danish Queen's disease. There was a queen in Denmark who was barren and she wanted a child really badly. And then the stupid fool's belly blew up, even though it was empty ...'

'I didn't want it, honestly!' Midge was offended. 'Not at all — I was scared. I was scared to death!'

'What difference does that make now!'

Svetka threw the blanket back off Midge and kneaded her soft white belly. She touched her nipples, no longer swollen up like yesterday, but small and virginal.

'Good morning, Marx-Lukich!' Midge muttered to herself.

'You were born under a lucky star, girlfriend!' Svetka covered Midge up and tucked in the blanket. 'Sleep for a while, get some rest. And when you wake up, spare a thought for your life. You need to get away from the front as fast as your legs will carry you. While you're still in one piece. God won't give you two chances. He's watching all your tricks from up there, like Smersh ...'

'There is no god,' said Midge and turned away. 'I've known that for ages already. Almost a year and a half now ...'

'How do you know, you fool? No one can know that!' Svetka crossed herself and glanced at the closed door.

'They can!' said Midge.

And she gave a loud sneeze. As though the blue clay dust had got into her nose and throat again, like that time in forty-one, in July.

Chapter 5

In which *Deus conservat omnia.*

Day and night the herds poured through the village of Kondriushino, through the blue clay dust.

Stately Simental matrons from the distant shockworking Stalin Collective Farm (the former estate of Count Meshchersky), always so reserved and self-possessed, swung their stupefied heads in time to their faltering steps. Only a week earlier they were crushing the tall lungwort in the water meadows with their taut udders, but now they were fatally emaciated, like the vision of the seven lean years in the pharaoh's dream.

Plodding along dejectedly came the piebald and brown Kostroma cows from the Our Road Collective Farm.

Following on behind the cattle from Kostroma were the delicate little Dutch cows from the Fifteen Years of October Farm. Their languorous grandmothers and wary great-grandfather were once ordered by the diligent Tver landowner Tsitsianov-Topilsky from the low-lying polders where Rubens strolled in search of inspiration.

Dragging themselves along indolently came the round-faced, long-eared bull-calves from the livestock unit at the Red May Collective Farm. Sullen-faced drovers urged the little babies on with the handles of their whips.

Shaggy, cloud-white masses of sheep kept trying to run off on to the side of the road and nibble on the grass. Wise-bearded, disdainful billy-goats transfixed the pitiful bustle of flight with an ice-cold stare, their horizontal silver irises frozen motionless, like the eyes of an owl in daylight: they were from the former Giant Commune, now the Ear of Wheat Collective Farm.

And the rams with the dejected-looking faces between the spiral ringlets of their coiling horns, who wanted to sleep — they were probably from Red May as well.

A battered zinc milking-pail clattered and clanked as it tumbled over and over beneath their hooves, still with a thin trickle of milk dribbling from it. The milk didn't soak into the trampled clay, it lay there in round, flat blobs, blue at the edges like spilled whitewash.

The refugees hobbled along on foot and jolted along on carts. From Demyansk town. From the distant villages of the Valdai Territory.

The dry, rasping lowing of cows that hadn't been watered. The faces of people who didn't speak, entirely immersed in the agitated river current of the walking, the road, the dust. The wailing whinny of a frightened stallion. The occasional sharp crack of a whip – there were too few drovers, not nearly enough.

Herd upon herd upon herd.

They were driving them into the rear, to the east. Along the Novgorod highroad.

And the wild, dirty sunsets reached right up to the Great Bear, heaving and seething fitfully in the sky until the dawn, with flurries of summer lightning.

The land cowered back and huddled down. The west was driven on to the east, covering the Valdai Hills with the lifeless blue-grey haze of immense conflagrations, driving the cattle from the pastures, trampling village life into the ground. War was covering the land with the threadbare, unwashed tablecloth of its fatty, festive picnic. Making up the bed for its dead bride ...

In the spring of forty-one Midge's doctors diagnosed anaemia and avitaminosis and also – tentatively – tuberculosis. After consulting with her teachers, her parents sent the pale little eighth-class pupil to her granny's place in the Valdai region, to the village of Kondriushino – to drink the fresh milk there. The village had a good ten-year school. Her daddy came to see her in his MK once a month, wearing his civilian suit, bringing her sweets and cakes, and for Granny Alexandra the halva she was so fond of.

On the twenty-third of June Uncle Vlas the postman brought a telegram: 'Don't worry stop coming soon stop expect letter.'

The letter arrived three weeks later. Not from her parents, but from Aunty Klava, who worked in the same military factory as her mother and father. She wrote that it would be best for Midge to stay in the countryside, because as skilled specialists her parents had been sent to a different city by the management, on an assignment, probably for a long time. She said they would write from there themselves, but in the meantime they told Midge to do as her granny said and not to be afraid: they would drive the Germans out in a couple of weeks or so.

And then the herds started pouring through the village ...

Midge ran out on to the porch at first light. A boar as crimson as a red banner was dragging itself along over the debris of the smashed and broken ruts with a purple patch of dried mud across its huge underbelly. The elite breeding sows Ulya and Gulya, known to the whole of mankind from the Moscow Agricultural Exhibition, couldn't keep up with the boar and an elderly drover who was short of sleep urged them along with the butt of a rifle. Weak-sighted, with cold, fishy foreheads, churning their mature lard as they waddled along, the sows kept thrusting their snouts into the rubbish on the road and so, unable to glance around, they had gradually lost their suckling piglets – which had probably been baked on the bayonets of the herd's military escort by now.

Past the teacher's tall wooden house, past the school and the village soviet with the flag faded almost to white fluttering over the roof, with the bravura tempo of an approaching thunderstorm, the purple pedigree bulls of the United State Political Administration Collective Farm bore their certified carcasses along with pomp and dignity, the rings in their nostrils glinting with military steel. The curved daggers of their polished horns glittering. The bloody eyeballs, each the size of a blacksmith's fist, glowing a fiery crimson.

Stepping out after these celebrated sires came the three livestock specialists assigned to them in perpetuity, each of them with a Medal of Glory gleaming on his dusty jacket. The livestock specialists marched in line, like soldiers. They were securely armoured against being drafted. They swung their arms and sang: 'Little blood spilled but a mighty blow struck'. Just behind them a little light-chestnut filly in a well-maintained harness with swanky city-style leather blinkers was dejectedly dragging along an ancient light britzka. Its black lacquered doors bore some count's polished operetta-style crests in gleaming gold with two lions rampant and an inscription in Latin: *Deus conservat omnia* – *God preserves all things*. So he must be canning and bottling everything. Mounted on the britzka, glancing back all the time and shouting something incomprehensible, as though she was upbraiding the horses or goats in their own language, sat a drunk, middle-aged, bareheaded gypsy woman in a blue silk dress. Thrown across her plump shoulders she had a small black shawl of stamped velvet with silver tassels. With one bracelet-and-ring-laden hand the gypsy woman tugged occasionally at the slack reins like a man, at the same time giving suck to a sturdy curly-headed girl of about six who was sitting on her knees. The girl was toying with the nipple with her tongue as she studied her mother's golden necklace, pouring it from one swarthy little hand to another like a long, scaly snake.

Immediately behind the britzka the young pioneers from the city were striding out in regular formation. It was them the gypsy woman was shouting at. One pioneer a little shorter than the others occasionally beat on a little red drum with a single drumstick – a rattling roll. When he struck the drum, he laughed. And he ran his hand over the narrow, hungry back of his little head, cropped close to the skin only the day before.

'Now the end of the world is nigh, Russia is on the move!'

Granny Alexandra was crossing herself behind Midge's back.

'Noah's ark, forgive me, Lord! Michael, Commander of the angels, protect me from the Evil One, for the sake of my old years!' She turned Midge round to face her and made the sign of the cross over her forcibly, sticking her bunched thumb and fingers painfully into Midge's eye.

Midge broke free and ran down off the porch. She made her way across the flow of the herd to the village soviet hut with the faded flag fluttering over its roof. To where the army trucks were already waiting for the village lads. A driver in a military tunic and tall boots was sluicing water out of a bucket on to a black commanding officer's MK that looked exactly like her daddy's.

Midge felt shivers run up and down her spine when she stopped to let the billowing swell of cattle past. The dust in her mouth tasted bitter and made her throat itch. Midge sneezed and wiped away her tears with the palm of her hand. She sneezed again and again, lost now in a haze of tears, despairing of ever finding her way out of the maelstrom of animal flesh that snorted, chomped and stamped like an insatiable bog greedy for victims. The herds bellowed. The whip cracked. The dark terror of the cattle twisted and coiled like a whirlwind – terror at being torn away from the earth by the swirling eddies of the universal river of the approaching end.

Mincing along nervously like eligible young girls on high heels came a small herd of two-year-old heifers, swaying and lowing impassively. Under its thin nap the skin on their jaws and bony, innocent hips was a tender pink. Midge recognised the Smirnovs' docile heifer Zorka from the dark patch on her withers. She reached out her hand to stroke her, but the heifer shied away violently, jarring Midge's thumb painfully with her hoof.

Caught up by the tumultuous, almost mindless torrent of the commingled herd, despite herself Midge absorbed into her body the piercing currents of terror, the innocent animals' dumb grief. Knowing no God over them except man, delivered into his power by the land though once they were free, they had long ago lost their wild animal wisdom. Now two or three days of hungry flight was enough for them to forget the mammalian order maintained by man. The phantom of reason that had preserved their thoughtless, brutish calm was scattering like the dust of the road above the surging waves of starving flesh.

As she forced her way through the currents and eddies of the horned heads with their dull, dust-veiled eyes, past the cows' long tails and along beside their sharp, pimply spines,

Midge could sense the growing wildness in the domesticated cattle, like a disaster, like her own illness. In her months in the country Midge had grown used to respecting the working animals almost as much as people.

'Trouble, terrible trouble and woe!' Granny Alexandra said to God from the porch. 'They know not what they do, Thine archangels, O Lord! The bloodsuckers could at least have thought of turning the cattle towards the watering-place ...'

An immature Oryol colt as youthful as a cloud after rain suddenly reared up, thrusting his birch-tree legs with the golden, unworn shoes against an old cow's rump and whinnying at his own mischief. Summoning his light-chestnut brothers bunched together by the force of movement and an old, doomed, dapple-grey gelding to exult, attempting to rouse an unfamiliar pair of Kabardian amblers in white circus bridles with their bits smashed by a hasty drover, and with them, perhaps at the bidding of the rancorous and resentful god of cattle Veles, drowned in the Dniepr almost a thousand years before, all of the bellowing and wildly galloping herds and swirling flocks that war had scattered from horizon to horizon.

Across the plain with its fields of grain tinted by the dawn light and the blue hill with the bell tower that you could see straight through.

Through the little village of Veltso and the village of Kondriushino, woken early – four lines of houses with wide-open doors and shutters, with new fences and aimlessly bustling chickens, black old men and white young children.

Through the final entreaties, crosses and sobs of mothers.

Through the breath and the tears of the little girl Masha Mukhina. On the porch of the village soviet she sneezes time and again, clutching at the shoulder of the world-class lad Alexei Zvonarev. And she suddenly feels with her cheek that Alyoshka, who shares a desk with her in school, has shaved off the silky white hairs on his chin today – Midge loved to catch them in her teeth as Alexei kissed her cheeks when he saw her home after dances at the club. Midge sneezes, and the blue clay dust flies like the final dust of a sunset that has burnt out during the night. And the hard straps of his father's army haversack already hold Alexei's shoulders in their tight grip.

'Don't wait for me,' said Alyoshka. 'I won't come back.'

Midge stopped sneezing. Her nose, lips and breath have understood what Alyoshka said, but she still hasn't taken it in. And she asked him: 'Ah?'

He kissed her wet nose and walked towards the trucks.

With no talking or larking about the lads climbed into the back of a grey, rattling one-and-a-half-tonner. The little truck set off against the flow of the cattle tramping down the slope of the low hill. The cows scattered at a gallop and stumbled in the gutters at the edge of the road, staring and exposing the wide, hungry whites of their weeping eyes. They raised their snouts in a low, booming appeal for man's protection and justice. They quaked, scarcely able to straighten up their legs, their spines bent and sagging from the weight of their unmilked, inflamed udders.

The trucks moved ahead at low speed, honking almost without a break in abject and angry voices. Ahead of the wheels of the leading one-and-a-half-tonner the river of horned heads parted into two streams. The trucks and the commanding officer's MK were like three islands standing motionless midstream in a powerful river. As if she was looking out of the window of a train, Midge saw the earth itself moving together with the herd that was rooted into it, while the trucks rattled and swayed on the spot. They rattled and shuddered, sharp and angular, with their eyes flashing, and the earth beneath them, with the road, the ditches and the fields all round, with the bulls like boulders surrounded by the foaming waves of flocks of sheep, by the crimson, chestnut, milky-black, broadsided Simental and Kostroma breakers – the very earth was rolling on, sliding past under the wheels, rushing ever onwards like a flying carpet. Midge felt as though she herself was tied to the trucks that were leaving the earth and the road was slipping past, swaying and trembling, under her feet.

The islands of war swam upstream against the river of salvation, carving through it with the lifeless voices of automobile horns. Alyoshka and the other lads stood in the back of a truck, waving to their mothers and girls, swallowing the dust thrown up by the wheels. The commanding officer, with a sword-belt across his shoulder, was perched on the running-board of a truck, yelling at the boys who kept dashing in front of the one-and-a half-tonner.

Midge had known for a long time that people didn't come back from the war. Her neighbours and friends Senya Glazman and Vanya Enakiev hadn't come back from the Finnish war. And from what Alyoshka told her she knew about boys from the village who hadn't come back either – Goshka Veprev, the herdsman Vitya Somov, the Selivanov brothers Frol and Gordei. And many others, very many. The only one from Kondriushino to come back was Seryoga Evgrafov, the blacksmith, and he came back missing an arm. He sat in the club at the dances every Saturday, hiding away in the corner, nibbling sunflower seeds and dropping the husks into a jacket pocket with an empty sleeve dangling over it.

Midge's legs bore her along the road by themselves and she quickly caught up with the truck. She grabbed hold of the back panel and hung there with her feet trailing along the road, biting her lips, her chest slamming against the rattling, nail-studded board.

Alyoshka squeezed his way through to the back. He grabbed her by the left wrist and pulled her up.

Midge pushed off from the road with her right foot and she went flying along above the ground.

The truck jolted over the potholes. The planks smashed against Midge's ribs. Alyoshka was shouting something into her face. But Midge kept flying on and on.

Her body became weightless, spread out above the earth. She closed her eyes. She was soaring up close to the clouds.

Midge had dreamed about it a week earlier: she was holding Alyoshka by the hand and flying along. And she would never let him go. And nothing bad could ever happen to them as they flew on and on. Because Midge and Alyoshka were flying together, holding each other by the hand and a rainbow of joy filled all the sky above them.

The truck stopped. The commanding officer with the sword-belt ran up and grabbed Midge's right hand.

Alyoshka pulled her up. The sword-belted commander pulled her down. There was a nail from a plank sticking into Midge's side, and her throat felt hoarse. She couldn't see anything and she couldn't catch her breath. The rainbow collapsed and shattered into orange stars and blue shards.

The commanding officer was shouting and swearing. Midge's winged body was torn between the earth and the sky.

'*Mein Gott*! You ought to be ashamed of yourself! You're a Red Army officer! Leave the girl alone, she has a right to see them off! You have no right! Donnerwetter! Zuruch! Zuruch!'

She didn't recognise her teacher's voice. But she knew that Walter Ivanovich was the only one who could shout in German when he got carried away. He often used German words to scold the boys – when he was joking and when he was serious.

Alyoshka's fingers parted and Midge fell to the ground.

And when she opened her eyes she saw another dream.

The quiet teacher of German threw himself at the commanding officer and grabbed hold of his sword belt. The commanding officer pushed his weak arm away, completely ripping off the collar of the teacher's white jacket, the one that was always so neatly ironed and clean, and shouting: 'German spy!' Soldiers with rifles came running up. They twisted the teacher's arms behind his back. They dragged him to the commanding officer's MK and pushed him inside the black automobile. The first truck set off, followed by the second, with Alyoshka in the back. The trucks climbed the little hill above Lake Velets. Then they followed the car that was carrying away her teacher as it turned off the highway on to a forest track and disappeared behind a long alder thicket, gathering speed in sudden bursts as they went, as though they were alive.

Midge lay there in the rye along the edge of the road for a long time. None of the girls had stayed with her: they were frightened. The stupid fool had got their favourite teacher arrested – and for what? You have to use your head, even if you are a city-girl.

She realised it herself when her tears dried: she was to blame. For ever ... No! He was a spy! A traitor! He got what he deserved!

A month earlier Walter Ivanovich had kept Midge behind after school to resit a test. In Leningrad she always used to get 'exc.' for German, or at the very least 'v.gd.' In the village school she had slipped down to 'sat.', and sometimes even 'unsat.' Walter Ivanovich forced them to learn Goethe and Heine off by heart – kilometres at a time. And translate – in both directions. He composed the texts for dictation himself or made them up as he went along. His mother was German, everyone knew him and respected him for his politeness and the neat parting in his white Ostsee hair.

'Richard Wagner is a great German composer,' Midge translated to herself, glancing sideways at her teacher as she tried to correct her mistakes. It was a good thing she'd made the sign of the cross over her fifth rib when she was sitting down at the desk, the way Alyoshka had taught her. 'His cycle of operas *The Ring of the Niebelungen* is known and loved by all musical lovers ...' music-lovers, you fool! 'Music-lovers not only in Germany, but in all the countries of the world. Especially famous is the great ... no, magnificent ... Flight of the Valentines ...' Oh no! 'Flight of the Valkyries ...' Vampires? Valekiras? Valekira – was there really such a name, she wondered. She'd written it down – so that meant there was. 'The flying Valekiras' from the opera *Tannhäuser* ... Valekiras, Tannhäuser – they were just trying to be clever and make people look stupid, why couldn't they just say it in simple Russian – Valya, Gesha ...

After he'd read Midge's translation, Walter Ivanovich went over to the corner behind the stove, where the phonograph stood. He wound up the rasping spring and put a record on. Midge felt the music seize her and she stopped breathing.

'I remember!' she said, slapping herself on the forehead. 'That's a great world-class record! It's "The Flight of the Valkyries"! You played it twice for us before, Walter Ivanovich!'

He pressed a finger to his lips: let's keep quiet. Crossed his arms and looked out of the window, not at Midge. He was standing, but Midge could see him flying through the sky. With his white parting. In a white cape. With a blazing torch in his hand – for justice, for our victory, for the worldwide conflagration! Against all these Finns, Japanese and Yakuts – only the Germans were on our side, a real friendly nation, class-conscious ...

When the music finished Midge went up and stood beside him. He drew the white curtain across the window. The curtains in the classroom had been put up by Valeria Isidorovna, the maths teacher, as black and vicious as an autumn jackdaw. Childless.

Looking at the floor, Midge said: 'Walter Ivanovich! Please kiss me. Just once!'

Instantly she was drowning in shame and confusion. Everything went dark.

'I can't, Mukhina,' he said calmly. 'You'll get pregnant straight away. And just think what kind of child you'll have! It will be German! Girls like you can do that, from just one kiss. And then you'll have a German, but you know, there'll be war soon ... And the war will be with the Germans, you know. Yes it will.'

'Why war with the Germans?' Midge asked, forgetting her rejection. 'Why would I have a German?'

'Because!' he turned to face her and pressed his forefinger against the tip of her nose.

Midge closed her eyes and kissed his soft fingers. How long they were. Petite little nails, so clean – so lovely!

He pulled his hand away. Turned pale. Like a sheet of paper, literally.

And suddenly with that same hand he slapped her across the cheek.

Walter Ivanovich hung his head. He blushed so powerfully that Midge could see the pink skin through his sparse, smoothly combed hair, and his parting turned crimson, like the scar from a blow with a cane.

'Why do that?' Midge asked quietly.

'So you won't watch from the bushes when I go swimming in the river at night with Valeria Isidorovna. So you won't put drawing-pins on my chair. Or knock on my window in the middle of the night, wrapped up in a sheet: poor Valeria Isidorovna drank all the valerian drops, it took me all night to revive her. But most important of all – so you won't run off to the war when they take me away in a black car, but wait calmly for your Alexei, he's a fine young man. You've too much energy, Mukhina. You're a skinny thing, but you're full of energy. You go dashing ahead when you don't even know the way. You fly ... But you have to walk on the ground, on the ground! Tame your conceit ... But I don't dare detain you any longer, *Fräulein*!' He inclined his silver parting towards her, gave a dull click of the heels of his white canvas shoes cleaned with tooth powder, took a step back and bowed, his long arms dangling formally in front of him. '*Auf Wiedersehen!*'

Midge took hold of his hand and lifted it to her lips. And with bitter-sweet relish she bit as hard as she could into the soft little pad of flesh beside his thumb. The warm skin yielded softly like rubber and then burst with the sound of a squashed cranberry.

She picked up her briefcase and went out.

In the doorway she turned round.

He was looking at his hand. The blood was dripping on to the floor.

'I forgot to ask, Walter Ivanovich,' she said, embarrassed. 'Who is she really, the Valkyrie?'

'You!' he said, shaking the blood from his hand. 'You are a Valkyrie. Take care of yourself, sweetheart ...'

And now they'd taken him away. Just like he'd said they would. The fool!

Midge turned over on to her back. Looked up at the clouds. They were running along the road of the sky like sheep, bunched together with their heads lowered. They couldn't care any more which way the wind drove them. They were big and they knew nothing would happen to them – they would just keep floating on and on until they dissolved painlessly in the sun and the wind. Or perhaps they would turn dark and become rain. Float along, scatter in the air, fall to the ground as rain – it was all the same to them. They didn't need anything. Like sheep when they've eaten their full and been gathered into a flock. And there was nothing the sun needed. Shining wasn't hard for him and he wasn't fed up with it yet, although of course, it was a bit boring. He was blind. It only seemed like he was laughing so happily. How could anyone blind be happy?

'*Ich weis nicht was sol es bedeuten*' – she heard Walter Ivanovich's voice say. 'I do not know what has happened to me. Heine, "Lorelei". What do you think, boys and girls, which of our girls is like Lorelei?' – and Walter Ivanovich had looked at her, at Midge.

The traitor!

Midge turned over on to her side. Lay face down. Turned over on to her side again. Started rolling, crushing the ripening rye under her body. As though it wasn't her own will making her roll. As though the wind was rolling her across the field.

She rolled as far as the edge of the road. She stood up, staggering, planting her feet wide. She waited a long time for the fields, the sky and the clouds that had hidden the sun to stop spinning round so shamelessly. She threw her head back and spat up at the sky. At the low clay vault with no lamp in it.

The road lay there empty and open, as though it had been trampled to death. The plump apples of horse dung were still steaming. There was yellow urine lying in the middle of the cowpats, swarms of little orange flies. As though the suffering of the mercilessly driven herds had been left behind in a dream somewhere for ever, and Midge's own fear had only been a dream, and the wound below her rib under her torn dress had already healed over, even though her side still smarted with every breath she took ...

About ten days after the day when Alyoshka was carried off from Kondriushino to the war and they took Walter Ivanovich away, Aunty Klava sent another letter. The military train in which her mother and father were travelling to their assignment had been bombed. Both Mukhins had been killed by the same bomb. 'I can't even come to see you,' her aunt complained. 'I'm crying all alone.'

Her teacher's things were collected by militiamen three days after he was taken away.

Alyoshka's killed-in-action notice arrived a month later, in August.

In the fields and in the woods and by the little river behind the washing line and at home, Midge kept repeating to herself the German word 'Valkyrie'. Waking and sleeping, staring into empty space, until her granny gave her a clip round the back of her head. Walking past his boarded-up house ten times a day, she repeated it over and over, chanted it. And later, after Alexei's killed-in-action notice – in an agony of hope, finding in it the strength to get up in the morning and do her work, to breathe and see the empty sky – VALKYRIE!

And in her semi-delirium, when Master Sergeant Bykovsky lifted her up off the bench at the railway station in Demyansk after he jumped off the military train to get some hot water for tea and she finally took flight in his arms, hearing Wagner's pealing thunder like the fluttering and flapping, trembling and quivering of wings behind her own back: 'What's your name, little girl?' – 'Vaal-kyrie-eee…'

And only after General Zukov's tear-washed gaze on the volleyball court set her truly free for flight did Midge learn that Walter Ivanovich was wrong: Valkyries were actually a bit taller, and wider in the shoulders, not to mention the hips, and they held some kind of long candle or torch in their hands, or maybe they had some special kind of clubs that glowed – anyway, even now it made her shudder just to think of it. Midge had come across them over Berlin: she was carried that far once early on, when she had no experience at all and didn't know how to get her bearings. She wished she'd never seen them at all, never run into their gang – then maybe she'd still think of herself as a Valkyrie.

A beautiful name! Or was it just some kind of job for them – go valkyrying or valkyrie a little bit, and Wagner will make you famous all over the world for no particular reason – that was the way things were with the Hanses, they wouldn't forget anyone if they'd done something heroic, even if they weren't fighting on our side, but for the Fritzes. She would never have believed they really did exist if she hadn't come nose to nose with them like that. And it isn't fair, by the way, that those stud-mares have music written about them, and some of us are fighting alone against Hitler using the same aerial method, and they still haven't printed a single portrait of us in the newspapers, there isn't even a song or a lousy little poem in the divisional newspaper, like they always dash off with ten exclamation marks about even the most useless Hero of the Soviet Union. They launched entire flocks of those Valkyries of theirs into the sky, but most likely in the entire Red Army Midge was the only one who'd mastered those methods of combat, and she was self-taught too, note that. Always all alone up there in the sky. That's of course if you didn't count that huge woman Midge saw floating over Leningrad on one of the white nights. True, she only saw her very vaguely. To this day she couldn't be absolutely sure if it really was a woman and if she was on guard over Leningrad that night. Really massive she was – something terrible! From up there she could probably shelter half the city with just her headscarf if she wanted. She had a sort of violet headscarf, kind of lilacish. Or maybe, of course, it was just the way the clouds came together in a special shape above the city – how could she ever tell now? But it was true that the woman sort of leaned down towards the city like a kind of canopy, trying to protect Leningrad with her huge, wide headscarf, or maybe trying to wrap it up nice and warm – it was hard to say. Or else it could have been those purple and pink clouds, but they lined up exactly like there was a living woman, word of honour, standing in the sky with her head bowed over Leningrad. Who knows! But that night there were no German planes in the sky over the city, that's for sure. Midge had made a point of remembering that. And it was a fact that apart from her Midge had never observed any other dubious-looking individuals – from the point of view of their proletarian origin – in the sky. Only this woman on guard and the Valkyries. But if this business with the strange lilac citizen seemed a bit fishy, with the Valkyries everything was clear straight away: there was a whole squad of them: about eight or ten, maybe, and all of them really hefty heifers, big square faces on every one of them and thighs so massive two men couldn't get their arms round them, it was a mystery how the officer Hanses managed to cope with them down in the dug-outs, on the trestle beds, she couldn't even imagine it, hell's bloody bells! And although Midge could never smell anything up in the sky either before or after that time, she immediately caught some kind of dark wind or maybe even an actual smell from that gang of bandits – a bit like undiluted triple eau de cologne. It was as if needles starting pricking her in the face, and all over her transparent body. But then again, neither before then or afterwards did she ever feel the bullets that simply flew straight through her unhindered, or the fireworks of the anti-aircraft guns or even the aeroplanes, any one of which could have cut her in half with its wing or ground her to powder with its roaring propeller – and she wasn't afraid of their smells either: not TNT or petrol or dynamite. But these creatures really did have a smell about them that wasn't Russian! When those invisible needles started flying – hell's bloody bells, watch out! That soon made it clear what that black city was down below: it was Berlin, sure as hell! They probably had it real cushy here – these fat-arsed broodmares with the big truncheons. And then it was as if the same will that lifted Midge up into the sky every time and guided her – with no voice or words, but very clearly all the same – explained it all to the crazy-girl in an instant: Seagull, get away from here. It was stupid for her to be flying towards them. She wanted to look into their shameless eyes, just to get a little feel of them, as they say. But it was as if a brake somewhere inside her squealed: leave it, don't be in such a hurry, you'll get your chance to teach them a thumping good lesson, but it's too soon, you can't handle the whole squad of them, they'll crush you. In reality, to tell the truth, Seagull didn't even have time to think about it and realise that consideration of the matter in question had been postponed, before someone or something turned her over on her back, looking up at the moon, and carried her off back eastwards, and that was that.

But even so, after that night, after the command's promises that an important, responsible mission with genuine risk and total glorious victory was still to come, for the first time Midge sensed at a level deeper than her mind that her dreams were not accidental, that they had been prepared by someone a long time in advance and the precise time and territorial location of her heroic feat would be explained to her by people wiser than she was. Otherwise, by the way, why would the goddess of war have preserved her to this day and hour? She could have abandoned her for ever on the forest track beside the river Mga or sent her to Germany as a prisoner. And why – let's just try to get to the bottom of it – was Midge not standing last in line on the volleyball court, as usual? Or had she figured it out in advance, so that the revolver doling out its strict justice would be thrust into the belly of the world-class lad Sevka Goryaev instead of hers? It was enough to make you laugh, for real. Although, by rights, it was his present – Sevka's, that is – that had got the battalion's last soldiers out of encirclement, otherwise they'd have been cut down by the machine guns of German patrols on the forest track as well.

No, carrying on this way will just set our heads spinning, comrades, trying to untangle where it all began and where it's all got to now.

For instance, take that time on the forest track. If not for Sanka Goryaev and Sevka and Commissar Chaban, who was due to die a terrible, shameful death, like Sevka, only two days later, if not for her senior comrades who had faced fire and were thoroughly battle-hardened, everything could have ended very badly or even worse. It was remarkable how the collective gave you confidence at the most difficult moment – it was like a law. Who are you on your own? Nobody! A zero without a digit, Stalin got that right. But in the collective you're strong, because your comrades won't let you down. That was what it said in the regulations, and it was funny but that was the way it always had been ever since the world began.

But by the way, the Hanses out on patrol were no cowards either. When Midge heard the words '*Hände hoch*!' loud and close up – from the front and the back and from the left, straight out of the forest – as if a noose had closed on the five surrounded soldiers – her hands went up on their own, and she got a cramp in her shoulder blades, as if an economical burst of German fire was just about to shatter her spine from a distance of two paces.

She was walking last in line. Ahead of her, without looking round, but with the back of his neck and bald patch showing crimson through his silvery mane, Commissar Chaban put his hands up. Cut off on three sides, the five soldiers left from the infantry detachment froze in the middle of the track with their hands in the air. Chaban swore long and slow, spat in front of his feet and hissed: 'I said we should go through the bog! But no, we had to take the track … Now we're fucked!'

That last word warmed Midge's ear as though she'd heard it for the first time – her ear began burning, and her right cheek too. Not because it was a swear word. The word had a meaning of its own, after all. And in that moment of burning shame she recalled how last night round the campfire, only two steps away from Midge where she was lying still awake on a pile of branches, as he moved his soaked foot-wrapping around over the flames Commissar Chaban had said: 'It wouldn't be too bad, but we've got a bint with us … She's only a little chit yet of course, but she's still a bint, no way around that. And a bint on board ship means trouble, it's a fact …'

Midge stopped breathing. She squeezed her eyes tight shut and held her body still, not moving a muscle so as not to let them know she was awake and could hear them …

The worst thing was, if that fool Sanka had blurted it out without thinking, or even Sevka – she wouldn't have minded, they were the biggest loudmouths around. But she absolutely idolized Chaban.

Chaban!

Chaban was Chaban.˙Her colonel.

Chaban had opened her eyes to life in the army. Supported her at a difficult time, prevented her from stumbling. And if not for him she would have done something bad to herself, it was a fact. Midge would have given her life for Chaban, easily. And he could say that …

The soldiers believed Commissar Chaban was the conscience of the battalion.

He was already grey-haired, but still strong, as solid as a block of oak. His belly, strapped in strict and tight with two shoulder belts and the fancy lacquered strap of a pair of captured Zeiss binoculars, and his red face, with the broad tubular veins pulsing on the forehead and his colourless eyelids without any lashes or eyebrows that seemed filled with the leaden suffering of a strategist biding his time, dispirited by their enforced retreat, even though it was wisely timed and well calculated, and the proud baritone voice with the trembling note of reproach, pleasantly poised, like an honoured vocalist's voice, and the triple pink chin above the casually unbuttoned collar of the army tunic, with the grey patriarchal fur growing in a clump – it all inspired a faith that was as necessary as breathing, faith in the imminent sudden arrival of the radiant goal of these temporary and therefore tolerable hardships, losses and shame. And even though as yet only he could clearly see the total, shattering victory over the enemy who was being lured deep into our territory, and the soldiers couldn't, weary as they were with longing for hand-to-hand death to glorify his strategic genius, everyone who met the direct gaze from below those eyelids weighted down by other people's alarmist disbelief, felt their heart tremble and they drove their weakness down into their heels, into their calluses, into the soaking tangle of their loose foot-wrapping, into the hole worn through the side of their boot, into the crack above the sole of their heavy, rough, half-rotten soldier's shoe that had been shattered in the retreat.

'My dearrr frrriends! My Rrred Arrrmy brrrothers,' Chaban's voice rumbled out above the ranks of the young boys, instantly quiet – even the toes on their sweaty feet were still. 'I believe you are tired! I know!' He walked along the line, pulling down the chin of his heavy grey-haired head with the swollen veins on the forehead and temples. He stopped. Gazed over their heads into the bright, tragically beautiful distance that shone into only his eyes. Ran his broad white hand over his cast-silver mane. 'Dearrr frrriends! This is a people's war! A holy war!'

With a feeling of personal involvement, Midge gazed into the commissar's mouth as she calmly and happily rummaged in her nose with her finger. Beside her the intellectual student Sanka Goryaev was trembling and clapping. A tear as long and fat as a saveloy sausage slithered down on to his lip.

'You must know the phrase –"duty first"'! Chaban dropped his head again and said nothing for a long time.

'He knows how to talk, the son of a bitch, you've got to give him that,' Sanka wiped away a tear and grunted as though Midge was scratching his back in exactly the right place. 'They say he studied at the academy. Hard as flint!'

Midge rolled her snots into little balls, but she stuck them back in her nose because she felt embarrassed: the assembled ranks were a sacred place.

'Victory is near!' Chaban took hold of his belt with both hands – firmly, confidently, commandingly. 'Soon we'll drive the vicious enemy from our sacred land! For the grief of our motherrrs! For the wounds of ourr comrrrades! For the tears of our childrrren and widows!'

And once again his head fell back on to his chest, as if all the hardships of every soldier's life and death lay on those broad shoulders of old oak that had matured and hardened under all the lightning strikes of the century, its heart burnt away to a black, hollow bitterness, but still the miraculously powerful and righteous force of mother earth forced its way up through it, just like in a fairy-tale.

'They say he drinks at least two litres a day, the poor guy's suffered so much,' Sanka sighed. 'But just look how he carries himself, Midge, even if he has been drinking. The old guard.

Not like you, little snot-nose, a hundred grams and you're as tight as a newt, it's a disgrace!'

She said nothing, just nudged him with her elbow. And she rolled the snot out of her nose after all and dropped it by her feet as if by accident.

'We have a phrase: duty first!' Chaban repeated. 'Are your boots worn out? I can see that! Did the sergeant not issue you any nice warm underclothes? Are you feeling homesick? I can believe it. My own hearrt's burnt to a cinderrr! Nothing left but a will of steel and pain for the Motherrrland! And invincible Stalinist faith in victory! Not boots!' He sliced the air with his broad white palm. 'Not weakness! Not alarmism! If anyone's tired, if your nerves have given out – then say so! I'll finish you off! Right here and now, myself! With this very own father's hand of mine!' He slapped his holster. 'Are your boots worn out? Take some boots from the enemy! Strangle him with your bare hands! Take his boots! Take his machine gun! With this very same hand!' He raised a massive fist above his bristling mane. 'The way we did in the year nineteen! Starving! Barefoot! Covered in lice! Where's your conscience, Soviet soldier? They give you vodka every day! Where's your honour, soldier? Drunk it away? Swapped it for an extra mouthful? Given it to the filthy Hanses?'

'No one here has!' The squeaky, breaking tenor of a platoon lieutenant.

'Then don't whinge!' Chaban was growling out the words hoarsely now, as if he was forcing them through a barrier of inhuman pain and drunken exhaustion. 'Then don't brrring shame on the rrranks! Forrwarrd, my brave boys! We won't dishonour our standard! We won't drop it! We won't give it up!'

He was shaking so badly now that his white mane split into two waves, revealing a red bald patch as they slid down like undercooked pancakes on to his small ears and temples. His crimson forehead was covered in sweat and his entire face glistened like fresh beef.

'Strong words!' whispered Goryaev, pale-faced. 'As solid as a strong stone wall, a colonel like that to look up to ... Doesn't spare himself, he's hot-headed! They say his heart's already damaged. The man's burning up, of course ... They say the doctors have already told him he can't go into the attack. And vodka's out too. Not a gram! Nothing but Armenian cognac, the quartermaster gets it in specially, two crates a month just does it, God grant him health ...'

Midge felt exhausted and stupid, she couldn't follow what Chaban was saying any longer. The massive block of dark, interminable necessity weighing down on her liberated her, assuaging the vague, semi-conscious pangs of her helpless anguish, which Midge defined to herself as a lack of class-consciousness and alarmism. Every time after Chaban addressed the assembled ranks she fell into a state of warm, thick quiescence that lasted for a long time. For an indefinite but vital period this calm drained her being clean once again of the alien time that was not burnt away in her unrelenting hour-by-hour perseverance, that she could not overcome – the time that smelled of vodka, gunfire and gaping entrails. It was as if it built up inside her day after day, month after month, constantly enlarging the oppressive lump in the pit of her stomach, so that it cost Midge a greater and greater effort to suppress her almost constant nausea.

The feeling of nausea didn't come from her throat or her belly, as it did every month during the woman's days of her mute body, as neglected now as it had been in early childhood. What made Midge feel sick was the senseless calm of evening, when Sanka and Sevka smoked because they had nothing else to do, or they caught up on their sleep, or it was the white face of the full moon, spreading its inaudible waves of piercing ringing across the sky, setting her temples hammering and bringing stinging perspiration to her eyelids. Often the hollow itching in the pit of her stomach and the sore feeling in her mouth would throw her into a cold chill when she caught the scent of forest moss or the smell of foot-wrappings, or just on their own. Perhaps the girl couldn't spot the reason, because she was too used to it. She first suddenly noticed this distressing illness or her body's habit of disobeying her, tormenting her and inciting her soul to mutiny early on that rainy morning when she woke up tipsy and battered with her guts tangled up in her belly and her nipples bitten and bleeding beside the snoring dark-faced company commander, who the evening before, after they buried her first loving 'husband', had brought her to his tent and ordered her to drink to the memory of Sergeant Bykovsky with him, just the two of them. Midge had felt afraid that she was being stalked, through the pain in her belly and breasts, by a death as dirty as she was and as pointless as the master sergeant's inglorious death away from the front line. And suddenly she realised death was what she'd come to the war for. But not that kind, hell's bloody bells! To fall in an attack, in a hail of gunfire, together with the Red Army, facing the enemy – but not to die from a dull, alien pain that wasn't even part of her, that had absolutely no legitimate right to her body, which meant it would do no good for anyone, bring no credit to anyone.

Leaving the company commander sleeping she quietly got dressed, slipped out of the tent and ran to the river. She took a long wash. She gulped down water, scooping it up in handfuls and eating it from her palms. She stuck her finger behind her lip, rubbed her teeth and her gums that were swollen and sore from the vodka. She flinched as she scrubbed her bruise-spotted hips, breasts and shoulders with sand, but not at the cold water, at her memories of the commander's caresses. With scrupulous fastidiousness she inspected her swollen groin, sorted her sparse woman's hairs by the braid and one by one, turning away from herself, but still she thought there was a bitter, corrosive smell that would not wash off, sharper and more acrid than the stench of a cesspool – it seemed to come from the deepest recesses of her body that was trembling, covered in goose pimples, that spread itself froglike to greet the water, hateful now for ever in its pollution, dirty and alien, stolen from her by a deception and now this second, unbearable, deception – and she didn't know what she should do so that all the filth of that terrible night would be carried away by the living stream and be forgotten, no more than a bad dream …

She pulled on her tunic, damp from the rain, and hastily tied together the end of the knicker elastic that the commander had broken – the white trophy knickers were a present from the deceased master sergeant – then tightened the belt of the breeches that hung loose on her hips and swept the water from her hair with her hands, squeezing out the long tails at the back of her head in her fist and fluffing up her wet hair like a boy as she walked along, then ran to the commissar's tent.

Chaban was sitting on a crate bearing the yellow Armenian cognac label under the tarpaulin canopy of his tent, wearing a white undershirt. He had just lathered up both his cheeks with a thick foam as silvery and massive as his damp mane of hair and made one stroke of his 'Solingen' nickel-plated German cut-throat razor from his temple downwards. His orderly, a lieutenant with a black moustache with curled-up ends, was holding up a broad oval mirror in a black lacquer frame in front of the commissar.

Midge ran up to Chaban from behind and beside the red and silver face of the commissar she caught a momentary glimpse of her own blue face on its crooked, greenish neck and the damp braids of hair on her forehead and her black lips and the purple patch on her cheek from when she turned her head away while the company commander was sucking on her skin as he searched for the girl's elusive lips.

She saw all that – and then saluted the battalion commissar. Suddenly remembered and stuck her forage cap on her head. Gasped and crossed herself.

The orderly dropped the mirror.

The glass jangled but didn't break. Now it reflected the grey sky. And the edge of the tarpaulin canopy. The mirror was quickly covered with raindrops.

'I'm sorry! I won't do it again!' said Midge's voice, 'I can't bear it any longer, pioneer's honour! Help me!'

The commissar laughed. Still holding the razor, he scratched his hairy chest and shook his heavy, massive head.

'Get away from here, you woman!' he said to the orderly, who picked up the mirror and wandered off, stumbling along as he wiped the mirror with his sleeve, then breathed on it and wiped it again.

Midge covered her face with her hands. The tears rapidly built up between her clenched fingers.

Chaban began shaving by touch, still shaking his head and chuckling in his throat.

'Want to go home? To mummy?' he asked gently.

'She's dead!' Midge couldn't take her hands away from her face.

'Is your father alive?'

She shook her head without speaking.

'Why did you come to the front? Who forced you to come? Who summoned you?'

His razor rustled and crackled over his neck. The stubble crunched with a quiet, damp, comfortable sound as it was cut. Midge wasn't afraid of the commissar, but her tears kept flowing.

'Eh? What for? What did you think you'd find? Eh?'

'The Motherland ... The Motherland ... To die ... for the Motherland!' She choked for a moment, expecting to hear those triumphantly reproachful words that expanded a man's chest, the ones he usually yelled out to the assembled ranks. Now he would start speaking at the top of his voice and the usual comforting stupor would come over her and she would be able to carry on living from day to day.

'For the Motherland is it? Then why are you blubbing?' He gave a short, dark, after-dinner laugh.

She waited a little longer for those words. But they didn't come – and suddenly she felt furious at the sight of his polished officer's boots.

'Why do they all pester me? What do they think I am? They've no right, they haven't.'

She finally showed him her face. Jabbed with her forefinger at her black lips and the patch on her cheek.

'Then don't let them!' He laughed again. 'If you don't want them touching you – don't let them, full stop! Or is that too hard for you?' The razor glinted even though there was no sunlight and left a broad naked swathe on the red cheek.

'But what if he's the commanding officer? What can I do? He's not going to ask, is he?' She twisted her forage cap in her hands, bold enough at this stage to force herself to smile at Chaban, realising he wouldn't punish her.

The commissar shaved without saying anything.

Midge twisted the cap in her hands, glad to watch out of the corner of her eye as he stretched out the skin of his second chin, catching it between his thumb and forefinger, and supported the cheek from inside with his tongue. And he shaved his neck right down to his chest, to the advance tufts of grey wool that stuck out from under his shirt, making his manly chest look like silvery chain-mail made of thick, powerful springs and covered with white canvas.

He wiped the razor on the towel. Slapped his glowing cheeks. Splashed some eau de cologne into his hand, rubbed it over his face and neck, ran his hand over his white mane.

'Wide and spacious is my native country!' said Chaban, and Midge started in surprise. In surprise and joy! There they were, the words! Such fine words, hell's bloody bells!

And instantly she could hear Lyubov Orlova singing: 'With broad forests, la-la-la, and streams ... Forests, heh-heh and streams ... Forests, heh-heh ...' Ah, now she remembered: fields! 'With broad forests, open fields and streams!' She could hardly hold back her tears of rapture.

'With broad ...' Midge was about to continue, staring Chaban in the mouth: you've got to feel who you're singing a duet with, catch the rhythm, hell's bells! After all, this is the most world-class song in the entire world!

'The Red Army is great!' he continued, gradually expanding his broad chest as he mustered the fiery timbre of exalted vengeance of his commissar's speaking voice. 'And there aren't en-nough women in the army! Not nearly enough women in the army, Comrade Private Soldier Maria Mukhina!'

The commissar's eyebrows were weighted down with

Midge's shallow lack of class-consciousness, her inadequate pride at fighting in the ranks of steel and even taking direct part in combat.

'I know how hard it is for you, daughter. I believe it!'

He dropped his head on to the edge of his silver chain-mail. A cut on his second chin oozed scarlet as it tautened like the master muscle of his indomitable commissar's faith. Tears sprang to Midge's eyes again.

'A com-mis-sar's thanks to you, my girl! I thank you with all my heart!' he threw his head back and looked up at Midge. A narrow drop of red crept over the steep slope of his double chin. 'Thank you, my dear girl, for bringing peace to a soldier's heart. You bring the kind gift of affection, as the people say. You share the warmth of your passionate Komsomol heart with your brother soldiers!'

He propped his hands on his knees and lowered his head again. The drop on his second chin blurred into a patch of red.

'You've got blood on you!' said Midge. 'You've cut yourself ...'

She moved closer to him and wiped his skin with the palm of her hand. Turned round, walked back to the place where she'd been standing and about-turned again, with a click of her heels.

It seemed as though any moment Chaban would sob out, 'My darling girl!', like Lukich on Saturdays, when he got pissed and started up his preaching and reduced himself to tears. 'My own dear heart's blood! It's hard for you, daughter, I know. But what's to be done? What's a soldier to do if he's going into action tomorrow? Eh? And maybe it'll be his last battle? Eh? What's to be done when his heart's on fire, begging for some affection, drowning in its sacred blood – for our land, for the tears of widows and orphans ...'

'I think it's disgusting!' Midge snapped. 'I'm still too young ...'

'Be strong, daughter!' Chaban said, slapping both hands down on his massive thighs. 'Have you never heard the phrase "duty first"? And if the Motherland or-rders it, we'll all rise up, every last one of us, in a mighty, indestructible wall ...'

He wasn't looking at her, but at her breasts, as though he could see the nipples bitten by the commander through the tunic. And she felt ashamed, ashamed of all the blue, red and black bruises ...

'I'm weak,' her lips whispered. 'Living like this makes me feel sick ...'

Chaban heaved a deep, weary sigh. But immediately jerked his head back up: 'Yes! One man on his own is weak! But the col-lec-tive ... The collective is a great force, daughter. Just look at the kind of people you have around you! The pr-r-ride of the army! Mighty heroes! Just think what an honour you've been granted ...'

'I'll kill myself!' she suddenly said firmly, looking the commissar straight in the eye. She could feel a tingling up and down her spine. Like that moment when she asked Walter Ivanovich for just one little kiss. She'd forgotten it, but now she remembered. She forgot it out of shame, so she must have remembered it out of pride. Pride in the disdainful death that would be hers, celebrating the hour of expiation in advance.

Chaban's mouth fell open. But then his eyes immediately narrowed and glittered. Midge couldn't stand up to that and she lowered her head. And everything that had risen up into her heart sank back into its customary oblivion, as if it was sinking down into a bog. She already knew, she could feel that if she couldn't stand up to the commissar's look, then she had no chance against his words ...

'We-e-ell, Mukhina,' he said, sighing loudly. 'I wasn't expecting that from a class-conscious soldier. Was-s-n't ex-pec-ting that ...'

'But I'm always for the collective!' Her voice was breaking. 'I am – pioneer's best word of honour!'

Midge suddenly realised who she was talking to and the way she was talking about things. Complaining. Gossiping. Betraying her army comrades. Like Murka the Cossack ataman's wife in the old folk play: 'You destroyed all our sweet life, so here's a bullet for you as well!' No, dear comrades, killing somebody for that wouldn't be enough, not even hanging would be enough. If anyone talked like that at school or at the pioneer meeting, she'd have been the first to vote for the motion: throw him – or her – out! Fling them out on their backside! Pull the bad grass out of the field! Eliminate it as a class – that's what Stalin wrote, and he was right!

'Feeling offended, are you? Who's offended you? The Red Army's offended you? Come to your senses, Mukhina! What are you raising your hand against? The most sacred holy of holies! And do you know, by the way, what that's called?' The narrowed slits of his eyes glinted again, like his war-trophy razor. 'First – desertion! Second – moral and social degeneration! Is that clear, Comrade Private Soldier? Or I shall I send you where you deserve to go? They'll soon sort you out there, they'll call you to account all right! Is that how you're posing the question, Mukhina? All right then, that's the way we'll decide it. You're forcing my hand. You are, don't forget that. I talk to her like a class-conscious, battle-hardened Red Army soldier, but what I'm really talking to is a shameless young hussy! Is that how it is, Mukhina. Look into my eyes! Look into my eyes!'

Midge lifted her head and immediately turned away: the commissar's gaze scorched her eyes like the flash of a shot at point-blank range.

'How did you come to slip down into this moral pit, daughter?' His voice trembled with warmth of feeling and Midge's tears began to flow. 'Do you want to bring disgrace on our glorious battalion? Endanger the entire division? Underrrrrmine the fighting efficiency of our arrrrmy?' Harder again now, without any trembling. 'Who are you worrrking for, you scum?' The hissed words lashed out from his eyes and scorched Midge's face with a dry, cold flame. 'Want to be court-martialled, do you? You've no one to blame but yourself ...'

He slapped his thighs again.

Midge just stood there, barely half-alive.

Gazing at her together with Chaban was the pioneer leader Volodya. And her dead daddy, who had been awarded an inscribed presentation sabre in the Civil War – he used to shave with a cut throat razor, a German one too, as a matter of fact.

And Stalin was gazing out at her from his portrait, the way he did at the pioneer rally, when they took the solemn oath.

'Perhaps there is something that's still sacred to you, daughter?' Stalin-Chaban's voice once again radiated warmth and affection from his broad, dependable chest. 'Surely your pure soul can't have become totally corrupted! I don't believe it! No, I don't believe it. So don't you go bringing disgrace on my grey hairs, my little girl! I implorrre you from the depths of a soldier's heart: be a man! Don't be a spiteful viper lurking under a log! Don't be a mouldy stain on the pure body of ourrr Holy Arrrmy! Become one with the fighting collective, let your soul take root in it! Hitch your youthful heart to our red banner for ever. Let the truth of our banner – our faith is sacred – be your guiding light for all time! Your light, Mukhina! And not darkness! Our leader and teacher himself sees you from the heights of the Kremlin!' Chaban dropped his head again so mournfully that it seemed he would never be able to raise it again. 'Remember this every moment, daughter' – no, it did rise, thank God. 'Don't be pitiful scum. Be a faithful support to our leader. He believes in you, after all. How will you answer the leader, Maria Mukhina? Now that you've realised the full depth of your baseness – how must you answer? Eh? Well? We-eeeell?'

'Always prepared!' her dry, bitten lips whispered as her legs began to buckle under her.

'Louder, private soldier Mukhina! Louderrrr! Moscow can't hear you!'

'Always prepared!' Midge roared, glaring at Chaban with eyes that saw nothing, and saluting him once again.

'That's my girl, Murka!' he laughed and stood up. 'Only remember: never raise your hand in salute to a bare head. Put your cap on. I know you're one of us, one of our own through and through. I've had my eye on you for a long time, Mukhina ...'

Midge put on her forage cap. Tugged down the front of her tunic. Looked up at the face with the distant odour of cologne. The cut on the commissar's second chin was already covered by a scarlet scab. She no longer remembered that she had just wiped away the blood, touched the skin of her massive master – her kind master. He radiated calm – from his smiling eyes, his regular breathing, the manly smell of his eau de cologne, the noble fumes of cognac on his breath, his weary soldier's body. She wanted to press herself against him, to hide herself under his arm. She would have just fitted perfectly, disappeared head and all. Although, of course, it would be better if he wasn't Commissar Chaban, but simply Walter Ivanovich ...

'I believe in you, daughter. You won't hurt a soldier's feelings. Our soldier is a holy man, remember that. Our people are pure gold. With them beside you there's nothing to be afraid of, they can put up with anything. Go on now, daughter, go on. Keep the sacred faith. And always remember – your commissar is the closest family have. At war he's your father and mother. And his order is the order of the Motherland. The most import-ant thing is to respect your comrades – then your authority will always be high. And if any questions come up along the way, never be afraid to come to me. We'll help, we'll set you straight. Right, run along and fight.' He hugged Midge gently round the shoulders, pushed her away and gave her a fatherly slap on her backside, adding a pinch to keep her mood up.

And off she ran, smiling, cursing herself and shedding sweet tears of repentance. That was always the way it was. You always thought you were a big girl now, all grown-up, but some good, kind person only had to explain things to you properly – and it took away all your resentment just like that and you understood immediately that you didn't understand before what the most important thing in life is. And why did it all happen? Because the most important thing isn't you, but the collective. The girl's senior comrades had been hammering that into her stupid head for fourteen years already, but she was still like a little baby, like some kind of crazy-woman with no class-consciousness at all. Oh no, cross her heart, this was going to be the last time. Disgracing yourself like that, it just wasn't on! – upsetting a world-class commissar like that so much he almost cried, and him with a bad heart too ... And all because of what, hell's bloody bells! Got bitten, did she, got bruises and bites all over her? And what if he was killed tomorrow? Then she'd be ashamed she ever snitched to the commissar about her own senior comrade. And if you couldn't stand army life, then you shouldn't have come to the front line, miss frothy and fancy, you slovenly slut.

That evening the company commander summoned her.

As she entered his tent Midge put her forage cap on her head, saluted and immediately took off her belt.

And while he kneaded her thighs and bit her breasts and stuck his fingers in everywhere, she saw Commissar Chaban's strong, honest face in front of her and she wasn't afraid of anything any more. On the contrary, Midge felt glad she wasn't letting him down with her stupid petty resentment and she never would let him down, he could count on that and pass it on to Comrade Stalin ... Oh, God! Mummy, why does it hurt like that, why, what for? Duty first! That's the phrase – duty first. Duty first! Duty f-f-f-first! And – full stop! Full stop! Fu ... Oh, I just can't, I can't – carry – on – please – Comrade Commander – a bit – gentler – please – plea-ease – don't – don'tdontdontdont – do ... do ... do ... aaabubbbbe-eh-eh – bite my fingers in my mouth – hard – harder – so it hurts more than he hurts me there? Harder – hurt – harder hurt – I'll die – die – dying – dieayeayeaye – I'm sorry – Walter Ivanovich – forgive me, please – I won't do it again – Walter – I won't – shout – I won't – pioneer's – best – word – of – honour – oh God – Mummy – what fo-ooor...

How could she have put up with it if not for Chaban?

...And now he'd put his hands up for the Germans too. Just like Midge, the cowardly little girl. Like all the soldiers who were surrounded.

Or had he thought up some cunning tactical move? She'd have to wait and keep her eyes open, not be caught napping. The Hanses searched their prisoners quickly and dexterously. Threw their rifles and pistols at the foot of an old spreading fir-tree. Midge was the only one they didn't bother to search, the officer flung her out of the line, saying something in German that Walter Ivanovich hadn't taught them, and it made the soldiers in the patrol guffaw like schoolboys laughing at a dirty joke. But Sanka Goryaev just had time to give her a smack on the backside, pressing Sevka's flat present lying in Midge's arse-pocket into her skinny buttock. And he whispered: 'Cigarette-lighter!' – then hurriedly drew himself to attention at the threatening shout of a German who had released the catch on his sub-machine gun.

The enemies were standing with their backs to Midge, their sub-machine guns trained on the other four prisoners. The officer in the smart peaked cap thoughtfully propped his highly polished boot on a wide, low tree-stump, leaned his elbow on his knee and leafed carefully through the documents confiscated from the surrounded men.

'Commissar?' he asked, nodding to Chaban, and without waiting for an answer he carried on leafing through his officer's papers.

The officer gave a short laugh and glanced again at Chaban, who had lowered his chalk-white face on to his chest. Then he stuck the commissar's identity papers into the front pocket of his uniform jacket and took out a pack of cigarettes and a lighter. Without hurrying, still showing no interest in the prisoners facing the sub-machine guns, he took the last cigarette out of the pack and threw the empty box on the ground. He clicked his automatic lighter, lit up and started to cough. Leaned his elbow back on his knee and carried on studying the Red Army soldiers' papers.

Then Midge suddenly realised why Sanka had said that – 'lighter'.

The brothers Goryaev had delighted Midge by presenting her with the toy only two weeks ago. It was a magnificent gift – fit for a general.

At first that was what Sevka Goryaev thought it was, the small, obviously woman's pistol with the rich white gleam of nickel that he'd found in the pocket of a German sergeant-major captured on the road – a cigarette-lighter. He decided to show off and light his roll-up with it – and at point-blank range the little pistol had killed his informer before he could even get him back to base – very annoying!

Along the way the two brothers had played tricks on the entire company with the toy. Of course, they'd taken the bullets out of the little cartridges and stuffed the half-empty cases with grey cotton wadding out of a firm little pillow that Sevka had. When they'd had their fun they presented the lady's Walther to the delighted Midge as she stood there laughing with cotton wadding in her eyes and nostrils.

'Exactly your size, could have been made for you, this little Wally,' said Sanka, nudging Midge in the side with the short, stubby barrel of the little pistol

'Go forth and multiply!' Sevka declared. 'Just make sure you love the little child like a son and take good care of him!'

Midge gave the brothers her secret flask filled with pure spirit – something she had left over from her first 'husband' – and she swaddled the little pistol in a clean handkerchief so that its little muzzle protruded like a tiny face, kissed it on the sight just above its forehead and began cradling it in her arms like a doll.

Since then she had never been parted from her son. And she loved him more and more. Sanka and Sevka quickly taught Midge how to cock the pistol and fire it, how to clean it, load it and empty it if she needed to. And they gave her two clips of cartridges: one with live rounds and the other with blanks containing wadding from the little pillow, for a bit of fun when the right moment came.

But the right moment had never come and for several days now the pistol in Midge's pocket had been loaded with real bullets.

The patrol officer leafed through the soldiers' papers, smoking and coughing.

The sub-machine-gunners stood with their feet planted wide, keeping their guns trained on Commissar Chaban, Sanka, Sevka and the company commander, who had lowered his head on to his chest, like Chaban.

Sanka Goryaev caught Midge's eye and smiled and winked at her. The Hanses guffawed again, as if their officer had told a joke.

Chaban was white. Midge could sense with every nerve in her body the way he was suffocating, the way his bad heart was straining. And she heard his fatal words again somewhere inside herself. And in her right ear Walter Ivanovich commanded her: 'Mukhina – come out to the blackboard!'

Midge slowly walked up to the officer, who didn't even glance at her – he was turning the pages of Sanka's papers, she noticed the photograph – took out her pistol, pulled back the catch and fired three shots, one after another, from below up into the face leaning over the document. As she did it, out of the corner of her eye she saw Sanka and Sevka throw themselves on one German patrolman while the company commander and Chaban knocked the other one off his feet: all he had time for was a short burst with his sub-machine gun up into the low clouds.

With a single long burst of fire Sanka Goryaev finished off both German soldiers right there on the ground. The long retort of the echo popped and crackled along the forest track and was tossed up into the sky.

'Now – quick – run for it!' Sanka commanded, grabbing up their identity papers from the broad tree stump and wiping them with a scrap of green moss as he set off.

They ran for a long time, first along the track, then through the forest, along a path. Chaban just barely kept up, but they didn't have to wait for him. The commissar's face had turned crimson again.

That night by the campfire when they took out the flat nickel-plated flask that Sevka had discovered in a German soldier's pocket and poured the first drink for Chaban, he handed the mug to Midge without speaking.

'Oh no, Comrade Commissar!' She jerked away from him across the ground. 'That's not right!'

'Drink, Midge!' the company commander ordered her. 'Drink for victory soon. For a long, peaceful life for us all ... When happiness will come to all of us ...'

She drank. It didn't make her gasp.

The German vodka smelled of the bog.

Midge thought for a moment and said: 'Water, comrades! Bog water at that.'

Sanka raised the flask to his nose. He swore, swung his arm and tossed it into the bushes.

Midge began to shake.

She saw the German officer's ear again. A big, clean German ear with a petite little brown mole on the soft lobe.

She barely managed to run a few steps away from the fire before she fell on all fours and then she just kept on and on puking up the German water and her own fear. Ears with brown moles flapped in front of her eyes like wings. 'Happiness ... When happiness will come to all of us ...'

The German hadn't even stirred at Midge's first shot. As if he was still reading the Russian Red Army soldier's papers and wasn't interested at all in why his smart new cap with its springy hoop and shiny peak had gone flying up off his head, tousling the sparse grey hair around his bald patch with the bullet hole, and ended up hanging on a branch of the fir tree under which the sub-machine-gunners had dumped the prisoners' weapons at his command. At the second shot he began to slump, although Midge missed and the bullet didn't go into his mouth like the first. But the final blow threw him on to his back, with blood streaming from the black third eye in his forehead.

At that moment Midge couldn't see a thing. The blood was rushing to her face, filling her mouth with a bitter taste, coursing down to her belly and rushing back up to join the crimson haze veiling her eyes. 'Happiness ... Happiness will come to all of us ...' Midge knew it never would. Never while she was alive. Never anything except the bitter, sickeningly sweet swaying of the wave that was buoying up her heavy body, bloated now for ever with someone else's blood, with cold fire and black blinding light – I didn't mean it – I'm sorry – I'm sorry – I'm really sorry – it's the first time – I won't do it again – Uncle German – a mole on the lobe of his ear – on his warm, tender little lobe – sorry, I'm sorry – better kill me instead! – I'm sorry – I'm sorry ...

Sanka Goryaev picked her up in his arms and carried her to a gully with a stream. He washed her face as if she was his little sister.

'I was the same the first time,' he said, running his damp palm over her forehead and cheeks over and over again. 'Probably everybody is, that's the way it's supposed to be. Don't be upset, Midge, there's no need. That's where we'll all end up. If you didn't get him, he'd have got you, you know that. Midge! Don't. Come on, that's enough now ...'

'That's where we'll all end up ...' Where?

Midge suddenly felt calm. Because when she thought for a second about 'where we'll all end up', all of them – that meant together, then, didn't it? – she seemed to catch a sideways glimpse of it out of the very corner of her eye, or perhaps she didn't really have time to see it, but she managed somehow to sense it with her memory or her hope – a kind of bright space without any pain or hostility. Maybe that was the world-class way victory shone from the distance? What other kind of joy could it be? The same for everybody, enough for everybody – that was the most important thing, that was what she mustn't forget. 'When happiness will come to all of us ...'

An hour later she was sleeping soundly on the dry hump under a pine tree, covered with Sanka's padded jacket.

In the morning Midge no longer remembered the third eye in the German's forehead, or the taste of the bog water from the flat nickel-plated flask, which was what had really started the whole silly business.

And when after two days of marching through the forest the five encircled soldiers reached their own side and a smart, erect, genuine military commander embraced commissar Chaban and all five of them and they were immediately given a day's rations and billeted in dry dug-outs for the night, and in the morning taken to the assembly point in the back of a smart one-and-a-half-tonner and led straight into the bathhouse, which turned out to be the village bathhouse built just before the war by a rich local collective farm, spacious and clean, as though the encirclement and the German patrol and the forest track and the war itself had never existed, Midge realised what it was as two hefty waitresses from the officers' mess lashed her with four twig besoms and scolded her for being so skinny and pale – she guessed this was that bright and peaceful, radiant space that Sanka had spoken about down by the stream: 'That's where we'll all end up ...'

That very night the soldiers from the encirclement who had trickled into the village a few at a time out of the forests and bogs, were roused by an alert. They were formed up on the volleyball pitch by the school, which was now something between a barracks and a hospital for dog-tired soldiers exhausted by the retreat. Some of them had been feeding themselves up on state grub and catching up on their sleep for more than a week already and it cost the acting commander a lot of hard work to shake each one of them awake and then reply to his angry swearing: 'General Zukov's arrived. There's going to be an inspection. Get up, General Zukov's arrived ...' The general – that was all they needed right now!

The surrounded soldiers who had just joined the spa resort collective had already heard plenty of insightful opinions about the new commander in chief: 'Zukov will soon straighten things out, don't you worry! Under Zukov we'll move straight into the attack, that's what a colonel was telling me, in just three days' time, the order's already been signed, they've already got the planes in the air, they've even given him special powers ...' There were no planes patrolling over the rest home yet, but the German shells weren't flying that way either and there were no stray bullets whistling through the air above their heads. There were already enough men for two companies gathered in the two-storey schoolhouse and many of them thought they were about to be collected together into a mighty strike formation and that would start the rout of the entrenched enemy at Leningrad, and then victory wouldn't be far away.

But why did it have to be at night? Why couldn't they let people get their sleep? The higher up an officer was, the less patience he had, everything had to be done at the double, at a gallop: just hand it to him on a plate!

When Midge ran out on to the sports ground in front of the school, buttoning her collar as she went, Zukov was already striding along beside the volleyball net in the yellow light of his black MK's headlamps without looking at the ragged, higgledy-piggledy line of soldiers and officers as they shuffled around, sorting themselves out along the yellow sandy border at the edge of the pitch. 'Attention!' the commandant of the assembly point, an elderly man in a cap with a crumpled peak, called in a dull voice that lacked the tone of command. 'I said attention! Who's that coming late?'

Midge installed herself on the left flank, beside a short, stooping squad commander who gave her a cheery wink and nodded at Zukov with a smile as if to say: now we're in for a real treat, eh? Midge shrugged. She only dared to glance at Zukov sideways, as if she was letting him know she was overjoyed to see him, but she knew her place and wouldn't make a song and dance about it, that wasn't allowed, especially in formation. What made the officers happiest of all was when a soldier stood smart and straight and looked straight ahead and didn't grin from ear to ear the way some rickety old clowns did – and he had a grey moustache, getting on a bit, and a front-line shoulder too, that was obvious, seen plenty of action, he might even be a regular officer.

'Have you seen him before, son?' the elderly man asked Midge.

'What's that to you, granddaughter!' said Midge, offended.

Hearing her thin voice the old man looked her over again from head to foot then snorted and shook his head, flapping his lips like a horse.

'How did you end up here?' he asked, still shaking his head and looking at Midge with an odd, childish curiosity and pity, as if he was watching a sick monkey in a zoo.

'How – ask the cow!' Midge retorted. 'If you learn too much, it'll make you old before your time.'

A tall boy with commander's pips on his collar installed

himself on Midge's left. Then Sevka Goryaev came running up.

Commissar Chaban came out on to the porch of the school. He was smoothing down his silver mane after moistening it over the wash-basin and looking around him unhurriedly, screwing up his eyes into a squint of authority as if he couldn't see or understand very clearly what was going on, shielded from the bustle of the petty ranks by the impregnable dignity of a senior regular officer.

Then Midge heard General Zukov's voice for the first time. It sounded like the falsetto tenor of a vicious fish-wife making trouble in the queue for macaroni, as if it was strangled by fury; it didn't suit this paunchy, bandy-legged man with the huge stars on his collar. His head, with its shaggy eyebrows and long, pointed, pink-shaven jaw, was set directly on the broad chest of a ponderous, clumsy circus strong man, as if it was lying on a table – he ought to have growled, not squealed.

'Put your cap on! Get in line – at the double!'

And Midge turned her face away when she saw Commissar Chaban take a few quick steps and start trotting like a new recruit, twisting his heavy shoulders towards Zukov as he ran and raising his broad white hand to the peak of his cap again and again. Zukov was striding along the sagging volleyball net without looking at Chaban, with his hands clasped behind his back.

'Eyes right! Attention!' the commandant shouted quietly. 'Comrade Commander in Chief!'

'Belay that!' Zukov waved his hand in the air and went over to the right flank of the line, jostling the open flaps of his greatcoat with his knees as he walked. The headlamps of his MK were shining along the line, but it had fallen back and no matter how Midge stretched out her neck, she couldn't see the general any more. Not him, not Commissar Chaban, not the company commander, not Sanka Goryaev. She only saw Sevka. He was standing to the left of Midge, he'd squeezed his way into the line from somewhere behind just a moment ago, like a genuine scout. To the left of Midge, with just one man between them. That boy-commander. If only she could move closer to him so at least she could feel the elbow of a tried and trusted fighting friend, but now it was a bit awkward: the general didn't look like he was in a very good mood, judging from the way he'd screeched at Chaban.

But good old Sevka just took a step backwards and then took the place beside Midge, neatly nudging the strange young commander aside. If only he'd known what that move would cost him!

Suddenly she heard swearing from the right flank – in the general's thin squeaky voice. And a quiet shot. A revolver from the sound of it

A silent flutter ran through the line. Midge held her breath along with everyone else.

'Something's not right down there, seems like,' Sevka muttered.

Another shot rang out. It sounded like the same one. The same low, workmanlike sound. There was no swearing. And again that flutter – like a general gasp of amazement. Shivers ran up and down Midge's spine.

Trying not to accept what was already clear to her numb body, Midge gazed fixedly at the MK's blinding headlamps. Perhaps she was trying to go blind. There were yellow rings in front of her eyes. Apart from the piercing glare of those two headlamps, everything blurred and merged into the darkness. Her stomach churned and she felt sick.

After the third shot Midge wanted to piss. The old man on her right had lowered his head and was crossing himself with small, rapid movements. Suddenly he spoke into her ear: 'Pass it along: he's shooting every third man.' She turned her head mechanically and said to Sevka's shoulder: 'Every third man.' He nodded without speaking. His arms hung loose at his sides.

Midge was afraid she'd spill a bucketful into her boots, she felt so afraid. But only a few drops oozed out and ran down her left thigh in a fitful, indecisive dribble. She just thought how strange it was that it flowed all on its own without asking whether it should or it shouldn't, it couldn't give a damn – but what couldn't?

Sevka was shuddering as though he'd been bathing in cold May water, opening the new bathing season, and he still had to stoke up the bathhouse stove.

Shots rang out every thirty or forty seconds, sometimes more often. When the darkness froze in silence for an eternity, Midge realised quite consciously that the general was reloading his revolver. He must be carrying cartridges in his pockets, he knew he'd be needing a lot.

Then another shot. And another. A screech and swearing – then a shot.

'If he kills me,' Sevka began, but he was shaking so hard he couldn't go on. 'If they kill me … If they …'

He grabbed hold of Midge's sleeve near the elbow. The piercing frosty chill from his fingers cut into her arm, ran up to her shoulder and spread across her taut chest in a rash of searing goose-pimples.

'Name!' came a voice from the right.

Midge couldn't turn her head. Another dribble flowed down her left thigh. Hot.

'Where's your company, Savichev?' the general's voice sliced effortlessly through the darkness. 'Where – I can't hear you! Speak louder!'

'My company fell on the Mga, Comrade General …'

'Why are you still alive? Traitor!'

The shot left Midge's ears blocked.

Sevka hiccupped.

The old man on the right sighed and mumbled: 'Receive the soul of Thine innocent servant Savichev, oh Lord!'

'Name!' came the strident voice from the right, closer now. 'How many guns did you leave to the enemy, gunner? Louder. You were happy enough to help the Germans. Now you can answer for it to your Motherland, you coward!'

Silence. A shot.

Midge's legs buckled under her. The old man's hand held her up by the shoulder. Sevka Goryaev suddenly started smelling so bad that Midge had to hold her nose.

General Zukov shot a battalion commander called Strunin.

The commander slumped to the ground right there in the line, without falling forwards or backwards, like the others. The line staggered to the left. Midge took a step too, or rather the old man with the moustache dragged her closer to him.

'Name!'

'Goryaev Vsevolod! I have an old mother, Comrade General!'

Sevka was gasping for breath. Midge held her nose, struggling to prevent herself from being sick.

'You stink-king cow-ward!' the general said disdainfully. He was standing only three steps away from Midge, but he still hadn't seen her. Standing there with his revolver in his hand and swearing. And Sevka was listening to his abuse, looking into the general's eyes, standing strictly to attention.

Midge suddenly realised that now she would kill General Zukov. With her beautiful petite pistol. Shoot him. Through his tautly braced paunch strapped in by the new, pinkish pig-skin belt and the massive sword belt under the imperiously parted flaps of his greatcoat. She was going to put a hole in him, it was a fact. And the blood would spurt out of the hole in general Zukov's carcass just like it did out of the German officer on the forest track by the Mga, hissing and foaming on the sand of the volleyball court. The blood of Commander Savichev and the other executed soldiers from the encirclement, and that portly elderly man whose right leg was pointing at Zukov with the toe of its boot turned towards Midge.

Yes, she had to kill him. He was walking along the line and shooting people. He could go on walking and shooting, shooting until he ran out of cartridges. But then he'd fill up the cylinder of his revolver again. And start walking and shooting again. Until he came to the end of the line. And then he'd form up a new line. And start walking and shooting again. Until the war ended. And when the war ended he'd declare a new war and start walking and shooting again. So that his paunch would always be strapped in tautly by his sword belt. He was sure all the blood he'd drunk would stay inside him for ever and give him a second life. A third life. A tenth life.

How many soldiers did he have to kill – the enemy's and his own – in order to become immortal? He was the only one who knew for certain. And he would become immortal – on granite pedestals, on plaster plinths, on the pages of books and the screens of cinemas – for all time. And the line would never, never end, the war would never end. Unless Midge's hand popped out of her arse-pocket holding the small pistol, still warm from her frozen buttock: she had already moved her forearm behind her back and slapped the pocket to make sure that sleepy dolt Wally was where he should be.

So that her eyes wouldn't give her away to Zukov, Midge lowered her head, and stopped listening to his trilling obscenities. For a second the commander in chief's voice halted – as though a lark had choked on the deep blue yonder. Midge used her finger and thumb to lift the leather loop off the concave man's button of her arse-pocket.

The shot deafened her. Midge pulled her hand away, thinking for a split second that faithful little Wally had got impatient and fired before he was ordered. As if he'd farted without any warning.

Sevka Goryaev belched and swore long and obscenely. His voice slowly sank into a squeaky groan. And Midge stretched her neck out just as slowly, seeing how rapidly his tunic was turning black over his belly, but still not understanding what had happened to him, how the commander in chief had stained Sevka's belly and what with. Spat on him, had he? Like a filthy camel!

Zukov took a step to the right, towards Midge.

Sevka sank heavily to his knees and fell. He twisted his head round and it rammed into the spot where Zukov's boots had been standing a second earlier. His forage cap slid forwards off his head and lay there like a boat on the sand.

The brown hair on the back of Sevka's head began slowly standing erect. He never wanted to get a haircut, kept trying to grow a thick mane 'like Mayakovsky's'. He was always combing his hair and moistening it with water and he swore when he squashed his curls down with his cap … The day he gave

Midge the little pistol his hair was slicked back with captured brilliantine – like some American von-baron in a white dickey from Charlie Chaplin's films. The entire platoon had made fun of him, and Sanka had put his arms round his brother, licked the back of his head and snuffled like a cat.

Sevka's dead hair was alive. It rose up, growing into a coarse brush, which is what it really was, no matter how much he tried to coerce it in the name of fashion. The back of Sevka's tunic was burnt through at the waist by the bullet, just above his belt. There was a brown spot around the hole.

'Forgive me, Sevka!' someone inside said for her. She reached for her little pistol again, calmly trying to recall whether it was enough to release the safety catch or she had to pull back the breech bolt.

All those days in encirclement she'd kept the pistol cocked and ready. Her heart, driven on by her rapid, jerky breathing, had been cocked and ready too. But after a day spent in the forest camp and a night of childish dreams on a bed in the former school the rusty spring inside her had relaxed. Even now, after General Zukov's shot, as she watched Sevka's hair moving, she couldn't clench herself up into a tight ball of fear and fury the way you had to do for combat, in order to repel death and direct it precisely ... Was it cocked or wasn't it?

The commander in chief took another step to the right. Midge looked at his boots, illuminated by the headlamps of the MK. Damp green leaves and blades of grass had stuck to their tall tops. Midge looked at the lowest leaf – a triple leaf of stonecrop. She could feel the velvety softness of its little lobes, the sharp lettuce green, the gentle fresh taste with just a slight sourness, in such complete detail that she suddenly wanted to reach down and take the well-formed leaf off that burnished boot and lift it to her lips. Put it under her tongue and close her eyes.

That made her want to laugh. She got a tight feeling under her belly, the laughter rose up to her throat and Midge gasped out a short hollow growl. She jerked her shoulders. She didn't understand her sudden laugh, but she wasn't afraid of it.

But then she understood everything. Sevka's hair was moving, right? That meant he was alive, just pretending. And Commander in Chief General Zukov was pretending, of course. The cartridges in his revolver were blanks, sure as hell. And Sevka had torn the back of his tunic in the forest, when they bolted from the forest track where the German patrol officer Midge killed had been left to stare up at the sky with his useless third eye, the one with the beautiful innocent ear with the petite little mole on the lobe.

Midge stepped out of the line. Stepped on Sevka's outflung hand with her boot. He didn't budge.

'Arise, arise, ye working folk!' she ordered him. 'All right, that's enough you wanker, get up! You've had your joke, that's enough. It's not funny any longer! Come on now, or Walter Ivanovich will give you a good telling-off. Do you hear? Get up, get up, you shithead! Comrade General, order him, hell's bloody bells!'

She turned towards Zukov, looking up suddenly at the joker with her laughing blue eyes. She curved her neck and back coquettishly, sticking out her skinny backside.

The commander in chief looked at Sevka. His mouth was open. The drooping triangular jaw with the dimple in the middle of the chin was quivering, working itself off its hinges, chewing up the rough, hoarse scraps of obscenities.

'Comrade General!' Midge fixed him with the deadly sideways glance of a hardened three-year-old flirt begging for a sweet from the party table. 'Aw, please, Uncle Zukov!'

His face instantly went white then immediately began turning brown, as if it was secretly gathering an explosive crimson blush under its lilac skin. And then the commander in chief raised his head slowly, as slowly as if he was lifting up an impossible weight on to his shoulders, keeping his eyes fixed on the narrow back of the man he had put a hole right through. And then with the same agonising slowness he started raising his swollen eyelids towards Midge, and his face was deep crimson, like it would be in the bathhouse after a good long steaming.

There were tears like beads of glass in his blue eyes.

'Oh Mummy!' she shouted and clutched at her throat with both hands, scratching her neck as she tore away the invisible noose that had cut off her breath.

She fell face down in the grass and choked on the thick grains of the sand that was damp with Sevka's blood.

When Midge came round General Zukov was gone, together with that severe but just martyr's face weeping tears for everyone that was still burning in her heart and filling her whole body with a pleasant warmth. The black MK was gone, and the dead 'traitors' on the volleyball court. Her tunic was unbuttoned and there was someone's wet, repulsive handkerchief lying on her bare chest.

'How many more rotten vermin did he kill?' Midge asked the old man with the grey moustache who was leaning over her.

'You were the last. When you fell he just spat and got into his car ... He didn't even take down the names of the men he killed.'

'A dog's death for a dog!' Midge yawned and stretched. 'I feel sorry for Sevka, though, he was just in the wrong place at the wrong time. But it's a law, everyone says so: you can't make an omelette without breaking eggs. Even Stalin himself has emphasised that more than once.' She was already buttoning herself up, handing the old man his unnecessary wet handkerchief, 'Thanks, Uncle, I had a good sleep. Only I dreamed the same thing anyway: I was hovering above all of you, above that sports field, and I thought I saw Zukov, the darling man, get into his car, and the dead men being carried away, and you lifting me up ...'

'Don't lie!' the old man cried in surprise. 'Why talk such nonsense? It's a sin!'

'Why is it a sin, if I saw it with my own eyes? I was flying up there above you, and you took this handkerchief out of Sevka's pocket and wet it from a flask and slapped it on my chest! Are you going to tell me I'm lying?' Midge jumped to her feet and put her hands on her hips.

'Saints preserve us, what's happening in God's world!' The old man crossed himself, staring at Midge warily.

'Saints preserve us!' she said, teasing him. 'Of all the lot of you he's the only one who's really saintly, if you'd like to know – General Zukov. When he shoots people he cries – did you see that? That's what you've got to understand, you bumpkin!'

'The Kingdom of Heaven to Thy Martyrs,' said the old man, who was still crossing himself.

'Haven't you realised yet there isn't any god anywhere?' Midge laughed. 'I bet you're a Party member as well!'

'God gave us the Party too!' said Osip Lukich Plotnikov. 'And Lenin's from God too. And Hitler. And Stalin. And your saintly general. And God sent you to me, that's the only reason I'm still alive, because you flopped over and fainted. You stay alive too, daughter. Stay here with me. You'll be safe as houses the whole war.'

And he kissed Midge on the top of her head – just like Granny Alexandra ...

Chapter 6

In which Comrade Stalin wages war without leaving
the Kremlin star, where hot soup is brought
to him regularly in the lift, and Midge battles in the sky
above blockaded Leningrad for the Motherland and for Lusya,
but fails once again to carry out General Zukov's secret order.

That night Seagull's speed was absolutely incredible, special
top emergency speed, literally. Although to be honest, she
wasn't too concerned about her speed or her heading in the sky
– there was no effort, none of the usual impatience, the flying
just happened on its own almost without her. She was even
thinking it was all the same to her where she ended up, any old
dump would do. Hell's bloody bells, she was tired. She couldn't
even care if she found herself over Berlin again and those
vicious grey German women with the big clubs tore the little
bird to pieces – she couldn't give a damn whatever happened.
She felt no fury inside herself, no joy in battle, no passion –
nothing but a bottomless void. The sky just went on and on
rushing through her while occasional lights twinkled down
below on the dark autumnal ground, and then Seagull turned
right over on her back and started contemplating the stars
without trying to remember the names of the constellations or
watching where she was going.

When she heard General Zukov's voice she yawned and
turned over lazily on to her stomach. She forgot to respond
properly, to report in. She suddenly thought: it's only a dream
anyway – so who cares. A dream. It had always been a dream.
And in a dream there was no point in getting hysterical about
anything, everything would sort itself out somehow, it was a
waste of time getting all worked up when there was nothing
you could do about anything anyway. Whichever way you
looked at it, how everything turned out would depend on the

command's orders, not on your own individual will. So just carry on dozing, you slovenly slut, and don't go getting any ideas, don't go taking on any extra responsibilities. Not once in your life has it ever done any good when you got yourself in a lather and started taking undisciplined initiatives.

'Seagull! Seagull, come in!' The general seemed agitated. 'Where are you, Seagull? This is Number One, Number One!'

'Number One, I hear you, Number One, I'm not deaf,' she said, stretching and yawning again.

'Atten-shun!' barked the general. 'Straighten that back! Fuck you up your slippery arse and rip your womb out!' – He'd never been so nasty to her before, he seemed such a cultured man, clean-shaven.

'Yes sir, rip my womb out!' She drew herself up, gathering her misty jellyfish body into the pointed shape of an artillery shell and assuming a bearing towards the voice. Imagining to herself what a whopping slap in the face Walter Ivanovich would have given the general for talking to a girl like that.

The general continued the exchange in a calm voice. He'd obviously realised that he shouldn't push things too far this time.

'Seagull, do you see the objective?'

'I see the objective, sir!' She really could see the light over her native city. And in some miraculous way the restless light that glimmered like the scales of an immense fish or a stream of silvery milk suddenly flooded into her and its straight rays plotted out the shortest route. Filled with this light radiance, she felt like she was inside a glowing sphere gliding towards Leningrad along a highway of light. It felt easier to fly and there was something bubbling up from inside her body, like effervescent gas or the buoyant fury of battle. 'I see it, Comrade Number One! Permission to commence approach?' The columns of the searchlights above the town grew brighter and brighter in the autumn chill, like the trunks of erect young birch trees.

'Steady now, daughter. Careful, I'm engaging the afterburner!'

A whistling in her ears. The expanse of the night is stretched over Seagull like a black stocking. The dome of light over Leningrad is an icy toboggan slope. She mustn't miss that spire again, hell's bloody bells!

'Seagull, Seagull! We are approaching the target! Good luck to you, daughter! Forward!'

Spiralling around the towering rainbow-coloured helmet — faster and faster ... A vertical climb — done it! An intrepid somersault and then, pressing her insubstantial bluish palms together like a diver — only this time not on to the trestle bed again, dear sweet God, not on to the trestle bed! Here it was coming up already ... Hey! Hey-ey, hell's bloody bells! Oi-oo-oo-oo-oi-ee-ee-eekkk!

She was in! She'd pulled it off! Did you see that? She'd broken through this time! They'd been right to trust Seagull and give her the job, eh? If only General Zukov and Stalin were here beside her now — she'd have kissed them both, she was so happy, hell and damnation! Through first time, eh?

Like the bells of the vault of heaven, the rainbow dome hailed Seagull's appearance over Leningrad in a voice of bronze and gold, lighting up triumphantly in her honour in a slow, surging wave of azure-blue sheet lightning. And the flashes that burst out one after the other above Seagull's head drenched her in a warm rain of tender gratitude and selfless maternal happiness.

The weariness, the resentment and the fear are forgotten. There is nothing but joy. Nothing but flight.

Below her the dark expanse of the town spreads wider as it approaches — inspecting Seagull with the huge burning eyes of its searchlights while the ragged wounds of its fires blaze fitfully. Bombs explode with a boom and rancid smoke comes rushing up towards her, driven by the shock wave. Her flight becomes slower and more even. Now she can clearly see that this is the very centre of Leningrad. As black as the sky. The Neva with its bridges and over there the semicircle of Palace Square and the Peter and Paul fortress, masked with camouflage. And the anti-aircraft guns on the embankment: the fire bursts out of the long barrels in flashing dotted lines and a string of shells hurtling by close to Midge drenches her in an icy chill – the future death of some pilot Hanses hurrying on its way. The girl manages to touch the final shell in the burst of fire in flight and when she feels no burn or any damage to her pellucid, permeable body, she can't help laughing with her entire being, scattering the blue sparks of her gentle, inaudible joy into the night.

And as she glides on the slipstream of the shells that have flown past, Seagull suddenly realises that she is grown-up now. Completely and finally grown-up, like she had always dreamed. After all, when you're little everyone dreams of being big, right? But no matter how hard you try to grow up while you're little – you can pull out your milk teeth every single day with a piece of string tied to the door handle and let every kid in the yard take turns to stick a pin in your bare bum – sometimes she couldn't sit down for a week after all those tests of her endurance – it makes no difference, you still can't grow up ahead of time. But now you don't even have to put yourself through any tests: nobody is looking for any proofs that you love your Motherland and are always ready and willing to die for her. Quite the opposite, the Motherland actually demands that you mustn't throw your life away, you mustn't catch a bullet when there's no need. Only if some emergency comes up and you have to block off a gun port or something with your belly double quick, like the hero Alexander Matrosov – now there's someone she'd like to write to, not those poets from Ashkhabad – or, let's say, crash a burning plane into an enemy truck – which by the way is a lot more beautiful to look at and makes a lot more noise – but just like that, for the sake of it, uh-uh! Your soldier's life is genuine state property too, like a rifle or cartridges – you have to save every round for victory, and anyone who squanders the people's property is no better than a traitor and an enemy. But if there's no need to prove that you're one of our own, that you're always prepared, then why can't they just give you your orders nice and calmly, if you're already grown-up. Because she hadn't caught herself feeling any fear or crying any tears for a long time now – not since that night in forty-one when she first went soaring up above the earth. That was why she'd been chosen as a Seagull by General Zukov – for her fearlessness. It was quite possible in fact that all that business on the volleyball court had been arranged for just one reason – to test her. After all, even Walter Ivanovich hadn't wanted to believe in Midge's trustworthiness, he'd doubted her moral fibre. But now everyone in the world knew for certain, sure for ever that Midge could be trusted. And that, you slovenly slut, was why it had opened up to let you in, that dome of light over the city that has been entrusted to your tearless and fearless care, just think about that, hell's bloody bells!

From the west, out of the sunset that had turned cold and been hidden away in its locker, and simultaneously from the north, from the Great Bear that was pinned up on the sky like the disposition of firing positions on a commander's map, two squadrons of black bombers were moving in to attack the city. Junkers and Fokke-Wolfs. Seagull knows their silhouettes very well, she could never confuse them with our planes, she can recognise the sound they make from ten kilometres away. But today the droning of the Hanses' motors is different somehow, and she halts for a moment, trying to understand if the reason is the black wind, or some special order the fliers have been given, or maybe after all the black dragon is flying with his flock, and then today's battle could be the last one for her as well – or else it would be the last in this war – the one that brought victory. So before the battle started she had to call in home and see Lusya – if only for a moment. What if she never got another chance to see her? And anyway, she had to check how the poor thing was getting on. She was there all on her own in the flat now, literally, with no one even to clean up after her or get her a drink or say a kind word – something terrible it was. Of course before the Mitlyaevs were evacuated they used to look after her a bit, so they still had some sort of conscience left. The week before last everything was nice and clean in Lusya's corner, there was no smell, and she was nice and clean too, asleep in her little bed, she'd got washed before she went to sleep, not been too lazy, and that was the first sign that her petite little body was fighting for life, everyone knew that. And the lock that aunty had put on the sideboard in August forty-one was still hanging there, it never even entered the neighbours' heads that Lusya was taking rusks out of it through the back panel, they hadn't caught on and they were feeding her themselves too out of respect for her age, the number of times Midge had seen their salami skins in her bowl – they were real freaks. Only twelve days ago, the last time she dreamed of Leningrad from the inside, Midge had learned that the Mitlyaevs had gone away after all, escaped from the blockade, as the bosses were supposed to do, and of course they'd left Lusya behind like you'd expect them to, the egotistical swine. But then you couldn't judge people too harshly, they had two useless idle mouths to feed: Lyubka and Verka. A really gluttonous pair of twins they were – never mind that they hadn't even started school yet – people don't learn their appetite in school, it's a natural talent. They were just the same before the war, racing round the yard all day long with a sandwich and if you asked for a bite they told you to get lost. And what's more, they each had their own whopping great personal sandwich. Not one between the two of them so they could start taking bites from opposite ends – after all, it was more interesting that way, right? No, for those egotistic individualists everything had to be individual, even their toothbrushes and their towels – and all the way down to their salami. Where do people like that come from in this Soviet life of ours? Petty bourgeois, literally. But then of course, if you were honest you had to admit they'd never really liked Lusya. She was so open-hearted with them sometimes, so trusting, let them get away with all sorts of things without losing her temper, things that Midge, for instance, would never have forgiven: she had a weakness for young children, she had none of her own, she was lonely. Sometimes she would glance out of the corner of her eye at those fat fools with their massive great sandwiches and shake her head and gulp, but she'd never ask, she wouldn't lower herself: got to keep up appearances if it kills you, as they say. But it was as if those two did it on purpose, they never came into the room without a sandwich stuck in their faces. So of course Midge would yell to her mother: 'Make me one with salami, Mum!' – 'Wait a little while, love, it'll be dinner time soon. I'm not going to spoil you. If you get used to stuffing your face, how will you ever find a husband who can feed you? You'll spend your entire life all alone, like our Lusya...' That was one thing Midge had really been afraid of – an old age like Lusya's. What a stupid fool she was, eh? Now she'd give anything in the world without giving it a second thought just to live like Lusya lived then – with kind people who do nothing but give you respect every day and try to make your food a bit more interesting. And as for any egotistical twins who might happen to turn up and were always chomping on their triple-decker sandwiches every time you saw them – cheese on sausage with another wedge of sausage on top – well, not every last little thing in life can be wonderful, my dear comrades, you have to understand that! Especially since Lusya actually ate world-class grub, no worse than Lubka and Verka's, and if she did squint at their smelly old cervelat sausage it was because she was offended, not hungry. But putting up with that kind of insult would be a positive pleasure now, no two ways about it, Seagull had learned a thing or two, she knew well enough what was good and what was bad, she'd picked up plenty in the school of life, hell's bloody bells! Lusya, she must get to Lusya as quick as she could!

It was so wonderful the way everything had worked out, just like it had all been specially arranged! Sanka Goryaev was from Leningrad too, from the Ligovka district, but since he ended up at the front he hadn't been for a single stroll down Nevsky Prospect or along the embankments, or called in to see his family in Ligovka, and he'd stopped getting letters from them back in the winter of forty-one – something terrible altogether!

General Zukov could easily have entrusted Seagull, as a reliable comrade tried and tested in every respect, with

Moscow, for instance, where at that very moment despite the night-time conditions Comrade Stalin was sitting inside the big ruby-red star on the Spasskaya Tower of the Kremlin, smoking away on his pipe. Or he could have given her any other big strategic target to suit himself, he was the boss. But as far as that went it was really good that the star over the Kremlin was stronger than any armour plate, the whole company was in the know about that. Stalin was as safe as houses up there, you could say that for sure. They brought him nice hot soup in the high-speed automatic lift with special steam heating, right up into the star with a two-sentry guard, steaming hot so his stomach wouldn't get upset from eating too much dry food – it had a serious effect after all. One guy from Moscow had told her, as a big secret – he had a brother who worked right inside the Kremlin as a plumber. The leader would take a bite to eat and have a little break, then it was back to fighting Hitler. And he pressed all sorts of secret buttons that he had up there under the desk and when his hands were busy he used pedals – after all he had to sign orders and fill his pipe with tobacco all at the same time – the man was torn in pieces, literally, fighting on a hundred fronts at once, he didn't have enough time to wipe the sweat off his forehead – and he gave urgent instructions on the phone to his stupid oafs of generals, and on the telegraph – telling them who had to do what. And if he needed to issue some top-secret command urgently, then he could signal without leaving his desk – with that big ruby-red star of his, where he was stationed day and night: he could just turn out the light up there – and then switch it back on with the petite little black switch, turn it off – and then flick it on again. As good as Morse code any day! Much smarter than the signals corps! And what's more, they said that star threw its ruby-red light for a hundred kilometres or more, further than any searchlight. When Comrade Stalin blinked three times in a row at full power – then even the most cowardly general who'd been sitting in defensive positions for six months, a real parasitic sponger, started scratching his head: like it or not, launch your regiments into the attack, and nobody's interested in knowing how many cartridges you've got left, you defeatist waster, or whether your companies are only at fifty per cent strength or whatever. Where he can see from Stalin knows best, he's done all your thinking for you ages ago, weighed everything up, so stop spinning things out, the game's up anyway, and in this situation anyone would rather die a hero than be shot for desertion and alarmism, right? And if the Kremlin star flashed just once – that meant now withdraw to your previously prepared positions, and do things properly, without any panic, the party's over, they've put out the candles. Never mind if maybe some over-keen marshal or other has already penetrated enemy territory and is galloping full tilt for Berlin – draw sabres! – oh no, my little Cossack, you just calm down, cool off a bit, let the other forces move up, don't break formation, curb your obstinate individualism, don't go breaking away from the collective, hell's bloody bells! What is it Stalin teaches us? One man in a field isn't a soldier. He ought to know, no two ways about it, just which regiment and which division to sacrifice and exactly when for strategic goals, in order to finally grind the enemy down and catch him in a pincer movement with practically no loss of combat *matériel*.

That was the way Comrade Stalin, thanks to the Kremlin signalling system, managed to maintain at least some kind of order in the forces, without him they'd all have run riot on their free grub ages ago, like little children, they'd be all over the place. After all, when he's asleep every general dreams of sticking his own revolver into the belly of the hostile enemy Füeller and making him do a *hände-hoch* in his fancy trousers with the stripes down the side and gabble off his own bat, without any prompting: '*Hitler kaput!*' If Comrade Stalin wasn't sitting so high up above all the horizons, the generals would have gone crawling off in every direction, like cockroaches in the kitchen – you'd have one setting out for Japan without asking permission to settle his personal scores with the chief samurai and another deciding he liked the look of the fat trained elephants in India, which hadn't even done anything wrong yet, when he saw it in a dream, or maybe the

Arctic with its ice reefs – they were officers after all, so what could you expect! And how would we be able to manage all those Indian Yakuts of theirs afterwards, what would we feed them all on when they were captured, and where would we get enough agitators to hammer all that basic political literacy into the cast-iron head of the whole of mankind all at once – which, just between you and me, we really ought to have done ages ago – and where, by the way, would we put them all, you couldn't get all of them sitting round the feeding troughs even in the biggest zoo – and they just reckon let Stalin worry about all that, do they? Oh no, dear stripy-legged Comrades Marshal-Generals, it's too soon to let you out into the world on your own, you haven't read Stalin properly, haven't been paying proper attention. But as it happens, he wrote in his red book ages ago already, wrote it in great big tall letters, gold ones: 'If you don't know the ford, stay out of the stream!' Is that clear enough? You need careful watching, like it says in our song. That's why an old man who's already busy has to stay permanently at his post day and night because of a few comrades who have no class-consciousness – as if he had nothing else to be worrying about apart from your rotten lousy political shortsightedness. He can see straight through you, no two ways about it, just as well as Seagull can. Because it's a short step from slack discipline to treason – that's a law. Wind your foot-binding on wrong today and tomorrow on the march you'll get a blister – and you're already practically begging the enemy for mercy, without even noticing how you turned traitor, because you've fallen well behind – and you can't go another step to save your life, the very same as happened to Midge, by the way, in forty-one, in September, on the forced march. Thank goodness for Sanka, he lugged her piggyback all the way to the halt, otherwise the company commander would have shot her as a traitor to the Motherland, he already had his revolver out – he was really strict and just, the freak, liked to shoot the men who fell behind, just loved it, especially if a man was already wounded and essentially due to his own indiscipline he was already an enemy saboteur. After all, if they were held up because of him, the enemy could easily catch up with them and that would be curtains for everyone. That was how without even noticing it a man could actively assist enemy operations by complicating the situation of the entire unit, especially if there were just five cartridges for the entire company – not even enough to deal with men who fell behind. So all in all, whichever way you looked at it, there was no getting away from treason, it was always sitting there inside you just biding its time waiting to come creeping out and put the collective on the spot – just try proving afterwards it wasn't you who damaged your foot with that blister – you wound the wrapping on, that's a fact, and that means while you were winding it on you were already planning your black treachery. And no one's insured against it. Any second any hero can turn out to be a villainous traitor, and there you'll be eating your porridge with him from the same mess tin and not knowing anything about it, because he hasn't even guessed himself yet about his treacherous betrayal of the collective, the foot-wrapping has only just begun working loose and bunching up in his boot, and maybe they won't even announce the forced march until tomorrow, so how could you know?

But Comrade Stalin has an extra-keen nose for betrayal: look how many traitor-generals he smoked out just before the war started – something terrible it was! They pretended to be on our side, wanted to deceive the entire people, sold themselves to Hitler for extra rations – the stupid freaks! Enough to make you laugh. Any child could have figured it out: the moment you're appointed a general, you have to go and confess straight away, the same day, literally – they're going to shoot you anyway, after all, surely it must be better to do your duty with a clear Soviet conscience? No, comrades, we started trusting you a bit too soon, we relied on your treacherous consciences, but you're rotten to the core, just like any officer. It's a good thing we got on to you in time. Because Comrade Stalin summed up the situation correctly with his exceptional farsightedness: the better you are, the worse you are, that's a law. And by the way, he discovered that law himself, as it happens. It's still written there in the red book to this day: 'Better fewer, but better'. And that's why the poor old leader has to stand watch round the clock, looking out with his eagle eye to see where else an enemy has taken cover, where he should expect the next treacherous knife in the back to come from. And as far as that goes, it would be better if there were fewer of you military specialists to weigh the soldiers down, only we're prepared to hump the best ones along on our shoulders until victory arrives, since that's the way it's supposed to be and it seems like fighting a war without generals isn't allowed. Although, to be honest, it would be better just to be on the safe side to eliminate them as a class without any fuss and bother – it would make better sense, keep things in better order. And General Zukov on his own would be more than good enough as a specialist for all the fronts – where could you find another world-class general like that? He'd manage things for everyone, no two ways about it. If he was smart enough to learn how to command all the Seagulls that there were all on his own using the invisible method – and mind you, that's not counting the kind of forces that any fool could spot with the naked eye from a mile away – then together he and Stalin would be able to get any order to every single private soldier, even the most extra-urgent one, it was a fact. That way they could divide up the responsibilities between them: Comrade Stalin seeing everyone everywhere through his optical star up in the Kremlin, and General Zukov transmitting his commands to absolutely everyone using the modern invisible means for waging war. Then we'd soon have a whole new order, with ammunition and elastic for knickers. Yes, and by the way, think how much easier it would make things for Midge, with no snot-nosed lieutenants or knobbly captains or fat colonels and all the other poor excuses for soldiers. It was amazing really that he still hadn't thought of it himself, the amount of time he'd save for Midge's night raids if he made a right and proper decision like that, and the nervous strain he'd save himself, which was an important consideration for an experienced commander. After all, he could see perfectly well, he was watching every last one of us from his strategic star – that was why he'd been put in it. In fact he'd appointed himself the one and only seer straight through everything and that had terrified every last one of his enemies – our generals and the Hanses all at once. And what's more, he didn't need a map up there in his star, or a compass – he could see everything anyway, all the way to the horizon on all four sides. Without even leaving his transparent ruby-red headquarters, Comrade Stalin could territorially observe all of Europe through powerful optical periscopes – all laid out there in front of him, up to and including the Reichstag itself. And to keep his beloved observation post safe he had a hundred high-speed top-class fighter planes patrolling round the clock, every one of them with three cannon and five automatic machine guns into the bargain, and with tracer bullets, by the way. They keep on patrolling up there in the sky until they land on Red Square for a rest while another hundred patrol instead of them, for as long as their fuel lasts. And that's the way they keep the wheel turning without a break. That's why it says that in that favourite folk song: 'The beloved city can sleep in peace!' So Stalin's defence in Moscow was in good shape without Seagull, no two ways about it. That's concerning what we were saying about how come, strangely enough, Seagull wasn't personally entrusted with Moscow. As you can see, it's because unfortunately it's Leningrad, not Moscow, that's our weak link. And a bottleneck, as they say, at the same time. In the first place, it's been blockaded for more than a year: and by the way Comrade Stalin himself thought up the strategically essential blockade for the people of Leningrad specially in order to tie all of Hitler's hands and at the same time pin down his main forces, so the whole gang of them wouldn't make a push on the capital all at once. We couldn't put Moscow in danger, could we now, comrades, are you crazy or what? But someone had to be sacrificed, that was a law in strategy, otherwise the war wouldn't be fair, it would be breaking the rules and everything would get confused on the front and in Stalin's head too: the rules were the same for everyone, and you had to stick to them.

If you wanted your authority to be respected, by the enemy at least, then you had to throw him a bone, as they say. And in this regard, I'd like to emphasise that after all it's exactly the same with any vicious dog: if you don't throw it a bone when you climb into its garden to pick the apples, it's bound to start barking or maybe even give you a fundamental and irreversible bite. In war everything's just the same as it is in life: if you don't take any risks, you don't get to drink the champagne, as the people say. Comrade Stalin thought long and hard over which bone to throw to the fascist Hitler, and he decided on Leningrad. It was the only correct decision, comrades! If anybody can stand it, then Peter's city can, and that's a fact. For some reason at the present moment the most class-conscious proletariat is concentrated there, that was recognised ages ago. Peter's city will tough it out, it won't let the country down. It already showed everyone what it's capable of in the revolution — that's if it's inspired the right way, of course, and the sacred goal is explained in a politically literate manner, all right and proper. Although it's true it's not Moscow, none of your impregnable Kremlins in case the enemy breaks through the defences or dug-outs and no ruby-red bunkers up in the sky so if the worst comes to the worst you can pour boiling tar on the Hanses like they used to do in ancient times when they had similar bothersome sieges. In Peter's city there are no real defensive strong points — apart from Lenin's armoured car at the Finland station. Basically it's a pretty difficult situation, so let's look the truth straight in the eye, after all, I reckon there aren't any stool pigeons here. It's an exceptionally difficult situation. So difficult that if the enemy saboteurs who wanted to cause total panic had been able to spread their slander and defeatist misinformation freely in the newspapers the way they sometimes did in Midge's dreams, Seagull would have dropped her wings in despair long ago. And after dreams like that, anyone else in her place would have decided on the quiet that the defenders of the city of Lenin were already completely finished from the viewpoint of physical constitution and could hardly even stay on their feet, and that was only the ones who were still alive, you wouldn't even want to mention the rest. When you go hedgehopping above the streets of Leningrad, when you glance invisibly in at the windows as you fly up to your own house – or when you look through the walls by accident, the way it often just happens in a dream – sometimes you notice a state of business that just makes you wonder what kind of dream you're in this time around, you crazy-woman: a strategic, military dream or just a plain ordinary human dream, or even worse, a defeatist and alarmist dream. Walter Ivanovich had warned her: 'You go flying ahead when you don't even know the way!' – but she hadn't listened, it went in one ear and out the other, and now she had no one to ask advice from on that subject, anybody would just report it back to the right place straight away, the kind of hostile-defeatist thoughts you had in your head, obviously thoroughly treacherous with a core of predatory egotism. It was a good thing at least sometimes you could get hold of the Leningrad newspapers, that was the only place you could find out the truth about life in the city.

So how do the newspapers elucidate the matter in question for us? Simply, clearly, directly. The city, they say, is continuing to labour heroically despite the reduction in the norms of provisions and nutrition, as well as of food. The plan for defence products is being met by every factory, even the very weakest, the most pitiful little plant is fulfilling it by almost three hundred per cent, or even more. And what's more, as always the Komsomol is in the vanguard. Nothing about any dystrophic corpses and such, not a single mention, and there couldn't be any in a class-conscious Soviet newspaper, because there wasn't the slightest trace of panic in Leningrad, not even any isolated instances of irresponsible wrecking at work – everybody was united as one around the core of Party activists and they took a class-conscious approach, the way they ought to, that is, like Pavka Korchagin would in their place, or any other normal modest Soviet hero. When you looked at their photos in the newspapers they were just ordinary faces. You couldn't say they looked really fat, but they weren't any half-dead saboteurs either, not useless skeletons no good for anything, no fucking good even for the Red Army, as they say – *pardon madame*, of course, apologies for my French. Then how could you believe your eyes, if you weren't a rotten kulak spy, when you flew over the city and observed the bodies of dystrophics lying right there in the streets and in the flats in ordinary buildings that hadn't even been bombed? She'd guessed almost straight away, started feeling uneasy: there had to be some mistake here. Maybe there was something wrong with her eyesight, or maybe in this particular case the dream hadn't come out right, it was the wrong calibre. Maybe it was a combined dream? Half was ours, Soviet, and the other half was from the fascist propaganda, sent directly from Goebbels deliberately to scramble her brains by filling them with misinformation, hell's bloody bells! But to be honest about it sometimes you wouldn't catch on straight away, at first you took it all at face value – all these rotten deceptions of theirs. She'd fallen for it especially often at the very beginning, in forty-one: she'd believed her own eyes then, like a little fool, and so of course she used to get so upset she almost cried out of pity for the dead children in the bombed kindergarten, or the elephant in the zoo that been killed by a bomb as well. But then eventually she'd caught on somehow: what sense did it make if there was one thing in life and another thing in the newspapers? What strange ideas have you got in your head, you slovenly slut? It means the enemy's been able to twist you round his little finger like a fool if you're letting yourself think thoughts like that, you must be totally doolally. Even if it was only for a while and only in your own heart – you were still a genuine traitor if you'd let that vision of black corpses and green dystrophics get inside your head, if you hadn't managed to fight it off. And for that you should quite simply have been shot on the spot with no trial or investigation, all right and proper.

But joking apart, every child knows what a genuine native Leningrader ought to look like, a person who understands and realises what a great honour has fallen to his lot – to live in the city of great Lenin, especially in the period when it's blockaded by the enemy, which, by the way, happens to be a very fine and timely test of our class-conscious endurance. Nothing like it might ever happen again in all of the remaining history of mankind, and genuine Leningraders understood and appreciated that, they went all out to exploit their fortunate situation to demonstrate their devotion to the cause of Lenin and Stalin to the whole world. You only had to think about it — right now, at this very moment, the eyes of the whole world are on Leningrad! And the bourgeois are watching especially keenly. They're eaten up with curiosity, right down to the marrow of their bones inclusive: will the Leningraders hold out — or will they capitulate after all, like cowardly deserters? And of course it goes without saying that Stalin is suffering up there in his star, puffing away non-stop on his pipe, opening up the window and airing the place a bit and then filling his pipe with tobacco again — he's suffered so terribly, after all he was the one who set up this test for his beloved children, the Leningraders, in order to toughen them up even more for future feats of heroism. But even though he's suffering he's still patient, he holds himself back with all his might, he doesn't divert any troops from the other fronts to come to the help of Leningrad. After all, in his capacity as the leader of the peoples he really wants to make quite sure that he wasn't wrong to set up such a terrible blockade, that he got all his calculations right. The English and the French are probably having a bet on whether the Soviet people will manage to defend their beloved city — or will they surrender after all? Of course, both of them would like us to surrender. But we'll show them all what's what — the whole world all at once! After all, just how difficult would it be for us to save Leningrad, if the whole country came to the rescue? Dead easy! But then that's just what we can't do. We deliberately won't do that — just to show them! We've specially left just one narrow little road of death to supply the city with provisions: if it's a blockade, it's got to be a real one, hell's bloody bells, we do everything honestly, no messing about, so they won't go whispering behind our backs afterwards, won't point at us and say: they cheated the whole world. Oh no, there'll be no one finding fault afterwards, Stalin's thought the whole thing through, no two ways about it: the bombing every day, the massive air raids on Leningrad from all directions and the shelling – everything the way it should be in a genuine blockade, like it says according to all the rules and regulations. It gives us something to be proud of. We can tell the whole world. We proved it! We took it all, we didn't take any notice of all the moral losses, and we proved it: our people will survive a hundred blockades, a thousand if you like! Because a new nation has actually been born on the earth: we stopped being Russians ages ago, we're Soviet people, that's the whole point. That's as far as the nation's concerned, if that's what we're talking about. One genuine Soviet man is easily worth three or maybe even five old-regime Russians, and with plenty to spare. When they were building St Petersburg on the bogs they probably wouldn't have stood it for long on a crust of bread a day, they wouldn't have got much done, they'd have organised a rebellion and overthrown Tsar Peter – then there would never have been any Leningrad. But us Soviet people don't need anything – just as long as you know in your heart that everybody respects you collectively and individually, every member, that you're no worse than anyone else, that you can even give your life for the Motherland too, like the very finest, the most class-conscious hero, any day, any time – even if only by starving to death. And apart from that what does any man need? The collective is the most sacred thing of all. That's where we get our special pride from: everyone's proud of everyone else, even if he's the most emaciated dystrophic ever, it's a sacred right. That's why any Soviet man will tell everyone: 'A blockade? Always prepared!' Let them bomb every flat and every building individually every day, he'll say, we'll carry on living and working just to show them all what's what. Because even in his sleep every one of us remembers that phrase – duty first! And it would never enter even a deserter's head to ask: why do your duty? Duty to who? What for, hell's bloody bells? Everybody knows for sure your duty is your duty, you just do it! Like Pavka Korchagin believed. And that's why Stalin doesn't have to worry about a thing. He only has to give the order and we'll set up another fine world-class blockade in Moscow, if he needs it that urgently, and in Ryazan, and in every single little village. After all, there are class-conscious people living everywhere, nobody will ask any questions, their stern faces will just turn a bit more severe, every one of them will just close ranks even more closely around the Party activist core of trustworthy men and passionate young women who are always prepared, the way they should be. Because everyone knows Comrade Stalin is relying on us, on every single one of us and he's ready to work himself to a frazzle every hour of the day to prove to the whole world that our country's the only one where anyone can feel like a hero, a warrior, a trusty support to the beloved leader. After all, so far no one's heard anything about anyone setting up a blockade to match Leningrad during any war anywhere in Germany or France, or in America come to that, not even in our own dear Yakutia. Not even a nice petite one to begin with. No, you haven't got the guts for it, dear comrades, you couldn't give a damn for your self-appointed leaders, you don't want to go hungry for the honour of your Motherland, lose a little bit of weight – though it would do you good! In your world man is a wolf to man, Stalin explained that to us ages ago. But over here even in a blockade every step you take you see mutual assistance going on, that's all they ever write about in every newspaper, and we have comradely assistance being rendered here as well, helping hands all around you, on every corner, literally. And if somebody or other who isn't completely class-conscious yet suddenly out of the blue happens to lose heart and starts to panic, the rotten bastard, and lets his petty bourgeois nerves get the better of him – after all, we've still got all sorts of have-beens left over who haven't been finished off yet, there's no point pretending we don't, as well as kulak lackeys and putrid intelligentsia, there's still plenty of scum and human refuse dragging along behind us, pulling the entire consolidated collective backwards – and so if some piece of garbage like that decides to start sighing and wailing and then keel over like he's fainting or something, because he's supposed to be starving, then straight away everyone else will come to the dirty rat's assistance, all the ones whose health is still sound, no two ways about it, they won't lose their heads! They'll have that bastard standing to attention in front of Stalin's portrait in a trice, on a carpet as red as the blood of the heroes who fell for the revolution, and give the lousy freak such a tongue-lashing, such a working-over there'll be nothing left of the scummy bastard but a heap of dry dust. So what if there is a blockade, dear comrade, hell's bloody bells! Are we going to let some lousy blockade make us go around looking as miserable as sin? Right now, tighten your belt, you ignorant fat-bellied swine! Reducing yourself to a traitorous dystrophic state like that, it's enough to make a cat laugh. Two extra duty details! Ab-out turrrn! Into the mess and peel potatoes for the entire battalion, quick marrrch! On the double! Crouching! They'll soon knock all that silly nonsense out of you, you little shit. What was it our beloved Stalin wrote? If you can't do it – we'll teach you; if you don't want to, we'll make you. Trying to take cover behind other people's backs? Oh no, bosom buddy, if you bear the proud name of Leningrader, then please conduct yourself accordingly, stick to the rules, do things properly. You've got to be an eternal example for the whole country – whether it's through your labour or your external appearance makes no odds in this case. An example, a model – understand? Not a dystrophic, not a corpse. Why sacrifice your social dignity, comrades? Remember the way that favourite song of ours goes? 'Captain, hey! Captain, hey! Come on cheer up! Captain, hey! Smarten all your sad ideas up!' Try singing that to make yourself feel better and put yourself in a happy, politically literate mood. I can't, you say? You have to get past I can't. Like everyone else. So there! So as you don't get normal people all confused by going around looking like a corpse, especially soldiers who go flying past you on their invisible mission and see you wrapped up to the eyes in shawls so you can't even tell if what you're seeing is a granny feeling a bit chilly or just a plain ordinary saboteur dolled up for disguise.

There was one time, in December forty-one, when she definitely had a dream that wasn't hers, she almost guessed it straight away. Only the most hardened spy or left-over traitor-general at the very least, could dream that kind of nightmare horror. But to tell the truth, Seagull only realised it was an erroneous fraud afterwards, when the horror of it woke her up as Midge back on her trestle bed in the dug-out. And that time she didn't have any guest for the night sticking his officer's fingers in anywhere, it was that nightmare that woke her up, its pernicious vision was so entirely alien to a Soviet girl and on top of that she was crying – so much for dropping in for a quick look, eh? Of course, we're always nattering away with anyone at all, blabbing military secrets left and right, slagging off the command good-oh, but we haven't got a single ounce of vigilance – so now we've landed right in it, we should have been expecting it, we're right up the creek now with no one but ourselves to blame for the fact that any old saboteur can stuff even the most two-faced, slanderous dream into the head of the most class-conscious and irreproachably politically grounded soldier, like sawdust instead of baccy, up to and including even the most alarmist and defeatist nightmare.

But in actual fact, dear comrades, where could you have seen anything of the sort, just try thinking about that! Just imagine it, right there in front of your own eyes – whether you're dreaming or awake makes no difference in this particular case – even if you are invisible just at this precise moment, you've still got eyes, haven't you? – and there right in front of your eyes, and also – this is a point that ought to be emphasised – absolutely without the slightest twinge of remorse – a simple Soviet granny, wrapped up to her eyes in a shawl and all stooped over from old age into the bargain, suddenly out of the blue grabs a long knife off the kitchen table and without turning a hair cuts the rump off a pretty little girl, an obedient little girl she is too, she obviously hadn't done anything she could be punished for with that kind of excessive severity, especially under the conditions of a blockade of the city of Lenin by hordes of ravaging invaders. The little girl, by the way is lying right there on the kitchen table on her side, naked, with just her feet dangling over the edge a bit, and her eyes are open, and her little mouth too – she's not asleep. Bright little eyes they are. And little milk teeth in her mouth, sparkling like sugar – that means her saliva hasn't dried up the way it's supposed to in corpses, she's alive. And when the old granny wheezes and turns her little granddaughter over from one side on to the other to lay her out more handily, her little arms move about too, they haven't gone stiff, and her head falls back – with a stunted little plait of light-brown hair, and a blue bow with white polka-dots all covered with repulsive little 'seeds' – lice, that is, but you already guessed that – the lice from her little round head, you can see them so clearly, you just want to pick them off and throw them in the stove, even though the girl undoubtedly couldn't stand such a serious operation without anaesthetic, and that means of course she is dead, but she's only just died. Yes, look at that blue spot with the scratch on her left temple: she must have been up to some mischief, the little scamp, and she fell and hit her head on the corner of the stove, or maybe on that iron – and she gave up the ghost, as they say – of course it wasn't the granny who did away with her own granddaughter with that iron lying there on the table – what a ridiculous idea! Anyway Seagull wants to pick off those repulsive 'seeds' so they won't eat the dead little girl, in the first place, and so they won't go crawling all over the flat, after all the granny is still alive, she even looks pretty lively in this domestic morgue of hers, and consequently the old woman requires the best possible hygienic conditions.

And in addition, Seagull didn't immediately realise the little girl with the bow with those cheerful polka-dots wasn't alive, the granny didn't pick up the knife straight away. It should be mentioned that in Leningrad at that moment in time the overwhelming percentage of the population wasn't glowing at all. Blockade Leningraders aren't soldiers and machine-gunners, they're not Vaska Kolyvanov, you can feel his healthy body heat three metres away when you're awake, and in your dreams you can see it as a pink or green light over his head and shoulders. After all, so far at least the food situation's better on the front, let's look the truth squarely in the eyes on that one while no one's listening. That's why that citizeness, the old granny in that empty kitchen with eight primus stoves that Seagull flitted into so thoughtlessly, attracted by the flame of the oil-lamp as she was flying past the fourth floor, or maybe it was the fifth floor of the long, old-regime building on her own native Suvorov Prospect – no, the old woman wasn't glowing even a little bit, nothing but a bit of grey smoke trailing up over the top of her shawl-wrapped head and a few faint little scarlet sparks that flared up and glimmered feebly around her face, then went out straight away. A really feeble old granny, packed up so tight in her shawl she can barely even move, and she's wearing a warm plush coat and felt boots with galoshes, but the poor woman still can't get warm, even though the stove is burning in the middle of the kitchen, blazing full tilt and the water's streaming down the wall behind it, almost all the ice is melted already. No, the old woman isn't glowing, she's obviously not got long left. So Seagull didn't really notice that the little girl wasn't giving off any light either, not even a tiny little bit – as if that was the way it ought to be. But then, hadn't she'd always taken notice of little children and been delighted by how bright and colourful they were, despite the war – like flowers – even in Leningrad, in the blockade. In the beginning, in autumn, she often used to fly in through top windows and little chinks out of curiosity and she always really enjoyed watching the little children sleeping: only knee-high to a grasshopper, the tiny little flea, and so skinny already, almost transparent – too lazy to eat an extra plateful of porridge at the kindergarten – but the light he gives out when he's sleeping is like a lovely little lamp – the way it flows and swirls in golden waves, the way it blazes up into a rainbow – what a performer! She used to be surprised too: when she was little she must have blazed away brightly like that too – so where had it all gone to, she wondered, who'd taken it all away? But the old woman's little girl was as dim and dull as a doll. She ought to have realised how things were straight away, it was Seagull's bad luck she got so distracted. She'd only noticed the lice on her bow. But afterwards when Midge woke up she'd seen it: the child's eyes were cold and chilly – like meat jelly, literally. But at the time she hadn't been absolutely certain. She thought the old woman had laid the naked girl out on the table like that because she was going to wash her – over on the stove there was water in a saucepan with steam rising from it, and a second saucepan on the table. The old granny was going to wash her little granddaughter, that was good, but first she was going to pick all the lice off her head, do things right. But then the old woman picked up the knife. And the little girl lay there on her side on the table, facing the old woman and not making a sound. And what's more one of her arms was reaching up from the table – as though she wanted to give her granny a quick hug, have a little cuddle. The old woman wheezed and slowly, with great difficulty because her hand was shaking, she sliced a layer of flesh off the round, childish bottom that hadn't turned blue yet, pulling it away as she cut – the little girl didn't move. The old granny held the severed top of the buttock on a black, bloody hand with bony fingers – as if she was weighing it. She put it on a chopping board, skin upwards and meat downward – a little white mound, like a pie that hasn't been baked yet, taut and plump with its generous filling. She sighed with her whole body and started carving again, pulling the meat away by its edge, a broad oval slab with a rim of skin. It didn't bleed; the little girl lay there like a doll.

The knife scraped against the exposed golden bone.

Masha screamed. Seagull was scalded by a frosty blast that pierced her like a thousand knives.

On the table the flame in the oil-lamp blinked. The old woman lifted up her head.

The cold pain that filled her flickering, invisible body was interwoven with a blast of searing shame. She realised she'd been duped. But who by? Who, hell's bloody bells?

The stooped old granny wrapped up in the shawl had a thick young ginger moustache and orange stubble on her unshaven cheeks. While her face was in the shade Seagull couldn't see the moustache. The granny stared at the invisible Seagull – or through her – with the glazed, dull-green, dim and hungry hollows of her eyes, with the knife trembling in her hand, stroking her moustache with her red fingers, moving her swaddled head with difficulty as she listened. She sniffed her fingers, licked them and smacked her lips. Then she said in a thin, hoarse voice that really was an old woman's: 'Rats …'

Seagull made a dash for the window, for the crack between the padding and the frame, realising now that she'd been cruelly and contemptuously tricked and laughing out loud with the throat that she didn't actually have, due to the absolute invisibility of her entire strategic body. They'd made a fool of the gullible little idiot – like that time in the Leningrad Young People's Theatre when she'd taken a man dressed up as an old woman for a genuine Wicked Witch. For almost two hours the old spindle-shanks had chased young boys and girls round the stage like an enemy of the people, threatening to gobble them up. Midge and all the other kids in the audience had been worried to death, literally. She was still young and green then, only in the third class. Well, of course she started blubbing out of indignation and wanted to dash up on to the stage, her daddy had barely managed to hold her back: don't worry, he said, everything will work out fine, the militia knows what's going on. She was trembling all the way through to the end of the final act: what if the militiamen didn't get there in time? Look what a big knife the Witch has! And a sabre! And a pistol too! And then when they finally grabbed the déclassé bandit, and they brought the curtain down and the actors came out to take a bow, the Wicked Witch suddenly jerked off her shaggy wig – and there was a bald patch! Midge almost fainted. What kind of bloodthirsty actor could be so shameless that he'd play an old cannibal woman in front of everyone like that? A bald, respectable-looking man at first glance. But what was he really? Disguise him with a wig, put a knife in his hand, and you had a desperate saboteur! And now this scene in the icy kitchen had been set up by saboteurs as well. Deliberately – to confuse gullible people, to see if any of the neighbours would come in to ask why there was suddenly a smell of fried rissoles here inside the blockade. Their artistic director had just put a knife in the hand of the first Hans he came across and laid out a little rubber girl to go with the knife, like a mannequin daubed with red paint and there you had your comic scene. Especially for people with weak nerves: see what brutes the sons and daughters of the city of Lenin have become in the blockade, just look your fill, comrades, and then spread our hostile slander and misinformation all over the shop, if you're so morally unstable you can't even spot the Wicked Witch's moustache under her nose at two paces. And after all she believed it, didn't she? She believed it! The only thing that saved her was that Hitler's artistic director forgot to shave off his leading man's moustache and that had given his treacherous scheme away. You couldn't help laughing so hard it set your head spinning round and round – all their lying propaganda about icy walls and emaciated corpses with blue bows covered in lice in their hair. Seagull shook in a fit of hysterical laughter, covering her wild staring eyes with her transparent hands to keep out a strange incomprehensible horror as she went swirling round and round herself like a spinning top, deeper and deeper, burrowing down through the slimy bottom of the fascist dream and returning to her own natural reality. And when she came to on the trestle bed, back in her body, it was trembling and shaking as though the frost that transfixed her in the dream had got stuck in its bones, she lay there for a long time wiping away her stupid childish tears before she could suppress the laughter that was wracking her.

She'd really let herself down this time, hadn't she? She'd flown into someone else's dream! It served her right, if you're on a mission you've no right to get distracted. If she hadn't gone peeping into other people's windows like some crazy ill-mannered freak, if she hadn't gone trespassing in kitchens in the middle of the night, then she wouldn't have gone off course.

People's dreams didn't have numbers, your name wasn't etched into them with bleach like it was on your trousers or tunic – on every dream approved for your viewing according to the staff list – you had to keep your wits about you, not let yourself get caught napping, go for the target and not get sidetracked. But she'd gone off the rails, stuck her nose into someone else's window instead of her own – it was the light of a home that had drawn her, you see, like a stupid little moth – so now don't whinge if hostile propaganda has decided to exploit you for its own subversive purposes, caught the little bird in its mousetrap. You say it doesn't happen, comrade? Oh yes it does, hell's bloody bells! Old women in Leningrad don't grow ginger moustaches under their noses, that doesn't happen, but anything at all can happen to you in a dream, just you keep that in mind and don't forget it. They keep trying to hammer that into you idle prattlers' heads – vigilance and even more vigilance, day and night! Before you know where you are, you slippery slut, they'll recruit you and you'll be a traitor. And then even if you don't want to you'll go spreading rumours to cause panic and undermine fighting efficiency from the inside. And it all starts with what at first sight looks like an ordinary dream: what of it if a granny carves up her own granddaughter, if you get sick you can see worse things than that while you're delirious, a dream is a dream, hell's bloody bells. And that kind of shit can happen to anyone, absolutely anyone at all. And why? Because in the first place it's not just your friends and comrades you have to watch – you've no right to trust yourself either, not an inch. Not even your own eyes and ears. She knew that now. One more minute and she really would have believed that in Leningrad grannies with moustaches were as good as eating their own little granddaughters. That 'granny' had exposed her wolfish saboteur's face with the moustache just in time and taught the stupid girl a lesson for the rest of her life. And it was only typical that with that kind of slacking, something in the line of treason was bound to happen to Seagull sooner or later. But she was finished with all that now! No more going near other people's windows or doors or chimneys or candles burning behind curtains – uh-uh! – not for anything, not even if they're burning with a bright blue flame in there, not even then. She'd been taught a world-class lesson. And even though she'd immediately drawn the practical conclusions, taken due and proper note and learned her lesson, she went on twisting and turning from side to side on the trestle bed for another two hours at least: she was so ashamed!

The main thing she was ashamed of was that she really had believed it for a moment, she'd taken that transparent propagandist falsification for a genuine, honest Soviet dream. She hadn't bothered to use her brains a bit and try comparing a few facts – if she had, she'd have cottoned on to their pitiful set-up straight off. In the first place, to be absolutely frank about it, they could have made their amateur movie about the girl getting sliced up a bit more realistic, and then Seagull would definitely have fallen for it hook, line and sinker – but after all, the girl they used as bait was a bit lifeless and they didn't even have enough sense to shave off the main character's moustache to keep things secret. And in the second place all Seagull needed to do, not now when she was Midge again, but there in that frozen non-Soviet kitchen with the walls covered in ice like at the North Pole – all she needed to remember was: you used to have a bow exactly like that in your plait, you stupid idiot, when they sent you to the village to stay with Granny Alexandra. Mummy put a spare bow in the suitcase – exactly the same, light blue with white polka-dots. So it turns out that if it hadn't been you who caught tuberculosis in nineteen forty, you typhoid louse, but Verka Mitlyaev, say, or her plump sister Lyubka with her sandwich always stuck in her face – she could easily have been the first to pick it up from you; touch wood she wasn't, you lived in the same flat, almost like one family, except of course for the cervelat sausage – then Verka and Lyubka would have gone away to the village instead of you and you'd have been left behind like a stupid fool in the blockade with your stupid bow. Right? Right. That is, you could easily have ended up in that old woman's granddaughter's place in the winter of forty-one, that is right now – laid out on the kitchen table. Kind of difficult to believe, isn't it? Hang on though, that's just for starters. Now let's try imagining you're lying on the table, never mind if you're already dead, and then someone like Verka and Lyubka's grandmother Lizaveta Rodionovna all muffled up in a shawl suddenly out of the blue grabs the first chopper she can find and starts hacking up your backside for rump steak – on account of your own Granny Alexandra not being around (she's in the village like before, don't lose the thread, you slippery slut, she's dosing Verka and Lyubka with milk for their tuberculosis, after all, you're not ill, they're supposed to have got ill instead of you, you're healthy, it's just that at this particular moment you happen to have starved to death and you're lying on the kitchen table in front of Lizaveta Rodionovna – instead of Verka and Lyubka and that other girl you don't know with your polka-dot bow in her hair). It's nothing but a load of old rubbish, right? But all that's just for starters too, now we're going to dig a bit deeper, get down to the root of the matter. Although it's clear enough as it is that it just won't hold up, a simple, class-conscious Soviet granny can't just go chopping you up and carving you into slices like beef – is she supposed to be some kind of nutter? She went to school, didn't she, they taught her what's allowed and what's not allowed. And then think of all the times you went to the bakery to get her halva! And what if you did nibble a bit on the way back while you were climbing up to the fifth floor – she was always happy to give a child a treat, if only she didn't forget all the time on account of that powerful weakness of memory in her old brain. And you used to go to the library to get her novels by Dumas – she was so fond of them, the old bookworm, just couldn't stop reading … Or maybe she did notice you were pinching halva from the paper bag on the sly, sponging off her in her old age? Her halva was sacred to her, literally, and you used to nibble on it … But surely your disciplined dependability was more important than a piece of halva? After all, it was a rare day when you didn't go to the library for Lizaveta Rodionovna, literally! She could read a book in five minutes flat, even without her glasses she just raced through them … And by the way, right there in her kitchen, that was typical, because the stove was blasting away too: she used to feed it with books, she had *The Three Musketeers* lying there already torn in half so it would burn better and there'd be less smoke … But that won't hold up either, you can feel that, can't you? Lizaveta Rodionovna burn books? You must be out of your mind, dear comrades? Don't pile it on too thick, hell's bloody bells!

But now let's go a bit further. Now we're going to imagine that it wasn't the neighbour with the knife, not Lizaveta Rodionovna nibbling her halva over her novel, but your very own mother. Eh? Well why not, now we've got everything tangled up in such a heap? Never mind that everyone knows she's the kindest, the best mum there is. As a matter of fact, a mother is more sacred than anything else, she comes straight after the Motherland for everyone, that is, of course, after the Motherland and the collective, obviously – right there in third place according to all the staffing regulations, and that even applies to front-line conditions, never mind any individualistic feelings. What's sacred is sacred – but what's she going to do if she's on the point of starving to death and even though she's wrapped herself and her empty belly up tight in her shawl right up to her moustaches she still can't get warm? You're already dead remember, don't you go losing the thread now, and your mother didn't wait until she started carving you up and you didn't make a sound to be certain of your lifeless condition, that came earlier of course. So can she carve a little bit of meat off you then after all? Or not? But why not, if everyone can do whatever they like – the Germans are allowed to bomb the city of Lenin, and no one stops Leningraders burning the best books – even *The Three Musketeers* who, by the way, were always 'all for one and one for all', all right and proper. And what's more, not only can people burn everybody's favourite books, they can use their neighbours' little girls for meat before they even get cold or stiff after they die, while they're still warm, the way we've just been able to confirm on every point in our example with someone else's granny, Lizaveta Rodionovna. Remember the way the little girl hugged her granny with one arm when granny was taking the knife to her? You couldn't ever forget that, could you? And the bow, by the way – it was yours, wasn't it, so at that same moment your mum could have been wrapped up to her moustache like the old woman in exactly the same kind of shawl. Is that logical? Absolutely. Sometimes when Walter Ivanovich was in a good mood he used to smile at the entire class and say: 'If it says 'lion' on a cage with a tiger in it – don't believe your eyes. Is that logical, my red high school pupil comrades? Absolutely! So let's make a note of that!' And all the boys were always repeating his saying: 'You'll get unsat. in the test tomorrow, Midge. Is that logical? Absolutely!' – or something else of the sort, the stupid studs. So the main thing is not to believe your eyes. Otherwise you get confused, you can't see the wood for the trees and you'll never understand what's actually going on right under your very nose. That granny had a real genuine spy's moustache. That's what going on in the world, hell's bloody bells! But then, if Mum never had a moustache, that doesn't mean that she'd never have picked up a knife; a moustache is one thing, but a knife – begging your pardon – is a different matter altogether; 'you've got to sort the which from the what' – Mum herself liked to repeat that when Midge didn't understand something and she got one difference mixed up with another. So that meant she could quite easily have been in the kitchen instead of that old woman – even wearing exactly the same kind of shawl – she used to have an old one almost exactly the same, greyish-brown. Why not, if we've decided to look the truth straight in the face?

What's that, you don't like this, hell's bloody bells? You've started shaking again? You add it all up, add it all up and figure it out. If you're such a fool. If you could believe in rubbish like that in your dream, now you can believe in your own horrible fibs. Why are you trembling? Why are you shaking all over, still got your backside, haven't you? Started sobbing again, have you? Afraid, are you? It's impossible, you say? That's right, it's impossible. Especially since your mummy and daddy were killed in a bombing raid. And in general it's just absolutely impossible – full stop! A class-conscious Soviet citizen can't go gobbling up neighbours in a harmonious communal flat without even choking once, and especially not her own child – it's insane!

So how did you dare believe in such a nightmare? How could your conscience allow you to believe in a horror like that – with the little blue bow that never did anything wrong apart from that piece of peanut halva? How come you didn't realise what was what straight away when you saw your own little bow covered with those disgusting lice? What was going on in your dim-witted head? Go on now, cry, bite your hand. Next time you'll know better. At your age you should have figured out long ago what you ought to believe in unquestioningly if it's written in the newspapers and any commander will confirm it, and in which case it's your duty to close your eyes, forget all these enemy lies and calmly flit out of some enemy spy's dream back into your own class-conscious, one hundred per cent or more politically literate dream. And what's more, now you feel ashamed for thinking about your mum like that, imagining her in the place of the old woman with the moustache. Let's just hope the poor dead woman didn't happen to overhear such stupid, inhuman thoughts about herself, that she didn't happen to glance into Midge's nasty little head just at that moment – she'd never forgive Midge for as long as she lived, and what someone from the next world can do to punish those who are still here – that's a question science still hasn't answered yet, the scientists are struggling with it right now, a one-eyed captain told her that – it was only because his sight was so good, by the way, that he wasn't demobilised from the front: he could spot a mosquito a mile away and he was a great asset in the verification of data gathered by means of visual observation behind the line of the Hanses' advance trenches almost round the clock, that was why they valued him and they hadn't even done anything to him when he spent an entire week living on Midge's trestle bed, hiding from the command –

true, afterwards he had to lie and say he'd been looking for his other eye, the glass one, in the neutral zone all week, because he couldn't carry out his observations without it: it acted like a sort of counterweight for maximum sharpness of vision …

Midge fell asleep still crying, but already feeling half-reassured. And she dreamed of her mother, Zinaida. She dreamed of her for the first time since that day when Granny Alexandra had handed her aunty's letter without saying a word and Midge knew that her mum and dad were gone and they would never come back.

… The dense, sparkling, opal cloud of tender, loving joy descended directly on to Midge's trestle bed, consoling her for all the agonies tormenting her body and her soul, which instantly became calm and snuggled up against the cloud of happiness before her body. Midge sighed sweetly as she nestled against her mother's breast and put her arms round her, wiping away the tears from her cheeks on the warm cloud. She knew perfectly well she was in a dream, but the dream she was in was special somehow, not a plain simple dream or a strategic one, it was like some other kind of life – she was flickering between sleeping and waking, like the midday haze in summer that blurs the substance of visible life without transforming the material of wakefulness into a weightless, permeable condensation of light and shadow.

Her mum was looking at the ceiling of the dug-out, her face wasn't dark and her glance wasn't motionless like a dead woman's. And Midge suddenly felt that she wasn't Seagull at all and she never had been, that this loving warmth was the only thing she had ever been looking for in her flights, she longed to go to her mummy, to go home and bask in her warmth like this, to cry to her heart's content, calmly, knowing for certain once again that this warm tender feeling for her and this all-embracing, cherishing peace were all hers, her very own, and they wouldn't go away, they would never disappear, they belonged to her for ever by inalienable right and they would comfort her for ever, warming her and loving her, and the separation was only for a short while, soon Mummy would be with her again every day, every Sunday at the weekend and on weekdays too. And the only hint of alarm came from her mother's face that was turned upwards in mute anguish, a kind of alarm that was new to Midge, that carried some novel, otherworldly meaning.

'Mummy! When will you take me away? Mummy! My darling dearest Mummy ...'

Midge burrowed into the opal cloud, swooning into it, and instantly her being was permeated through and through with the remembrance of her family world, where she shared the same breath with her mother. How could she live without this? Without this, life was worse than death!

'When, Mummy? I've missed you so much!'

'Don't ask!' her mother said with a curt gesture of her hand, not looking at her.

Midge began crying even more bitterly, realising she would never know the things her mother couldn't talk about even though, of course, she knew everything.

'I've got nobody, nobody at all!' Midge almost shouted, sobbing and choking, then felt horrified that she was shouting at her mum and demanding what wasn't allowed, reproaching her – as if her mother was to blame for something. 'Not a single person left alive. Why did you let that happen, Mummy? What did I do?'

The cloud swayed and Midge was horrified to see that her mum was crying too, crying silently, profoundly, the way only grown-ups can – without seeking any consolation – after all, what consolation can a little girl possibly offer for the incomprehensibly huge and scary mystery of the remote, immense agonies of a totally different existence?

'You've got Mama Lusya,' her mum said with a sad smile, and Midge couldn't tell whether she was saying such strange words to comfort her or to taunt her, whether she was praising her or warning her of some danger that threatened – or whether she was simply making fun of her stupid little Midge. 'The sun's still a baby,' she added with a sigh, quite incomprehensibly now, almost despairingly – and the opal cloud began swaying again, as though it was seething from the inside, a slow, secret agitation began inside it — like in a saucepan of semolina coming to the boil — and it felt even more warm and sweet for Midge to be with her mummy, the currents of warmth that washed over her being from all sides made her feel even more tranquil, warming her through, bringing new life to old, deep-buried hopes and young, tender feelings for life that she thought she had lost and forgotten long ago.

But then the cloud began to fade and melt away. Horrified, Midge felt her essential substance and her vital energy, which had just been fused in tranquillity with the radiant cloud, begin to shrink, fitting into each other with a shamefaced snugness and growing cold as they sank back into the chilly waves of the vast, solitary emptiness of sleep. The silver sparks scattered and vanished under the ceiling of the dug-out. Midge was left lying on the hard trestle bed feeling heavy and out of place. She woke up almost immediately, but she brought with her out of her dream her mother's strange words about Lusya and the sun, like snatching a washed stocking out of the tub. By some miracle the warmth her mother had brought was still with her, and so was the certainty that everything would turn out really well in the end — there where her mum was, together with Mum, under her protection and according to her will. The most important thing now was to grasp the meaning of her mum's words, what they were really about, not just in the dream, and what she had to do now so as not to miss something important and at the same time not lose the solace and absolution the warm cloud had bestowed on her ... It was just a pity that Mummy hadn't said anything about Walter Ivanovich, after all she probably knew something at least, she had to ...

So one thing was clear straight away. Of course she ought to pay a lot more attention to Lusya, because Mum seemed to be angry that Midge didn't call in at Suvorov Prospect very often. Mum had probably reminded Midge about it because on her last raid Midge hadn't got home at all, she'd woken up straight away after that shameful business with the old woman with the moustache. Who could tell? But the fact was that Lusya was starving all on her ownsome on Suvorov Prospect and that meant as soon she got the chance she ought to give Lusya some proper attention.

And as for that, of course, it was really world-class that General Zukov had entrusted Seagull with Leningrad, the city that carried the name of the great Lenin, which was actually why it had got into such a terrible fix, as they say – out of the Hanses' hatred for that hateful name. Essentially, of course, there was really nothing to be glad about in that, especially if you were a patriot and you suffered for the Motherland on that basis, all right and proper. But on the other hand, if it wasn't for the blockade, even with fascist dreams in other people's kitchens where the mad raving Füeller had spread his shameless propaganda, the filthy scum, including blue bows for the total disorientation of the civilian population, and if General Zukov hadn't also allocated Midge precisely to that centre of population, Leningrad – then after all you'd only be able to day-dream about flying home from the advance line and your real dream would be something about Moscow all the time, according to orders received, with all those Tsar-Canons and cracked Tsar-Bells instead of living darling little Lusenka who you worried about all day and all night when you weren't really busy. Especially since it turns out you're not the only one who's afraid for her, Mum is too from somewhere up in the clouds. Or they could even have ordered her to have nothing but German dreams and taught her in no time at all, if they'd instructed her to fly against Berlin – and then there'd be nothing but dreams of Berlin all the time, with reichstags and swastikas and Hanses' round ugly mugs everywhere, the way it had already happened once – it still made her feel sick to remember it. But like this at least every now and again you could drop in at home to see who was still fighting the war in such privileged circumstances.

And so again and again and again Midge flies above her beloved Leningrad!

Would they let her go this time or wouldn't they? She was past Uprising Square now, there was Old Nevsky Prospect below and the Alexander Nevsky Monastery sticking up ahead. Would they really not let her have any leave of absence?

'One leg on – one leg off!' General Zukov's voice sounded a bit annoyed now, disgruntled, but once again Seagull could detect his kind smile behind the assumed severity. 'Three minutes for everything! ... Seagull, Seagull, this is Number One. Perr-mission for a three-minute absence without official leave! The assembly point is Palace Square. I repeat: be at Palace Square in three minutes! Dismissed!'

Dismissed! She was free!

But what was the sweet darling so happy about, playing those rolling, booming tricks with his voice and barely able to restrain his laughter? What a good man he was, how dear he'd become to her in these last few months – something terrible it was!

Seagull performs a triple somersault and goes hurtling downwards as though she's skiing downhill. The dark streets slide back and up underneath her. The swirling fires are left behind with the blinding spots of the gigantic searchlights, the broad swathes of smoke and the clouds of ash. She's going home!

Seagull could have found the window of her room on the corner of Suvorov Prospect and Seventh Soviet Street with her eyes closed. Snuggling up for a moment against the window pane – it was pasted over so that it wouldn't get broken by an explosion nearby, Mummy or Lizaveta Rodionovna had stuck the strips of newspaper on criss-cross – she could already sense living warmth inside the room. Lusya was alive! And it was only now that Seagull understood the yearning that had been tormenting her since the night before last, now that it was gone. She hadn't managed to get to sleep last night. Yesterday new reinforcements had joined the ranks of the company and from midnight until reveille a snub-nosed little lieutenant had wept on her breast as he told her about his first love, the beautiful girl in tenth class, Cleopatra Tyutko, who turned out to be a perfidious traitress and didn't show up to see him off to the front. Lukich was on duty at the advance line, so Midge didn't try to stop the snub-nosed boy from sobbing as loud as he wanted. She even took off her own tunic and knickers to get him to pay some attention to a girl at last, do the right thing by her and not keep her awake any longer. But the lieutenant needed to snivel urgently – double top-speed emergency, hell's bloody bells! Now and then he asked her: 'Are you feeling hot? It's all right, I'll go in a minute, let me just finish telling you everything and then I'll go. You can hang on for just a bit can't you? You don't mind!' The snub-nosed boy prattled on all night, didn't let her get a wink of sleep. He kept babbling into her damp armpit and she kept trying to figure out where that muddlehead Lusya could have got to. Because the night before last Seagull had almost arrived late at Palace Square, she'd rummaged through the entire flat, literally, trickled into every nook and cranny, but she still hadn't found her. What was going on? Had someone killed her? Eaten her? – Like that little girl with the blue bow. After all, the flat was empty, all sealed up, their neighbours had been evacuated. And by the way, if the seal was still on the door, that meant thieves still hadn't got in yet, right? Lusya couldn't have just flown out through the hole in the corner of the window-frame – she wasn't Seagull, not yet anyway. It was just like a bad dream, word of honour! Look, there was a puddle under the sink in the kitchen – that meant she couldn't have died of thirst. It was a mystery, of course how the water kept miraculously seeping through especially for Lusya, when the mains weren't working anywhere, but if the rusty pipe hadn't leaked, then Lusya couldn't have survived, it was a fact. No, she was here somewhere: her little turds were lying in the corner of the room and some of them were fresh. Pretty sort of turds, long and slim like the stones in figs before the war. The old woman was alive, she was! But where was the rotten pest, hell's bloody bells! The crazy freak hadn't really survived a year and a half of hunger to spite her enemies only to go missing for nothing when the blockade was about to be lifted any moment, had she? That was just plain stupid! And there were still three sacks of rusks lying untouched in the sideboard, her parents had dried enough for ten years before that rotten assignment of theirs was bombed to pieces, rest their souls – provided, of course, you took Lusya's modest appetite into account ... Lusya, come out, will you! You haven't gone out to the bread shop or the market – you have to use your head just a little bit, dear comrades! But what's the point in shouting when in your dream you haven't got a throat or a voice – nothing but a holy spirit, pardon the expression.

But still two whole days after Seagull's unofficial leave of absence in Leningrad Midge was cursing and nagging away at herself because she hadn't found Lusya in the empty flat – either alive or dead. But now, at the window of her own room she suddenly felt as light as she did that autumn evening in nineteen-forty when she carried Lusya into the house with her eyes already squeezed shut against Mum's shout: 'That's the last thing we needed!'

Seagull peered in through the window, but it was dark inside. She slid along the window frame and flowed smoothly into the room through the little triangular hole where the corner of the glass had been chipped off before she was even born. All her life Daddy had been meaning to replace the glass, he'd even bought a glass-cutter at a flea-market, but he never got around to it: his work was secret, so sometimes if there was an alarm they used to get him up in the middle of the night, they sent a special messenger, and sometimes at the weekend the telephone would ring in the morning and he'd say 'Yes sir!' into the receiver, stick his cap on his head and his Browning in his pocket – and then he wouldn't be back for a week, if you were lucky. The number of times Mummy had laughed about it: 'You're not meant to do anything about that window, Dad, living with you is just one long emergency!' But now it was no problem for Midge as Seagull, who she actually was, to get into her home without a key. She slipped through the crack between the black-out blinds. Home at last!

As she flew over the desk, she gently stroked the covers of her history text-books, glanced into the dried-up unspillable inkwell, touched her cotton dress on the hanger with her unfeeling lips – blue with white polka-dots. Mummy sewed it herself. The smell of childhood was still just barely discernible through the dust of neglect. By the thin, gentle light of her own shimmering, scintillating body – Seagull could see it so clearly here in the dark room that she was almost frightened by the long snaky fingers of her blue yet transparent hands and her long legs that were almost fused together into a mermaid's tail – but then she could see every polka-dot on the little dress and the familiar pattern of the wallpaper, those five-pointed red stars on the yellow circles, and even the deep scratches scarring the front of the wardrobe: MASHA. She'd scratched the first crooked letters of her life with the key of the room – on that day when Daddy first showed her how to write her name. Mummy had slapped her and made her stand in the corner. And now Seagull found it strange and funny to recall the delight with which five-year-old Masha had scratched the crooked lines, scraping through the furniture varnish and the tough wood fibres. What was so special about that? M-A-S-H-A. But Seagull, now, that was a different matter. Sea-gull! A proud, high-pitched call ringing out between the clouds in the open sky. Seagull! – and the black dragon bolts back to his secret aerodrome double quick – a bad dog knows what it's got coming, as Stalin wrote. But of course, she was Seagull!

Lying on the dining table, weighted down with the salt cellar, was Mummy's note. Seagull stretched out her hand to illuminate the page from an exercise book with the light from her own fingers and palm – like a pocket torch. The words that Seagull knew off by heart sprang out of the darkness:

> *Little daughter!*
> *Dad and I will be back in two weeks, we're going*
> *away extra special express. If you come back when*
> *we're not here there's butter in the kitchen between*
> *the double windows and boiled macaroni in the*
> *cupboard use plenty of butter when you warm it up*
> *don't be mean. Don't get up to any silly nonsense*
> *while we're away don't turn your room into a*
> *rubbish tip and don't argue with Lizaveta*

Rodionovna behave politely and stick to the rules.
Clean up properly after Lusya, brush your teeth in
the morning and at night don't be lazy. You have to
be someone we can be proud of, we're relying on you.
Kisses to our little Midge.

Mum and Dad

There was something added underneath:

P.S. Dad says you mustn't give the meat from the
soup to Lusya no matter what since in view of the
fact that very soon the food situation in the city is
going to be terribly bad. So gobble down your own
share and build yourself up. Dad and I will soon
drive the Germans out and come back home and the
very first Sunday we'll go to the zoo and all ride on
the roundabouts together. Be good!

There was a moist squeak from the corner of the room.

The moon-blue horse-shoe over Lusya's head glowed like the final fading scrap of flame over a piece of firewood. Lusya had sat up and frozen like a candle, making funny movements with her tiny hands, pushing and plucking at the empty darkness in front of her. She can sense me! How can she, can Lusya really see her owner the way her invisible owner sees her? But what if she can – what difference does it make anyway? After all, just because Midge couldn't see Lusya's weak little light until she became Seagull, that didn't mean Lusya had always been as blind as Midge was, did it? Take bats, for instance, they find their bearings somehow in the total darkness of their caves without being able to see, and the moles under the earth, not to mention simple earthworms, who don't have any eyes at all – even they can find their way somehow, they stay on the pathway of life, as they say – and without any help from anyone else. And Seagull can't even imagine any longer how she could have lived day and night without seeing the real light of people, animals, mammals and all sorts of botanical plants –

she'd got so used to the colourful beauty of it all. But maybe Lusya didn't have to get used to it, maybe she was born like that. Why not? After all, in a dream anything's possible.

Seagull glided over to Lusya's box. And then she started back, squeezing her mouth tight shut to stop herself screaming, completely forgetting that nobody would hear her scream, and anyway there was nobody to hear it in the empty flat.

The two newborn babies were sleeping with their noses nuzzling into their mother's belly as she lay there on her side. They were white like Lusya herself, both of them with a tender pink radiance like a soft cocoon around the petite little body and head. Lusya stretched out her pointed nose to greet her owner and twitched her silver whiskers, her eyes gleaming like little round pink beads – as if she was smiling. And Seagull squeezed herself up into a tiny ball no bigger than a baby rat and snuggled up against her large, warm maternal belly.

And again Midge felt she was under the protection of a mysterious and righteous power. The same as that moment in the pet shop when she held the snow-white creature with the pink eyes in both hands and pressed it against her chest for the first time – and suddenly she was swamped by a weightless wave of warmth that didn't weigh her down, it was the liberating promise of a long, dependable joy. She'd been surprised even then: would you believe it! How come that it wasn't her, the grown-up little girl, who was giving refuge to the stupid little rat with the straddled legs and the repulsive little tail covered in snake scales, but the other way round, this little thing as soft as dough, with its tiny, frightened little heart pounding as hard as it could under your human hands, fluttering all over so it seemed like it was ready to die any moment if it couldn't hide – it had even squeezed its eyes tight shut so as not to see its own immense death, not to feel anything, not to be alive at all! – it was this little thing with its startled fear, its helpless blindness, that was protecting you, sticking its wet little nose trustingly into the palm of your hand, comforting you, who were so huge compared to it and in doing this it drew down into itself from somewhere on high a great strength that towered up above the creature that had trusted it, as if it was on guard, as if it was responsible for the little mite to the whole world – and somehow she felt so sorry for herself that she cried, literally, comforted by a little rat – although it seems like there's no reason to feel sorry for you today, Masha Mukhina, quite the opposite: you got a five for singing for doing nothing at all – for your favourite song, 'Sleep not, arise now, curly head, for ringing in the workshops ...' But no, she just couldn't swallow that lump in her throat. How come it was here, in this illiterate rat – your sweet peace and complete, you might say completely grown-up, happiness? Where did it come from? It was in the delicate little whiskers, in the thin, pink, almost powerless fingers. And most important of all, that repulsive tail, that seemed to be the thing that was constricting her breath the strongest of all, and a tear came to her eye – she wanted so much to dress the poor naked thing, hide it away. But then the little mite pressed itself against your breast and froze, then squeezed its little beady eyes shut and started burrowing under your palm with its nose – and your eyes closed by themselves and your breath dropped down into your belly, and you were on the point of dozing off yourself and dissolving in the lovely, kind warmth. What's going on? After all, you're a human being, nature's top world-class achievement, eh?

The mother-of-pearl, sweet-berry, bready smell of mother's milk permeates and saturates Seagull in waves of warmth as if Midge is standing with her eyes closed beside Mummy under the shower in the bath, leaning back against Mummy's soft, slippery side as if it's a wall. Lusya is breathing deeply, her mother's heart is beating steadily. Her children twitch and shudder in their sleep and Seagull is upset that she can't stay with her brothers for ever. Funny, why is it that people have to be alone all the time except for dreams?

Midge-Seagull slowly pulls herself away from Lusya: it's time. The stream of protective warmth doesn't dry up straight away. She glides on it like a sea wave, soars round the room in circles as if she's reeling out an unbreakable spider's web behind her – Lusya's calm sleep flows through it to Seagull and straight into her body that glows pinker and pinker – sleep with no more concern for the children who have been fed, no more fear for her own little patch of safe space in the besieged city: Seagull will protect us, Midge won't forget us! This wave carries the warrior-maiden out through the little corner hole of the window-frame into the black sky – feeling reassured now and even a little bit sleepy. Lusya will be all right now, she's produced such fine defenders for herself, attagirl! Including Seagull that made three heroic warriors, just like in the folk-tale!

Well within the three minutes allowed by the general, Seagull finds herself hanging over the very centre of Palace Square. Even Walter Ivanovich himself would have been proud of such German precision, such punctuality, hell's bloody bells!

She hovers about fifteen metres above the Alexander Column – above the head of the bronze angel standing there stock still as if on guard, with a cross over its shoulder instead of a rifle.

'Seagull, Seagull. This is Number One calling!' – his voice doesn't stimulate her, it doesn't make her stand to attention and brace herself – she yawns and gives a sweet shiver, spilling the fuzzy, gentle electric glow of Lusya's affection down inside herself to the tips of her toes and back up again.

'Attention, Seagull! Prepare for immediate action.'

'Pre-pared for action!' she says, struggling to suppress the yawning of her incorporeal mouth, then immediately straightens herself up and corrects herself.

'Yes sir, Comrade Number One, ready and prepared for action!' But she doesn't really feel a single sound in that customary chime of her smart response. Lusya's soft, springy whiskers twitch in a silvery gleam, her pink sons sigh in their sleep, like tiny Lilliputian piglets. Seagull has no desire at all to go roaming around the night-battle sky in an extra special emergency search for their damned dragon. She'd like to go back to Suvorov Prospect, cuddle up against Lusya and go to sleep. And then wake up there, at home, in the morning – and not in a dug-out under some lieutenant who's already twisting and thrashing about on top of her like a bream in the fish shop on the corner of Seventh Soviet Street when the net has just fished it out of the marble swimming-pool aquarium that three-year-old Midge has pressed her nose against so hard there's no way they can tear her away – just look at the way it's flopping about, a bad dog knows what it's got coming, it can tell its funeral's coming up ...

'Attention, Seagull! Into action!'

She shudders and gathers herself into a fist, trying to summon up the furious hatred that has disappeared somewhere for the black dragon that she's never seen even once. The number of different monsters she's observed on the fuselages of the Hanses' planes – she spotted an orange tiger once, and once she chased after a buffalo with big horns half the night, and she remembers a panther as black as shoe-blacking on the fuselage of a high-speed Messerschmidt – but she's never set eyes on a dragon. She wonders how much more of this tail-chasing is left today, when will the moment arrive for her to wake up on her disgusting trestle bed – squashed flat and struggling for breath? Oh no, dear comrades, better to die as a falcon than live as a snake. What was the point Stalin emphasised in all this? If you're born to crawl you shouldn't fly! Golden words, hell's bloody bells, with them in your heart you'd just fling yourself into battle even against your own will, into the thick of the action – it was such a catchy expression!

And she takes on an elongated, bellicose appearance with the pointed shape of an artillery shell ready to smash into any target indicated in due proper order.

'My blessing for the battle, daughter!' the general sighs, as if he is handing over the reins of management to supreme justice – she'll sort things out somehow, the good Lord is no slouch, as they say.

A silence as immense as the entire vault of heaven that fits inside it and even higher – the silence between the general and Seagull, stock still now and stretched out into a glowing knitting needle – tautens her impatient yearning to a sharp ringing note throughout her tense being, sending clusters of blue sparks flying out of her body in the direction of her intense gaze – out into the menacing night. Into the sky, gashed through by the crossed wedges of the searchlights.

'Fire!' and off she flies like a bullet out of a sawn-off barrel – spinning like a top, whistling as she screws herself into the black wind.

The general shouts after her. Perhaps he even waves his cap, he could. But Seagull can't hold herself back and listen – and his voice fades away in the crackle of the anti-aircraft fire, the dull croaking of the shrapnel and the heavy rumbling of the shaken, suffering earth rising up from below.

She cuts intrepidly across the blinding streams of light from the searchlights, the incandescent tracks of the anti-aircraft shells – they're heading for a black bomber above her head, but they fly straight through Seagull without even tickling the transparent maiden – merely enveloping her in the momentary vortex of their movement as they pass. Above her head their explosions open out into fiery umbrellas. Seagull flies through streams of shrapnel, fading sparks from explosives and fused metal, bathing in them as if they are the powerful jets of a cold shower – to follow up after the steam room that has left her flesh languid and breathless, and she rejoices to feel the cold that is so good for her. A high-explosive bomb tumbles out of the belly of the black bomber and straight through her weightless, incorporeal body. If this wasn't a dream it would have sliced Midge in half, whistling and spinning on a slant like a roller – exactly the same length as the girl herself. But now she is Seagull, Seagull!

No, Seagull doesn't feel the jangling strings of machine-gun bullets from the plane with the heavy cross on its underside as they pierce her through – she has already flown on higher, laughing, invulnerable. The German is firing at a little fighter plane with a red cross on it that has wandered into the beam of a searchlight from the very ground that the half-pint is protecting against the roaring Fokke-Wolf with a transparent cockpit for the gunner, whose face Seagull can see so clearly, with the same hate as if she was looking through an optical sight. Maybe that's him, the dragon? If only she knew what he looks like, the freak, what plane he flies in. And in general if he's a man or really a dragon. She couldn't ask General Zukov, he was sure Seagull herself was already in the know. And anyway, of course, the black dragon must actually be the most important military secret of all, words like that must never be broadcast, otherwise your number would be up, sure as hell. So that meant the Fokke-Wolf could be him. All right then, that would be all the worse for him!

Seagull calmly focused her will into an intangible burning point and confidently directed her flight towards the transparent cockpit, head-on at the glass, hurtling towards it like a shot from a gun. In a second her entire being would penetrate his deadly glance, which kept eluding the gunsights of her eyes. Will you stop twisting your head around, you bat-faced bandit, look at me, you freak!

Just a moment before the pale face, when she could already make out the drops of sweat on his forehead above the bulging frog-dragon goggles, she suddenly realises with all of the body she doesn't have right now, that her heroic aerial ramming won't shatter the transparent cockpit or tear the enemy's head off and it won't bring down the Fokke-Wolf − it'll just fly through her in the same way as the incandescent bullets and the searchlight beams and the long blunt bomb that had probably already killed people down on the ground in the last few seconds − forgive me, dear sweet people, it's not my fault, I don't know what I can do: I can see everything, I feel like I could defeat all our enemies on my own single-handed, let alone just one dragon, but then I do something wrong again, I'm wrong myself, I just can't understand if I'm real at all or I don't exist either waking or sleeping ...

'Comrade Number One! Comrade Number One, this is Seagull! Please give me a reference point, Comrade Number One!'

'Seagull! Seagull! Here are your orders! The target is the black dragon. Forward! For the Motherland! For Stalin!'

The same thing that's been happening every night these last few weeks. Every night.

Every night she's over Leningrad – up among the anti-aircraft fire, the howling engines, the chattering bursts of machine-gun fire, the piercing glances of hate, desperation and ultimate terror. The girl believes that she only has to catch the enemy's glance, as empty as the barrel of a revolver pointed at her face, in the sights of her will, and the force of his black power will instantly be reduced to ashes by her overwhelming truth. Every night, again and again the flesh and substance of her dream pierces the bodies of dragons with crosses, with tigers, panthers and rampant lions drawn on the fuselages she can penetrate so easily, like the night air and the black smoke of the explosions, as if she really is the only one alive in the battle-sky – a concentrated focus of the all-permeating pain – any moment now the others will dissolve in the beams of the searchlights, the dream of the sick earth – she only has to get them to face her pain, fearlessly exposed. Every night, neither conquering nor surrendering, pierced and shredded by fire, steel, lead, the insanity of evil – remaining invulnerable and eternal, feeling guilt for everyone she has not been able to save. Every night.

So it wasn't for nothing that ever since she was little she'd dreamed of being a flyer and attended the gliding club without missing a single session, she hadn't skipped even one, and once she even went on an excursion to the flying club, where she touched the levers in the cockpit of a genuine biplane, and the fact that its motor had been taken out didn't really make the slightest difference.

Midge didn't argue with Lukich any more, they lived together in untroubled harmony for month after month. And every time as she flew out at night to carry out General Zukov's secret order, Midge said goodbye to Lukich like a dearly loved friend.

That was why the freak was crying openly and wiping the tears off his moustache in the mental vision Midge saw when she was striding along to her execution, as he and Sanka

Goryaev and Sevka and General Zukov carried along the comfy, cheery little coffin with the heroic body of the world-class girl Midge — supported on crystal pillars — to the strains of the tedious funeral march and the frisky 'Rio-Rita'. She wanted so much to give the old man a big heartfelt hug, to press her cheek against his, but it would be a shame to spill the roses on the ground — Midge was covered all over in white roses, after all — Walter Ivanovich would have been so delighted!

She didn't notice that her steps sometimes slowed down — in time to the funeral drum and the deep-voiced trumpets — and sometimes went dancing and flying along, when the vivacious 'Rio-Rita' got the upper hand. It seemed to her that she'd already been wandering for years along the level road that the Germans had rolled smooth to last for ever, but the glittering noon would never end, never wane.

Chapter 7

In which a cricket prays for Midge
and Smersh-with-the-Portrait turns up his toes
in front of the bride of his dreams.

In the blackened, crooked and cracked little bathhouse where Captain Smersh had set up his quarters, Midge immediately felt like she was suffocating in the scorching heat of the man's anger. It was the smell of a full-grown mouse caught in a mouse-trap.

'Hoping I'd give up waiting, were you?' The captain launched straight into the interrogation, fixing Midge with a sullen glance from under his brows. 'Been covering up your tracks? Working on your story? We've had our eye on you for a long time, just remember that, we know every last little thing about you ...'

Smersh was perched sideways on the bench by the little window – a scrawny man with a round, balding head, scowling fastidiously as he cleaned his richly burnished famous inscribed presentation revolver with a grey handkerchief. He poured some milk into a mug from a cracked earthenware jug, drank it down in a single gulp, like home-brew, then went back to his revolver.

The midday sun forced its way into the bathhouse through the grime and soot of the narrow little window, laying its unfastidious light across the heap of leafless twig besoms by the wall and the long-dead triple-winged spider's web in the corner, with the ragged holes made by flies that broke through it with impunity. Under the ruined little stove a solitary cricket was praying brightly in its sleep. The stove shelf was as black with soot and smoke as if the retreating Germans were not the only ones who had scorched the inside of this abandoned bathhouse at the back end of the Pskov province village of Shisyaevo through and through, as if the Varangians, the

Mongol horde and the Knights Crusaders had all thrust their flaming torches into it as well. As if not a single war since the creation of the world had bypassed these fissured walls, and the flames of every internecine war and every armed conflict had gone out of their way to force themselves into the innocent bathhouse and deposit their generous coating of greasy soot on the bench, on the ceiling and on the hard whiskers and steep knees of the unsingeable cricket who was now praying for Midge.

There was a bast-fibre washcloth hanging above the unbroken window. Green and thick with mould, like that clammy jellyfish – little Midge had burnt herself on it when she was on holiday with her mummy and daddy in the NKVD sanatorium in Sukhumi. The huge jellyfish had been tossed up on to the beach by a wave and three-year-old Midgelet had immediately stood on it with both her little feet and jumped up and down. And now here they'd met again – would you believe it!

Just above the wisp of bast, the haughty, principled profile of Comrade Dzerzhinsky glared out from a piece of paper nailed to the wall – a page from the magazine *Ogonyok*. The entire division knew about the portrait with the long nostril and the little beard. And about the special one-off Tula-steel revolver with the inlaid handle. People's Commissar Ezhov himself had conferred the inscribed presentation weapon on Smersh when he was still private soldier Kuznetsov, for preventing a mass escape by dangerous convicts – dekulakized peasants.

The captain was also well known for his monkish indifference to the conditions in which he carried out his assignment and his love of cold milk with ice – it had to be straight up from the cellar that very second. Everyone knew he didn't smoke or drink and never ever swore, and though he shaved punctually before breakfast and after supper he still couldn't subdue the rampant furry growth on his face. The division knew everything about Smersh. The way they knew from school about the infinity of the universe – believing and not believing, knowing and not knowing. They told stories about the captain's habits the way they did about the singer Klavdiya Shulzhenko's holiday fun and games – smiling the same way Pushkin's serf nurse Arina Rodionovna smiled at the mischievous pranks of her brilliant charge at the Mikhailovo estate.

Before the captain appeared Sanka Goryaev had discovered that when he was close to the front Smersh-with-the-Portrait preferred to be stationed in barns, sheds and uninhabited bathhouses. That when he pronounced sentence he glanced up at Comrade Dzerzhinsky and blew his nose with agonised groaning and gasping into a damp handkerchief and squeezed a fluey tear away from his eye with his finger. And if he felt like it, when he was in the mood, as they say, he would carry out the sentence with his own hands. Right there on the spot, no messing about, by the wall of the same bathhouse, still gasping and blowing his nose. Curiously enough, the captain took aim without shutting his left eye, using both eyes at once. And when he did it he looked off to one side a bit, as if he was cross-eyed. And so the shot always came unexpectedly. They said it was easier to die without the final terror. And not once had the presentation pistol ever happened to miss: it dispatched you straight to heaven, no screams, no twitching and jerking. It never caused any trouble or upset for the personnel: just carry the executed man away and bury him – only twenty minutes of spade-work – real world-class Smersh efficiency.

Tactfully ignoring the captain's first meaningless questions, Midge wiped her nose rather loudly on her sleeve, holding the dangling cuff of her over-size standard issue soldier's tunic in place with her finger.

'Attention!' the captain shouted without looking at Midge, continuing to spin the cylinder of the revolver and force his finger, wrapped tightly in the handkerchief like a condom, along the white grooves. 'Straighten that back!'

Midge drew herself up even more erect. Raised her head with a sigh. And stared at the little window behind the captain's back. It was light out there beyond the dirty glass, nice and bright.

Captain Kuznetsov gave a wet snort. Politely set the oil-stained handkerchief to his nostril. With every moist sobbing breath he was drawing Midge's secret intentions out of the air, she thought, so she tried not to project her thoughts far beyond her forehead.

The captain's runny nose was an army service injury, like other people's wounds or concussions. The Siberian had got chilled through by the cold wind up on the Yamal peninsula, where he was serving as an armed guard near Labytnangi. The convicts there had invented a saying: 'The Yamal escort has special rules: one step left or right is escape – so fire!' The final diagnosis of 'chronic rhinitis' had triggered an inner crisis and self-reassessment that had re-shaped the young soldier's entire view of the world. In particular, as Kuznetsov grew stronger and matured year by year under the influence of the diagnosis, little by little he won the exceptional right in the fighting collective, confirmed by a certificate with a big seal, to remain unaware, so to speak, of the smell of his own boots and foot wrappings, to be above such things. And once he made it to officer's rank, he really did forget all about those pearly-white Labytnangi nights when his army mates used to stifle his brazen snores by covering his face with his own legendary foot-wrappings that whiffed of the gas condemned as inhuman by the Geneva Convention.

And now the captain's forgetfulness was making Midge's throat itch too. Her eyes watered. And then she sneezed. Trustingly, like a child.

She gulped in air – and erupted again. This time with painful desperation. She froze, holding her mouth shut and not breathing, squeezing her eyes shut. The sly mousy odour slithered into her ears too, and under her tunic. She felt an urge to dash outside.

The captain was watching Midge sullenly, working the large knots of his jaw muscles so hard that his ears wiggled. He was pondering some arrogantly sober idea. The corner of his upper lip twitched. The jet-black gypsy stubble bristled on the captain's patchy, frost-bitten cheekbones.

The girl trembled and wheezed hoarsely. Struggling to check the murderous third sneeze. Since she was little the third one had always been the most disastrous. She couldn't hold it in, had to let it out — stop up your ears, brothers, this cannonade will rattle your eardrums for you, no two ways about it. And Midge herself had absolutely no say in the matter, it was just her constitution, as they say. An inherited allergic response, something terrible it was. She got it from Granny Alexandra together with the mole under her left eye. Granny Alexandra always enjoyed a real good sneeze, even though she was a cultured village teacher and she'd been decorated into the bargain, awarded a certificate from the people's Commissariat of Enlightenment, Lunacharsky himself had signed it. Granny used to sneeze heartily and admonish Midge strictly: don't you ever go behaving like that!

'Be-lay that!' the captain ordered, dumbfounded at the thought of Midge's third detonation. 'Who d'you think you are, girl?'

Midge waved a hand woefully in the air. She was blinded and choked as the roof of her mouth strained greedily to catch that critical grain of dust that would spark a response. She rolled her eyes up agonisingly and stretched her arms out like wings. Her spirit was soaring through the sky like in her dreams, far out of reach of Smersh-with-the-Portrait and this whole war.

The delicate streams of air under the vaults of her larynx finally merged together. The shell of liberation detonated with a flash and the shock wave from the high-explosive sneeze slammed into the walls of the little bathhouse, setting them shuddering. The glass pane from the little window fell at the captain's feet and broke crookedly in half.

Once freed of her explosive charge, Midge went limp. Her little head surfaced on its weak green neck like a water sprite emerging from a duckweed-covered pond. She fell on the bench by the door and leaned back against the wall, rolling up her sky-blue eyes. She sang out, as if she was tipsy.

'Nev-er mind, little Com-rade Cap-tain. You don't mind me just having a bit of a sneeze, do you? I really have to, hell's bloody bells … I'm sorry about it, Granddad, I'll try to keep qui-et as qui-et, eh? All righty?'

And she dropped her head like a swan, tucking it in under the wing of her little white handkerchief, glad that Walter Ivanovich couldn't see her at this particular snotty moment in her life – he'd have put her straight out of the room.

She had no strength left to be afraid. And so she believed that her choking sneezes just before she died would be forgiven. Or maybe Smersh-with-the-Portrait would take pity on such a petite, dutiful, snot-nosed little girl, especially since she wasn't even the slightest bit guilty.

Trustfully pandering to the latent paternal feelings of the latest master of what remained of her life, Midge took off her forage cap, stuffed it under her belt at the side and sneezed twice again, sobbing, squeaking and clucking without holding back, letting it rip, taking shelter behind the drenching spray of her juvenile anguish against the dry nose of Comrade Dzerzhinsky with the long black nostril: no doubt he'd look down disdainfully on the snivelling little milksop. The same way she got used to defending herself against being told off at school and at home when she was little.

'On your f-f-feet! Atten-shun!' the captain roared in a whisper. 'On your f-f-feet I said, you bitch-ssh!'

Midge leapt up. She broke into a sweat and her next sneeze, already ripening, was gulped back down. The captain's whisper swished through the air like a scythe – Midge was frozen to the spot. Her belly quivered: this was the end – court martial – execution. And no swaying on golden chains in a coffin with white roses, saboteurs didn't get coffins. And the smell in the hut didn't come from the mice, it came from Midge, no two ways about it – from Midge's own rapidly approaching death. She'd have to train another flying ace for General Zukov and his nocturnal aerial battles. And how would Lusya manage back there in Leningrad, alone with the little children? What a time to choose to have them, the crazy freak

But since it was the wall for her for sure, Midge decided even more firmly not to ask forgiveness for anything – why should she, *merci beaucoup* with tassels on! And not to answer the captain's mean, underhand questions. And absolutely not to sign a statement: she'd say she was illiterate, hell's bloody bells! That was the last piece of advice she'd been given that morning in the dug-out by Vasily Kolyvanov and Sanka Goryaev, whose old present had really helped keep Midge going, lying there in her back pocket. Twice it had saved her life: yesterday night and that time in forty-one, on the forest track near the river Mga. And it surely wouldn't betray her now, it certainly wouldn't miss its owner's forehead at point-blank range, no two ways about that!

Watching furtively to make sure the captain didn't notice, Midge moved her right hand behind her back and checked that the little 'Walther' was where it should be. It was lying at attention in the arse-pocket of her sagging breeches, as though it remembered yesterday's unforgettable feat of heroism on the dark forest road and was quietly rejoicing over it.

But Midge was not feeling glad.

There wouldn't really have been any need for her to hide anything from some normal person or even, say, from an officer. No doubt the whole company, probably even the whole division, already knew about Midge's feat of heroism in the dark yesterday from internal intelligence. That was how come Smersh-with-the-Portrait had got involved, because of the way our own idle tongues are always wagging. Just what was it she'd done, if you figured it out commonsensibly? What was the big deal? Some pissed Hans had got what was coming to him – and that was all. And basically, if they had normal front-line soldiers working in Smersh, Midge might not even have sneezed the moment she went into the bathhouse to be run through the mangle. No, she understood perfectly well, she could tell from the deadly smell: Smersh was no laughing matter. There was no way you could expect anything to be normal round here. But keeping shtoom, now – that was a much better idea. If you didn't you'd get wound round his little finger before you even noticed, you'd just end up dead, and all for nothing. Yes, stand there and say nothing. And if it came to it ...

Her hand reached towards her back pocket again. But it fell away under the captain's gaze.

And again the cricket, that lifelong happy hermit, began chanting his psalm in the silence. And without speaking out loud Midge suddenly said to someone – perhaps the little fool of a cricket, perhaps herself, or perhaps Walter Ivanovich, who had been smiling down at her gratefully and reassuringly from the sky above since the night before: 'There is no god!' And just as unexpectedly her tears began streaming down of their own accord.

In the evening of the day before yesterday, Midge had been sent to take a package to the divisional headquarters in a village way back in the rear.

'There and back – like a shot!' The company commander wagged his finger at her, pulled on his trousers, ran the palm of his hand over his moustache, spat into the corner and cheerily tugged down the front of his tunic.

Midge listened to him with half an ear as she slowly cooled off on the broad bunk, with her weary thighs spread wide. With one hand she stroked her belly, which the commander had pounded to a pulp, and with the pale index finger of the other, black-rimmed under its gnawed-down nail, she absent-mindedly traced the golden knots in the planking wall of the commander's spacious log hut.

'Listen to what I'm telling you and leave that wall alone!' Major Gnedko shouted. 'At least cover yourself up and don't lie there shamelessly like that! No sense of shame or conscience left in you, thank God, lost every last little drop of it, you have, fucking hell! The things war does to people – it's beyond all sodding comprehension! Cover up your twat, I tell you, you little minx!'

Midge began laughing, a low, rippling laugh. She pulled on her knickers, rejoicing in the springy dependability of the elastic that her unhurried host had not torn, and began lazily buttoning up her clothes – yawning and missing the stretched and grimy, well-thumbed buttonholes.

'As soon as it's dark – you fill up on spuds and away you go, straight down the German road.'

Midge nodded, hiding a yawn behind her hand. Gnedko had called her in twice already today: first after breakfast and then just before lunch the knobbly old goat had got the urge again. So this was the third time, to help him sleep and speed her on her way. For over a year not a single bullet, mine or piece of shrapnel had touched the major, the only one like that she'd known in all that time. The rest were all in their graves, where they ought to be. But what world-class lads they all were, really interesting men, all so presentable! So how come he was the only one with such reliable special privileges, she wondered.

'Only don't turn off the road, or you'll get lost, sure as hell. Seen what they did round there? Cut loads of dead ends. But you just press right on, the dead ends have nothing to do with you, forget them. Just cruise right past and don't turn off. And don't go falling asleep out in the woods, under some fir tree: just look at you, you can hardly keep your eyes open! Don't sit down on the damp ground at all. You fool. You'll get yourself a chill in your bits and pieces in no time. Then afterwards we'll have no end of bother with you out here on the front-line. The number of times that Lukich of yours has asked me on bended knees to let him go and live in a normal soldier's dug-out, says he can't stand it any more in that den of vice. So what am I supposed to tell him? Midge is a human being too, right? So we have to settle things the best way for people. Who else is going to agree to look after you but some guy with a concussed noddle? So naturally I threatened him with the punishment battalion and threw him out ... Hey, are you asleep?'

She jerked her chin up and started fiddling with the buttons on her chest again, but she couldn't wheedle them into the buttonholes. The commander pulled her breeches on for her and buckled the belt, swearing as he talked through his gritted teeth: 'Just what did I do to deserve you, you anaemic little mermaid?'

His grouchy concern brought Midge fully awake and she was instantly cheerful and lively. She gave Gnedko a smacking kiss on his moustache and hung with her arms round his neck, kicking her legs up and squealing like she did with her daddy when she was little.

'Enough of that silly nonsense!' the commander yelled at her.

And when she stood back down on the floor, sad and sulky now, he handed her a sealed package: 'Hide it properly, you little baggage! So they won't find it even if they search. Come on, think of something!'

Midge took the package with the thick blob of sealing wax and stuck her tender pink anaemic tongue out at the commander. She pulled up the hem of her tunic and her white soldier's shirt, stuffed the military secret inside her belt and her knicker elastic and tucked everything back into place, taking her time. Ignoring the major's laughter, Midge saluted him smartly, swung round on her heel, lifted up her left leg and hopped along the line of the narrowest floorboard from the table to the door just to see if she could, and naturally she won her bet with herself. Then she hopped over the broad doorstep and continued her pranks by jumping down from the porch on one leg – smartly and merrily, like a genuine one-legged invalid.

Midge had forgotten a long time ago how to blush and feel embarrassed when she fastened and unfastened her clothes in front of men. Since that night her first front-line husband, the thirty-year-old Master Sergeant Bykovsky – the one who picked her up at the station in Demyansk, where Midge had already been raving for a day and a night in the delirium of acute pneumonia – had fed her diluted neat spirit and gently, lovingly raped her. Bykovsky had got Midge into the infirmary and when she recovered he put her in the company's battalion cookhouse as a kitchen girl. When she'd put on some weight, he decided to make her his 'sweetheart'. The next day a Messerschmidt flying by had shot the master sergeant in half on the road. When she heard about it, Midge nodded indifferently – she'd known since that morning the stupid sergeant would get his comeuppance, one way or another.

The secret package quickly crumpled under Midge's belt. The sealing wax grew warm against her body and stopped scratching her belly-button. It was dark and damp in the wood. With a full belly now and still feeling sleepy, Midge lowered the flaps of her forage-cap over her ears and half-dozed as she walked along, taking advantage of the Germans' sound construction work: the road was as even as an asphalt-coated highway, the Hanses had built it to last. In the darkness it served their enemy Midge the way honest Germans know how to serve, as if it couldn't tell whose boots were tramping along it. Midge just kept walking on and on, yawning every now and then. The route through the wood was straight, with occasional gentle bends – a boring walk. In order to keep sleep at bay Midge took out her favourite petite cigarette lighter and began scraping the little wheel against the German flint as she walked along – striking a flame then blowing the delicate petal of fire off the wick, like off a candle on the cake baked by mum for her birthday.

Midge didn't smoke, but she'd already accumulated about thirty cigarette lighters at least – an entire collection of them. It was an established tradition for Sanka Goryaev to egg on every new lieutenant from the reinforcements to bet on an open-ender: if Midge downs a full glass of vodka in one go – I win, if she chokes on it, you win, and they always forced the greenhorn to give his cigarette lighter to Midge, who didn't even smoke – so the whole thing would be twice as upsetting for him. And Midge got to keep the cigarette lighter as a souvenir. After all, a lieutenant's life lasted no longer than a child's delight with a clockwork toy anyway. These open-ended bets quite often led to a brief and sad night-time friendship between her and the lieutenant – until they were soon parted for ever.

Apart from her mysterious elephantine ability to gulp vodka straight down like water for a bet, what delighted the lieutenants about Midge was her fantastic fearlessness in battle conditions. Somehow the little girl Masha Mukhina, only seven classes old, managed not to be afraid that the bursts of German tracer bullets would kill her. When they went whining over the heads of the machine-gunners as if they were angry because they'd missed, down in her trench Midge laughed as if she was being tickled. And she could feel the fine white hairs rising up as springy as pine needles on her back, along the row of rounded bones in her narrow spine. And when she fired she clutched the handle of the machine gun tight and ground her teeth – she shot at the teeth of the vampires lurching into a drunken psychological attack from out of those rich German bogs. Sometimes she could even see through the gunsight that she hit the teeth – and then she lowered her head and bit the sleeve of her tunic that was dry with dust and tasted bitter with the death of enemy strangers.

After one battle Vasily Kolyvanov came up to her and said: 'If you hadn't covered us today, we'd never have got out alive. Not me or Starostin either. It's a fact. So here, this is for you!'

He unpinned the 'Valour' medal from his broad chest and pinned it on Midge. She took out a little mirror, looked at Midge with the medal in it, straightened up her forage cap, leaned her little head to one side – and suddenly burst out laughing. She took off the medal, tossed it up and down on the palm of her hand and jabbed Kolyvanov in the belly with the pin.

'It won't do,' Midge explained. 'Think about it. As soon as all these medals and decorations start clattering and clanging about on me at night, the Hanses'll plot the position straight off from the sound and they'll bomb some heroic lieutenant's arse to hell. Why don't you give me your lighter instead, Vas, you know I love them, and your lighter's world-class.'

Kolyvanov shrugged and without saying a word he gave her his faithful cigarette lighter that was famous throughout the whole machine-gun regiment. That was the toy Midge was amusing herself with now in the wood. For what must have been the hundredth time she lit the wick and puffed it out. And then scraped the wheel against the flint again. A little shower of startled sparks gleamed briefly, but no flame was born. She gave the rough, ribbed little wheel another turn. Again sparks – and darkness. Midge looked around, maybe for the first time in the last half hour.

Oh no! She'd lost her way, hell's bloody bells. She was obviously lost. Must have wandered into a side-road, a dead-end, the crazy-woman. Dense forest all around her, but by now she should be able to see the lights blinking in Shisyaevo, where the new divisional commander had taken the two-storey school building as quarters for himself and his staff. The colonel didn't like darkness, and the Germans didn't bombard the rear-line village, they didn't want to waste shells. So His Excellency the Headquarters Staff lit up all sixteen windows bright and clear in the long schoolhouse in the depths of the Pskov woods. The divisional commander worked at night. And he smoked a pipe. Like Stalin.

Midge went up to a tall fir-tree, gave it a friendly hug and pressed her cheek against the warm dry bark. She realised she'd have to walk back the way she'd come. She sat down on the roots covered with pine needles and burst into tears, but immediately jumped up and started laughing.

Walking confidently along the road with a bit of a stagger, as if he was on his way to a date with her, she saw a tall officer. He had no cap on his head, but his boots struck against the road Russian-style.

Midge immediately felt calm and courageous. She walked out into the middle of the road and set off towards the man, staggering just like him, readying herself to bump into him like one drunk into another and blast him with a salvo of swear words prepared in advance – give him something to remember her by, just for a good laugh.

The man waved to her from the distance and shouted something either happy or sad – she couldn't tell which. He slapped his pockets, took out his smokes and scraped away with his lighter for a long time, getting nowhere.

Midge went up to him and took out her favourite cigarette lighter again, the one Kolyvanov had given her. She decided to tell her own fortune: if the lighter worked, then she'd have a regular little fling with this tall, impressive, jolly officer; if it didn't, it would turn out just a stupid load of nonsense. But to tell the truth, it wasn't really very honest of her, because apart from the time on the road just ten minutes earlier the efficient little toy had never let Midge down: its wick flared up at the very lightest pressure on the little fluted wheel and the flame was tall and clean, with a point like the tip of a penknife. And as she gave the unknown officer a light Midge was already priding herself in advance on the way he would envy her the lighter and preparing a disdainful reply to his stupid childish admiration.

'*Sehr gut*!' He shook his clearly illuminated head of bright-white Ostsee hair with the officer's parting and brushed a shred of German wooden *ersatz*-tobacco that had been tossed up by the strong flame off his braided-silver major's shoulder strap. And he raised Walter Ivanovich's blue eyes, with the whites reddened by schnapps, to look into Midge's dumbstruck face.

The string of obscenities simply flew out of the young machine-gunner's narrow throat like a sparrow. She didn't even have time to wag her tongue once. She blasted it out – and the German's eyes swung in towards the bridge of his nose as if he'd been punched by a boxer.

'I'm sorry,' Midge mumbled, blushing. 'I didn't mean to. Don't take offence now, Comrade Major! What do I mean, comrade, hell's bloody bells! It's just that you look like someone else – something terrible!'

The officer bowed to the *fräulein*, with his head formally inclined and his arms dangling in front of him. He clicked his heels, turned sharply round, clicked them again and set off down the road, walking straight and sober.

Midge set off in the opposite direction.

But about maybe three seconds later she remembered the little Walther in her back pocket. She took the pistol out quickly and went dashing after the German, firing and swearing through her sudden tears of angry girlish shame.

The answer was the roar of a heavy Parabellum. But the major was almost dead already, and the bullet smashed into the solid German road beside his polished boot. The polite German staggered and howled, returning Midge's glorious obscenities in the same order as they'd been flung into his face. The final 'hellss-ploody-pellss' was cut short by his death rattle. Midge squeezed her eyes shut and fired another three times, yelling after her bullets: 'Traitor! For your shameless eyes! For Stalin! For all of you billy-goats!'

How did a German major come to lose his way on the German road, even if he was drunk? Midge didn't bother trying to answer that question. She didn't feel sorry for the German, she didn't even feel ashamed of her seventh-class fear at the sight of the lovely parting in her young village teacher's hair. The idea of Walter Ivanovich, from whom the major was almost indistinguishable, took fright at itself and darted away into the darkness of the past. Midge kicked the major's shiny jackboot, put another bullet in him just to make sure – into the heart – and walked out of the dead-end, somehow miraculously divining the shortest route to the headquarters village where the divisional commander was waiting for the important news in the package hidden under the elastic of her captured knickers by a fourteen-year-old fool.

But after she'd handed over the package at headquarters she suddenly felt unwell and was almost sick on the carpet. The colonel's adjutant with the long moustache gave Midge some water to drink and laid her out on the divan in the teachers' staff room, which was now the waiting room, with a carafe on the table. He listened patiently to her lamentations about a young SS major 'with white hair' – the adjutant realised he must be SS from what she said about the 'petite' black uniform – and suddenly he decided to act according to instructions, and as soon as she left he phoned Smersh …

In Captain Kuznetsov's dark little bathhouse the cricket chirped as Midge gradually began to realise she was finally sunk. She'd really gone and done it this time! Sanka had warned her today that Smersh's men had failed to find any body and only a couple of days earlier a young, blond, blue-eyed major had disappeared without trace somewhere in the area of the German road. Midge had been there. She was alive. Which made her look very, very suspicious in a situation with so many idiotic coincidences.

'So are we going to clam up?' The captain asked her, already hating Midge's innocent, blank expression. 'Hand over your weapon!'

Unthinkingly obeying the steely commander's tone in his voice, Midge took out her little Walther and put it on the captain's table.

'That's a bit better,' he said, then he opened the pistol's breech and sniffed it. 'Who did you shoot at? Your own brother, a Soviet officer! You killed a real major, one of ours, and you hid the body. And now you're lying and saying he was German. Right? Tell me! Well?'

The captain smashed his revolver down on to the bench. He blew his nose into his oily handkerchief in a menacing trumpet-blast.

He was tired of shouting furiously and smashing his revolver against the table. No one had ever loved him, the poor orphan, a balding thirty-seven-year-old man with a grey face as boring as his handkerchief. When he was young he had been afraid to love girls because he was so insignificant in their eyes. Up in the north he'd had no chance for anything like that. And now there was war. And this girl standing before him, whom he knew by reputation as a harmless, silly, undiscriminating, promiscuous minor, turned out to be a wonderful beauty out of some Russian folk-tale. With the clear, sky-blue eyes of a faithful wife, quietly loving, coolly affectionate and hot-blooded at the same time. She would love her legitimate husband as fatally as she was destroying her own beauty in this desperate war with her fury, cursing and vodka – Captain Kuznetsov realised that from the very first glance. And he decided to marry Midge. And to get started right away. Here at war. In this stuffy little abandoned bathhouse. Get married for real, for the rest of his life. And take his wife in with him, into Smorsh. And take her around with him everywhere – instead of the crumpled and tattered portrait of Dzerzhinsky with his skinny goatee. His young wife would read out the sentences in an agitated, earnest Komsomol voice and he would carry them out.

The captain reached out a hand and pulled Dzerzhinsky off the wall. Tore him up and threw him out of the window.

Midge stopped breathing. She realised Smersh had totally flipped his lid.

'Mukhina!' the captain said in a muted voice, looking away from her. 'My dear Maria Ivanovna! Please don't be angry with me for yelling at you. I took a great liking to you straight away. Let's get the colonel to marry us tomorrow. Eh? I really do love you — here, look!' He crossed himself three times and bowed low to her from the waist.

Midge fainted, falling back on to the bench by the wall.

The captain took out a comb and combed a few hairs over his bald patch. Poured out some milk from his earthenware jug and lifted Midge up in his arms. Sat his insensible bride on his knees and began kissing her little blue fingers. The cricket under the stove emitted lengthy trills of approval.

When she came round Midge smiled quietly. Squeezed her nose against the captain's neck. Kuznetsov stroked her back and coaxed her: 'When the war's over, we'll make ourselves a nice quiet life. OK? I'll treat you like a queen. I'll go for the potatoes, I'll watch the cattle ... You don't believe me? You don't know what I'm like! I'll make *pelmeni* so tasty you'll be begging me for more. Do you want some milk?'

He picked up the mug from the table and began carefully feeding Midge milk, a sip at a time, so that the cold liquid brought up from the cellar by the doddery old man who owned the sound wooden house next door wouldn't chill the girl's delicate pink throat, from which poor Kuznetsov's nostrils caught the scent of her breath, mingled with the sweet milky smell.

When she felt calmer Midge kissed him on the cheek and said: 'No, Comrade Captain. Let's not. I don't love anyone yet, not my way. When I fall in love I'll get married straight away. But I can't do it just like that. Please let me go, I'm very tired.

You turned out a real world-class comrade. But if you like I can lie down on the bunk ...'

She got up off the captain's knees and picked her Walther up off the table.

'You're lying – you'll never leave here!' The captain cried joyfully. 'I caught you and you let the cat out of the bag! I caught you out properly, didn't I?'

He still didn't know which way he was going to turn this unpleasant situation. He'd really shot wide of the mark this time! No, there was no way he could let the little tart go now: she'd trumpet his proposal round the entire division. What could he do now?

'Belay that!' he ordered quietly, certain that Midge would drop the pistol. 'Atten-shun!'

His voice broke and turned squeaky. Midge laughed. She stuck the pistol in her back pocket, buttoned up her tunic and stepped towards the door.

The captain sprang from the stool to the table and grabbed up his revolver.

'Stop – I'll shoot!' he shouted, this time in a man's voice. 'Get away from that door, you bad bitch! And don't try any tricks – I'll shoot without warning!'

Midge screwed up her eyes and set her hands on her hips, mentally running through the most scathing words, the ones that stung men's coxcomb vanity worst of all. She pressed her lips together – and ...

'Ma-sha!' the captain groaned like a sick cow. 'Don't destroy my life, my darling! At least let me kiss you just once ...'

He threw his revolver back down on the table in annoyance: he hadn't expected to hear himself say that.

Midge took out the Walther and clicked the catch, lining up the last cartridge that the captain hadn't noticed.

'Kill me!' said Kuznetsov, nodding. 'I don't care any more ...'

He rubbed his dry little hand hard across his lips, opened his arms wide and walked towards Midge as if he was going to a hero's death – with his eyes squeezed tight shut.

Midge retreated with the pistol held out in front of her,

stepping backwards until she had her back pressed against the door. The key jabbed into her backside and her trembling finger squeezed the obedient little Walther's sensitive trigger of its own accord.

Sanka Goryaev's joke cartridge went bang – and Captain Kuznetsov's face was covered with a black film of dirty gunpowder and fibres from the cotton wadding shattered by the blast got stuck in his teeth, bared in the smile to precede a kiss.

Convinced he'd been killed outright, Kuznetsov groaned, clutched his face in his hands and fell on the ground. The captain turned up his toes in front of the bride of his dreams, shuddering once before he lay still, expecting to die completely for his untimely, shameful love.

Midge sank down wearily on to the floor by the door and inspected her gift pistol melancholically. She looked at the captain without any surprise and seemed to see the German major again – in the captain's place. And suddenly she felt so sorry for him she could cry, the way she had in the divisional commander's waiting room. The merciless machine-gunner wished the other bullet had been a blank, not this one that had saved her from a kiss, but yesterday's, the one that killed the tall, handsome, blue-eyed Walter Ivanovich who had bowed so low to her on the forest road, as if he was thanking her from the bottom of his heart for the death he would die a moment later with Midge's curses on his lips instead of the kiss he had deserved for so long. Midge realised yet again, as she had yesterday when her teeth chattered against the edge of the glass of water in the divisional commander's waiting room, that she would love the dead German – Walter Ivanovich, that is – who had died for her for the rest of her life, she would never forget him now as long as she lived because of the drunken ss officer the day before yesterday (if not for him, then Walter Ivanovich would still be alive for her today) – now she would remain empty and cold for all of her long, lonely life, like one of pitiful Kuznetsov's boots. Again and again she had searched in vain for Walter Ivanovich in her nocturnal flights, and now yesterday she had killed him here on earth.

The tears poured down from her eyes of ice on to the white barrel of the cold Walther ...

Kuznetsov raised his head with a groan and let it slump back on to the floor.

'Stop that!' Midge ordered. 'Get up, you witless wanker! Take me to the guardhouse. Well? D'you hear me? I want to go to jail! Get arrested! Get executed, hell's bloody bells!'

The captain gave an aggrieved moo. He started fastidiously picking out of his mouth the cotton wadding from Sanka's little cushion that the good-for-nothing from Leningrad's Ligovka district carried to and fro with him throughout the whole war.

'Arise, you starveling from your slumber!' Midge threw her forage cap at the captain. 'Come on, do your officer's duty! I'll get undressed ...'

She pulled her tunic up over her head together with her shirt. And Kuznetsov slumped back down from his sitting position, his lowing cut short by the sacred milky-white light of her breasts.

'Well!' she shouted. 'Quickly now, military-style, hell's bloody bells!'

And she began pulling off her boots.

Kuznetsov got up. Shook his head and spat into the corner. Sat down on the bench by the little window. Put his revolver away in its holster.

Midge's tears began falling more rapidly, like rain.

'Go away!' Kuznetsov begged her, unable to tear his childishly hungry gaze away from her.

Midge began shaking her head and put her hands over her ears. She sobbed silently, but the rhythm of her heart said: 'My white-haired darling ... My white-headed boy ... My white-headed love ... White Wally Walter! mister von-baron Walter von Schmalter! My love, my only one, my white dove, my white sugar-sweet love, my sugar-lollipop on a stick ... Walter! Where are you, my beloved? I know you're here with me ... You're in me for ever – do you hear me, you little twerp? Come to me now, come! Oh! Walter! Waa-a-a-aalter ...'

Her whole body was swaying, with her arms thrown back

behind her head, with her eyes closed, she was beautiful, with her high-arching brows and the blurred scarlet patch of her insatiable mouth. And the captain suddenly felt more afraid than he had during his recent imaginary death.

The half-witted cricket filled the bathhouse with his quiet, devoted praying.

Midge began getting dressed.

She picked up her pistol and put it away, fastened her buttons, stood up and went over to Kuznetsov with an embarrassed smile.

'Forgive me!' she said, laying her hand on his shoulder. 'I'm just a stupid fool.'

She kissed the captain on the side of his head and walked out of the wooden hut.

Chapter 8

The final chapter. In which Midge will never die.

She had no time to be frightened or even to hear the crunch and squelch as the bone of her forehead was crushed in and back. She heard nothing but the shudder and boom of a bell. An immense bell with no clapper that enveloped the sky above her and the whole of the earth. At the centre of the round earth, slumped on to the breechblock of the machine gun, lay her bullet-pierced head with her motionless little body.

The dead girl was amazed at how the bullet that flew in through the aperture of the gun-sight could have grazed the armoured screen of her 'Maxim' but not ricocheted away. The damn fool thing had pierced the keen-sighted machine-gunner neatly between her eyes with a damp rustling and bubbling. As if someone had stuck a hot, fat finger into a cold, bottomless void − as if that was where the fatheaded idiot was supposed to be: Hi there, shitface − been expecting you for ages!

The incandescent crimson booming of the bell expanded outwards and upwards. As she struggled painfully up through the darkness and the dense, stifling, viscous sound, up towards the dome of the empty vault, Maria saw the light of heaven above. It was calling to her through an opening in the dome − and she rose towards it, becoming lighter and lighter, like in her dreams − and then she crept out, flowing through from the dark, dense sound into a sky of light.

At the zenith of the vault of heaven, which was made entirely of rainbows fused together, the sun, with its thick, faceted rays reaching down to the very earth, came flying motionlessly towards the girl − moving low, like an airship. Around it the stars gleamed and glittered as they did around the moon at night, each of them with a rainbow of its own − blue, green and red ones, and many, very many, silver stars that were small but unbearably bright. And everything around and within her weightless flying being fell silent, and the girl halted in space, at the centre of naked existence. And the trees of the forest below her, and the figures of people and every single blade of grass in the meadow, everything was enveloped in radiance from every side. Revealed in its power and glory, without shadows, the world lay open to her gaze, bathed and enveloped in streams of truth.

Glancing back, once again she saw Midge lying below, and Lukich crying beside her. And tender maternal affection for him caught her up and lifted her still higher. So high that the black wings of a swift flitting past as it dodged about below the clouds over the battlefield clipped straight through her incorporeal throat, which seemed to contract in pity for the bird, so defenceless against the whistle of the bullets and the shrapnel, against the flashing and stench of the bursting bombs.

Maria did not know that a strange new power had arisen within her – in place of the wretched fears and dismal oppression of the girl left behind on earth. And the majestic power spoke from the very highest depths: 'Now. Yes!'

The scattered sounds of battle flying in all directions suddenly formed up around her into a ring of agonisingly regular vibrating sound. Maria could not tell if it was the song of a choir of frightened birds following the rhythm of the battle, or the complaint of human torment from the earth, from the ditches, trenches and shell-craters where living and dead human bodies lay concealed, or perhaps the sounds of the forest, maimed by the blind impact of lead and steel, blending into the summons of a lingering groan. She knew only one thing: there was no more need to stagger wildly, waking and sleeping, through the scraping and screeching of these streams of death, there was no point in seeking a rendezvous with the empty gaze of non-existence, which did not exist anywhere. She had to see, and see clearly with all the freedom granted to her, the tempestuous, turbulent, seething stream of time's lethargic, incandescent necessity. Its current was in every drop of blood. In the body of a blind bullet and a man's final scream. She had to be with no one, and with everyone that her new-born tenderness could see.

She knew now that once, or perhaps only a moment ago, she herself had exhaled from the motionless flux of the celestial rainbows everything that she could now see so clearly. Through her own will she had set the girl Masha's little body at the centre of the earth where she could see it plainly – and assigned to her a life so painful that Midge was forbidden to know of her own pain, for it was too much for the mind to bear. And she herself had created the damp clayey earth of the parapet under the cooling housing of the silenced machine gun. And Lukich's childish weeping in his suffering was also a function of that same single, transcendental power. Everything that was had been invented by herself at one time, like the double knot in the elastic of the flimsy white knickers, that kept breaking again and again – it had been untied again by her own free decision. And someone else would knot together a different pattern – for unprecedented, unexpected pain and tenderness, for the liberating glance of love – a tormenting, bright delirium of time, which craves again and again the taste of rational flesh to feed the joy of its pitiless flame, for the smoke breathed by the insatiable sky in its striving to sate itself. The sky is a greedy child in the womb of Maria's infinite being: for after all, she has always heard the steady pulsing of the sun within herself.

Now Maria knew it: happiness was about to arrive.

All she had to do was rise a little higher and embrace the foolish little sun. Return with the radiant infant to a place where there was not even a trace of the heavy boots on the thin little legs of the exhausted little girl, or of anyone else's heavy breathing on her badly bitten lips. Where noon had still not been born, with its fat-bellied, brazen, eternal infant in the heavenly cradle, blowing rainbow bubbles and smiling as if he's dreaming, and worrying his mother's breast like a hollow rattle containing the dried-up pea of her heart. Where the piteous, guilty groaning of the violated earth cannot be heard.

But somehow this faint lament, languishing in resignation as it repeated in interminable circles like a worn record, would not let the girl rise higher. It pierced through her long-awaited tranquillity with its helpless demand, like a hungry infant's cry of senseless anger.

When she realised that she had halted motionless at the centre of God's amusements, her being was instantly shrouded in the cold shadow of her former fears, which had not after all been completely exhausted in the course of her life with people and at the moment of the final blow. Distancing herself in annoyance from her deceitful, clinging temptation, she waited to see what a higher power had in store for her – for after all, there should be no barriers for her, should there?

But now the will that she had already recognised as the new essence of her being seemed to recoil a little distance away from her. And the universal anticipation that was focused on Maria not only from above, but also from within her own conscious-ness, was shot through with a surprising, incongruous-seeming slyness that now, after everything, felt almost insulting.

Feeling a light pricking in the spot below her ribs on the left where formerly her body and her heart had been, covered by the dress that was torn on the nail sticking out of the side of the one-and-a-half-tonne truck when they were driving Alyoshka away, the girl suddenly realised – guessed – that the sly, patient anticipation of the force that was guiding her was giving her a sign. Meanwhile the voice of earthly suffering, barely audible only a moment ago, entered into her as palpably and hotly as if she possessed flesh again, and was again accepting her forsaken pain through her old wound.

But why? What for? When now everything was absolutely clear?

As if in reply to her question, the pain instantly vanished. But the sly anticipation focused on her became more mocking and demanding.

And again her throat was pierced through insensibly by the swift that could not see her. As though attempting to support this pitiful creature as it flew along, demented by the roaring din and fire of earth that seemed everlasting to its mind without memory, she stretched out her hand after the bird, and although she was too late to touch it, she distinctly felt something glowing fly out of her fingers and fuse with it, and the bird soared upwards, breaking out of the dead space, abandoning the circling of its hell. How simple! – she thought, laughing at something she didn't understand and noticing at the same time that when she transmitted the gift that she herself did not understand to the swift, she sank down lower above the battlefield. But then why did she suddenly feel as if it was easier to breathe?

And suddenly they fused together inside her – the wound that had flared up again and the calm power that could direct itself, unrestrained by anyone, loving and choosing the peace or the pain, the pitiless light or the consoling night. And Maria had no more guides, no more commanders. There was only the necessity to travel. A single flickering point of light in space, born from her own long dreams.

Joy transfixed her, blinding her for an instant.

Joy at her unbearable compassion for those who did not know the great secret. Whose blind, weak, common voice she could hear once again, as if it arose within her own unique being. And she followed it, floating where it led.

Slowly circling down over the field, over the black fire and red churned-up clay. Over the figures stumbling as they ran – they fell, leapt up, casting clouds of flame and glittering bursts of gunfire ahead of them. She floated lower and lower, closer and closer to them, and now she could already make out the faces of the screaming men. As though she had just woken from a sound sleep, she had to force herself to remember which of them were screaming and groaning in Russian …

Where the radiant, invisible girl flew by above the battle, people ran after her as if they were following armoured corridors impenetrable to the flying lead. In thin little streams, following each other in threes and fours, some on their own, or in a broad rank that was absolutely impossible in battle. Regrouping as if following orders, not knowing, unaware whose will was leading and watching over them, the soldiers rushed forwards – and they did not fall, they saw the flashes of explosions close beside them – and they remained protected against oblivion.

She led them and directed them along those same paths and tracks followed by future time, still unknown to anyone, as it extended its power across the earth, through the battlefields, avidly mastering space – consuming without malice the pain and hope of all who had been chosen as its sacrifices …

On one of the recent anniversaries of the lifting of the blockade of Leningrad, one of the veterans gathered round the modestly festive table at the reunion of the Red-Banner Fifty-Second Infantry Guards Division, a retired captain and professor of the Russian Academy of Culture, the quite charming Moisei Budulaevich Khabibulenkovas, told me in confidence: 'I know that writers always like to exaggerate – just to make sure things get across. Well, I couldn't care less about that, but with your permission I would like to clarify one small point. When we ran to that breach, firstly the snow was up to our knees, for a start. And secondly, I don't know about anyone else, but I saw her with my own eyes. She was flying, I don't deny that. But firstly, she wasn't completely transparent, for a start. Apart from her arms and legs I could see other parts as well – but let's follow Mayakovsky's advice and not swear in front of the newly-weds. But what amazed me most of all, young man, was something they'll never allow you to write about. And that was the white flag. You'll never believe it! Nobody does. Can you imagine it? Instead of a red flag in her hands she had some kind of rag – begging your pardon – tied to her leg, and the string was dangling down as well. Do you understand the political implications of that? Leading people into battle – with a white flag! It's inconceivable! And while not many of us actually saw her – mostly officers and a few privates who also had higher education, thank God – everyone was flabbergasted by the white flag, literally everyone! It was sort of double, like a torn skirt or maybe a pair of football shorts. But just why was it white — that's the question! Anyway, you won't believe it, but everyone who went running after those knickers survived. Right beside me, literally just two steps away, there were explosions, groans, death — but there was I running along like I'm taking the test for the work and defence health standards. Nasymbaev survived that time. Traugot and Fokin — practically all the officers. It was this very day, the day of the main breakthrough. Only you'd better not write about that — the white flag: we might just be misunderstood. The war and the blockade are sacred ... But you know, by the way, the Leningrad front wasn't the only place I caught sight of her. I remember one night before we advanced, the time we destroyed the enemy's Kozlo-Popovsky group, I walked to the next village. And let me tell you, the way lay through a wood. But that's a different story altogether ...

P.S.

Wearing a canary-yellow towelling dressing-gown and tattered slippers on bare feet, walking with a shuffling but firm stride, the petite snub-nosed woman with the heavenly glow in her eyes and the short, straw-coloured hair came out to meet me in the narrow corridor of her dark flat on the second floor of an annexe sandwiched between the fireproof walls of Dostoyevsky's district in our own Palmyra of the North. I was cheered to see in her face the familiar, fearless determination of the front-line soldier, that makes it equally simple to kill a living man or to save him. Feeling that accustomed inferiority of the post-war generation for whom our fathers fought, I clicked my heels and gave the lady a brief officer's bow.

'Mag-nificent!' she shouted in my face, setting my arm and my entire being trembling with her commander's handshake. 'The only genuine stylist — just like myself! Your story's world-class! Only three comments on the text. Three! Oh, how I suffered with the others, how much I had to rewrite for them —

pages, literally pages for some ... Mag-nificent! Please, come through!'

The young man floating in the air in the lotus position in the corner of the corridor continued calmly playing the flute. He politely allowed me past him into the room and without removing his lips from the short black flute slowly floated in after me and hovered above the table, without unfolding the petals of his legs and continuing to improvise on themes from ancient Chinese classical music.

'This is Petya!' she shouted. 'Finish up now, son, time to come back down to earth! At least say hello to our guest, be polite!'

Without even shaking his head, the levitating Petya continued weaving his melody in the former tempo.

Using a hairpin to stuff the anti-nicotine cotton-wool into the cardboard tube of her 'Belomor' *papyrosa* with incomprehensible swiftness and categorical passion while the song of the ancient Chinese aesthetes showered down on her from Petya's celestial heights as she sat there at the immense table covered with manuscripts for the collective anthology of which, fortunately for me, she was the editor, she took great delight in retelling to me my own sentimental story about three friends from the city, one of whom hanged himself at the very beginning of the narrative and another drowned himself, which was the part my editor and benefactor opposed, wishing in this way to preserve my first masterpiece for the printing press and save it for our grateful people, and praising me, I repeat, so lavishly as she did so that I found myself dabbing at my eyes with the paper napkin I had just been sniffing to soften the effect of the vodka she had poured for me, scarcely able to suppress the indecent sounds expressing my own involuntary catharsis. Eventually, orientally embarrassed by this excess of praise, I was relieved to be able to go the shop with one of my co-authors in the anthology, who had been driven demented by the undeserved eulogy to my talent, to get a bottle of 'sadness remedy', as she put it, thrusting into my moneyless pocket the five roubles that was adequate to the order in those times of stagnation. Stung into preserving his independence, my colleague, subsequently a hard-core truth-lover, and then a major publisher, bought a *'panzerfaust'* of strong white wine and then I passed that evening so crucial to me enveloped in sunny-golden shot-silk, laurel-wreath tones, without interrupting for a single moment the unconstrainedly brutal monologue of the front-line authoress about the business of war.

After that I began visiting her home regularly, shamelessly exploiting Valentina Vasilievna's exceedingly generous interest in my modest talent, which I realised was undeserved even then, and which remains incomprehensible to me to this very day. I heard more and more new stories from her life at the front and as a writer, and also from her work-experience, as they say, in the people's court – she had been a real live judge! Both Valentina Vaslievna herself and her son, a genuinely educated and cultured man, benevolent and wise, temperamentally taciturn and in the delicate susceptibilities of his soul the absolute antithesis of his mother and a mag-nificent scholar of oriental and even occidental philosophy, were my teachers for a long time.

During the final months of her life Valentina Vasilievna got the idea of writing a new story – 'The White Walther' – about events that are not mentioned in her well-known books. She began writing drafts. But as ill-luck would have it, she broke her arm.

'My God!' I ask him today, 'Why did you have to torment a person just before she died? What else could a front-line veteran, a writer, and a judge actually learn from new pain and suffering? What new insights did a broken arm bring to Valentina Vasilievna's weary soul? Or do you not feel pain? Or do you only discover wisdom through our sufferings? Or perhaps we mortals do not know what pain really is? Is it not perhaps Your love, despairing on the road to Calvary, that stings man again and again – like a reproachful wife, like a child demanding from a young, downtrodden single mother a different kind of attention, affection and discipline, not womanish but totally dependable, the kind only a father could give? But then are You not our Father, Lord? Do You Yourself not prefer the freedom of the seducer and payer of alimony, buying freedom from Your hungry offspring with crumbs from the table of infinite existence, knowledge and bliss?

'Resign yourself, proud man!' replies the front-line authoress's neighbour Fyodor Mikhailovich Dostoevsky, as he lifts the hem of his prisoner's overall, not to wipe away his tears, but to wipe clean Rodion Raskolnikov's conscience-stricken axe. A familiar argument. And probably the only one, when even today You still have the arms of half of humanity twisted behind their backs.

As she waited resignedly for her arm to heal so that she could carry on with her work, Valentina Vasilievna told me about things she was not destined to put in writing. About her close friends at the front line. About her women-friends, not all of whom managed to get through the war unsullied like Valya. About the miniature, nickel-plated trophy pistol with which she really did shoot the German officer, as my story – which is also not my story – tells, and so saved her army comrades. I listened without interrupting, at the same time focusing my willpower as Petya had most kindly taught me to do and alternately shifting the large prehistorical oak cupboard nicknamed 'Slavs, arise!' closer to the bed and moving it back into the corner with short, vigorous passes of my right hand. Paying no attention to my progress in non-literary matters, she stuffed one 'Belomor' after another with cotton wool and coughed up weighty obscenity.

When I heard her story about how the unfortunate soldiers who had been surrounded were executed – not, in fact, by a general, but by a marshal, whose name I have been obliged to change here by a single letter in the name of consciously adopted artistic license (the marshal did not actually kill unarmed Soviet soldiers and officers with a revolver as my story has it, but with a Browning automatic – I confess and repent) and I shuddered at the tale, I could not help asking the writer if I had misheard the name of the renowned military commander, whose photographs are still highly regarded by long-distance lorry drivers as icons of a guardian angel equal in potency to portraits of the leader of the peoples himself. Her reply to me was a quite unprintable tirade, and what's more she added, as if she were speaking from the bench of a people's judge, with the modest but impressive halo of the carved oak crest above her head – 'Why, both of that butcher's arms are soaked up to the elbows in blood!'

It would be superfluous to describe my admiration for Valentina Vasilievna's bravery in calling the famous memoirist a bloody butcher at a time when the people used to read his 'Reminiscences' from cover to cover in a single reverential breath, hoping to discover behind the inarticulate ramblings of the martyr who spent his whole life spilling other people's blood that very same single, eternal, original truth that the boyars concealed from the good little father tsar.

And was that not perhaps why Valentina Vasilievna's arm was broken – Zhukov learned that the keen-sighted machine-gunner had finally decided to make a contribution in writing and add a truthful line to the long list of victims in the marshal's service record – long before *glasnost* was announced by his former colleagues? Of course, by the time the unfortunate Valentina Vasilievna missed her step on the steep, dark stairs in front of the door of her flat, the marshal, lying under his granite slab heaped high with bombastic roses and principled carnations, must have already fallen into slumber and forgotten how obsequiously the magic flute, that ancient companion of psychopropedeutic mysteries and master of tamed demons and trained cobras, had chirruped at his funeral procession 'like a bullfinch' as the mocking future Nobel Prize-winner put it from the distance of our ally America. And he probably never remembered the little girl who had fainted at his heavy blood-spattered boots almost forty years earlier even once in all of his glorious martial career. And yet no one can prove to me that the soul of the leader who loved people so insatiably was not wandering that day through the broad streets of the purgatory city for the salvation of which from the

Germans the marshal had been prepared to pay so much cheap Soviet blood. And so it might have happened to glance in at the gloomy staircase of the little annexe in one of the steep enclosed courtyards of Raz'ezzhaya Street just at the moment when the petite forearm of an elderly woman slipped down along the yellow-lacquered banisters and got stuck between the cast-iron stalks of the openwork decoration, and it would only have had to twitch a hair in her nostril with a light breeze to make her give a massive sneeze, and …

But let us leave aside this so-called 'mysticism' – there is quite enough of it in the story. It is far more fitting for us, as materialists to the marrow of our so far – thank God – sound bones, and quite adequate for the consummation of the plot, to assume with sober medical correctness that the life-saving faint that was mercifully triggered in Valya's brain by the blast of black terror also gave the first impulse to the writing that was to become her life and awoke her passionate talent. And since she actually died the traditional death of writers from a stroke, for which the ground could very well have been laid by that same first blow from the marshal's hand in the autumn of nineteen forty-one on that volleyball court, then however you look at it, it would seem that the name of Valentina Vasilievna, machine-gunner, writer and judge should be entered into the list of victims of the marshal's court-martial justice – as the last, credo, credo!

I prayed for this to the marshal and his present commanding officer, comrade God, as the unlubricated infernal device squeaked below the floor of the brightly lit hall of the crematorium, making the professional truth-lovers and prophets of the Union of Soviet Socialist Writers cringe when the coffin with the body of the front-line authoress was dispatched on its final mission – beyond all battle-fronts at once.

And I remembered then the very funny way in which Valentina Vasilievna had concluded her oration at the recent funeral of an old poet: 'Goodnight, dear Leontii! All the best!'

My humble greetings to you, mag-nificent Valentina Vasilievna!

All the best to you, where they don't kill or lie or betray, where there is nothing but double-filtered and distilled, ninety-degrees pure, absolutely genuine Good. Isn't that so?